Praise for Debra Webb

"*Trust No One* is Debra Webb at her finest. Political intrigue and dark family secrets will keep readers feverishly turning pages to uncover all the twists in this stunning thriller."

—Melinda Leigh, #1 *Wall Street Journal* bestselling author of *Cross Her Heart*

"A wild, twisting crime thriller filled with secrets, betrayals, and complex characters that will keep you up until you reach the last darkly satisfying page. A five-star beginning to Debra Webb's explosive series!"

—Allison Brennan, *New York Times* bestselling author

"Debra Webb once again delivers with *Trust No One*, a twisty and gritty page-turning procedural with a cast of complex characters and a compelling cop heroine in Detective Kerri Devlin. I look forward to seeing more of Detectives Devlin and Falco."

—Loreth Anne White, *Washington Post* bestselling author of *In the Deep*

"*Trust No One* is a gritty and exciting ride. Webb skillfully weaves together a mystery filled with twists and turns. I was riveted as each layer of the past peeled away, revealing dark secrets. An intriguing cast of complicated characters, led by the compelling Detective Kerri Devlin, had me holding my breath until the last page."

—Brianna Labuskes, *Washington Post* bestselling author of *Girls of Glass*

"Debra Webb's name says it all."

—Karen Rose, *New York Times* bestselling author

GONE TOO FAR

OTHER TITLES BY DEBRA WEBB

Trust No One

GONE TOO FAR

DEBRA WEBB

This is a work of fiction. Names, characters, organizations, places, events, and incidents are either products of the author's imagination or are used fictitiously. Any resemblance to actual persons, living or dead, or actual events is purely coincidental.

Published by Thomas & Mercer, Seattle

www.apub.com

ISBN-13: 9781542091770
ISBN-10: 1542091772

Cover design by Shasti O'Leary Soudant

Printed in the United States of America

There are many amazing people in my life, but one in particular has always had my back.
He has cheered me on when I succeeded and picked me up when I failed.
I cannot imagine this life without him.
I love you, husband!

Take my hand and you will be invisible.

1

Today

Saturday, April 17

7:15 a.m.

Birmingham

The rear passenger door slammed, and she was alone in the back seat of the car. The driver glanced at her in his rearview mirror.

She looked away. Pretended she wasn't afraid. But she was. She had never been more afraid in her life.

This neighborhood was one she'd been to before but only to this one house. The house where bad things were kept secret . . . where empty eyes stared out from the walls and something evil lived.

Her body began to shake. She tried to stop it. Couldn't.

No one else is going to die. No one. Not again.

She told herself these things over and over. Today it would end.

No more hiding the truth. No more secrets.

Her gaze shifted to the bag on the floor. She'd never seen this bag before. Plain. Black. Like something for carrying a laptop.

She glanced beyond the car window to the house. This might be her only opportunity to look inside. Snooping in other people's bags wasn't a very nice thing to do. She'd been taught better. But she had to be sure.

After leaning forward, she unzipped the bag with shaking hands, then pulled the sides open wider.

The shiny blade of a big knife reflected the sun streaming through the windows. Duct tape and a large crumpled garbage bag were stuffed beneath it.

A new blast of fear rushed through her veins.

No. No. No. She shook her head. *No!*

No one else could die.

I don't want to die.

Turning fourteen hadn't made her as brave as she'd thought. She had to run . . . she should never have taken that call. She should have stayed home and not sneaked out of the house.

She had to find a way to contact her mom and . . .

The car's rear passenger door opened once more.

It was too late.

2

Five Days Earlier

Monday, April 12

10:30 a.m.

Leo's Tobacconist
Oak Grove Road
Homewood

The two victims were secured to chairs and then shot execution style—in the back of the head. With no exit wounds, the weapon was likely a .22. Something small caliber and intended for up close work. The typical MO for these types of kills. The medical examiner and the Crime Scene Unit had been summoned.

Detective Kerri Devlin turned her full attention back to the responding officer as he described the events that had occurred before she and her partner received the call.

"Tara McGill arrived on the scene at nine thirty to prepare for opening at ten. She entered through the rear exit." Officer Eugene Franklin gestured to the door at the back of the stockroom. "According to McGill, all employees come and go this way. Once inside, she discovered the owner, Leonard 'Leo' Kurtz"—Franklin pointed his notepad to the older victim, sixty to sixty-five maybe, seated nearest him—"and the other male victim just as you see them."

"You ID'd the other guy yet?" Luke Falco, Kerri's partner, asked.

Franklin nodded. "This is where things get interesting."

Though the second victim looked vaguely familiar, Kerri couldn't place him. Young, late twenties or early thirties maybe. Unlike the older vic, who wore dark-blue trousers and a lighter-blue button-down open to the center of his chest, where gold chains dangled, victim number two wore a business suit—the kind that wouldn't be found on some rack in just any department store. Frankly, the man didn't actually look like the type to drop by a smoke shop, but then you never knew. With all the bad press about vaping, maybe some millennials were turning to custom-made, organic tobaccos. In any case, Leo's was the place to shop in the greater Birmingham area. The oldest tobacconist in the state, in fact. Everyone who was anyone who had a fetish for tobacco, cigars, pipes, and/or fine liquors came to Leo's. The city's elite, mostly the old guard, kept the business thriving.

Kerri lifted her gaze to Franklin's. "How interesting?"

"As in"—the uni's eyebrows reared up his forehead—"he's that new DDA everyone's talking about. The rich one from up north." He indicated the dead guy in question. "Detectives, meet Asher Walsh, deputy district attorney, Jefferson County."

"Well I'll be damned." Falco shot Kerri a look that said: *So this is why we're here.*

"That's pretty damned interesting," Kerri agreed, surprised she hadn't recognized him. Then again, with his head dropped forward, the mask of death had bulged and discolored his facial features.

Her partner was right; Walsh was definitely the reason MID had been called. The Major Investigations Division wasn't just another part of Birmingham PD homicide. The division comprised the top detectives from BPD as well as the surrounding communities, including Homewood, Mountain Brook, Vestavia, and Hoover. Their job was to handle the investigations that impacted more than a single jurisdiction—the high-profile cases to which the powers that be wanted undivided attention provided by handpicked assets from across the greater Birmingham area.

Cases like this one.

Kerri crouched and took a closer look at the vic's face. With his chin to chest and body in a seated position, hands secured behind his back, ankles bound to the chair legs, it wasn't easy to estimate time of death. Judging by the lividity in the downturned face and along what she could see of the throat, he'd been dead possibly ten hours or more. And he'd died exactly where he was, seated in this ladder-back chair in the stockroom of an establishment with deep roots in local history.

Kerri hadn't met Walsh personally. She'd seen the news about him joining the DA's office. The son of wealthy Bostonians. Harvard educated. After a stint clerking for the Massachusetts supreme judicial court, rather than go into practice in his father's prestigious firm, he had accepted a position in Birmingham, Alabama. According to the national and local media, it was a major coup for Birmingham and an up yours to his domineering father.

Now, a mere six months later, he was dead.

"What the hell did you get yourself into, Mr. Walsh?" she murmured before pushing to her feet. She turned to Falco. "One of us should let the LT know."

Lieutenant Dontrelle Brooks was not going to be happy to hear the news. As with Walsh's arrival in Birmingham, his abrupt departure would make national headlines. The theories about his death would get messy. Something else that usually went along with the sorts of cases assigned to their division.

"I'll call him," Falco offered.

"I'll interview the employee who found the bodies." Kerri was more than happy for her partner to brief the LT.

"The ME is on his way," Franklin said to Kerri as Falco headed for the door that led into the front retail shop.

Kerri nodded. "What about cell phones?"

"We found the shop owner's cell phone behind the bar," Franklin explained, "but if Walsh was carrying one, we haven't found it yet."

He was a DDA; he would have a cell phone. It was only a matter of finding it. Unless, of course, the shooter had taken it. In that case they'd have to wait for his phone records, which would be requested as a matter of standard protocol.

"Thanks, Franklin. Keep looking for that phone. We have boots on the ground going from door to door?" She'd asked the responding officer to call for additional backup in hopes of getting on top of the situation sooner rather than later.

"Yes, ma'am," he assured her. "No hits so far. Most of the shops along this block close earlier than this one and weren't open until just a few minutes ago, so no customers in the parking lots or employees hanging around outside. At least none we've found."

She gave him a nod and turned back to the victims. The shop had closed at ten last night. If her estimation on time of death was anywhere near accurate, the murders hadn't occurred until well after the shop closed. With the rest of the shops in the area already shuttered for the night, there might not be any witnesses at all. They could hope for security cam footage, but there were never any guarantees with these older shops and neighborhoods.

"I'm ready to talk to McGill."

Franklin jerked his head toward the door that separated the stockroom from the public space beyond. "She's at the bar."

"Make sure the outside perimeter remains secure now that the other shops are open for business, and let Detective Falco know when the ME arrives."

"Yes, ma'am."

Before turning away, she asked, "Do we have an ETA on the Crime Scene Unit?" Generally, they arrived about the same time or shortly after Kerri and Falco did. A call en route got a unit moving ASAP. Apparently there had been a glitch this go-around.

"I checked with dispatch to find out what the holdup was and learned there's a major pileup on 280. Our guys got caught up in that, but they'll be here in the next few minutes."

Kerri nodded. "Good."

She followed the route Falco had taken. She spotted him through the storefront windows, standing outside, his cell tucked against his ear. Brooks was likely warning her partner about how sensitive these sorts of cases were. How they had to be exceedingly careful. No leaks. Keep the press at bay until an official statement was released.

It wasn't like they hadn't done this before. Ten months ago, the first case she and Falco worked together had involved the top echelon of Birmingham society. An ache pierced Kerri's heart. That case had stolen the life of Amelia, her precious niece . . . it had taken a terrible toll on her family, and she'd been saddled with a new partner she hadn't liked. She gave her head a small shake. Turned out that new partner was the best thing to happen to her, professionally and personally. He was a great partner and a good friend. She was lucky to have him.

She glanced to the far end of the bar, where Tara McGill waited, her elbows on the counter, her face in her hands. Long blonde hair streamed down her back. The dress was short and tight, the sandals slinky. Kerri imagined all the employees who worked here were attractive and probably female. The older men who frequented the place with its vintage, tony appeal would prefer to be catered to by women.

Kerri settled onto the barstool next to McGill. She looked up, tears blackened by her heavy mascara, and eyeliner stained her cheeks.

"Ms. McGill, I'm Detective Kerri Devlin. I'd like to ask you a few questions about this morning."

She nodded. "Okay." More dark tears rolled down her cheeks. "Who would do this?"

"We're hoping you can help us find that answer." Kerri reached across the bar and grabbed a couple of napkins for McGill. "How long have you worked for Mr. Kurtz?"

McGill swiped at her cheeks, then dabbed at her nose. "Two years."

"Do you have some idea about how many people the shop employs?"

McGill considered the question for a moment. "There's five or six who work part time and two of us who are full time besides Leo." She drew in a big breath. "I just don't understand. Everyone loves Leo."

Obviously, there was at least one person who didn't. Or maybe it was simply a matter of wrong place, wrong time. Kerri doubted that scenario. This execution had been planned and carried out carefully. "Any trouble with customers or suppliers?"

"Never." McGill shrugged. "I mean, I've only been here for two years, but all the people I've encountered say the same thing—Leo is the best. Some have worked with him since he opened the place forty years ago. A lot of the customers have been coming here all that time too. It's just crazy."

"No issues with any of the employees, past or present, that you're aware of?"

"No. Nothing."

"What about family troubles? Issues with his significant other or current love interest?"

McGill moved her head side to side. "Leo is—*was* single. His partner died like five years ago, and he never wanted to be with anyone else." She sighed. "The man was a true romantic. And he didn't have kids. He always joked that this place was his child." She made a sound that fell short of being a laugh. "He would say the business just kept growing and never let him down."

"Best friends?"

McGill summoned a watery smile. "We—those of us who work here—are his friends. And his customers. There's no one else I know of."

Which could mean Leo was a loner in his personal life. Or just particularly discreet.

"I realize you've probably already done this with Officer Franklin," Kerri said, "but I need you to take me through your arrival this morning. Tell me everything you remember. Sometimes after such a traumatic event you recall more when you've had a chance to regain your composure."

McGill fiddled with the wad of napkins. "I parked next to Leo's car at like nine twenty-seven. I know that because when I saw his car, I was surprised that he was here already. So I looked at the time on my dash to make sure I wasn't late. I didn't recognize the car parked next to his. The silver Audi, I mean. Leo drives that old four-wheel-drive Bronco. I think it's about as old as he is . . ." She blinked once, twice, then swallowed hard. "Was."

"Did you have to unlock the door to come inside?"

McGill shook her head no. "But I didn't think anything of it since the boss was here. I came inside. Stuck my purse in the locker I use. There's a whole row of them by the coatrack at the back door." She paused, reviewing the next moments before speaking again. "The first thing I saw was the two chairs with hands tied behind them." She made a face. "I thought, *What the hell?* I walked over to the chairs and around in front of them, and there was Leo. I didn't know the other man. It took me a minute to understand they were dead. I was like in shock or something. I kept thinking this can't be real. No way." Her hands sliced through the air, punctuating the statement.

"Did you touch either one of them—maybe to see if they were still breathing—or move anything near where they were seated?"

"No." An adamant shake of her head. "I just stood there trying to get past the shock. I kept telling myself I should scream or do something, but I couldn't move. Then I used my cell to call 911."

"Did you work yesterday, Tara?"

She nodded. "I closed with Leo last night. I left about ten thirty."

"Was there anyone besides you and Mr. Kurtz here at that time?"

"Only Lucky. He closed last night too."

Falco came inside, the ME, Dr. Jeffrey Moore, and one of his assistants right behind him. Two steps behind the threesome were a pair of evidence techs. *About time.*

Kerri turned her attention back to McGill. "Lucky?"

"Lucky Vandiver. He's in college and works here part time." She rolled her eyes. "His family is like megarich, but his daddy insists he work a real job while he's in college. I think his daddy and Leo are friends. The way I heard it, Leo hired Lucky to do the cleanup every night. He sweeps, mops, cleans the bathrooms. All the dreaded shit no one else wants to do. Lucky says his daddy likes torturing him, but—between you and me—he's just a selfish, rich brat. Whatever his father hopes to gain by forcing him to work here, I think he's wasting his time."

Nothing wrong with teaching a kid to work, but Kerri could see how Lucky might not appreciate the lesson, particularly if he was on the spoiled side. "When did Lucky leave?"

"The same time as me. He always tries to talk me into letting him come over to my place for a drink." She shook her head. "I made that mistake a couple of times. He's a good time—if you know what I mean—but he likes the powder, and I am not into that stuff."

"Powder?" Kerri knew what she meant, but she needed the woman to say it.

"Cocaine. He's one of those social users. His parents would kill him if they knew." She shrugged. "I swear, the guy's an idiot. He's got it all, and he does everything possible to screw it up."

"Did Mr. Kurtz know about his drug use?"

Her eyes widened as she moved her head adamantly side to side. "No way. He would have fired him. He's big-time anti–illegal drugs. Tobacco and alcohol are . . . *were* the only drugs he believed in."

"Do you recall if the clothes Mr. Kurtz has on are the same ones he was wearing when you left last night?"

Her breath caught. "I didn't think about it until you asked, but yes, definitely. He always wears blue on Sundays. For the customers, he said." She smiled sadly. "His philosophy was that Sunday is the worst day of the week because you spend it dreading Monday."

Kerri had spent her fair share of Sundays dreading Mondays. "You're certain the navy trousers and light-blue shirt are the ones he wore yesterday?"

McGill nodded, then abruptly stopped. "He never got to go home. Someone must have come in last night after I left and done this. Maybe someone with the other guy." McGill clasped a hand over her mouth and said, "Oh my God," through her fingers. "If I'd been later leaving, I could be dead too. Maybe that other guy was just a late customer."

Kerri didn't bother explaining who the other victim was. *No leaks.* It was better that McGill didn't know his identity. For now, anyway. His face would be plastered on the news soon enough. The next question was an awkward but necessary one. After all, the woman had used her cell phone to call 911, which meant she'd had it in her hand. "One more question, Ms. McGill. This one's a bit sensitive, and I need your honest answer."

She stared wide eyed at Kerri.

"Did you take any photos of the bodies?"

McGill's weepy expression shifted to horror. "Oh my God, no! Who would do that?" She shuddered visibly. "I can't even imagine."

"You'd be surprised." Kerri saw it all the time.

McGill pushed the cell phone lying on the counter toward Kerri. "Have a look for yourself."

Since she'd offered, Kerri checked her call log, text log, and then her photos, recent as well as deleted. No pics of the victims. Just to be certain, one by one she tapped the woman's three social media apps and viewed the last posts on each. Nothing since nine o'clock last night.

Kerri placed the phone on the counter and slid it back to its owner. "Thank you."

"If we're done," McGill said, "I really, really need a drink."

"Just a couple more steps." Kerri pulled a clean page from her notepad. She placed the page and a pen on the counter. "I'd like you to make a list of the other employees and their phone numbers if you have them. Put a star next to the names of folks who have worked here the longest or were closest to Mr. Kurtz."

McGill nodded and picked up the pen.

"I'll be back in a few minutes," Kerri assured her as she slid off the stool.

She made a pass through the public space. The bar was vintage, like an old speakeasy from a century ago, with lots of wood, glass, and leather. The mirrored shelving behind the bar was loaded with classy-looking, high-end bottles of whiskeys and other liquors. Beyond the bar was a small kitchen. A side hall led to the restrooms. The room hosted intimate groupings of tables scattered about. Display cases of cigars, pipes, and tobacco blends. The entire atmosphere was very European, from the wood floors to the coffered ceiling. A large fireplace stood at the far end of the space. This was no typical smoke shop. This was a gathering place for the wealthy and famous of Birmingham to indulge in their habits.

Not the sort of place a double homicide of this nature was expected to happen unless there was a robbery, or the owner was involved in some illegal activity. Drugs, prostitution, human trafficking. There were all sorts of possibilities.

But what the hell did the new hotshot DDA have to do with it?

Kerri made her way into the stockroom. The evidence techs were already doing their thing. Falco and the ME hovered near the bodies. Other than the two vics, this back portion of the building held what one would expect. Supplies for the store as well as a walk-in humidor. The first she'd seen. There was an employee area near the rear exit. The lockers McGill mentioned and a long coatrack that extended from the lockers to the door of the restroom for employees. A narrow row of well-stocked shelving separated the area from the rest of the space. A round table with chairs—two of which had been used to secure the victims—stood in one corner. The employee break area, she supposed.

Moore glanced up from his examination of Leo Kurtz. "Detective, long time no see."

Kerri smiled. "I took a vacation with my daughter during her spring break. The first one I've taken in far too long."

"She called me every day," Falco added.

Moore laughed. "A truly dedicated detective can never fully let go of work."

Kerri couldn't deny that allegation. She'd always found putting work on the back burner more than a little difficult. Moving on to business, she asked, "You have an estimate on time of death?"

Moore's assistant came through the rear exit with a gurney. Falco had obviously shared the need to be discreet. Hopefully the assistant had moved the vehicle fondly referred to as the meat wagon around back as well. The fewer people who noticed that detail, the better.

"For now, I'm going to say between ten last night and two this morning. I'll have something more definitive after I've done a thorough exam."

"We're in the ballpark," Kerri agreed. "The employee who found the bodies this morning worked until ten thirty last night."

Moore nodded. "Falco says we'll need something on these two rather quickly." He looked to Walsh. "I suppose he's the reason."

"He is," Kerri confirmed.

"The chief will probably be giving you a call," Falco warned.

Moore chuckled. "I'm confident he will."

Deep in the pocket of her jacket, Kerri's cell vibrated. She stepped over to the break area to take the call.

A glance at the screen and recognition flared. Her daughter's school. Her brain instantly cued a shot of adrenaline and a burst of apprehension. "Devlin," she said rather than hello.

"Ms. Devlin, this is Joslin Farrington."

The assistant to the head of the school. Kerri held her breath. "Has something happened to Tori?"

Haunting memories from last year—Amelia's murder—ripped through Kerri.

"No." The single syllable sounded oddly uncertain. "She's not hurt or anything, Ms. Devlin."

A pause while Kerri's heart rate raced higher in spite of the news.

"However, we do need you to come to the school as quickly as you can. It's quite urgent."

Rather than demand more information, Kerri said, "I'm on my way."

Heart pounding, head spinning with the possibilities of all the awful things that could happen at school these days—even a posh private one—Kerri jerked her head at Falco, and he joined her near the door between the stockroom and the front retail space.

"What's up?"

"Tori's school called. Something's happened. I have to go. Now."

"Go," he urged. "I've got this."

"Thanks."

"Call me," he said to her back. "Let me know what's going on."

Kerri didn't take the time to respond. She had to go . . . she had to go now.

3

11:50 a.m.

Brighton Academy
Seventh Avenue
Birmingham

In the twenty minutes required to reach Tori's school, Kerri had imagined a dozen ways that her daughter could be in trouble. She'd turned the radio to a local channel and got nothing. She'd resisted calling dispatch since an explanation would be required if she asked questions about any calls to the location.

My daughter's school called. I think she's in trouble. Have any codes been issued for Brighton Academy?

Kerri exhaled a lungful of air as she made the final turn from Twenty-Fourth Street onto Seventh Avenue. The air immediately sucked back into her chest on a vicious gasp. Three BPD cruisers as well as a fire and rescue vehicle littered the street in front of the school's main entrance.

Kerri didn't remember parking . . . had no idea if she'd locked her vehicle or even closed the door. Heart in her throat, she was on the sidewalk and bounding toward the main entrance before her brain caught up with the rest of her. A uniformed officer stood at the double doors.

"I'm afraid the school is on lockdown, ma'am," he warned as she approached.

Kerri shifted her jacket to reveal the badge clipped to her belt, and the uni immediately opened one of the two doors.

"Straight ahead, Detective."

Inside, Kerri hurried down the hall, past the rows of bulletin boards filled with news postings and announcements of upcoming events. The bright overhead lights reflected against the shiny terrazzo floor. The bulletin boards transitioned into surprisingly good watercolor paintings posted on the clean white walls. Any other time she would have paused to check coming events or to admire the artwork. She couldn't take the time now. She had to know if Tori was okay.

At the far end of the main corridor, where the wide stairs led up to the second floor, more uniforms were stationed. A long strand of yellow crime scene tape looped from one side of the corridor to the other, blocking the entrance to the staircase and the exit to the inner courtyard beyond it.

What the hell happened here?

Kerri's heart was thudding ineffectively by the time she reached the door to the school's main office. She walked inside. The lobby was empty save for Detective Wayne Sykes and Nile Foster, the head of the school. The two men were apparently waiting for her. She looked from one to the other. "Where's Tori?"

"Ms. Devlin," Foster said, "we need to speak in my office."

Kerri held up her hands. "Just tell me what's going on."

"Devlin," Sykes said before Foster could respond, "one of the girls in your daughter's class was badly injured in a fall down the stairs. You probably know her, Brendal Myers."

The name clicked into place. Tall, slender, pretty. The Myers family was one of the top donors to the school. "What happened?"

The mother in her wanted to demand to know if Tori was okay, but she'd already been told her daughter wasn't injured. No matter, whatever had happened, Tori was somehow involved; otherwise Kerri would not have been called. That was the part slashing her insides to shreds.

Sykes jerked his head toward Foster's private office. "Let's take a moment and talk about this."

Rather than argue, Kerri went into the office. Taking a seat wasn't possible, so she stood there, waited for Foster to close the door behind Sykes.

"Brendal's parents are on their way. They were in Montgomery for a meeting. Thankfully there's an aunt who could go immediately to be with Brendal at the hospital." Foster rubbed at his forehead. His hand visibly shook. "We're still investigating exactly what happened."

"That's where your little girl comes in," Sykes said.

A new kind of apprehension expanded in Kerri. "Tori would never—"

"No," Sykes said, cutting her off midsentence, "I'm not saying she pushed the Myers girl, but Tori and two other girls were on the landing with Myers when it happened."

"Pushed? What the hell is going on, Sykes?" A knot formed in Kerri's stomach.

The detective gave a nod. "Like I said, when Myers fell, there were three people standing around her. Tori was one of them."

The apprehension vanished, instantly replaced by ire. "Where is she?"

"Peterson is talking to her. We figure she'll be the one most likely to give us the whole story, you being a cop and all."

Kerri understood exactly what he meant. Livid, she swung her attention to Foster. Her protective mother instincts overrode more than a decade of hard-earned cop reflexes. "And you allowed this?"

Foster looked from Kerri to Sykes. "Detective, you assured me Tori's mother wouldn't have a problem with you proceeding with the questioning." He turned back to Kerri. "I'm so sorry. I don't know what to say."

Kerri bit back the curse that perched on the tip of her tongue. It was done. “Take me to her. *Now.*”

Sykes exhaled a long breath. “This way.”

The office phone rang, so Foster stayed behind to take the call. Kerri followed the other detective into the main corridor. At that point she couldn’t stop the words from tumbling out. “What the hell were you thinking, Sykes?”

He stopped, did an about-face, and glared at her. “Look, we got a girl critically injured. And we got three other girls who know what happened, and not one of them is talking. Of all people, you should understand the urgency of the situation. What if it had been your kid rushed to the hospital?”

Kerri took a mental step back. On one level, he was right. Anytime a minor was involved in an incident, it was the waiting for a parent to arrive that often hindered the investigation. Gave the child time to grow more afraid or confused and to possibly make up a story. Parents wanted to protect their children—even if that child had committed a crime. Not to mention the idea that no child wanted to admit his or her wrongdoing in front of a parent.

But Tori was a good kid. An excellent student. She wouldn’t lie or cause any sort of trouble. Ever.

“Don’t give me that shit, Sykes.” Kerri wasn’t letting him off the hook so easily. “She’s a kid. Easy to manipulate. That’s the reason we have rules and procedures. You know as well as I do that anything she has said to you up to the point where I’m in the room is inadmissible.”

“Yeah, yeah, come on.” He started moving again. Paused two doors up and on the other side of the corridor.

The counselor’s office.

Kerri knew the counselor, Anna Leary, fairly well. If she was with Tori, Kerri had nothing to worry about. Leary would never permit a child to be manipulated or badgered. For now, Kerri breathed a little easier.

The secretary wasn't in the small waiting room, so Sykes went straight to the door of the counselor's office and knocked before opening it.

Kerri's gaze landed on Tori, seated in one of two chairs in front of Leary's desk. She took in the red, swollen eyes and the tearstained cheeks. A new burst of fury ignited inside Kerri. The counselor sat behind her desk, and Peterson stood next to her chair. He hadn't taken a seat, a blatant demonstration of authority. He stood on the counselor's side of the desk. Two against one. He glanced at Kerri, then to his partner. Visibly attempted to gauge just how much trouble Kerri was about to start.

"She hasn't threatened to shoot you yet," Sykes said with an attempt at lightheartedness.

Peterson shifted his attention to Kerri again. "You would've done the same if it had been my kid."

"Get out," Kerri said to the man, who knew better than to pretend he hadn't crossed a line. "My daughter and I need the room."

"We'll talk later," Leary said to Kerri as she stood. "Let me know if you need me or want to discuss the past twenty minutes."

Twenty minutes. Peterson had been grilling Tori for twenty damned minutes.

Kerri gave the counselor a nod and waited until the three had left the room before she allowed herself to really look at Tori.

Her fourteen-year-old daughter appeared inordinately small in the upholstered wing chair. Her thin arms were crossed over her still mostly flat chest, and her face revealed exactly how terrified she was. Before Kerri could speak, Tori launched out of the chair into her mother's arms and started to sob.

For a long while, Kerri held her and whispered soothing words. Her own tears flowed down her cheeks. Whatever had happened, Tori was not responsible. She would never purposely hurt anyone. Kerri realized that most parents would believe as much when it came to their offspring, but she didn't just believe it—she *knew* it. Like the rest of the family, Tori was still struggling with her cousin's murder. This child didn't have it in her to hurt anyone.

When Tori's shoulders had stopped shaking and her hard sobs had diminished, Kerri ushered her back into her chair and took the one next to her. "Tell me what happened."

Tori stared at the floor. "I'm . . . I'm not sure."

Kerri's heart twisted. Tori's inability to meet her mother's gaze warned this was not entirely accurate. "Take your time," she said softly. "Who was with you, besides Brendal?"

Tori's thin body jerked at the mention of Brendal's name. "Is she going to be all right?"

Kerri gave it to her straight. "I don't know. Sykes said she was critically injured. We'll have to wait and see what the doctors say."

Tori swiped at her eyes, then met her mother's gaze. "Sarah, Alice, and I were coming down the stairs, headed to our next class, when we ran into Brendal on the landing. She was going upstairs for science."

The ceilings were high in this historic building, which made the staircase from the first floor to the second a double set. At the midway point there was a landing with windows that overlooked the center courtyard.

"What happened then?" Kerri coaxed.

"The same thing Brendal always does." Tori bit down on her lower lip to stop its quivering. "She makes fun of everyone. She's a serious bully." She shrugged. "I mean, I wouldn't have wanted her to get hurt in a million years, but she's so mean to anyone she feels is beneath her—which is most of the other girls in our class. She's always been that way, but she's worse now."

Kerri and Tori had talked about bullies at length many times. Whenever there was an incident at a school anywhere, they had the talk. There was so much more that needed to be done to stop this sort of thing, but Kerri wasn't going to pretend to have the answer. It was an ugly problem without an easy or quick resolution.

"Was Brendal bullying you?" Kerri couldn't help holding her breath. Though Tori hadn't mentioned anything of the sort, she might be less inclined to share with her mom, being a full-fledged teenager now. Adolescents didn't always share everything with their parents during this often-difficult phase in their lives.

"She treated me no differently than she did everyone else." Tori let go a long breath. "Lately, it was Sarah she really went after."

This was news to Kerri. Sarah Talley had been Tori's best friend since kindergarten. Sarah was shy and quiet. Never got into trouble. Always an honor student, like Tori. Kerri was surprised Sarah's mother hadn't tried to intervene.

But then maybe Sarah hadn't told her mother.

Before Kerri asked the really painful question, she ventured into less delicate territory. "Alice is the new girl who started Brighton this semester? The one you spent the night with a couple of times?"

Tori nodded. "Alice Cortez. Remember she moved from Mexico last year, like August, I think. Her parents died, and an uncle took her in. She went to another school before this one, but it didn't work out."

Kerri remembered Tori coming home all upset and sharing the sad story the first day of school right after the semester break. She'd taken it upon herself to befriend the new girl when others weren't so quick to do so.

"Was Brendal bullying Alice too?"

Tori shook her head. "Alice ignored her. It was mostly Sarah she'd been hounding really hard lately." Tori averted her gaze, stared at her hands. "That's all I know."

Kerri recognized the lack of truth in her daughter's final statement. Tori wasn't a very good liar. Or maybe Kerri's skills at spotting an untruth were just particularly well honed. Either way, there was more.

"I understand this is difficult," Kerri assured her. "I also know how it feels to want to protect someone you care about. But sometimes you can't do that. Protecting someone is different from covering for them. Which girl are you trying to protect?"

Tori clasped her hands together in her lap. When she finally lifted her gaze to Kerri's, more tears flowed in little salty rivers. "I swear I don't know if anyone pushed her. I know I didn't, but I was so focused on how Brendal was lashing out that I can't be sure who did what. It all happened really fast."

Kerri nodded slowly. "All right. *If* you didn't see what happened, I can understand your hesitation to hazard a guess."

Tori peered up at her again. "I swear I can't be sure." She glanced around the room before meeting Kerri's gaze once more. "I wouldn't want to get anyone in trouble unless I'm certain."

Kerri squeezed her daughter's hand. "If you're not certain," she said carefully, "then you shouldn't say one way or the other. What did you tell Detective Peterson and Mrs. Leary?"

"I told them the same thing I told you. I don't know who pushed her or if anyone did. I was watching Brendal's rant, and suddenly she was going backward. Her back was to the steps going down. Maybe she backed up or leaned the wrong way and lost her balance. Maybe it wasn't anyone's fault."

Kerri nodded, mostly for her daughter's benefit. "That's possible. There wasn't anyone else in the halls? A teacher or another student who might have seen something?"

Tori moved her head side to side. "The bell had already rung."

Not the answer she'd hoped for. Kerri tried to think of any other possibilities. Janitor? Librarian? Another student late for class? But why wouldn't they have come forward?

Because there was no one else. Kerri felt the additional weight settle on her shoulders.

"What's going to happen now?" The fear in Tori's eyes twisted Kerri's emotions to the snapping point.

"Stay here for a moment while I speak to the other detectives." Kerri stood and turned toward the door.

"I just want to go home," Tori whispered, her eyes squeezing shut against the new flood of tears.

"I'll take you home as soon as I can," Kerri promised.

She stepped out of Leary's office, closing the door behind her. Sykes, Peterson, and Leary were crowded into the tiny waiting room. No doubt straining to hear through the wall.

"Did she tell you anything?" Sykes wanted to know.

Kerri shook her head. "She didn't see what triggered the fall. She was looking directly at Brendal, and suddenly she was tumbling backward."

Peterson nodded. "That's the story she's stuck with from the beginning."

Kerri wanted to tear off his head and spit down his throat. "Have you considered she might be sticking with it because it's the truth?"

Sykes held up a hand before Peterson could spout whatever had his face turning an unpleasant shade of reddish purple. "The trouble is, Devlin," he said in a weary voice, "that's what all three of them are saying. Having one girl not be sure is to be expected, but all three?"

The knot reappeared in her gut. "Sarah and Alice have already been interviewed as well?"

Sykes nodded. "Mrs. Talley was in a PTA meeting in the cafeteria. The Cortez girl's guardian came immediately when we called. You're the only one we had trouble reaching."

"Funny," Kerri tossed back at him, "I don't have any missed calls from you."

Sykes and Peterson exchanged a glance; then both men shrugged.

Didn't matter. Kerri knew exactly what had happened. Or, more accurately, what hadn't happened. "So, Tori was the only one questioned without a parent or legal representation present?"

Sykes and Peterson shared another look.

"I am so sorry," Leary said. "Detective Sykes—"

Kerri held up a hand to the other woman. "I'm aware of what happened." She turned to Sykes. "You have my daughter's statement. I'm taking her home."

Sykes and Peterson started to argue. Kerri ignored them. Before she walked away, another thought occurred to her, and she turned to Leary once more. "This is one of the premier private schools in the state. Sending my daughter here costs a lot of money. Are there no cameras in the halls?"

A new kind of outrage roared through Kerri. This should not have happened, but since it had, where had all the teachers been? Had no one been watching four girls who were obviously late for their next class? One of whom was yelling at the others? And there were cameras. She knew this, but the realization had only just now plowed through all the emotional junk clouding her brain.

Leary seemed to struggle to find the wherewithal to answer the question. "There are cameras. Yes."

"We've already reviewed the footage," Sykes explained. "The positioning of the camera on this first floor is so that the coverage stops at the top of that first landing. All we can see are the girls' feet. We can't tell who did what. The camera on the second floor reaches onto that same landing but on the other side. There's nothing useful on that footage either."

A shroud of frustration closed in around Kerri. "We're leaving. When you want to speak to my daughter again, you ask me first."

She ignored the detectives' complaints and went into the room where Tori waited. "Let's go."

Tori grabbed her backpack from the floor and followed her mother.

In the corridor, Mr. Foster was speaking quietly with Sarah Talley's mother. Sarah clung to her mother like a terrified toddler. If Renae Talley noticed Kerri and Tori exiting, she gave no indication.

Kerri had no idea where the third girl, Alice Cortez, was. Maybe in the other counselor's office. There were two available at all times.

Tori stared at Sarah, but the girl never looked her way.

"Come on." Kerri put her arm through her daughter's. "We'll get this figured out."

Outside, two uniforms were attempting to hold back the reporters who had descended on the scene like a committee of vultures desperate for the remnants of the tragedy. Kerri ushered Tori to the passenger side of her vehicle and hoped like hell the reporters didn't capture a photo of her. She did not want Tori to be the face of this tragedy.

When they reached the street, Kerri turned right without stopping. The reporters had already surged in that direction, but she got away before they managed to reach her vehicle. As a detective Kerri had encountered most of the reporters more than once, and, unfortunately, she was the only detective who drove a vintage Jeep Wagoneer. It wouldn't take a resourceful reporter long to figure out who had driven away in the vehicle. Even less time would be required to determine that Kerri had a daughter who attended this school.

She silently swore at herself for hanging on to this damned thing all these years.

"What do we do now?"

Tori's voice sounded so small Kerri wanted to pull her into her arms and rock her the way she had when she was a baby. "We're going home. Sykes and Peterson will sort this out. They're good detectives." She said this despite how pissed she was at the two of them just now.

Tori stared out the window. Kerri wished she could reassure her that this would be over soon, and all would be fine. But she wouldn't lie to her daughter. It would take time, and the process would be painful. If the Myers girl died, things would get exponentially worse.

Bully or not, Kerri prayed the girl pulled through. No matter that she was mean, she didn't deserve to die as penance. No parent should have to suffer through that kind of loss. Kerri had watched what it had done to her sister and her brother-in-law. She wouldn't wish that pain on anyone.

Her cell vibrated and she considered ignoring it, but it could be Falco. She'd promised to call him. She fished for the phone in her pocket, checked the screen. Falco's face flashed there as another insistent ring vibrated the device.

"I'm leaving the school now," she said rather than hello.

"Is our girl okay?"

Falco and Tori were close. That was something else Kerri appreciated about her partner. Tori's father, Nick Jackman, had moved to New York and started a new family with his second wife—the woman with whom he'd cheated on Kerri. Tori had desperately needed someone to fill the void he'd left. Falco had stepped up to the plate. Kerri couldn't ask for a better surrogate father for her daughter. Especially since she didn't have the time or the inclination for any sort of relationship other than family and work.

Not that she would anyway. Allowing herself to trust someone that deeply ever again wasn't very likely in the foreseeable future.

"She's okay. We'll talk about it later."

"Got it." He cleared his throat. "I know you have your hands full, but we have a development here."

Kerri took a moment to reorient her thoughts. She rarely permitted her mind to shift so fully from a case. "You found a witness?"

"Nope, but I found Walsh's cell phone. It was tucked into his sock like a backup piece."

Smart guy. That said, sometimes intelligence wasn't enough to keep you alive. "And?"

"The last call Walsh made was to a number I recognized."

Kerri braked at an intersection and waited for her partner to say the rest.

"Cross," Falco announced. "Our dead DDA spoke to Cross at ten o'clock last night."

Sadie Cross. Now there was a surprising turn of events. Cross was a former BPD detective. She'd worked for the department for more than a dozen years, and then she'd walked away. Everyone said she hadn't been the same since that last undercover operation. She'd gone missing for nearly a year and come back with no memory of what had happened to her during that time and very little recall of the events that had occurred while she was under deep cover for the four months prior to vanishing. Cross was an odd sort. She rubbed Kerri the wrong way.

But Kerri owed her.

Whatever Cross had to do with this double homicide, Kerri had no choice but to give the woman the benefit of the doubt. She damned sure had no right to cast the first stone.

"You talked to her already?"

"We should do this in person. I can go without you, if that would be better under the circumstances."

"No. You're right. We should talk to her together. I'll pick you up." Diana, Kerri's sister, was always more than happy to spend time with Tori. Kerri glanced at her daughter. "I'll drop Tori by Diana's for a little while."

Tori looked at her. She didn't say a word, but the unspoken demand was written all over her face.

You're going to leave your traumatized daughter to work on a case?

What kind of mother did that?

4

12:30 p.m.

Sadie's Loft
Sixth Avenue, Twenty-Seventh Street
Birmingham

Sadie stared at the news flashing on the screen. There had been a double homicide at Leo's. The victims' names hadn't been released yet. Sadie didn't need anyone to tell her what had happened.

Walsh was dead.

He'd said they would talk this morning about what he'd learned in his meeting with Kurtz, but he hadn't called. There was no need for her to try calling him. He was dead. She knew it. The only way he wouldn't have called or shown up this morning was if he was dead.

"Son of a bitch!" She clicked the remote, turning the television screen to black.

She had told him. Damn it. She'd told him more than once. This thing he wanted to do was not a good idea. Not for someone like him. He didn't know how to dive into the deep water like this without ending up shark bait. He didn't have the experience. Just a lot of ambition and fearlessness.

Idiot.

Sadie closed her eyes and blocked the image of his face. Too damned young to die. He wasn't even thirty. So damned determined to be the big hero.

"I'm the perfect example of how that shit works out," she muttered.

Now the cops would be crawling all over her ass. She'd been extremely careful—as always. No phone calls unless they used burner phones. No emails or text messages. They'd met in private. No one could know she had spoken to him, and yet there would be no way to hide that fact after what he'd done.

He'd called her last night from his personal cell phone. She'd jumped his shit, but he'd been too excited to care. He was close, he'd said. Kurtz had agreed to talk with other small, independent business owners he'd suspected were dealing with the same concerns. More importantly, Kurtz had found a potential source they were going to confront.

Now Walsh was dead.

The investigating detectives would find the call. No matter if Walsh deleted the call and her number from his call log; they would find it in his phone records.

What she needed was a logical explanation for why he had called her. A call to a wrong number wouldn't have lasted three minutes or so.

Damn it!

Sadie grabbed her smokes from the table and tapped one out. She tucked it into the corner of her mouth and flicked her lighter. Savoring a long drag, Sadie allowed the chemicals to fill her lungs with the comforting promise only nicotine could make. She didn't worry about lung cancer. It wasn't like she was going to have a long and prosperous life. It was a miracle she wasn't already dead.

Plenty had tried to make her that way. Not that she cared. She didn't. Another day lived was another day she had to find ways to distract herself from the bits and pieces of the past that haunted her. She wasn't suicidal or anything. She just didn't care. She was done.

Done. Done. Done.

Her father slipped into her thoughts, and she dismissed him. He'd given up on her long ago. They hadn't spoken in what? A year? He'd likely be happy once she was out of the way. Then he wouldn't have to be disappointed in her anymore. She couldn't screw up her life any worse if she were dead. She could no longer embarrass him. His life would certainly be less complicated.

Are you married? No, no, I'm a widower. Any children? No, no children. My only daughter passed away.

How nice that would be for him. He wouldn't have to explain who his daughter was. Where she lived. What she had done since quitting the Birmingham Police Department. The only question that might crop up was how she'd died. He wasn't above making something up to cover that detail. Cancer like her poor mother? Hit and run? Robbery gone wrong?

But she wasn't dead.

Truth was she didn't really understand why. She should have died the day she vanished all those years ago or on any number of other occasions before and since. She'd taken a bullet more than once. Had multiple car accidents—usually while chasing bad guys. Somehow, she had survived them all.

"Your luck won't hold out forever," she muttered as she drew more smoke into her lungs. The upside was then she wouldn't have to bother with all *this*.

The DIY route had never been an option. She might be a lot of things, but she wasn't a quitter. In her opinion, going the suicide route was being a quitter. Taking the easy way out. Leaving the rest of the world to clean up your mess.

Nope. She wasn't a quitter. Her plan was to piss off the whole world, and then maybe one of these days someone would do it for her.

Easy peasy.

She crossed the room and parted the blinds on a window overlooking Sixth Avenue. No cops yet. Her phone hadn't rung, which was strange. The detectives investigating the case should have called her number already to find out who she was. Unless they hadn't found Walsh's cell phone. Or he'd deleted his call record.

If either of those scenarios was the case, it would buy her some time.

She drew her fingers away; the blind snapped into place, sending years of dust filtering through the air. Turning her back, she braced her hip on the window ledge and looked around the room. Really, she didn't have it so bad. She had this place. It wasn't much, but it was hers. Damned sure was more than her father would have given her—seeing that he had basically disowned her and all.

Pauley Winters, a former cop and the best damned PI in the state of Alabama before his death, had left the building and his business to her when he'd died last spring. He'd been her best friend and the closest thing she'd had to a real parent since her mom died. Her father had changed after his wife's death. Pushed Sadie away, grown hard and cold. Not even when she'd joined the Birmingham Police Department could she please him. She'd even gone into narcotics to impress the revered DEA special agent in charge Mason Cross. She could be a big undercover hero like he once was.

He hadn't been impressed.

Thinking about her father and the past had her stomach cramping. Sadie pushed away from the window and went to the sink. She needed coffee. Too early for a whiskey. She'd allowed her alcohol consumption to get out of control for a while. She wasn't going there again. Her father would be waiting in the wings to put her in rehab for the third—no, fourth—time.

"Bastard." She poured water into the machine. A few scoops of grounds and then she pushed the "Brew" button.

The only thing worse than living through the haunting memories of those missing months was rehab. She'd spent more than enough time in hospitals and rehab for a dozen lifetimes.

She walked to her desk and shuffled through the files there. Her last case was closed. Nothing new had come in. That was the way of a small private investigations firm. It was feast or famine. Pauley had explained the instability of the business was the primary reason he'd bought this building. The pub downstairs was the only one of its kind in this neighborhood. Very Irish, very vintage. He had leased it to a real Irishman years ago. The money from the lease provided sufficient income for scraping by if nothing else panned out.

Lately, Sadie had come to appreciate her old friend's foresight. Barely a month after Pauley died, she had walked away from her damaged career at the BPD and taken over the PI shop. Pauley had left it to her, after all. Why not? She could be her own boss. Do things her own way.

Funny, her father—the man she hadn't been able to impress with her law enforcement career—had suddenly been beyond pissed off that she'd left it behind.

Sadie shook off the memories. She poured a cup of coffee and walked over to the wall next to the door, the one that stood between her and the alley. No windows on that wall. She used it like a massive bulletin board for her cases. But at this end, next to the door, was her ongoing, four-year-old-plus *personal* case. The one that haunted her sleep and gnawed at her every waking hour.

What in the world happened to Sadie Cross?

The answer to that question was the one—however remote—real reason for her to have even the slightest desire to continue breathing. A little less than five years ago she had taken what would turn out to be her final field op with the BPD. Deep undercover. Inordinately dangerous. Four months in, she'd disappeared. Nearly a year after vanishing she'd reappeared as if an alien spaceship had dropped her back on the planet. Those missing months had stolen the person she had once been. Had taken more from her than anyone knew. She'd come back an empty shell. Her stellar law enforcement career had suddenly become that of a file clerk digging through dusty cold case files.

Now she was here. Filling the emptiness with booze and what Pauley had left her until she could find the truth.

She couldn't really say why it mattered, but somehow it did. She stared at the timeline she had created. There were dozens of sticky notes on the wall. Red, yellow, and purple. Even a few pink ones. A couple of light-green ones. All were pieces of her shattered memory. Scattered fragments. Nothing, not counseling, not regression therapy, had unearthed more than mere slivers of recall. This past Christmas she'd considered going back to the guy who had done the regression therapy three years ago and trying again, but then he'd died. Car crash. He'd been the only one of the shrinks she'd seen that she had liked . . . trusted just a little. She'd considered requesting her files and the audiotapes of her sessions after his death, but she'd never bothered.

She'd let it go. Wouldn't help. The shrinks had reached a certain point, and her mind had blocked any further progress. There was a brick wall inside her head, and nothing or no one seemed able to get her past it. Maybe the truth was she didn't want to know whatever was beyond that brick wall. It wasn't like she could change whatever had happened during those missing months.

Sounds and images whispered through her mind, making her flinch.

She had survived. The only question was why.

"Just another mystery in the life of Sadie Cross."

She stared at the colorful notes, some faded with age. Did it actually matter what had happened during those lost months? Probably not. She wasn't a cop anymore. It wouldn't fix the canyon-wide rift between her and her father. Damn sure wouldn't help the failed operation. Still, part of her wanted those weeks and months back. It was her life, and whatever happened, she wanted to know and understand it. To log it in like the rest of her days. If she was going to continue breathing, she might as well have the whole story.

The regression therapy shrink, Dr. Oliver Holden, had told her the memories behind that wall were either gone for good or there to stay. Trying to dig them out was in all likelihood a pointless endeavor. If regression therapy hadn't resurrected them, they weren't coming. The trauma could be too much for her to handle. The mind's ability to block something like that was powerful.

Denial was an incredibly strong cognitive process.

The soft chime of the alert that someone had approached the fire escape sounded. She went to her laptop and checked the camera. The stairway down to the first floor, to the pub, had long ago been closed off to allow for a private living space on the second level. This upstairs loft—her dusty, disorganized home—was entered via the fire escape in the alley. Since that access point created a vulnerability all its own, she'd taken precautions with plenty of added security. Like cameras and motion sensors.

Frustration furrowing her brow, she watched the images on the screen. Kerri Devlin, followed by Luke Falco, climbed the rusty iron stairs. At least now she knew who had landed the double homicide at Leo's Tobacconist.

"Shit."

She would have been far happier if it had been anyone else. Luke Falco she liked, sort of. It would be harder to lie to him with a good degree of success.

She needed to lie. Not that it was anything new.

She lied a lot.

It was necessary. Or, at least, less complicated.

Equally troubling, Falco and Devlin were good. By far the best of the lot at the BPD.

The knock came. *Knock. Knock. Pause. Knock.* Sadie stared at Falco's face on the screen. She might as well get this over with. Even if they went away, they'd only come back again later.

At the door she disengaged the multiple dead bolts. Heaved a massive sigh and opened the door.

"What do you want?" She never minced words. Ask the question, get the answer. Done.

"We need to talk."

Falco was usually direct as well. Most of the time anyway. She glanced at Devlin. "Fine. But make it fast. I have shit to do."

She turned her back and walked over to where she'd left her coffee on the counter next to the sink. Like most lofts, the space was one big room with only a dinky bathroom closed off with its own walls. She liked it. The place suited her personality. Urban. No fuss. She kept the lighting dim, almost dark, on purpose. People were nosy. Especially detectives.

"I'd offer you coffee"—she held up her mug—"but you won't be here long enough."

Falco closed the door and locked one of the dead bolts. He knew how she was about security. Your ass didn't go missing for nearly a year—most of which time was a blank—without becoming a little paranoid about security. Not that she was afraid. Not really. Death wasn't such a bad thing. It was the stuff they did before they killed you that typically sucked.

"Do you know DDA Asher Walsh?" Devlin asked, opting not to drag her feet and going straight to the point.

Good.

"No." Sadie wasn't dragging hers either.

"Come on, Cross," Falco griped. "You were the last person he called."

She shrugged. "Was my name in his contact list?"

"You know it wasn't." This from Devlin. "Cut the crap, Sadie. Why did Walsh call you?"

There were moments like now when Sadie wished things were back to the way they used to be—when she had no friends. Any facsimile of friends she'd ever had had dropped out of the picture after her disappearing act. Some of those so-called friends actually had the balls to believe she'd fallen off the radar on purpose, then returned when things didn't work out. Yeah, right. People were so quick to condemn anything they didn't understand.

She should have learned her lesson about friends. Allowing Falco so close had been a mistake. Then he'd dragged Devlin with him. Damn it.

Maybe the term *friends* was a bit of a stretch, but these two humans knew her better than most. Most *living* humans, anyway.

She thumped the coffee mug down on the counter and crossed her arms over her chest. "He wanted information." Sadie cocked her head. "You know," she said to Devlin, "like you did last year when your niece was missing. When I helped you out of a really fucked-up situation."

Funny how people never remembered that kind of shit unless it suited their purposes.

Falco shook his head, but before he could go busting her chops, Devlin walked toward Sadie. Brushed past her and grabbed a mug and poured herself a coffee. Then she sat her skinny ass down on the sofa. The one Sadie had helped Pauley retrieve from a curb over in Mountain Brook and haul up those damned rusty stairs. It wasn't that he couldn't have bought a new one, but he'd sworn the brand of this sofa made it worth the trouble. It barely had any wear, but the people in the multimillion-dollar house had no longer wanted it.

Pauley had been like that. He'd liked saving things. Like broken detectives.

"I've had a really bad day," Devlin said, dragging Sadie's attention back to her. "I had to pick up my daughter from school after one of her classmates fell—possibly with some assistance—down a staircase. Because DDA Walsh went and got himself murdered, I had no choice but to dump my traumatized child on my sister's doorstep and come here." She produced a fake smile. "Now stop wasting my time and tell me the rest."

Falco chuckled. "Damn, Devlin. Why don't you tell it like it is?" He strode over and poured himself a coffee and then sat down next to his partner.

Knowing a stalemate when faced with one, Sadie decided to throw the pair a bone. If it got them the hell out of here, it would be worth it. She strolled over to the chair that had once been a recliner but no longer worked other than as a chair, dropped into it, and hung her hands between her knees.

"Walsh had visions of grandeur. He wanted to make a big name for himself really fast. And he wanted to get dirty doing it. Two of the biggest things on people's minds these days are drugs and human trafficking. We all know the drug cartels are eyeball deep in the human trafficking as well as the drugs. You stamp out one, and you stop the flow. For a while anyway. The ambitious DDA made no secret of his stance against drugs."

"The Osorio cartel," Falco suggested. "He knows you got in once, and he wanted to pick your brain."

"Right," Sadie said with all the sarcasm she could muster. "Apparently someone forgot to tell him that my brain got damaged during that operation. It's full of pieces from that time period that don't fit together or make any kind of sense. Like someone lost part of the puzzle, and now it doesn't come together in a complete picture."

"When did he first contact you?" Devlin asked.

Sadie stared at the other woman. As much as she didn't want to like Devlin even a little, she did respect her. Devlin had learned a hard lesson last summer. She'd picked up her own shattered pieces and gotten on with her life. That was the thing about being a cop; sometimes it broke you into a million little bits.

"About a month ago." Sadie leaned back in the chair and forced her body to relax. It sucked that Walsh was dead. He'd really wanted to do this thing. He'd wanted to help her in the process, but she'd told him he was painting a serious target on his back. Dumb-ass rich boy. "He wanted to know if I would walk him through anything I remembered about the Osorio cartel's compound and the operation."

After an expectant second or two passed, Devlin asked, "Did you?"

"I told him what everyone else already knows. I only have fragments of memory, and they're foggy and blurry and completely unreliable."

This was not the whole truth. She had told him this at first—two months ago—but he'd just kept coming back, and finally a month back she'd shared shit about her past with him. Shit she hadn't shared with anyone since the regression therapy.

Shit that probably got him killed.

"Did he contact you again after his initial visit?" Falco placed his mug on the table at the end of the sofa. "I'm guessing when we check his phone records, last night's call won't be the only time he called you in the past month."

Sadie shrugged. "He called me several times, usually with this burner phone he used. He wasn't prepared to accept that I couldn't remember anything useful. I told him that even regression therapy hadn't pulled it out of my head, but he just kept prodding me. Some people just won't listen if the words you're saying messes with their plans."

"What did he want last night?" Kerri sipped her coffee, her gaze never leaving Sadie's.

Here it was. The moment for another piece of the truth. Devlin and Falco were good detectives. Relentless. They would figure it out eventually or bug the hell out of her until she told them what they wanted to know just so they'd go away. She had no interest in prolonging the misery.

"He said he believed he'd found an inside source. Possibly related to the distribution of illegal drugs in Birmingham. He and Leo Kurtz were going to confront this source. Walsh would offer a deal for cooperation. The usual bullshit."

"You have any idea who this source was?" Kerri nudged. "Man? Woman?"

Sadie laughed, the sound as dry as the leaves would be in Alabama's relentless summer heat. She actually couldn't remember the last time she'd experienced a real laugh. "He referred to the person as 'the source.' Never indicated male or female. Obviously since you're here, the source wasn't interested in the deal he had to offer."

Devlin glared at her with that holier-than-thou attitude. But they both knew the real story. Devlin was no saint. She had secrets. Sins. Everyone did. She'd gotten her hands dirty at least once, by God.

Falco braced his elbows on his knees and studied Sadie over the rim of his coffee mug. "Was anyone else besides Kurtz—another business owner maybe—involved in or cooperating with Walsh's plan?"

"If that was the case, he didn't share the information with me." This was not entirely true. Drawing other business owners out of the cloak of fear and secrecy was the goal, but she had no idea if Kurtz had even started attempting to bring others to the table. Either way, she needed to follow up on a couple of things before she gave them too much.

"Was Walsh's boss aware of this investigation?" Kerri asked.

"I don't have a clue. I assume he was, but Walsh never mentioned him. My impression was that this was his baby. He wanted to rock it all by himself at least until the op found its legs."

"We need your help with this."

The idea that these words had come from Devlin surprised—no, shocked—the hell out of Sadie. Maybe the detective really was off her game after whatever happened at her daughter's school.

Sadie went with the flow. "I'll tell you like I told Walsh. You can ask me anything you like, but I can't guarantee I have the answer. At least not an answer I can produce."

"I'm sure you can answer this one," Falco said. "What's the number of the burner phone he used? We'll need to get those records. See who else he called."

She rattled off the number. "But don't waste your time. I already pulled the records. He only called me with that phone. If he had another one, I don't know about it."

"You can email me a copy of the records." Devlin stood. "Thanks for the coffee. Keep in mind we'll have more questions."

Falco pushed to his feet. He grabbed Devlin's mug and carried both his and hers to the sink. The guy was too stinking nice for his own good. Years of undercover work had done shit to him too. Maybe all the being extra good these days was about making amends for something he'd done during that time. It happened. Going undercover was sort of like acting. If you wanted the Academy Award, you had to buy all the way into the part. It had to be real. Had to be you. Sometimes you did really bad shit to give the best performance.

"This case is going to be all over the news, Cross," Falco offered. "The chief will be breathing down our necks."

"I'll make you a deal." Sadie looked from Falco to Devlin. "You make sure no one knows about the calls between Walsh and me, and I'll cooperate fully. But I don't want my name anywhere on the official reports."

Devlin and Falco exchanged a look. Devlin took the initiative. "You have my word."

If there was one thing Sadie understood with complete certainty, it was that Devlin would not lie to her. As far as she'd fallen last summer, Devlin still had this idea of what a good cop was supposed to look like, and she tried her best to live up to that image.

Sadie wished she could make her see that the ideal was not realistic. A good cop did what had to be done, and sometimes it wasn't good at all, only necessary.

"We're square then," Sadie agreed. "I'll reach out to my sources and see what I can find for you."

This was something Sadie did have, if nothing else. She had invaluable sources. All from the most unlikely of places. Not only were they reliable; they were damned good. Not a single one of her sources had ever let her down, which was far more than she could say for most of the friends she'd ever claimed.

"That would be very helpful," Falco said.

"Yeah, yeah." Sadie got up and moved toward the door. "You'll owe me, I know."

At the door she reached for the top dead bolt, and Falco said the rest, "I already owe you, Cross. I haven't forgotten."

She turned to him. "I'm sure you haven't." Her attention drifted to Devlin. "You should remember the people who do you favors."

Devlin gave a nod. "I haven't forgotten either."

Sadie reached for the door again. "Just one thing." When both Falco and Devlin met her gaze, she continued, "Anyone associated with the Osorio cartel is utterly ruthless. I mean, the kind of evil you don't even know. Those people will do anything to protect themselves. You should watch your backs."

"Got it," Falco confirmed.

As they filed out the door, Devlin paused. "You should watch your back as well. We may not be the only ones who know Walsh came to you."

Sadie was well aware. This was yet another reason she had to find a way to put all those pieces together.

Whatever was happening, it was no doubt prompted by her past.

5

3:00 p.m.

Office of the Jefferson County District Attorney
Richard Arrington Jr. Boulevard North
Birmingham

Kerri sat behind Deputy District Attorney Asher Walsh's desk and surveyed his office. The usual government-issued furniture. No upgrades for the wealthy Bostonian. The only concession to his prestigious background was the framed diploma from Harvard Law School. Nothing else.

The bulletin board was plastered with newspaper articles about drugs and human trafficking that had captured Walsh's attention since he'd landed in Birmingham. So far, the contents of his files and his desk drawers were immaculately organized if lacking in any useful revelations.

One by one Falco moved through the books—mostly law books—filling the shelves along the opposite wall. He opened each one, looking for anything that might be hidden. Then checked the shelf before sliding the volume back into place.

Walsh's assistant, Louisa Allen, eyes red from a recent bout of tears, had unlocked the desk and left Kerri and Falco to do the necessary search. The press conference had happened at one thirty. The district attorney, with the sheriff and the chief of police as well as the mayor, had announced the somber news. Because of Walsh's strong and well-known antidrug agenda, the mayor, Emma Warren, was calling for a joint task force that included the DEA. Though she was well aware of how capable the BPD's Major Investigations Division was and the wider jurisdiction, she felt the death of DDA Walsh was a message, and the city needed to respond to that message with a show of force and unity in a much broader fashion.

Until this proposed task force was set in motion, Kerri and Falco were to carry on.

Warren didn't seem to be satisfied with the knowledge that the MID was made up of good cops from Birmingham as well as the surrounding communities—including the Jefferson County Sheriff's Department. She understood their jurisdiction was all-inclusive. The former mayor, the chief of police, and the sheriff had spent years developing this division. It was a fairly new concept, yes, but it had worked well so far. Being new to the office of mayor, Warren obviously wanted to prove she was not only paying attention but engaged and more than happy to ensure her predecessor's legacy still met the needs of the community.

However much she disagreed with the decision, Kerri had to admit it was refreshing to have a woman—especially a minority woman—in the city's most powerful office. With a law degree as well as one in psychology, Warren had spent her entire career working hard and supporting the community. Rarely a day passed without one effort or the other putting her face front and center in the news. Even at sixty, her sophisticated beauty had captured the media's attention. Her rhythmic and appealing ability to articulate her message made any audience want to join her cause. The candidates who'd run against her hadn't stood a chance.

Emma Warren was an inspiration to all women despite being on Kerri's shit list at the moment.

Shifting her focus back to the matter at hand, Kerri considered that she had executed a thorough search of the desk drawers. No hidden alcohol or drug stash. No porn. Just the usual pencils, pens, notepads, erasers, paper clips. The guy was over-the-top well organized—almost as if he didn't actually work at this desk. One drawer contained files. These, Allen had explained, were his current working files. Oddly, none were related to the Osorio cartel or any other for that matter. In fact, none were related to illegal drug activity at all.

This didn't surprise Kerri any more than it suggested Cross had lied about Walsh's interest in the Osorio cartel. Frankly, there was no readily identifiable, logical motive for Cross to try to mislead them. But what it did illustrate was that Walsh's research into the cartel was off the record. Not exactly what Kerri would expect from someone with a burning desire to prove himself in a professional capacity. Why the secretiveness—even with his colleagues?

On the other hand, nothing they had discovered suggested the loss of a friend or loved one to drugs or human trafficking, which might imply a personal mission. And yet, based on what they knew so far, this—whatever it was he'd gotten himself into—was in all likelihood *personal.*

Maybe there was no particular event that had lit a fuse under his personal mission. But that wasn't the norm. When someone went about an undertaking like this in such a secretive and aggressive manner, there was typically a very personal motive.

She and Falco had only to find it.

They hadn't interviewed the DA yet. Lockett was in a meeting. Allen would see to it that they got a moment of his time as soon as he was available.

She scanned the notes written on Walsh's blotting pad once more. The few scattered words didn't provide anything useful. There was a phone number jotted in one corner, but it was his dry cleaner's. The in- and out-boxes stationed at the front of his desk were empty. Allen said he stayed on top of the paperwork.

The one framed photo on the desk was of him and some of his law school buddies—this, too, was according to Allen. There was no photo of his parents. He had no siblings. Allen was developing a list of friends and colleagues with whom he associated frequently and any particularly troubling cases he had worked since his arrival in Birmingham. Kerri wasn't expecting anything useful since the woman had already stated that she couldn't think of any such cases off the top of her head.

The door swung open, and DA Luther Lockett entered. Kerri straightened and rose to her feet. Lockett was a large man, tall and broad shouldered. Back in the day, he had been a quarterback for the University of Auburn's Tigers. In Alabama, besides politics the one thing folks got extra hot and bothered about was the rivalry between the Auburn Tigers and the University of Alabama's Crimson Tide. Football was practically a religion around here.

Lockett swung the door shut and glanced at Falco before resting his full attention on Kerri. "Detectives." He thrust his hand across the desk and gave hers a shake. Then he did the same with Falco. "I'd like an update on what you have so far."

He settled into a seat in front of the desk and waited expectantly.

"At this time, sir, we don't have much. We've asked Mrs. Allen to prepare a list of DDA Walsh's cases as well as his friends and colleagues. We've also requested his phone records, and we're currently looking for any notes he may have left related to anyone he intended or expected to see last night. There was nothing about the meeting with Mr. Kurtz on his calendar. No phone calls or texts between him and the other victim. Our first goal is to establish a connection between the two victims."

Lockett gave her a nod as if he approved. "You may or may not be aware that Asher made his thoughts regarding gun control public in a recent interview. His feelings on the matter are not popular here in the South. You will certainly want to add that possibility to your list of potential motives."

"In another recent interview," Falco said as he approached the desk, a book in his hand, "Walsh mentioned that he wanted to do all in his power to stop the flow of drugs into the country. He seemed very determined on the subject."

"And human trafficking," Kerri added. "Putting an end to the sale of humans was another of his goals."

They'd watched all five of the interviews Walsh had done with local news channels since settling into the DA's office.

Lockett nodded. "We all come into this world of law enforcement and prosecution with big ideas about change. But we can't always attain the first goal we set. Sometimes not even the second or the tenth. But we can do our very best. I had high hopes for Asher. He was a brilliant young man." He seemed to reflect for a moment. "As you can imagine, when my DDAs are working on cases, I'm not always aware of blow-by-blow events. I trust my people to do their jobs and to keep me informed. I have no doubt you will discover whatever Asher was working on with Mr. Kurtz relates to his duties here. He was not the sort to go off half-cocked."

"I'm certain you're correct," Kerri agreed.

When the silence grew awkward, she went on to assure him, "We'll do everything we can to find the shooter as quickly as possible."

"Well, then"—Lockett pushed to his feet—"I'll leave you to it." He hesitated at the door. "I'm confident you're aware of Mayor Warren's desire to take this investigation to the next level. Whatever comes of her suggestion, I want the two of you to push onward until you're told differently. Do not allow what you hear in the news to slow you down. Every member of the media wants to be the first to find the answer. Ratings, you know."

"Understood, sir," Kerri said. If Walsh had been going after one or more drug cartels, the mayor would no doubt insist on being involved with the investigation. After all, one of her campaign platforms had been her determination to stamp out illegal drugs. Like Walsh, the mayor took a strong and very public stance on human trafficking. And why wouldn't she? The number of female victims was nearly triple that of male vics.

When the door had closed behind Lockett, Falco opened the book in his hand, *To Kill a Mockingbird*, by Harper Lee, and removed a photograph. "Take a look at this."

Kerri stood as her partner moved closer and passed the photo to her. She studied the image, which showed Walsh with an older woman of sixty or so. The woman wore jeans and a sweater. Her long gray hair was a wild mane of loose curls, and the expression on her face warned she didn't care. On the back, the photo was dated four years ago.

"There are some similarities between the woman and Walsh," Kerri pointed out, "but this isn't his mother." She'd done some research on the vic's parents. The mother was very attractive and dressed with expert style. Elegant would be the best way to describe her. The father, too, was very polished, sophisticated looking.

"It's his aunt." Falco flipped open the book's cover. "This is who gave our vic the book. Read the note."

> *Asher,*
> *You are too good for this profession you've chosen. But if you're going to do it, do it with all your heart.*
> *Love,*
> *Aunt Naomi*

Kerri looked from the note to Falco. "Maybe this is his mother's sister? Based on the photos of the mother I found on the internet, there is definitely a resemblance."

"Check this out." Falco turned to the next page in the book and offered it to Kerri.

She exchanged the photo for the book, then scanned the copyright page. "First edition."

"Signed by the author," Falco pointed out.

Sure enough, there was the icon's signature. *Be the best you can be.* The words were addressed to a Norman Taylor.

Before Kerri could ask, Falco explained, "I googled Norman Taylor. Like the author, he died a few years ago. He was in his nineties. A retired Birmingham attorney. A *big deal* attorney. Big supporter of the civil rights movement in the sixties." He held up the photo of the woman, Naomi. "This Aunt Naomi is Norman Taylor's daughter."

"So, it's possible Norman Taylor is Walsh's maternal grandfather." The memory of documentaries Kerri had watched about the civil rights movement era in Birmingham gave her chills.

"The mother's maiden name wasn't Taylor, but the photo and the note seem to suggest the two were related somehow," Falco agreed. "The question is, Why does no one here—where our vic worked—realize he had a connection to Birmingham? Think about all the hype when he first arrived, Devlin. And those interviews we watched. No one—not even Walsh himself—mentioned a personal connection to Birmingham."

Falco made an interesting point. Kerri pushed the chair she'd vacated into the desk. "Could be this Naomi is just a friend who calls herself his aunt." Her sister Diana's kids had always called her longtime best friend Jennifer Aunt Jen. "Either way, we should find out about this Naomi Taylor."

"We could ask his assistant," Falco suggested.

"Good idea. Ask her." Kerri flashed him a smile. "Use that formidable Falco charm. She'll never be able to resist."

He chuckled and headed for the door. "Funny, it never works on you."

"I'm immune." Kerri shook her head, then studied the photo from the book. She'd learned not so long ago the one thing she could count on was that everyone had secrets.

Good or bad, rich or poor, there was always more to the story. Asher Walsh and family would have plenty.

—

Taylor Residence
Eighteenth Avenue South
Birmingham, 4:00 p.m.

"This is it?" Kerri looked beyond her partner to the house on the right of the curb where she'd eased to a stop.

"It is," Falco confirmed. "The residence of Naomi June Taylor. Sixty-two years old. Never married. No kids."

Walsh's assistant had no idea who Naomi Taylor was. They'd had to look her up through the DMV and old newspaper articles about her father. She was a retired law professor from Samford, her and her father's alma mater. She drove a vintage Mercedes and had three tickets for speeding in the last two years. About a dozen outstanding parking tickets.

Kerri surveyed the place. "Looks a little run down."

"Not exactly a premier neighborhood, but it had its heyday in the fifties and sixties." Falco reached for the door.

Kerri climbed out and met him at the front of her Wagoneer. "Even now, there's certainly something to be said for that view of the city."

Beyond the houses lining this side of the street was an incredible view of the Magic City sprawled across the landscape. At night the lights were likely something to see.

"It ain't shabby," Falco agreed as he adjusted his jacket.

One of the things about him that had driven Kerri crazy when he was first assigned as her new partner was his manner of dress. The cocky attitude and laid-back, I'm-down-with-it lingo weren't so in your face unless he opened his mouth—which he did quite frequently. But there was no way to ignore his wardrobe. The beat-up leather jacket and the worn-out jeans, wrinkled tee. He hadn't looked at all like the typical detective representing MID. Still didn't. She'd felt certain they would never make it as a team. She'd said as much to Lieutenant Brooks at the onset. Luke Falco just wasn't what she had expected in a partner.

Kerri had been wrong. She'd learned very quickly not to judge this particular book by his cover. Falco was loyal, caring, and relentless. He was a damned good detective.

She would without condition or hesitation dive into any situation with him.

He was the one good thing that had happened last year.

He knocked on the door of the Taylor home.

The house appeared to be circa 1950s, possibly older. Redbrick. Some peeling white paint on the trim. A few torn screens on the windows but nicely landscaped. Colorful spring blooms filled the flower beds and window boxes. Kerri wasn't that good with the names of flowers, but the ones with the blue blooms were very pretty and the most prevalent in the landscaping. Obviously, those were the homeowner's favorite. Kerri thought Diana had those same flowers blooming in her yard.

The lawn was neatly manicured. The trees were peppered with spring's fresh green leaves. The whole picture reminded her of all the things she needed to do around her own house.

Maybe one day.

The door opened a crack, revealing a single blue eye beneath the brass chain stretched tight across the narrow space. "If you're selling something, I'm not interested. If you want to acquaint me with God, don't waste your time. He and I don't get along."

Kerri showed her badge. "Ma'am, I'm Detective Devlin, and this is Detective Falco. We'd like to speak to you about Asher Walsh."

The door closed once more, followed by the sound of the security chain rattling before opening again. Ms. Taylor might be in her sixties, but she had a lean figure and an alert, watchful gaze. An attractive woman with silver hair and blue eyes. The pink sweater lent a feminine softness to her faded, comfortable jeans and casual white tennis shoes. Fashionable pearl-rimmed glasses sat on her keen nose, making her eyes look even larger. Those large eyes were a little red. Maybe she was suffering from allergies, or maybe she'd already heard the news about Walsh. Unless she avoided the television and radio altogether, it was doubtful she'd missed the press conference.

The lady gestured toward the room on the left. "Please, join me in the parlor."

"Your flowers are beautiful, Ms. Taylor." Kerri settled on the small sofa that was more like a love seat. The many windows in the room filled the small space with light. Houseplants were scattered about. The lady had a green thumb or a housekeeper with one. Either way, she liked her plants.

"I learned long ago that gardening was the best sort of therapy for quieting the mind. Beats the hell out of Prozac and isn't illegal. Would you like tea or water?"

Sharp witted as well, Kerri noted. Not that she'd expected anything less from a law professor.

"I'm good. Thank you," Kerri said as Falco sat down next to her. He declined the offer of refreshments as well.

Taylor relaxed fully into her chair. "A friend in the mayor's office called and told me what happened to Asher." The facade of strength never faltered, but emotion glittered in her eyes. "I knew a bad end was coming. It was only a matter of time. I warned him, but he was as stubborn as I am, so there was no stopping him from charging forward."

Falco shot Kerri a look. "Can you explain what you mean, Ms. Taylor?"

"Let's start with the fact that he was even in Birmingham. Do you think that young man came here after graduating at the top of his class at Harvard and then clerking for a Massachusetts Supreme Court justice because it was the best he could do? Please. The opportunities available to him were endless."

"Did he come to Birmingham to be near you?" Kerri asked. The lady had no children or family remaining in the area as far as they had found. "You're related to him in some way?"

"I suppose that played a small role in his decision." One elbow propped on a chair arm, she clasped her hands together in her lap. "When he was a child—until he was fifteen—he came for a few weeks each summer. But then his father decided he didn't really want anyone making the connection between the Walsh family and this one, so the visits became shorter and far less frequent."

"Then you are related to him," Kerri offered. "On his mother's side?"

"His father would say not, but it's true. Lana and I are sisters. When I was only two, our mother left my father and me. She moved to Boston to go to college. She was very young when she had me. Her greatest wish was to escape her southern heritage and pursue a different life. Eventually she married again and had another child, my sister, Lana—Asher's mother. To make a long story short, I grew up here with my father, and Lana grew up in Boston. Our mother insisted we know each other, so she'd fly me up to Boston each summer. Lana and I kept in touch to some degree until our mother died. After that, not so much. We had very different pursuits. As my daddy often said, my little sister got my mother's looks, but I got her brains. I became a law professor, and my sister found herself a rich husband. Her husband doesn't like me. I'm certain I don't meet his high standards." She made a soft sound, a sort of laugh. "I suppose it's only fair since I literally despise the bastard."

Kerri bit her lip to hold back a smile at her bluntness.

"But they allowed Asher to visit you," Falco noted.

"Only because they wanted to jet all over the world, and Asher, being quite the handful, made traveling difficult. Mother died before he was born, so there was no one else save nannies, and I don't think they liked the idea of anyone knowing so much about their private lives. Asher was one to repeat every word he heard his parents say. It was quite a problem until the desire to have a car outweighed the boy's need to annoy his parents."

"He stayed in contact," Kerri said, "even after he stopped visiting so often?"

"Not at first." She sighed, a sad smile furrowing her face. "Hormones, you know. The teenage years are fraught with love and loss. But by the time he was in law school, he found his way to me again. I think he realized we were very much alike."

"How so?" Kerri asked.

"Our determination. Our love of the law. Most of all, I think, was our distaste for the privileged class."

"People with money," Falco pointed out. "But his father is very wealthy, and he went to Harvard."

"And his distaste grew. No one was more surprised than me when he chose to move south rather than join his father's esteemed firm. Leland had been planning that moment since Asher was born." She gave a small shrug. "Granted, I imagine his father was more surprised. In fact, I'm certain he was gobsmacked. I was quite overjoyed."

Kerri steered the conversation back to the present. "Once he moved to Birmingham, did he spend a lot of time with you?"

"There's a condo he leased, but he rarely stayed there. It was more for appearances, in my opinion. He spent most of his nights here. I knew there was trouble when he didn't come home last night. I scarcely slept at all. I wanted to call him, but he'd asked me not to. He had an important meeting. He assured me he would explain everything today."

Kerri's instincts moved to the next level. As cooperative as this lady appeared, she knew the law. Obviously better than most. To go beyond the room she'd invited them into, they needed a warrant. *Or her permission.* She seemed all too happy to talk, but she might very well balk at anything more. Still, it never hurt to ask. "We were planning to visit his condo next. Perhaps that's not where we need to start. May we see his room here?"

Ms. Taylor sat forward in her chair. She stared silently at Kerri for a long moment. "You do whatever you have to if it helps find who took Asher from me. He was a brilliant young man with a bright future ahead of him. More importantly, he was a good person. He wanted to help others and to rid the world of drugs—he was very antidrug—and other evils. Truth is, Detectives, he was too good for this world." She stood. "His room is on the right at the end of the upstairs hall. I'll make tea."

Falco followed the lady from the room. "Is there any way I can help?"

"No. No. You go along and do your job, Detective. I've been making tea since I was old enough to light the stove."

Kerri climbed the steep stairs slowly, studying the framed family photographs. There were several of Walsh when he was a kid but only one of Lana, his mother. The photo appeared to be thirty or so years old. Lana and Naomi stood in front of some historic building that was obviously not in Alabama. By the time Kerri reached the landing, Falco had caught up with her. The house appeared to be trapped in its last update. The seventies, she decided, considering the owl accents and geometric shapes and patterns in some of the paintings. No recent upgrades or decorating.

"You think there's any chance the lady actually knows what Walsh was doing with Kurtz?" Falco asked.

"I have a feeling she knows a great deal, but like any good lawyer, she's not going to tell us anything before it's necessary."

There were four doors along the narrow hall. The first on the right was a pink bedroom with lots of lacy curtains and shabby chic linens. The gold shag carpet screamed more of that seventies vibe. The perfume bottles on the dresser suggested it belonged to the lady of the house.

The next door was a large vintage bathroom complete with a massive soaking tub. Across from the bathroom was a second bedroom. This one dark and masculine with heavy antique wood furnishings, including a four-poster bed. The musty, closed-up smell was indication enough that it had likely belonged to Naomi's father.

The final door led into the largest of the bedrooms. Across the room a door to an en suite stood ajar. An open set of bifold doors displayed shirts and suits and a few pairs of jeans. Though still dated, the furniture was newer than the other furnishings in the house. This was likely the room Walsh had used when he'd visited growing up as well as since moving to Birmingham. This space was another indication of how much Naomi Taylor adored her nephew. She'd given him what was obviously the owner's suite.

Falco opened a dresser drawer. "Looks like Mr. Walsh was as organized at home as he was at work."

Kerri glanced at the neatly aligned hangers in the closet once more. "I think we can safely assume the man liked all things in their place." Neat and reserved.

The walls were a pale, almost white shade of blue. No shag carpet in this room. The hardwood floors were scuffed and scratched from decades of life. The bed, dresser, bureau, and night table were all crafted in the rock maple of the early to mid-twentieth century. Kerri remembered her grandmother having bedroom furniture exactly like this.

She went to the nightstand while Falco moved through the dresser drawers. Each drawer would be emptied and checked top, bottom, and sides; then the removed items would be replaced as they'd been found. They inspected between the mattress and box spring as well as under the bed. While Falco examined the floor for any loose boards, Kerri walked through the bathroom and checked the small cabinet and inside the toilet tank. There weren't many other hiding places.

Back in the bedroom, she walked to the closet and started the process of examining every pocket in his wardrobe. When Falco finished with the floor, including scrutinizing the ventilation ducts, he joined her at the closet. The space was only about five feet wide and maybe two feet or so deep. Nothing like modern walk-in closets. Falco settled onto his knees and began checking the shoes lined in a well-ordered row along the floor of the closet.

The edge of something yellow caught Kerri's eye. Whatever the glimpse of yellow was, it was at the back of the closet. She struggled to part the abundance of clothes. When the view to the back wall of the closet was cleared, she spotted several squares of yellow. *Paper.* A frown tugged at her brow. Sticky notes. Lots and lots of sticky notes.

"Have a look at this." She held one side of the hanging garments back and waited for Falco to stand.

He reached for one of the notes. "Osorio." He stuck that one back to the wall and snagged another. "Cross." His gaze shifted to Kerri. "We need to get these clothes out of the way."

They removed the items from the closet, piling them on the bed until the closet was empty. Most of the back wall was covered with sticky notes and photos and news articles.

"This is the case he was working on," Kerri murmured, stunned by how much research the man had done into the Osorio cartel and potential connections to Birmingham. Most of the articles were about the cartel. Sticky notes listed names and locations. Dates. All sorts of information that likely tied together somehow but showed no logical order in its current context.

"We need to talk to Cross again," Falco said. "If how many times her name appears here is any indication, she knows a hell of a lot more than she's telling."

"I picked up on that." Kerri had suspected the woman was not being fully forthcoming.

Her cell vibrated. She dragged it from her pocket and read the text message there.

When are you coming home?

Tori.

"Let's document all this," Kerri said. "We'll do a walk-through of the Kurtz home to see if there's anything related to this, and then you go talk to Cross. I need to get home sooner rather than later."

"Everything okay?"

Kerri had allowed this case to push the incident at her daughter's school away for a while, but it was still there. Writhing and expanding in the back of her mind, warning there was a strong possibility that some aspect of her and her daughter's lives was not ever going to be okay again.

"I don't know yet. I hope so."

6

7:30 p.m.

Devlin Residence
Twenty-First Avenue South
Birmingham

Kerri placed her weapon in the lockbox on her bedside table. Heaving a big breath, she peeled off her jacket and tossed it onto the bed. They'd found nothing to indicate anyone had been in the Kurtz home since the owner had left yesterday, headed to his place of business. Not a single sticky note or anything else regarding Cross or a drug cartel similar to what they'd found in Walsh's closet was discovered. A forensic tech would do a sweep, and she and Falco would have another look.

But not tonight.

Most disappointing was that they had found nothing that even hinted at whatever had been happening between Kurtz and Walsh. No indication that Kurtz had been doing anything other than enjoying life or that he'd even known Asher Walsh.

The stop at Diana's house was the same as always. Diana pretended she was great; the twins—her boys—were great. Robby, her husband, was great. The dance studio to which she'd dedicated her life building was great.

Everything was great.

Kerri wondered how much of Diana's prescription medication it took to make everything great.

She rubbed at her eyes and reminded herself that she would probably need more than medication if something happened to Tori.

Rather than hide in her room and worry about all the things that were wrong in her life, Kerri made the short journey to her daughter's room. She hadn't said much on the drive home. Myers remained in critical condition according to the television news report she'd caught a glimpse of at Diana's before the channel had been changed. She had hoped Sykes would offer an update, but no such luck. She should have known better. Her daughter was a person of interest in the case, which ensured Kerri was excluded from ongoing details.

She rapped on the closed bedroom door.

"Come in," her daughter called in that resigned tone that said, *You're going to anyway; why bother knocking?*

Kerri opened the door and walked in. Tori leaned against a stack of pillows on her bed, her laptop perched on her waist.

"Anything interesting on social media?" She'd done her homework at Diana's. A crystal ball wasn't required to know she was almost certainly searching for anything new about her injured classmate.

And maybe whatever gossip had cropped up about the incident.

"Nothing I want to talk about." Tori closed the laptop and held it to her chest like a shield. "What's up?"

Settling onto the side of the bed, Kerri studied her daughter for a moment. Same dark blondish-brown hair as Kerri. Same brown eyes. Tall for her age and thin. And smart. Tori was really smart. Far smarter than her mom or her dad had been at this age.

"Have you recalled anything about what happened that might affect the investigation?"

Tori stared defiantly at Kerri as if she hoped to back her off the subject. Not happening this side of the grave.

Admitting defeat, Tori muttered, "Someone in Brendal's family posted on Facebook that her condition is unchanged. Critical. And she's still unconscious. They're asking for prayers." She blinked rapidly to hold back the emotion shining in her eyes. "I don't know why anyone would pray. All that praying I did for Amelia didn't help one bit." She glared at Kerri again. "I probably wasn't doing it right. Maybe because I never really went to church much."

The easiest way to release guilt was to heap it onto someone else. "Your father didn't want you encumbered with religion." Although Kerri had been raised in church and old habits died hard, she hadn't disagreed with him entirely. "We can pray together if you'd like."

"Forget it."

For about five seconds Kerri allowed her daughter to stew in her latest excuse for why she felt so miserable. Then she asked the question to which she desperately needed an accurate answer. "Do you feel like what happened to Brendal was in any way your fault?" Kerri held her breath. She didn't want to believe her daughter capable of this sort of violence—and she didn't—but she did need to know what had happened.

Horror claimed Tori's expression. "How could you ask that? Of course not!"

"But there's something you're not telling me, Tori. Something that's bothering you. It feels to me like you're battling some amount of culpability."

Since hitting fourteen, Tori had become more secretive. It was normal. Kerri understood this. Until this year, she had known all Tori's friends—girls and boys—her daughter had gone to school with since kindergarten. But everything was different now. After elementary more kids had merged into the private school Tori had attended her entire academic life. There were a lot of new names and faces.

Kerri and her sister had gone to public school. Diana's kids did. But Tori's father had insisted their one and only child would go to private school. To the same one he had attended. Funny how that fancy school hadn't done one damned thing for his moral code, or perhaps he had missed that part. Either way, Tori was happy there. Her friends were there. The one good thing her ex had done in the divorce was agree to pay the tuition until Tori graduated. The concession was not for Kerri's benefit or even for Tori's. It was for his own. Nick couldn't have his child attending public school. Even one he had abandoned emotionally and geographically.

"I told the police the truth," Tori said, fresh tears gathering in her eyes. "I don't know what happened. One second we were all standing there, and the next Brendal was falling down the stairs."

Her voice shook on the last word. She swiped at her eyes.

Kerri gave her a moment to compose herself. "Your new friend, Alice . . . do you like her? I mean, really like her the way you do Sarah?"

A shrug lifted one thin shoulder. "I guess. Sarah and I have been friends forever, so it's hard to say that I like Alice the same. I haven't known her that long. She's pretty and smart, but she doesn't make friends easy. She likes being the center of attention. That turns a lot of people off."

Unquestionably. "So, she isn't shy?"

Another of those noncommittal shrugs. "She's just, you know, different."

Brighton was particularly well known for its diversity. Kerri couldn't see the difficulty Alice had making friends as being related to her ethnicity. "Different how?"

"She's bossy, sort of."

A new student coming in with a *bossy* attitude would certainly turn most students off. "Bossy how?"

Tori heaved a big sigh. "How do you think? She likes to tell people what to do. She says she's a princess." Her lips bit together, and her eyes widened.

Obviously, she'd told Kerri more than she'd intended. "A princess?"

Tori moistened her lips. "That's supposed to be a secret. I wasn't supposed to tell."

"I won't tell anyone," Kerri promised. "Whatever you tell me will stay between us as long as it has no bearing on what happened. I have—we both have an obligation to share anything that relates to what happened to Brendal."

Tori fingered the edge of her laptop. "Alice said she was born to rule, but that something happened and changed everything. That's why she was sent here. Away from her home until the trouble is over. The story about her parents being dead is like a cover story. Her parents are dead, but they died a long time ago. She was sent here for protection from whatever is happening back in Mexico."

Kerri nodded. "Anything is possible. Sometimes, though, people make up alternative stories when the real one is too painful."

"I think maybe that's what she's doing." Tori's gaze met her mother's. "I didn't really believe her story about being a princess."

Kerri waited for Tori to go on, but she looked away instead. "You and Sarah have spent the night with her a few times." Now that Kerri thought about it, a couple of months had passed since the last time. Alice had never come to their house for a sleepover. Kerri had no idea if she'd gone to Sarah's.

"Her house is kind of creepy." Tori chewed her lower lip a second before going on. "I don't like going there. I think Sarah has gone a couple times when I didn't."

"It's a nice neighborhood." Kerri made it a point to familiarize herself with the homes and neighborhoods of her daughter's friends if going to the home came up.

"It's not that. The house is pretty and all, but it's creepy inside."

"Creepy how?" This was news.

"There's all this religious stuff. Her aunt and uncle are deep into it."

"That made you uncomfortable?" This was the South. Most folks went to church. Tori had gone to church with Sarah several times. Diana had crosses and at least one picture depicting Jesus in her house.

Tori nodded. "It's just different. Can we please not talk about this anymore?"

"Okay. For now. But I need you to think over those moments before Brendal fell and tell me anything at all you remember that's different from what you've told me so far. Detectives Sykes and Peterson will be talking to you again. Count on it."

Shrug number three. "'kay."

"I'll go work on dinner." Kerri stood. "Feel free to come and help."

Kerri left the door open to emphasize her invitation as she headed downstairs. She had always trusted her daughter. Tori wasn't one to keep things from her. Only that once when she'd kept quiet about the man harassing Amelia. Kerri couldn't believe she would hold back anything important ever again. Not after losing Amelia. The loss was still fresh in all their hearts.

But she wasn't foolish enough to believe her daughter might never make the same mistake again.

In the kitchen, she browsed the pantry offerings for inspiration. She really, really needed to do some shopping. Maybe she would try one of the online delivery services that were so popular now. Or maybe the pickup option. Diana raved about both. Kerri's cell vibrated. She dragged it from her pocket. *Falco.*

Her thoughts instantly shifted to their case. "Hey. Any revelations from Cross?"

Kerri supposed it was possible Walsh had zeroed in on Cross, since she'd worked all those years undercover going after the big drug runners. Whatever the case, she was holding back just how well acquainted she was with the DDA.

"I haven't been able to track her down," Falco said, frustration simmering in his voice. "She's not home and not answering her cell. Maybe she's tied up. She doesn't usually ignore my calls. I'll keep trying."

Kerri's first instinct was to assume the woman was avoiding them, but she pushed the conclusion aside. Reminded herself that she owed Cross the benefit of the doubt. "You think she has reason to not want to talk to us?"

A couple of seconds of weighty silence passed between them.

"Yeah. I do. Knowing Cross, she's conducting her own investigation into Walsh's death, and she doesn't want us involved."

"She was a cop for too many years not to understand how unproductive that would be." Kerri was all too aware of how truly ineffectual and dangerous choosing that route could be.

"Maybe there was something between her and Walsh. Maybe it's personal."

"Walsh was what? Five or six years younger than her?" When they'd first met, Kerri had believed Cross to be older than her. Not that thirty-something was so old, but Cross looked closer to forty. Her career—and the drinking and smoking—had taken a toll on her. In all fairness, the woman had gone through hell. Abducted and held hostage for nearly a year. She'd come back damaged, physically and emotionally. Who wouldn't look a little older under those circumstances?

"You know what they say," Falco tossed back. "Age is just a number."

"Yeah, well, he doesn't seem like her type."

"I have to agree with you there."

A comfortable silence settled between them. Sometimes when they were working a case, they didn't say a word. Just did some thinking, but those quiet moments hummed between them—like music no one else but the two of them could hear. Maybe this connection they had was like Kerri looking through the pantry—it prompted inspiration.

Sometimes it even felt as though this thing went beyond work and friendship, but she kept that idea at bay. Always. She didn't want to lose this man as a professional partner or as a friend.

"You guys had dinner yet? I'm only a couple of blocks from that sandwich shop Tori loves. I could pick up dinner. Try and cheer her up."

The first real smile of the day touched Kerri's lips. "That would be great. Diana wanted us to eat with her crew, but Tori just wanted to come home. Maybe she'll open up more to you." Kerri told herself the best part was that she wouldn't have to cook. But the best part was that Falco was a member of their family now, and there was no denying the fact even if she had felt so inclined.

Tori adored Falco. From all indications, the feeling was mutual. Kerri would trust this man with her child's life. No question. Whatever haunted him from the part of his past he didn't like to talk about, he was a good guy.

The past shouldn't rule the present.

Not that she was so good at keeping it in the moment, but Falco was deeply burdened with his past. She doubted he would ever share all of it with her.

"You got the drinks covered?" he asked, drawing her thoughts back to the moment.

Kerri opened the fridge and double-checked how much beer she had on hand. A six-pack and a couple of cans of cola. "I do."

"See you in half an hour, then."

"Thanks, Falco. You're the best."

"If you think I'm good now, wait until I tell you what I found out from Sykes."

Tension slid through Kerri. She leaned against the counter. "When did you talk to Sykes?"

"He called wanting to know more about Tori. If she has a temper. If she gets along well with others. You know, stuff like that."

Fury belted Kerri hard in the gut. "Are you kidding me?"

"He didn't want to ask you. He was afraid you'd punch him."

Damn straight she would have. "He can't seriously think Tori had anything to do with what happened."

"I don't believe he's leaning in that direction. He just wanted to ask me the things he was afraid to ask you."

Kerri knew the drill even if she didn't like it one damned bit when it involved her daughter. "And what did you tell him?"

"That Tori is the sweetest, kindest kid I know. No drugs. No alcohol. No problems whatsoever. Sykes even said the questions were ridiculous, that he knew you'd be on top of any issues. But he had to ask."

"Thanks for telling me. I'll try my best not to punch him next time I see him."

"He and Peterson think it was the Talley girl."

Kerri couldn't see that scenario. At all. "I'd wager they're wrong on that one. I've known Sarah since she was five years old. She isn't violent or mean or hurtful in any way. What did he say about the other girl, Alice Cortez?"

She's a princess. Kerri couldn't shake that part of what Tori had told her.

"Only that everyone they've interviewed so far sung Cortez's praises. And, apparently, she wasn't the one Myers was bullying."

Kerri's gut clenched in rejection of the concept Sarah Talley would hurt a fly much less another child. "There is that," she confessed.

"Turning in at the sandwich shop now."

"Okay. I'll see you in a bit."

She ended the call and placed her cell on the counter. Could persistent bullying really push a typically good kid to go that far?

Kerri closed her eyes. Of course, it was possible. Basically anything was possible.

She could only imagine what Sarah's mother was feeling right now. She had tried twice to call and check on Sarah and had to leave a voice mail each time. Kerri wondered if she should be worried that Sarah's mother hadn't called to inquire about Tori. Maybe.

She decided it wasn't personal, just instinct. Fear. Denial. Hope. Anger. All the emotions any mother trying to protect her child would experience.

Worse than any of that, the Myers family was faced with the possibility of losing their child.

Whatever happened . . . all involved were hurt.

7

10:30 p.m.

Taylor Residence
Eighteenth Avenue South
Birmingham

Sadie watched the headlights go out in front of her. The other car had rolled to a stop a few yards from hers. She opened her door and got out. The interior light remained dark. A car's interior light was the fastest way to get yourself noticed on a stakeout. She'd learned that as a surveillance virgin with her first BPD partner.

A lifetime ago.

She forced the memories away as she walked through the darkness to the passenger side of the other car—a beat-up yellow VW Beetle. She opened the door and got in. Like hers, the interior light remained dark.

"You've gotta find yourself a less conspicuous ride," she told her colleague. "This thing stands out like a lone duck in a pond full of hungry alligators."

"I can't part with my baby."

Sadie shrugged. "A couple cans of spray paint would take care of the problem."

He grunted and changed the subject. "Anything exciting happen?"

"Not unless you count the two kids playing porch pirates after the mail was delivered this afternoon. Little bastards."

Heck Keaton surveyed the house Sadie had tasked him with babysitting every night until this was over. "She come out today?"

"Nope." Sadie and another of her resources were taking care of the day shift. She wanted eyes kept on the Taylor house at all times. Until she had this figured out, it was the least she could do.

Sadie opted not to mention the lady had had visitors. Nothing Sadie hadn't expected. Falco and Devlin were thorough. "Hopefully this will be another boring night detail."

"Let the boredom come." Heck chuckled. "I'm prepared. Back seat's full of Red Bull and candy bars. I may never sleep again."

Heck—this was his actual name—Keaton was a former marine. He'd lost a leg on his last tour in the Middle East, but one would never know. The prosthetic worked for him as if it were his own flesh and bone. He worked out religiously. Had the muscled body to prove it. It was the PTSD that gave him the real trouble. The meds kept him leveled out most of the time. When it didn't, he disappeared. He said going off into his hiding place was better than the alternative. He didn't trust himself around people when he got like that. Unbalanced. Unable to hold it together.

Sadie never doubted him. He'd worked for Pauley for six years before Sadie took over the business. If Pauley said he was a good guy, he was a good guy.

"Call if anything comes up." Sadie reached for the door.

"Sorry about your friend."

Hand on the door handle, she hesitated. "Life sucks that way sometimes."

"Yeah."

Sadie climbed out of his car and got back into her own. She glanced at the house once more before pulling away. She was halfway down the block before she turned on her headlights. Traffic was light as she drove to her place. Didn't take ten minutes. She rolled into the alley and parked. She locked the doors and headed for the fire escape. No one had been near her door or the fire escape since the last time Falco had banged on her door at seven. He'd called her a half-dozen times. She would get back to him in good time. It wasn't like she didn't know what he wanted. His and Devlin's visit to Asher's aunt had obviously turned their attention back to Sadie.

She unlocked the multiple dead bolts and walked into her loft to the sound of her security system's hyperbeeping. Entering the code shut the thing up. She locked up and tossed her backpack on the sofa. She needed a drink. If there was any chance at all of her sleeping, she'd have to get ahead of the demons.

After grabbing the bottle she'd started on last night, she walked to her checkerboard pattern of sticky notes and photos on the wall, which represented her missing ten months. She tilted up the fifth of bourbon and chugged a long swallow. As the burn flowed down her throat and into her empty stomach, she wiped her mouth with the back of her hand.

"Come on," she murmured. "Do your magic."

Knowing the buzz would soon begin, she studied the images of the faces she had reason to believe were involved in whatever had happened to her. Her gaze stalled on *his*. Eddie's. Eduardo Osorio. The only son of the most dangerous and powerful cartel leader in Mexico. He'd lost his wife only a year before the undercover operation had been launched. Sadie was no fool. Her commander hadn't picked her for the assignment because she was the best detective on the team. Her likeness to the target's deceased wife was undeniable. The powers that be had wanted to get Eduardo Osorio's attention, and it had worked. He'd taken the bait like a starving rat.

A shift in her chest had her tilting up the bottle once more. She closed her eyes and let the burn overtake the memory. Her mind took her to the one constant in the fragmented pieces of her memory.

The mask. White. Horns sprouting from the sides and curling over the top. Soft, childlike voice instructing her to eat . . . to drink . . . to listen.

The masked child, or whatever the hell it had been, had come to her so many times. Sadie had recognized the person was female, small. Maybe a kid. But everything around the visitor was a blur. The memories were scattered and cloaked in darkness. The occasional sound or image. Sensations. Fear. Pain. Need. Panic. And occasionally hope.

All of it nothing more than pieces she couldn't seem to put together.

"To hell with it."

Sadie turned away from the mishmash she'd worked on for nearly three years now. The first year back from that dark place she'd been too much of a physical and emotional wreck to focus on anything. Over the past thirty-six or so months, the one thing that had kept her from admitting defeat was her refusal to give her father the satisfaction of knowing she'd given up.

She would not give him that. Ever.

The neck of the bottle hanging from her fingertips, she decided a long hot shower was necessary. She'd finish off the bottle and hopefully sleep like the dead for a few hours. She'd promised herself she wouldn't let the alcohol lead her anymore, but this was different. This was just for sleep. She rarely drank before or during work. She'd narrowed any serious drinking time down to a limited hour or so before bed.

It's a start, right? She'd even gone to AA a couple of times. Needed to go more—she got that. And she would. She definitely would.

As long as she was breathing, she had an obligation to do right by Pauley. He'd left his business and this place to her.

And she needed the whole truth. All those missing pieces. Some part of her wouldn't let go of the idea that those pieces were essential to something she didn't fully understand.

With Asher's murder, those pieces were even more important. Something or someone from her lost past was relevant to his death. She had to find that thing or person. Maybe the whole concept was simply a reason to seek revenge. Revenge was a powerful motive.

The warning that someone was on the fire escape chimed. She stalled. A fist against the door confirmed it was neither cat nor another four-legged animal.

Pound, pound, pound. "Cross, I know you're in there."

Falco. Sadie gritted her teeth. She was not going to answer his questions tonight.

She started forward once more, and the pounding began again.

"We know you were working with Walsh more closely than you told us," he said, the hushed accusation leaching through the wood of the door.

Sadie turned around and moved toward the sound.

"I understand," Falco said, his voice softer now, "what it must have taken for you to trust him."

She pressed her forehead against the cool wood surface and closed her eyes. He couldn't possibly.

"I just need to understand what he was doing. It's the only way we can find his killer. You know that, Cross. You have to help us. We can't help you unless you help us. You can count on Devlin and me. You know that."

Sadie twisted around until her back was against the door, then tipped up the bottle and guzzled another deep swallow. With the fire burning in her gut, she slid down the door until she folded into a heap on the floor.

"Go away, Falco. I don't need your help. Or Devlin's."

"We know about Naomi Taylor. We found Walsh's working notes at her house. We need to understand what the pieces mean, Cross."

Join the fucking crowd.

"I'll call you tomorrow," she lied. Anything to get him gone. She needed peace. Darkness. Quiet.

"What time tomorrow?"

Sadie gritted her teeth. "Just go, Falco, before I change my mind."

He knew she would too. There were only a handful of people, and several of those were dead, who understood her. Falco was one of them. He even knew a few of her secrets.

But not all of them.

Hell, she didn't even know all of them.

"Tomorrow, Cross. I need to hear from you tomorrow."

"Yeah, yeah."

She listened to the clomp of his footsteps fading down the stairs. The security system chimed again, confirming he'd gone.

Good. She angled up the bottle once more and focused on cutting her own path away from here.

8

Session One

Three Years Ago

"I am Dr. Oliver Holden. With me is my patient, Sadie Cross, age thirty-one. This is regression therapy, session one."

The sounds of rustling papers float up from the recording.

"Sadie, are you ready to begin?"

"Guess so."

"I want you to close your eyes and relax. Allow your muscles to loosen. Start with the muscles in your neck and shoulders. Let them soften; release any tension. Slow your breathing. Slow and deep. Now your arms. Allow them to lie beside you. No tension. No anticipation. Just lie there. Deep breath. Slower. In . . . out. Your legs should be relaxed. Soft. Pliable.

"I'd like you to count down in your mind, starting with three hundred. Slow, going down, down, down. The numbers slip away. The thoughts and senses that hold you to this time and place are slipping away with the numbers. Away. Away. Away."

Slow, deep breaths whisper from the recording.

"It's eighteen months ago, Sadie. Fall. September 7. Remember September 7?"

"Yes."

"Tell me about that day."

"I was working undercover to infiltrate the Osorio drug cartel." The pitch of her voice rises as she speaks.

"Deep breath, Sadie. I'm with you. Tell me where we are."

"At the dump where I lived for my cover. Shitty little place in Druid Hills." A gasp rises in the quiet. "He's there. He came back. Like he said he would."

"Who is *he*, Sadie?"

"Eddie—Eduardo Osorio. My target."

"Your target." Pause. "What do you mean by *target*?"

"The son of Carlos Osorio, the leader of the largest, most ruthless drug cartel in Mexico. Their reach extends up into the United States. From Atlanta to Houston. New York to Chicago. Everything in between," Sadie explains. "Their primary base of operations in the Southeast was Atlanta. Had been for years. But, at the time of the operation, they were moving things for some unknown reason. Here. To Birmingham. Eduardo did all the face-to-face business. His father never left their Mexican compound. He was too afraid of being executed or grabbed by law enforcement. Still is, if he's alive."

"You'd met Eduardo before?"

"Yes. He stopped at my food truck every time he was in Birmingham. That was my cover: food truck operator. I stationed my truck near his hotel. He always stayed at the same place. A strange ritual that could've gotten him killed but he didn't appear worried about it. He gave the impression of being fearless. Fierce. Powerful."

"You sound as if you admired him." Holden's tone is tinged with a note of surprise.

"It was my job to understand him. To know his MO. How he moved, reacted."

"All right. Explain to me how you were ordered to approach this target?"

"I was tasked with finding a way to get close to him. To lure him into trusting me. The goal was to get invited back home to meet Daddy. No one had ever gotten into that compound and survived to talk about it. I wanted in. Whatever it took."

"Why was Eduardo back in Birmingham on this particular day?"

"It was Friday. I was supposed to go home with him for the weekend. He said he'd come, but I wasn't sure. It was happening faster than any of us anticipated."

"Who is *us*, Sadie?"

"The task force. We expected the infiltration to take far longer."

"To what does the task force attribute this unexpected success?"

Silence.

"Sadie?"

"He . . . Eduardo became attached to me far more quickly than expected. I reminded him of his late wife. That was why my commander fought so hard to keep me on the task force. I was the perfect bait."

"I see. Did you go home with Eduardo? To this compound in Mexico?"

"Yes."

"How did you get there?"

"He had a plane waiting at the airfield, and that was it. I mean, I was in, and a lot of things could've gone wrong. If I was caught . . . I couldn't let that happen." Her respiration audibly accelerates.

"Slow your breathing, Sadie. Relax. You're safe. You're happy. Tell me what happened after you landed in Mexico."

"We drove to the compound. His father wasn't happy that Eddie—Eduardo brought me. He was suspicious. Nothing I hadn't expected. I was prepared for his suspicions. I walked right up to him and hugged him. I told him how nice it was to meet him. My actions surprised him. He wasn't sure what to make of me."

"What did this compound look like?"

"Very large, which we knew. Grand. Countless acres surrounded it. Armed guards were everywhere. Along the outside of the perimeter wall there were a dozen different kinds of booby traps. Those guys weren't playing."

"Who else did you meet, Sadie?"

"Eddie's daughter, Isabella. She was maybe eight or nine. This was new information. No one was aware he had a child until then. There was a wife who died but never any intelligence about children. Eddie eventually told me that he kept his child's existence a secret to prevent her being abducted and used against him. I was surprised he'd been able to maintain the secret so well. I figured she'd been homeschooled. She probably was never allowed off the compound."

"Did his little girl like you, or was she shy?"

"She liked me. That first day she took my hand and led me to the dining room to sit next to her at dinner. I'm not very good with kids, but she didn't appear to notice."

"How are you feeling, Sadie? You don't seem nervous about being at the compound."

"We drank champagne on the flight. He wanted to celebrate. So I was chill."

"What was he celebrating?"

"I don't know for sure. Maybe some big deal."

"Did you meet any other relevant players during the meal?"

"There was only Carlos, the little girl, Eddie, and me. Besides the staff, of course. There were people running about, serving the food. Keeping the glasses filled." Sadie pauses as if examining some memory in particular. "It was a little awkward because the kid kept watching me so closely. I guess she was curious."

"What happened after the meal, Sadie?"

"We had a drink with his father. Then Eddie took me to his room to wait while he tucked Isabella into bed."

Sounds of leather squeaking. Fabric brushing.

"You're growing agitated, Sadie. Did being in his room make you nervous? Remember, you're only viewing a memory. You're not actually there; you're here, in my office with me."

"No, I wasn't nervous. I had slept with him before."

"Then why do you feel ill at ease at this juncture in the memory?"

Long pause with the sound of increasingly rapid breathing.

"Slow, deep breaths, Sadie." Holden speaks softer. "You have no reason to be afraid. This is only a memory you are visiting."

"I should have gone. Before . . ."

"Relax. Loosen your muscles. You are safe. I'm still with you, Sadie."

Pause. Slower, deeper breathing.

"Now tell me; why were you afraid?"

"Because I knew what he was going to do."

"What was he going to do, Sadie?"

"He came back to the room, and he just stood there, watching me."

"Why did you find this troubling, Sadie? What was going through your mind?"

"I should have killed him then."

Pause.

"But you had attained your goal, had you not? You were inside the compound. You had met Carlos Osorio. Why would you have compromised your cover?"

"Because that was . . . where it began."

"Where what began, Sadie?"

"Me . . . becoming invisible."

9

Tuesday, April 13

8:00 a.m.

Birmingham Police Department
First Avenue North

"I don't disagree with you, Devlin."

Kerri searched her partner's face. They should be working on their assigned case; instead she wanted his thoughts about Tori. He and Tori had talked about what had happened at school over dinner last night. He'd spent a great deal of time afterward just reassuring her. There was no question he'd formed an opinion. But he was holding back.

"We've worked together almost a year, Falco. Don't try faking me out. This is my daughter we're talking about."

Feet propped on his desk and hands clasped behind his head, Falco held her gaze a second or two before confessing, "She's not being completely forthcoming. You're right. Is that what you wanted to hear?"

"We need to know what she's holding back." Kerri almost felt as if he was fighting her on this. Maybe not fighting, but definitely too restrained, which was not like him at all.

His feet hit the floor, and he leaned forward. "Does that mean it's relevant to the actual event—Myers falling—I can't say. You know how kids are. Hell, they hate a lot of people at this age. They're also embarrassed by their own thoughts. Maybe she wished Myers would be hurt somehow. The girl hurt Tori's friend, which hurt her." He turned his palms up in question.

Kerri made up her mind then and there. "I'll be back."

"Dev . . . lin," he warned, drawing out the syllables as she walked away.

She ignored him.

Across the bullpen in their own cubicle, Sykes and Peterson were huddled over their case board. Kerri cleared her throat, and the two jumped apart as if they'd been discussing the latest issue of some porn magazine.

The instant their gazes crashed into her, they sidestepped toward each other in a perfectly choreographed routine, aligning their shoulders to block her view of the case board.

"Anything new on Myers?" She'd checked with the hospital this morning, and the girl's condition had been unchanged. An old friend with whom Kerri attended college worked at the hospital. She'd been more than happy to share an update. She didn't have to know Kerri wasn't involved in the investigation. The subject never even came up. The other woman simply assumed, which was what Kerri had hoped for.

Sykes made a face. "You know we can't talk about this case with you, Devlin."

Peterson crossed his arms over his chest. "Unless you've got something new to share."

Anger sparked inside her. "Let's just hope I'm never assigned a case that affects either of you, because I'll have a difficult time forgetting this."

It was a childish tactic, but she was desperate. This was her daughter's life. The dread on Tori's face when Kerri had taken her to school this morning had been very nearly more than she could bear. A part of her had hoped Tori would break down and spill whatever she was holding back. But she hadn't.

If she had nothing to hide, there was no reason she shouldn't return to school.

Still, Kerri felt enormous guilt for sending her in to face whatever music the other kids decided to play today. Kids could be so cruel.

Being a teenager sucked. It had two decades ago, when she'd been in the midst of those angst-filled years, and it did now.

Sykes and Peterson shared a look, then stepped apart, allowing her to see their case board.

"As you can see," Peterson groused, "we got nothing more than we had yesterday."

Kerri moved closer to read the scribbled notes visible just over Peterson's right shoulder. Details about Alice, the new girl to the group. "What have you learned about Cortez?"

"Not a whole lot." Sykes followed Kerri's gaze to the girl's photo. "She was homeschooled when she lived with her parents in Sinaloa. She moved to Birmingham last fall and started school at Walker Academy. She transferred to Brighton in January. The teachers love her. She's reportedly brilliant and extraordinarily well behaved."

The girl couldn't make friends, according to Tori. Kerri frowned. "Why the move from Walker to Brighton?" Walker was regarded with equal respect. Brighton leaned more toward the arts, while Walker was better known for the sciences. "Was the academic philosophy not the right fit?"

Peterson shrugged. "We have no clue about the philosophy, academic or otherwise. Some people send their kids to public school." He arrowed a look at Kerri, she rolled her eyes, and he went on. "According to the principal—"

"School head," she corrected. The term was once *headmaster*, but that had changed in recent years.

"Whatever," Peterson bounced back. "Alice Cortez claimed there were big problems at the school. She didn't like the atmosphere. She feared for her safety."

A problem at the previous school and now this? Interesting. "Was she involved in any sort of incident?"

"Nope," Peterson said flatly.

"But there were a couple of incidents while she was there," Sykes confessed with a sideways glance at his partner.

Kerri lifted her eyebrows in question. The two didn't appear to be on the same page as far as sharing was concerned. Strange. They were usually like an old married couple—in it together until the bitter end. "And?"

"Two kids tried to check out"—Sykes made air quotes—"just before Christmas break. Her guardians decided Alice was right that the atmosphere was all wrong."

Obviously, the suicide attempts weren't successful, or the devastating events would have been all over the news. "Did Alice know either of the students involved?"

"Walker is a lot smaller than Brighton," Patterson grumbled. "How could she not? But she says she didn't really know them."

"Have you interviewed the two students at Walker?"

"Can't get past the parents." Sykes shook his head. "You know how rich people are. They want to keep their secrets. Don't want anything like that on the kid's personal record. Might keep them out of an Ivy League institution."

To a degree, this was true of any parent. Sykes should know that. He had three kids of his own. No one wanted their child to carry any sort of shame for the rest of their lives. At least not as long as unfair social stigma existed.

Kerri argued, "Then you can't be sure Cortez didn't know the students or play some part in their decision to, as you say, check out." Was throwing another kid under the bus necessary to rule out the possibility of Tori's involvement in this nightmare? The idea cramped inside Kerri.

Had she become that parent?

Could she do the same with Sarah Talley? A kid she had known for nearly a decade? Tori's friend?

Nothing about this was simple and certainly not painless.

"Did Tori say something that suggested Cortez might be that kind of kid?"

The question Sykes posed was the same one Kerri would have asked had their roles been reversed. "No." She opted not to mention the comment her daughter had made about how creepy the Cortez home was. "Tori's statement hasn't changed."

Peterson eyed Kerri speculatively. "Are you and Talley's mother close?"

She took a moment to consider the question. "We're not close as in best friends or anything like that. We've known each other since our girls started kindergarten together. Our kids have had countless sleepovers. We've spent plenty of time together on the soccer field when our girls played. We've worked together at school fundraisers." She shrugged. "I suppose that makes us *mom* friends. Why do you ask?"

"No reason," Peterson lied. "Just another blank to fill. You know how it goes."

If it was just another blank to fill, why the obvious lie? The untruth had shown in his flinch and the diverting of his gaze. Kerri couldn't be sure if he'd been attempting to prompt some sort of reaction from her or if Renae Talley had maybe said something negative about Tori. The latter made no sense. What could she possibly say negative about Tori?

"We should get going." Sykes moved around Kerri and reached for the jacket hanging on the back of his chair.

"Yeah." Peterson skirted his desk and grabbed his own jacket. "See you later, Devlin."

Kerri gave a little wave as she watched them go. Oh yes. Those two had wanted a reaction. She ignored the emotion coiling in her gut. She refused to give them any sort of ammunition.

She would ask Renae herself. They'd been friends for years. No reason they couldn't talk about this.

"You ready?"

Falco's voice snapped Kerri from the troubling thought. "Yeah. Sure."

For now, she needed her mind on this double homicide. Tori would never hurt anyone. Whatever happened, the trouble lay with someone else.

The problem was the other girls' families were likely thinking the same thing.

Leo's Tobacconist
Oak Grove Road
Homewood, Noon

After a call from the Crime Scene Unit as they left the office, their first stop was a return to the residence of Leo Kurtz to meet the forensic folks. His home was like his Bronco. Vintage with a definite collector's appeal. The place was small but elegant in an understated way. The sort of home, Kerri considered, perfect for a single man or couple who had no desire for the burden of a larger property.

Despite their second look, unless the forensic sweep underway turned up something, the place was clean of anything useful to the case. Definitely nothing to suggest any sort of tie-in on Kurtz's part with drug activity or any ongoing relationship or connection to Walsh.

Thankfully, Kerri and Falco's second stop proved a bit more fruitful. Tara McGill had come through like a champ. All eight employees of Leo's Tobacconist, including McGill, had been seated around the bar. Officer Franklin had waited with them to ensure no one went into the stockroom or the office and that no one compared stories.

Franklin continued to babysit while Kerri and Falco used the employee lounge area for a sort of interrogation room. So far, every single person they had interviewed had said the same thing. Leo was a great guy, an amazing boss with no known enemies. There were no problems whatsoever. Until George Caldwell was up. Caldwell had worked for Kurtz the longest. When he joined Kerri and Falco in the stockroom, his unease was immediately visible.

As soon as the preliminary details and questions were out of the way, Caldwell blurted, "Leo was a little distracted lately. I can't say why; I only know he seemed worried."

Kerri shared a look with her partner. No one else had mentioned any concerns.

"Did Mr. Kurtz say he was worried about anything in particular?" Falco asked for clarification. "Or was this your personal feeling or assessment?"

"He didn't say anything," Caldwell admitted, "but something was wrong. He wasn't himself. I've known him too long not to have noticed. So yes, this was my own assessment based on what I saw."

"Any reason to believe he had financial problems?" Kerri asked, no matter that the bank and credit card statements she and Falco had pulled showed a hefty savings and practically no debt. "No recent breakups, personally or professionally?"

Caldwell shook his head. "Leo was set. He'd saved well and invested even better. He didn't need to keep running this place. He did it because he loved it and wanted to keep us all in jobs. He'd been single since his partner died."

"No one he dated or went out with even occasionally?" Falco asked.

"No one. I don't think he felt the need. This place was his life since he lost Perry."

"Perry was his life partner?" Kerri knew the answer already, but confirming was always the best practice. Perry Sager and Leo Kurtz had been together for thirty years. Neither had extended family, only each other and this place.

"Yes," Caldwell said with a nod.

"You can't think of any reason," Kerri pressed, "that explains this worry or distraction you noticed?"

Caldwell shrugged. "In my opinion, it was probably Tara. I don't think she was living up to his expectations in her new position as assistant manager."

Now they were getting somewhere.

"I've been thinking about Tara," Falco said. "Of all the employees here, you've worked for Kurtz the longest. Why weren't you his assistant manager? Why Tara?"

Exactly, Kerri mused.

"My ticker," Caldwell explained. "I'm on medication for my blood pressure and my heart. If I'm going to keep working, my doctor says I have to limit the stress. Leo wanted me in the position, but I had to turn him down." He sighed. "I couldn't take the risk."

Falco glanced at Kerri, and she threw out the next question. "Why didn't you mention your concerns about Mr. Kurtz the first time we spoke?"

He sighed again, gave his head a shake. "I was in shock, I guess. And it didn't seem relevant when compared with murder. But then the idea just wouldn't let go. It kept eating at me. I had to tell you, whether it was relevant or not."

"You didn't talk to Tara about this?" Falco presented the next logical query.

Another shake of the older man's head. "I didn't see the point. Especially now. If she wasn't living up to his expectations, it was irrelevant with him gone."

Understandable. Kerri said, "We'd like you to make a list of any friends or close associates Leo had—besides his employees. If you have phone numbers, that would be great as well." If he had concerns, as Caldwell suggested, maybe he'd shared them with a friend.

"Sure thing, but I have to tell you, we"—he patted his chest—"were Leo's friends and associates. Outside this place, he always said that anyone else was just an acquaintance."

McGill had said basically the same thing. "Any names you can come up with may prove useful." Kerri passed Caldwell her card. "We may have other questions later."

"Of course." He nodded adamantly. "Anything I can do to help. I loved Leo like a brother."

Falco pushed back his chair and stood. "Thank you, Mr. Caldwell. Please call if you think of anything else."

"Believe me, I will." Caldwell got to his feet. "I want whoever did this caught. Leo was a good man. He didn't deserve to go out this way."

When he'd exited the stockroom, Falco said, "That leaves us with only Lucky Vandiver."

They had saved him for last. Mostly to make him sweat. McGill had stated that the young man and newest employee of Leo's was a coke user. He had a couple of public intoxications on his record. One public disturbance. Clearly the man had issues, including a temper.

"Let's find out what he has to say," Kerri said.

Falco walked to the door that separated the stockroom from the retail shop. He opened it and stuck his head out. "Yo! Vandiver, you're up."

Her partner waited at the door until Vandiver swaggered in, then he closed it with a firm thud.

Vandiver took a seat across the table from Kerri. Falco leaned against the wall a few feet away. Kerri allowed a moment to visually assess the twenty-three-year-old. Shaggy blond hair. Bloodshot blue eyes. He looked as if he hadn't slept in days. The Rag & Bone Henley—she'd spotted the logo on the hem—paired with the probably equally expensive jeans looked as if he'd slept in them for a couple of days already. Daddy made him work, but Kerri doubted Lucky had bought his wardrobe on his minimum wage salary.

"Mr. Vandiver," Kerri began, "thank you for coming in today."

One shoulder rose, then fell with a careless shrug. "It's not like I could say no."

This was mostly true. "Are you certain you don't want an attorney present?"

Kerri asked this question of everyone they'd interviewed as part of the preliminary prep before moving into the more relevant questions. With this guy, she felt the question was particularly important for setting the tone. She would wager every cent in her bank account that he hadn't told his father about this command performance. Whenever a person hid something like this, there was a reason—a motive. In a murder case, every motive had to be analyzed.

Even those that might turn out to be irrelevant.

Lucky shook his head. "Don't need one."

Which meant he didn't want to tell his father, because then he'd have to face his interrogation. Kerri had a feeling Lucky—Lucas Lorenzo Vandiver, actually—would rather face a firing squad than his father.

"All right. Why don't you tell me about Sunday night?"

He stared at Kerri. "Where do you want me to start?"

"When you arrived at work."

"I came in at six. I bused tables and loaded and unloaded the dishwashers. Around nine I started the cleanup. I left a little after ten. Same time as Tara."

"Was there anyone else here besides Leo when you left?"

He shook his head. "He was alone in his office. I know because I asked him for an advance on my pay."

"Why did you need an advance? You just got paid on Friday, right?"

Lucky shifted in his chair and stared at Falco. "The usual reason. I was broke. You never got paid on Friday and was broke by Sunday?"

Falco didn't bother responding.

"Did anyone else hear this exchange?" Kerri asked, drawing his attention back to her. Tara hadn't mentioned it.

He shrugged again. "I don't know. Ask Tara. She's always nosing around."

"You needed to score some blow?" Falco asked.

Vandiver's eyes widened. "What? No, man. I don't do that shit."

"That's not what we heard," Falco argued. "We heard you're a regular cokehead. Daddy probably doesn't know that."

Vandiver made a sound of disbelief. "Don't believe everything that bitch Tara tells you," he warned. "She's crazy."

"Why would you think Tara would suggest such a thing or that she's crazy?" Kerri asked. "Obviously Mr. Kurtz trusted her, since he made her an assistant manager."

Vandiver snorted. "Did you ask her how she got that position? I'm guessing she was on her knees at the time."

Falco walked to the table and flattened his hands there, leaning toward Vandiver. "What're you saying?"

Vandiver turned his face up to Falco's and laughed. "I'm saying she would do anything to get ahead, including say shit about me. She's like that. How do you think she got the job and not George?"

"Mr. Caldwell turned down the offer," Falco said. "He didn't want the added responsibility."

"Yeah, he would say that," Vandiver scoffed. "A guy's gotta save face."

Kerri could see how others might think as much if Caldwell hadn't chosen to share his health issues.

"So, you don't like Tara," Falco said as he straightened away from the table. "Is that it? She's in with the boss and maybe she wouldn't do you any favors."

"Like I said, she's a bitch. If you really knew her, you'd get it."

"Did Mr. Kurtz give you the advance?" Kerri asked.

Vandiver's attention shifted back to her. "Sure. He was nice like that. He gave me a hundred bucks."

"What did you do with the money?" Falco tossed out, leaning toward him again.

Vandiver smiled up at him. "That's none of your business, man."

"We both know you probably rushed out to meet up with your favorite supplier," Falco pressed. "Why didn't you just get what you needed from Leo?"

"Are you fucking kidding?" Vandiver stared at Falco as if his head had done a three sixty right there on his shoulders. "Leo wasn't into drugs, man. He would have canned me on the spot if he'd known . . . fuck." The guy snapped his mouth shut.

"Your father and Mr. Kurtz were friends," Kerri stated.

Vandiver blinked. "Yeah. He knew my old man's an overbearing asshole."

"Did Mr. Kurtz ever mention any concerns he had in his own life?" Kerri asked. "Maybe he seemed distracted or worried lately." She opted to throw in Caldwell's comments for a reaction.

"As far as I know, he didn't have any. Leo was cool like that. He didn't let shit get to him. He just rolled with it, you know?"

"Had you ever seen Asher Walsh in the shop before?" Falco asked.

They had asked each employee this question as part of the preliminaries, and none had seen Birmingham's new DDA before. It was possible Kurtz and Walsh conducted their meetings after hours or away from the shop.

Vandiver cut Falco an annoyed look. He appeared to still be pissed that Falco had suggested his former boss would sell drugs. "No. Never. The only time I ever saw him was at that big party my mom had for my dad's birthday last month. Leo was there too."

Kerri looked from Vandiver to Falco and back. "Walsh was a friend of your father's?"

Another of those lackluster shrugs. "I don't know if they were friends. But my dad knows everyone who's anyone. Hell, the mayor and every other *boss* in town was at his party."

"Thank you, Mr. Vandiver. If we have other questions, we may need to speak with you again." Kerri passed him a card. "Please feel free to call us if you think of anything else you want to tell us."

Vandiver took the card and looked it over. "Can do. If you call me, just be sure you call my cell phone and not the house. My dad is not a nice guy."

"I'll keep that in mind," Kerri assured him.

When he had swaggered away, she turned to Falco. "We should talk to his father."

Falco nodded. "I'm down with that."

Kerri stood and pushed in her chair. "If McGill and Kurtz were intimately involved on some level, maybe she knows a little more than she's shared."

Falco grinned. "Count on it."

"She may have been pressuring him for a raise or some other benefit that had him doubting his decision to promote her into management in the first place. That could explain what Caldwell noted about his old friend."

"Either way," Falco offered, "McGill needs a little more of our attention."

"No question."

The door opened, and a tall man with salt-and-pepper hair walked in. He wore a designer suit that spoke volumes about where he shopped, and he carried himself like a military general. Maybe Vandiver had decided to summon the family attorney.

A little late.

"Detectives," the man announced, "I am Special Agent in Charge Mason Cross, DEA." He produced his credentials, then repocketed the leather case.

Cross? DEA? Kerri extended her hand. "Kerri Devlin."

He shook her hand, then reached for her partner's.

"Luke Falco. I've heard about you, Agent Cross."

Kerri considered her partner, but she supposed it made sense. Falco had once worked under deep cover with narcotics. He likely was acquainted with a number of DEA agents.

"I apologize for barging in like this," Cross said. "But we need to talk before this goes any further."

"This?" Kerri pulled on her jacket.

"This investigation," he explained. "The DEA is taking lead. We hope you'll continue to support our efforts to solve this case."

What the hell? "Agent Cross, I'm afraid you've been misinformed," Kerri countered. "This is a homicide investigation. The BPD's Major Investigations Division is lead."

"Perhaps there has been a lapse in communication, Detective. You may not be aware that Asher Walsh had stumbled into an ongoing DEA operation. We're not sure yet how Mr. Kurtz was involved, but the investigation is ours. As I said, we appreciate any support you'd like to give us. But we'll need you to take a stand-down. All movement related to his case will need to be approved by me first."

Falco stepped into the conversation. "If Walsh had stumbled into your op, why wait until he's murdered to make it known? You're a little behind the curve, Agent Cross."

The older man smirked. "Falco. I know that name. You made quite the reputation for yourself a few years back down in . . . where was it? Mobile? Although I respect your impressive record in my world, this is *my* world. We clear?"

"Very," Falco confirmed.

Kerri, on the other hand, was not clear at all about this turn of events. "We'll check back with you, Agent Cross, after we speak with the chief."

As far as she was concerned, the chief of police trumped some federal agent in charge any day of the week.

10

1:30 p.m.

Birmingham Police Department
First Avenue North

"This is what the chief wants." Lieutenant Dontrelle Brooks didn't look any happier about the decision than Kerri or Falco.

She wanted to scream. The joint task force was a go, and DEA Special Agent in Charge Cross was lead, just as he had warned.

"This is our case, boss," Falco said. "It's a homicide, and we haven't even confirmed a connection to drugs."

Brooks leaned back in his chair and studied Falco. "So, you're suggesting Agent Cross made up this whole ongoing op story just to steal your double-homicide case."

"That's not what we're suggesting," Kerri countered. "What we're saying is that since the homicides are two locals, we should be lead. Cross and whoever else the mayor and the powers that be have decided needs to be involved are welcome to play with us too."

Kerri liked the new mayor's plans and goals, but having one who wanted to run the police department, too, was crossing the line. Wasn't that the way of things now? Everybody thought they were better at policing than cops. Cops were suddenly the enemy.

Brooks turned up his palms. “This is what the chief wants, and this is what we’re going to do. End of story.”

Kerri glanced at Falco. He looked even more irritated than she was.

“The first task force meeting will be at four this afternoon in the main conference room. Be there and be nice.” Brooks looked from Kerri to Falco and back. “I don’t want to hear about you two unless it’s news that with your gracious and insightful cooperation the case has been solved.”

“Yes, sir.” Kerri turned to go.

“Do not push the boundaries on this one,” Brooks warned before she could get out the door. “Mayor Warren is watching the department closely. No missteps. No ignoring orders. She wants to see team players, and so do I.”

This time Kerri didn’t bother with a response. She walked out, Falco close on her heels.

“You know they’re going to leave us out of the loop every chance they get,” Falco muttered.

As much as Kerri didn’t want to go straight to that conclusion, she’d worked with various federal agencies enough times to know he was right. “That’s exactly what they’ll do.”

Rather than go back to their cubicle, she headed for the exit. They didn’t have a lot of time before the task force meeting, and she wanted to talk to Sadie Cross first.

Once they were outside, she asked, “Why didn’t you tell me Cross had a father who lives right here in Birmingham and who’s DEA?” It hadn’t been until they were driving away from the tobacco shop that Falco had announced: “Oh, by the way, Agent Cross is Sadie Cross’s father.” The concept was startling considering the two were polar opposites.

Falco followed Kerri through the parking area. “No reason. It never came up.” He stopped at the tailgate of her Wagoneer. “It’s not like we've talked about her family. We haven't even talked about her that often. Not since the Abbott case."

Flashes of memory from those days and weeks tore through Kerri; she blinked them away. "True."

She walked around to the driver's side and slid behind the wheel. Usually Falco did most of the driving, but with the tragedy at Tori's school, Kerri needed her vehicle handy in the event she had to leave suddenly. Her chest tightened with the thought. Tori had been far too quiet this morning. The atmosphere in the house reminded her of this time last year after Tori's father had left. The somber silence and unspoken anger were hard to bear.

This time instead of anger it was fear pulsing in the silence. Kerri did not want her daughter to be afraid. She didn't want her to be unhappy or sad or hurt. But how could she protect her from all that life had the potential to hurl at her?

She couldn't. No parent could.

Sadie's Loft
Sixth Avenue, Twenty-Seventh Street
Birmingham, 2:00 p.m.

Falco pounded on the door again.

Kerri ended her third call to Cross's number. "Did she tell you what time she would call you today?"

"Nothing specific." Falco glared at the camera above the door. "Open the damned door, Cross. I know you're in there. Your ancient Saab is in the alley."

Kerri scanned the alley below. The Saab was parked beneath the fire escape. Unless Cross had left with a friend, Falco was right. She had to be in there. Avoiding them, most likely. She thought of Mason

Cross. Strong build. Obviously intelligent and good at his job or he wouldn't be in charge of the Birmingham district office. Dressed like a general, only in civilian clothes. Fierce attitude. One of those guys who went strictly by the book and thought he should be in charge of any given situation. Supremely uptight and no doubt completely ruthless.

Then she thought of Sadie Cross. A total contradiction to her father. So laid back she was practically in a coma. Thin to the point she could just disappear. Dressed like a street dweller. Capable of anything whether it was legal or not. The one thing the two had in common was obvious intelligence. Unlike her father, Sadie Cross expected nothing of anyone. Her resources were like her, ragged, unkempt, but incredibly smart and capable. That was the strangest part about the woman and her group of misfit resources—they were like this unexpected group of geniuses who had somehow fallen out of accepted society.

Falco pounded on the door again. Kerri jumped at the sound. "If that doesn't get her attention, she's either not at home or dead."

The sound of dead bolts sliding snapped their gazes back to the door. When the door opened, Cross stared first at Falco and then at Devlin with enough irritation to blast them off the landing.

"It lives," Falco griped.

"What time is it?" Cross asked, her voice rusty.

"Two o'clock," Kerri said. The woman looked hungover, seriously hungover. Her hair was mussed. Her clothes the same ones she'd been wearing yesterday. Actually, it was difficult to tell about the wardrobe. Ragged jeans and tees were her usual attire. As were the well-worn sneakers.

"I need coffee." Cross gave them her back and disappeared into her perpetually dimly lit loft.

Since she'd left the door open, Kerri and Falco followed.

"You were supposed to call me," Falco reminded her.

Her hands shook as she attempted to pour the water from the carafe into the coffee maker. Water splashed on the counter.

"Give me that." Falco took the carafe from her and finished the job.

While he scooped coffee grounds into the basket, Kerri said, "I met your father this morning."

Cross's bloodshot eyes shifted to Kerri. "Aren't you the lucky one?"

Falco shoved the basket into the machine and started the brewing process. "He took over our case. The DEA is now lead."

"Surprise, surprise." Cross reached for her cigarettes and lit up. "That's what the old man does when it serves his best interests."

The smell of coffee drifted into the air. Would never be enough to block out the smell of cigarette smoke. Kerri got the distinct impression that Cross was trying to kill herself. In Kerri's opinion there were far easier ways.

"What was the deal between you and Walsh?" Falco demanded. "No more beating around the bush, Cross. I want the truth. All of it."

"Give me five minutes, and we'll talk all you want." She walked across the room, leaving them staring after her.

She grabbed a black tee from the pile of clothes on a dresser. Scrounged for a pair of jeans and underwear and then disappeared into the bathroom.

Kerri shook her head. "Has she always been this hell bent on killing herself?"

Falco shrugged. "I don't know. Maybe a little."

He'd told Kerri as much as he knew about Sadie Cross's story. Deep cover cop. Things had gone to hell, and she'd ended up damaged goods. Apparently, she and her father were not on good terms. He didn't approve of her lifestyle, Kerri imagined. She didn't have to know the man to recognize he likely approved of very little. Since Cross was an only child, he had no doubt attempted to mold her into something that resembled his image.

Clearly, he had failed miserably.

Then again, Kerri wasn't exactly the perfect parent. She had no right to judge anyone else. Except that she already disliked Mason Cross. Immensely.

While they waited, Kerri wandered around the space. There were windows facing the street. None that overlooked the alley, thus the cameras. Cross kept the blinds closed tightly. Her furnishings were sparse and had seen better days. The kitchen area was more a kitchenette with a small peninsula skirted by a couple of stools. A television. Music system. All looked to be from the previous decade. A movable whiteboard—the type on legs with wheels—she likely used for cases stood in the corner near the door. Lots of filing cabinets lined the wall, fronted by a massive wooden desk that might actually be an antique. The top was cluttered with papers and file folders. An empty whiskey bottle lay on one end. No glass or cup.

This would certainly explain the megahangover.

The bathroom door opened, and Sadie Cross emerged, dark hair wet, clothes as wrinkled as the ones she'd been wearing before her shower.

"Pour me a cup, Falco."

Judging by the urgency in her voice, Kerri figured she felt on the threshold of death's door. Since Kerri was closer to the counter, she grabbed a mug and the carafe and poured the hot liquid.

Cross came straight to her and took the mug. It wasn't until after she'd finished off the first cup that she spoke. "I haven't heard anything new from my sources. I told you why Walsh was talking to me. I said I'd call you if I had anything new, but I don't. What is it you want from me?"

Falco kicked off the questioning. "You and Walsh were working on an off-the-record case."

"I told you that already," Cross growled.

"Like I told you *already*," Falco said, "we saw the case board he'd made in the back of his closet. Whatever the two of you were doing was a lot bigger than you led us to believe."

Kerri added, "It was dangerous, and it's likely the reason he's dead."

That part was a no-brainer.

Cross poured another cup of coffee, took a breath before meeting Kerri's gaze. "I'm not stupid, Devlin. I know he's dead because of me. I told him what he was doing was dangerous, but he didn't listen." She walked over to the whiteboard near the door, pulled it aside, and gestured to the wall. "Look familiar?"

Kerri moved to her side and stared at the wall, which looked very much like the one in Walsh's room at his aunt's. Sticky notes, photos, newspaper articles were stuck to the wall. The name that jumped out at Kerri was *Osorio*.

"This is the operation you were working on when you disappeared," Falco said, his gaze roving over the notes and photos. "I remember it was all over the news when the son, Eduardo, disappeared." He turned to Cross. "That was months—close to a year—before you resurfaced."

Cross cradled her mug. "And these"—she gestured to the wall—"are the pieces I can remember from those lost months. Everything else is a fog."

"How did you and Walsh meet?" Kerri decided Falco was right. Walsh and Cross obviously had a thing. He'd been digging around for information about the cartel, and he'd discovered the operation from four and a half years ago. What better way to learn details than by getting close to a member of that op?

"He came to me. *Like I said.*" Cross's attention remained on the many fragments of her past she'd lost. "He claimed he'd come to Birmingham for a purpose: to stamp out the Osorio cartel's connections here."

So the hotshot had an agenda after all, Kerri mused.

Falco scoffed. "Did you remind him how many have tried?"

Cross grunted. "He was well aware."

"Why?"

Cross looked to Kerri. "Why what?"

"Why the Osorio cartel? Why Birmingham? Why do this off the record? We've found nothing in Walsh's background that gives us any sort of motive."

The last part was the big question in Kerri's opinion. As a part of the district attorney's office, Walsh would certainly want to see that crime was stamped out—that justice prevailed and the law of the land was upheld. It was the whole purpose of the DA's office. Why now? Why here? *Why* this particular criminal element? Where was the fire that fueled his passion? The match that lit the fire? Something or someone had to have triggered his decisions.

Cross shrugged. "No clue. All I know is I never met anyone who wanted to stamp out the big drug sources—particularly the Osorio cartel—more than Walsh. Whatever his motives, he was over-the-top antidrug."

She turned and walked away from the wall of fragmented memories. Poured herself a third cup of coffee and focused on downing it.

"Why would you lie about how involved the two of you were?" Kerri joined her at the counter. "Is there some reason you didn't want to share with us what he—or the two of you—were doing?"

Cross, her expression locked down like a vault, stared at Kerri. "I said I would check with my sources and see what I could find out. Otherwise, *now* you know what I know. Can we move on?"

Kerri shook her head. "Then why feel as if his death is on you? You said he's dead because of you. What was he working on specifically? How exactly were you helping him? You're sharing only vague details, Cross. Reluctantly at that. And what I'm reading in your body language isn't vague at all. His death affected you deeply. Why, if—as you say—you don't really know anything at all?"

"Maybe you're not as good at reading people as you think. You got it wrong this time."

"I am not wrong."

Cross plunked the mug down on the counter. "Trust me, Devlin. You do not want to go down this path. You have a daughter. She needs you."

The words took Kerri aback as nothing else the woman could have said or done would have, but she rallied. "Don't use my daughter as an excuse to avoid the truth. You know we're investigating this case. Why leave us in the dark?"

"I thought you said dear old Dad took it from you."

Kerri held her stare until, remarkably, the other woman flinched.

"Fine. Just remember that you asked for this." Cross looked from Kerri to Falco and back. "Walsh believed that someone in a powerful position in Birmingham helped the Osorio family forge a path through Birmingham as their major channel of distribution. He wanted to find that link no matter the cost. You happy now?" Cross waved an arm at the dozens of sticky notes on her wall. "This isn't going to help you solve your case, but if you start asking questions on the subject, it will get you dead."

"He's been here only a few months," Falco argued before Kerri could respond. "He came to this conclusion that quickly when no one else had?"

"Maybe the link is in the DA's office," Kerri offered, barely keeping her voice level as anticipation pounded through her veins.

Cross held up her hands. "I don't know who he suspected; he wouldn't say. All I know is he wanted my help. I made the mistake of agreeing, and now he's dead."

"He got too close to the truth," Falco said.

Kerri turned to him. Her partner was right. It was the only reason to bother eliminating such a high-profile target. "Your father said Walsh's murder was because he'd stumbled into an ongoing DEA operation. If that's what happened, why wasn't Walsh working with him instead of behind his back?"

Cross thought about the question for a bit before answering. Kerri wondered if she was putting a story together or collecting her thoughts.

"The DEA and every other law enforcement agency you can name has wanted to stop the Osorio cartel for years," she said finally. "Walsh wanted to stop the people in positions of power who support the cartel, starting here. Those two goals aren't the same."

"Why do you say that?" Kerri asked.

Cross stared at her. "The ones Walsh wanted to stop are people the world around them believes in, respects. Except they have no idea that some of those icons of trust and justice wear masks that conceal the worst kind of evil."

11

2:30 p.m.

Brighton Academy
Seventh Avenue
Birmingham

Tori kept her head turned down as if reading while she surveyed the other tables in the library.

They were watching her.

All of them.

"I'm terrified for you," Alice whispered.

Fear slid icy cold through Tori's body. She turned her head just enough to look her friend in the eye. Alice was the only person who had sat down at Tori's table.

No one else was speaking to her . . . just watching her. They were all watching her. "I don't want to talk about it."

Alice pretended to read her book, but, like Tori, she wasn't. Enough. Tori had done nothing wrong. She lifted her gaze and scanned the tables. Faces instantly turned away, heads tilted downward. Tori gritted her teeth. She had gone to school with most of the kids since kindergarten. How could they believe she had done something so terrible?

She lowered her gaze to the printed pages. "I didn't do anything."

This was the truth. She'd never laid a hand on Brendal. She'd argued with her, sure. The girl was mean. She loved to hurt people. Tori's mom had taught her to stand up for herself and her friends. She wasn't going to stand by and allow some bully to just say whatever she wanted without speaking up.

"Maybe you just need to tell the truth."

Tori's gaze jerked toward Alice once more. From the day Alice started at Brighton, Tori had been in awe of her. She was so beautiful. Her long dark hair and intense dark eyes were like exotic or something. She had those lips celebrities paid big money for and extralong, thick lashes. Tori's stomach cramped. She didn't remember a lot about her grandmother. She'd died like seven years ago. But she did remember this funny rule she'd always recited. *Pretty is as pretty does.*

Alice wasn't as pretty as Tori had thought.

"What do you mean?" Tori said this louder than she'd intended. She lowered her voice. "I did tell the truth."

"Did you?" Alice's dark gaze was laser focused on Tori, as if she could see inside her brain. See her thoughts.

"Of course I did. Why would I lie? I didn't—"

"Everyone knows, Tori."

Alice didn't look away, didn't blink. Her gaze was hypnotic. It drew Tori and at the same time terrified her.

"I . . . I don't know what you mean."

Not even a blink. "They know Brendal had figured out your secret. She was going to tell the whole school."

Impossible. The only person who had known was dead. Tori had confided in her cousin Amelia. No one else in the whole wide world knew.

Unless . . .

Alice nodded as if reading her mind. "Yes. Sarah knows. She's always known."

Tori swallowed back the awful taste suddenly filling her mouth. "Sarah is my best friend. She wouldn't say anything to hurt me."

"Are you certain?" Alice countered. "She goes to that very strict church. They don't accept just anyone, you know."

Tori's heart beat faster, throat tightened. She struggled to draw in a breath. "You're wrong." She stole another covert glance around the library. Some still stared at her and whispered behind their hands to their tablemates. Faster, faster, Tori's heart pounded. "No one knows."

"I know. Remember?"

The air stalled in Tori's lungs as her gaze swung back to the other girl's. "I don't want to talk about it anymore. No one knows. Not even Sarah." A tiny burst of anger gave her courage. "You're lying."

Tori had seen Alice talking to Brendal. Lots of times. At least for a while. Then Brendal had started her usual mean crap, and Alice had ended up all alone again. Tori had felt sorry for her. She'd invited Alice to sit with her and Sarah at lunch again—despite how Alice had blown them off for Brendal. Sarah hadn't wanted to. Not at first anyway.

But it was the right thing to do. *Wasn't it?*

"I do know. You just don't remember what happened that night." Alice smiled. "Doesn't matter, why would I ever tell? I'm your friend. I love you. But they see it. Anyone who really looks can. It's so obvious. They probably think you and Sarah—"

"No," Tori snapped. "Sarah and I are best friends. That's all."

"Has anything like Brendal's fall ever happened to anyone you and Sarah know?"

Tori shook her head. "Things like this don't happen at Brighton."

As hard as she tried to focus on the words printed on the pages, Tori's mind wouldn't latch on to them. It was like looking at a foreign language. Alice still stared at her. She could feel her gaze burning her cheek. Had something happened between her and Alice one of those times Tori had spent the night with her? She'd had weird dreams when she'd stayed at Alice's house. But this wouldn't have been a dream. Worry tore at her. She didn't dare ask Alice to explain what she meant.

"This is going to destroy your life, Tori. Your family—everyone here—they're all going to be shocked and believe the worst. That's what people do. Someone has to take the blame for what happened."

Terror rose in Tori's blood. Her throat tightened to the point she couldn't speak.

"I know you've thought about this before. When your father left. And then when your cousin was murdered."

The whispered words echoed in Tori's ears as if Alice had shouted them.

"You're thinking it would be easier not to have to deal with it. I understand. I would be terrified too. It would be so humiliating if they learned the whole story about who you are."

"You can't tell," Tori warned, finally finding her courage once more. "Whatever it is you think you know, you can't say a word."

Alice's lips formed another of those sad smiles. "Don't worry. I would never tell anyone. You can trust me. I won't let you down. Whatever you decide, I will never tell. No one ever has to know the whole truth. Unless . . ."

Tori blinked. "Unless what?"

Alice leaned closer. "Unless Sarah already told them."

"I'm telling you," Tori argued, "even if she knows, she wouldn't do that. We've been best friends too long."

"She told me before that night."

The words stabbed deep into Tori's chest. This wasn't possible. She couldn't be sure Sarah even knew. They had never talked about it. Alice could be lying . . . she could be trying to make Tori say something she didn't want to say. "I don't believe you."

"How do you think I knew? That night—when it happened—you didn't notice I wasn't shocked?"

Tori couldn't remember. *What was she talking about?* Fear pounded in her veins.

"You have to decide, Tori." Alice glanced toward the door; her breath caught.

Tori followed her gaze. Sarah closed the library door behind her and started toward their table. The thrashing in Tori's chest seemed to rise into her throat.

"You have to decide," Alice repeated. "Either tell the whole truth and face the consequences or . . ."

Tori's gaze collided with hers once more. "Or?"

"Or take yourself out of the narrative. That's the simplest solution."

12

4:15 p.m.

Birmingham Police Department
First Avenue North

The task force meeting started off exactly the way Kerri had imagined it would. Mason Cross and his team were lead. The DEA had been investigating the Osorio cartel throughout its steady surge into power—for nearly a decade. More recently, local agents had been following a newly discovered connection in Birmingham upon which Asher Walsh seemed to have stumbled. How Kurtz came to be involved was unknown at this time.

This new connection could lead them to the main artery pumping drugs through the Southeast. It was immensely important that no one got in the way.

Like the BPD.

Kerri and Falco were to continue their pursuit for any information about Leo Kurtz and how he and Walsh connected. At this time, other than dying together, there was no proof the two men were involved whatsoever. Agent Cross even went so far as to suggest the execution of Kurtz was nothing more than staging to throw the DEA off track. At any rate, for Kerri and Falco it was hands off where Walsh was concerned.

Funny, Kerri decided. If the DEA had been following the movements of the cartel as their stronghold in the Southeast increased, why didn't they know more about the takeover in Birmingham? The transition of power from Atlanta to Birmingham? These were things, apparently, that Walsh had learned in his short time in Birmingham. The details weren't quite adding up in Kerri's opinion. The DEA's primary focus was drugs. They should have been on top of this rampant spread of the Osorio criminal organization throughout the Birmingham area.

Then again, it was certainly possible that the DEA knew far more than it was sharing. In fact, it was entirely likely.

Cross stood at the front of the conference room, that military bearing of his exuding power and confidence. He spoke as if he had the whole situation sized up and the perfect operational plan nailed down and already well underway.

Ultimately, for Kerri, the burning bottom-line question was, *How could the upper echelon of the BPD not have been aware of any sort of ongoing operation?*

Even with a black op—one completely undercover—certain powers that be were made aware. The mayor may or may not have been briefed. But the chief of police would have known. He may not have been aware of all the dirty details, but he would have been provided a vague overall snapshot of the situation. It was the only way to prevent agencies and departments from stumbling over and into each other.

Based on how curiously quiet the chief had been so far, he'd been as in the dark as anyone else on this. Kerri had never seen him so subdued during a major briefing.

As if she'd said the words out loud, Falco glanced at her. She and Falco understood something was off with this situation, and it was a hell of a lot more than mere territorial issues.

Kerri surveyed the others present. If Sadie Cross was telling the truth and Asher Walsh had thought someone in a position of power in Birmingham was involved with the cartel, then it could be someone in this room at this very moment. Special Agent in Charge Cross, the chief, and the LT—Brooks looked over his shoulder at her as if he, too, was aware of precisely what she was thinking. Maybe she was just too easy to read. The mayor sat next to DA Lockett. Seated behind the Jefferson County sheriff were three other DEA agents. Any one of these people could be wearing that mask Sadie had mentioned.

Kerri's attention shifted back to the mayor. Emma Warren was sixty. Attractive. Long dark hair that lay in waves around her shoulders. Being married to one of the wealthiest financial geniuses in the Southeast allowed her to wear a high-end designer wardrobe and live in a multimillion-dollar mansion. Warren donated her salary as the mayor to support a brand-new endeavor: the Women of the Future mentoring program. Three students, grades seven through nine, were chosen in January each year for the program. Mayor Warren would mentor one, while two other prestigious and powerful women of Birmingham would mentor the other two.

It was an exemplary program, and frankly Kerri had no reason not to like the woman beyond her public decision to ensure a task force investigated this case rather than merely the BPD. Kerri supposed she should be grateful the investigation into the murder of a high-profile citizen wasn't on her and Falco.

Except she wasn't.

Agent Cross continued to drone on about the terrifying statistics of drugs and human trafficking and how the cartels were the main drive behind those ugly crimes. Kerri attempted to stay on task, but her thoughts drifted to her daughter and Brighton Academy. She'd sent a text to Tori at lunch and asked how her day was going. Her daughter's response had been a thumbs-up. Kerri hoped that was the case, but she knew too well how these things went. Rumors would be rampant. Fingers pointed. Accusations thrown about.

She closed her eyes and tried to view the situation objectively. Tori and her friends had been the ones huddled with the Myers girl when she'd fallen. Of course, they would be the center of gossip and innuendo. Kerri forced her eyes open. How could something as seemingly simple as a disagreement between middle schoolers have evolved into something so devastating? The four girls had been standing on the landing. Based on the security camera angle, the leopard-print flats worn by Brendal Myers had been heels toward the camera, which confirmed she'd stood with her back to the descending steps. The other three, including Tori's black Converses, had been toes toward Myers in a sort of semicircle.

The only conclusion could be that the three had ganged up on Myers somehow. Even as Tori's mother, Kerri couldn't deny the way it looked—at least from the perspective of the shoes the girls had been wearing.

It looked bad. No question.

But the video surveillance showed Myers's right foot coming out behind her as if she'd taken a step back and hit air rather than lost her balance due to being pushed. The movements hadn't been frantic or clipped. Right leg had swung back ever so slightly, and then she'd tumbled down. The other three sets of shoes had remained exactly as they were for several endless seconds. Then, Tori in the lead, the three had rushed down the stairs. As the girls came into view, the camera captured the stunned expression on Tori's face. Sarah's and Alice's faces had been tilted more downward, so deciphering their expressions was basically impossible.

"You ready?"

Kerri pulled free of the troubling thoughts. The briefing had ended, and folks were filtering out of the conference room. Falco stood over her, his face showing the concern she heard in his voice. He was all too aware of her dilemma.

"Yeah." She stood. "Look, do you mind if we drop by your place to get your Charger? There's something I need to do, and then I'll catch up with you."

They were working on the list of Kurtz's friends that George Caldwell had provided. Based on what the employees, including

Caldwell, had stated so far, the list likely comprised customers with whom Kurtz had associated more than others or for a longer period of time. There appeared to be no friends outside his employees, customers, and business associates.

"No problem." Falco eyed her speculatively. "But I would like to know where you'll be."

They were partners. No secrets. They'd come to that agreement after their first big case together. With the caveat that they wouldn't discuss the distant past. Meaning Falco's undercover days. No reason to, she supposed. Whatever he'd done in the past, good, bad, or indifferent, she trusted him completely.

"I've been trying to check in on Sarah Talley, but her mother isn't returning my calls. I thought I'd stop by. I need to look her in the eye and get her take on what's happened."

"You know Sykes and Peterson won't like it."

"This is about my daughter. I don't care how they feel."

Falco nodded. "Got it. I'll carry on with that list."

His face told her he wasn't particularly happy about their going in separate directions. He was worried. Hell, she was worried, and she damned sure didn't like anything about this.

In the corridor outside the main conference room, the chief and the mayor were in deep conversation with Cross and a couple wearing visitor's badges. Kerri was too far away to read the names written on the badges, but the stark pain on the woman's face was telling enough even before Kerri recognized her.

The mother, Lana Walsh.

The man was the father, Leland Walsh. There was some resemblance to the murdered DDA in his profile. The sharpness of the nose, the thick eyebrows.

"Walsh's parents arrived last night," Brooks said quietly as he moved in shoulder to shoulder with Kerri. "The chief will be giving them a full update. As will Agent Cross, apparently."

The LT's tone hinted that he wasn't too thrilled with Cross, either, but he was far too diplomatic to say as much.

"Everyone is watching." Brooks looked from Kerri to Falco and back. "Stay inside the lines on this one."

Kerri nodded. Falco did the same.

It wasn't until they were past the painful huddle in the corridor that Kerri could breathe again.

The only thing people were watching more than this investigation was the incident at Brighton Academy. It was all over the news, including the video of her loading Tori into her Wagoneer and speeding away.

Worry chewed at Kerri's ribs. How in the world could she fix this?

"I need to pop into the ladies' room," she said to her partner. What she needed was a moment.

Falco nodded. "I'll meet you outside."

He strode on to the stairwell exit as Kerri moved toward her destination. The hydraulic wheeze of the ladies' room door closing behind her followed Kerri into the first stall. She closed her eyes and pressed her forehead against the cool metal. She needed a moment of total silence to quiet the worries spiraling out of control in her head. The hydraulic wheeze sounded again, followed by heels clicking on tile. Kerri ignored the realization that she was no longer alone and worked to calm her thoughts. Tori would never hurt anyone. She was a good kid. A happy kid—at least as happy as teenagers could be. She needed her mother to be strong. To be there for her.

Kerri drew in a deep breath. Losing it wasn't going to help her daughter.

She squared her shoulders, reached back and flushed the toilet, and then exited the stall. A woman stood at the row of sinks, her head bowed. Kerri looked away, walked straight ahead to the first porcelain bowl, and went through the motions of washing her hands. Another deep breath. She forced the lines of worry on her face to relax. Everything would be okay. Sykes and Peterson would find the truth—she would help—and Tori would be cleared. Life would go back to normal.

Kerri would not allow any other outcome. *Good. Okay.* She had to go. Falco was waiting.

"You're working on my son's case."

Kerri's attention shifted to her right. *Lana Walsh.* If Kerri hadn't been so flustered, she would have recognized the elegant suit the woman wore. *Damn.*

"Yes." Kerri grabbed a paper towel and dried her hands. "Detective Kerri Devlin."

The mother moved closer, her eyes searching Kerri's. "I need you to do something for me, Detective Devlin."

Kerri wadded the towel in her right hand. "I'll help if I can, ma'am."

"Find who did this. Don't be distracted or fooled by theatrics."

"I'll do my best," Kerri assured her.

Her face gripped by misery, the other woman nodded. "Thank you."

Kerri gave a nod and made her exit.

When she reached her car, Falco was waiting, leaning against the front fender.

"I have a message from Lana Walsh," Kerri announced. At her partner's raised eyebrows, she went on, "I ran into her in the ladies' room. She wants us to find who did this and to not be distracted or fooled by theatrics. Who do you suppose she's talking about? The task force or maybe her sister, Naomi Taylor?"

Falco grunted. "Could be both."

"Maybe," Kerri agreed.

He pushed away from the vehicle and started around the hood. "For the record"—he paused before getting in—"I'd do the same thing you're planning. Make Talley talk to you, Devlin. To hell with what Sykes and Peterson think. To hell with this case. I've got this."

Just another reason she was grateful for her partner.

Talley Residence
Twentieth Street South
Birmingham, 5:30 p.m.

Renae Talley's SUV was in the driveway.

Kerri parked at the curb and climbed out. Tori usually went home after school. But considering what had happened, she had gone to Diana's house. Kerri would pick her up after work. Tori loved her aunt Diana but didn't like having to change her routine. Kerri pretended it was all good. The truth was she felt completely incompetent as a mother just now. She was supposed to protect her daughter from things like this. Be there for her . . . instead she was at work. Long hours. Every day. Renae Talley, on the other hand, was a registered nurse and married to a surgeon. The couple had decided Renae would be a stay-at-home mom until Sarah went off to college.

Even if she'd had that luxury, Kerri wasn't sure she would have chosen to stay home rather than continue her career. Her family had always been a great support system. If Kerri was caught up in a case, there had never been a need to worry about Tori's well-being.

She closed the door of her Wagoneer. But Kerri's situation was quickly changing. Her father had died a few years back, her mother years before that. Diana was scrambling to keep her life together after her daughter's death. And Tori's father was in New York. A band tightened around Kerri's chest. Life happened. The only choice was to go with the flow and to be prepared when change shifted the circumstances.

Easier said than done.

Kerri rang the doorbell and waited. This was the first time she'd left messages for Renae and failed to receive a response. But then this was the first time the stakes had been so inordinately high. With them seemingly on opposite sides of the challenge.

The door opened, and Renae stood face-to-face with her. She didn't smile as she typically did. Her hair and makeup and the casually sophisticated attire were the usual fare. Her long elegant neck and squared shoulders spoke of her confidence and years of ballet. She and Diana had attended the same dance school back in the day. Renae was older than Kerri and Diana. She'd been married many years before her first and only child had come along. Unlike Kerri, who'd married right out of the police academy and gotten pregnant soon after.

"Kerri." The one glaring absence in Renae's manner was that usual spark of happiness to see the mother of her daughter's closest friend.

No smile. Not even a hint that she was glad Kerri had stopped by.

Kerri's heart sank. "Renae." She drew in a breath and reminded herself of Falco's words. *Make her talk to you.* "I've been trying to reach you. How is Sarah doing?"

"She's as well as can be expected."

If anything, Renae's posture had grown even stiffer. Her lips thinner and tighter.

"I wanted to speak with you about what happened at school. We've always discussed whatever was going on in our daughters' lives." Kerri hated that her tone sounded a little hopeless and a lot uncertain.

Renae seemed to realize how visibly out of character her reaction to Kerri's visit was. "Of course." She stepped back, opened the door wider. "Come in."

As soon as she'd closed the door behind Kerri, she added, "Sarah is lying down. She came home very tired. I'm certain it's depression." She exhaled a weary breath. "Who wouldn't be depressed."

"It's a terrible situation," Kerri agreed.

"Would you like tea?"

That was another thing. Renae was a tea person. Kerri couldn't recall ever seeing her with a mug of coffee. Hot tea was one thing Kerri had never learned to enjoy. It was like wine; it gave the appearance of a bit more sophistication. Coffee and beer drinkers were a little less classy.

"No thank you."

"Join me in the kitchen," Renae suggested. "I really need tea."

Kerri followed her through the family room into a kitchen that would make any chef jealous. Lucky for Kerri, she wasn't a chef.

While Renae lit the flame under the kettle, Kerri slid onto a stool at the island. "I'm sure Sarah is as devastated by what happened as Tori."

Renae leaned against the counter next to the stove. "Unquestionably. Do you have any news on Brendal's condition?"

"Unchanged. I'm hoping for better news soon."

Renae gathered a cup and tea bag. Her hand slowed as she reached for a spoon. She lowered it to the counter and turned back to Kerri. "Sarah is frightened. Terribly, terribly frightened."

"Tori too," Kerri commented. "We've all just started to heal after Amelia's death and now this."

"Sarah said Brendal had given Tori a hard time about what happened to Amelia. Did you know that?"

Kerri schooled the surprise that streamed through her. "Tori didn't mention it."

Renae poured the hot water into her cup before turning back to Kerri. "Brendal is a bit of a bully. Even when she was just a toddler, she pushed the other kids around. You know we attend church with Brendal and her family."

Kerri had forgotten. "I see."

The other woman seemed to catch herself. "I didn't mean to speak ill of the poor girl. But everyone knows how Brendal is."

Kerri held up her hands. "No, I get it. I've heard the same thing from others."

A frown marred the older woman's perfectly smooth forehead. "Really. Have you been talking to the other parents?"

"No, no." Kerri shook her head in emphasis. "I meant I've heard people make those sorts of statements before. Before what happened."

She shrugged. "You know, like on the soccer field. At the Christmas program rehearsals."

Renae nodded as if Kerri's explanation seemed plausible. She went on, "Brendal has always been the chosen one. At church and at school."

For a moment—a single moment—Renae allowed Kerri to see and hear a hint of jealousy. Then she banished it and smiled. "I guess when your daughter is as beautiful as Brendal and, my word, as intelligent, it just makes sense that she always rises to the top. You certainly can't blame a child for being all she can be."

A lone nod seemed an adequate response. "Tori told me what a terrible time Brendal had been giving Sarah recently. I know that must have been difficult for her. Sarah is such a sweet, kind girl."

A cloud of uncertainty passed over Renae's face before she could stop it. "You know how girls are at this age. All those hormones." She made a tsking sound. "I don't know how any of us survived it."

Kerri pinned on a sad smile. "It really is a difficult stage."

The silence went on for a beat or two too long.

"I'm certain you know Sarah would never hurt anyone, not even someone who had been unkind to her."

"Never," Kerri agreed. "She and Tori are very much alike in that. They are too kind and far too sweet to hurt anyone."

"Tori hasn't mentioned the issues she was having with Brendal of late?" Renae reached for the spoon again and added sugar to her cup. "A lot of the children are talking about it. Sarah has been very worried about her."

"We've discussed at length how hurtful bullies can be." The answer wasn't really an answer, more an avoidance of the question since Tori hadn't mentioned any such issue. In fact, she'd said Sarah was the one on the receiving end of Brendal's recent attention.

Renae picked up her cup of tea. "Young girls do like their secrets."

Kerri somehow managed a vague tilt of her head. "Tori learned a hard lesson last year about keeping secrets, even the seemingly harmless kind."

Renae only smiled before sipping her tea.

Again, Falco's words reverberated inside Kerri. "I'm glad the girls were able to give coherent statements after what they went through."

This was straight-up fishing. Kerri hoped like hell it worked.

Renae shook her head with the same weariness and sadness she'd been wearing since she'd opened the door to Kerri. "Sarah can hardly remember anything. She said it happened so fast. Everything was just a blur. Of course, she's never experienced any sort of trauma like this."

"As a detective, I've tried to impress upon Tori the importance of paying attention to the details. You'd be surprised how much happens in a split second that we don't see if we're not paying attention."

Renae set her cup aside. "I'm sorry. I really should check on Sarah now. We'll have to talk again soon."

Rather than push more questions at the other woman, Kerri followed her back to the door. Renae opened it, but Kerri hesitated before leaving. "Maybe the news will be better next time. Tori and I sent flowers to the hospital. As soon as Brendal is well enough, we're planning a visit."

"Brendal can't have visitors yet, but Sarah and I visited her parents yesterday. They're holding up as well as can be expected."

Kerri had known Renae wouldn't be able to let the comment pass without a comeback of her own. "That was very thoughtful of you."

They said their goodbyes, and Kerri headed for the street.

How the hell had Renae and Sarah managed a visit with Brendal's parents? Kerri gave herself a mental kick. What was she thinking? The two families attended the same church and Dr. Talley likely knew everyone in the hospital. Did Sykes and Peterson know about the visit? No wonder Renae hadn't returned her calls. She was too busy making sure her daughter was in the clear.

Aren't you doing the same thing?

Kerri refused to consider her investigative attempts to be the same as Renae's obvious steps to set the stage for her daughter's innocence.

By the time Kerri reached the sidewalk she was mentally kicking herself. Of course Sarah was innocent, and so was Tori. This situation was getting to her, making adversaries of longtime friends.

Tires squealed as a car screeched to the curb in front of her.

"What the hell are you doing here, Devlin?" Peterson shouted out the driver's-side window as he lowered it.

Damn. She was caught.

Sykes was out of the passenger-side door and striding her way. "You know better than this, Devlin," he reminded her. "This is interfering with an investigation."

"Seriously? Renae and Sarah are our friends. I wanted to check on Sarah."

"Maybe that's the way of it," Sykes said, "but you know better than this."

"I didn't talk to Sarah."

Peterson was out of the car, standing in the huddle now. "You cannot do this shit, Devlin. Stay away from the Talleys and the Cortez girl and her folks."

"What the hell?" She looked from Peterson to Sykes. "You two know me better than this. It was a quick visit. No big deal."

"But it is a big deal," Sykes countered. "Brendal Myers just died. Until we can rule out foul play, this is a homicide case."

Sykes had lost her at *died.*

Brendal Myers was dead.

Regret, horror . . . fear all twisted inside Kerri. *Dead.* Those poor parents. Air forced its way into her empty, starving lungs. This was the worst possible news.

Kerri had to get to Tori before she heard this some other way.

As she drove away, leaving the two detectives glaring after her, she recognized she could no longer put off calling Tori's father about the situation. He had a right to know. But first she had to call Falco.

She needed to hear his voice.

Swanner Residence
Twenty-Third Avenue South
Birmingham, 6:30 p.m.

"Hey," Kerri called as she entered her sister's kitchen. "Sorry I'm late." She forced her lips into some semblance of what she hoped was a smile. She couldn't talk about what she'd just learned. Not until she was alone with Tori.

She had to be strong. Keep it together.

Diana and Jennifer Whitten—Jen—were seated at the island. Jen was like another sister. She and Diana had been best friends for as long as Kerri could remember. Sadly, Jen was the only person Kerri knew who had worse luck with men than her. She'd been married and divorced three times. Kerri had long ago lost count of her numerous and often short-lived relationships. Everyone had their weaknesses, and men just happened to be Jen's.

"No worries. Tori's playing video games with the boys," Diana said. "You want a beer?"

Kerri shook her head, barely holding herself together. The last thing she wanted to do was fall apart in the middle of her sister's kitchen. Diana had enough hurt of her own to suffer. "Thanks, but I just want to get home."

Jen frowned. "If you're not willing to have a beer with us, things must have been really shitty today."

Jen had always been on the blunt side. It was one of the things Kerri and Diana loved about her. At the moment she had no idea how right she was. "Really, really shitty," Kerri confessed, her voice brittle.

Diana pressed her fingers to her lips for a moment as a realization sank in. "It's the Myers girl. She took a turn for the worse?"

Kerri nodded stiffly. "She died."

Everything inside Kerri had expanded and swollen to the point she felt ready to choke to death. Her heart thumped so hard she could scarcely think. Between the Talley house and here she had called Falco and given him the news. He was coming over as soon as he finished for the day. He would help navigate the new direction this tragedy had taken. Tori would need them both.

"Oh my God." Jen was off her stool and rushing around the island to give Kerri a hug before the words stopped ringing in the air. "I am so sorry, sweetie. This is hard, I know."

Diana joined the hug. "We'll get through this. Tori will be okay."

Kerri closed her eyes tight to hold back the emotion burning there. If she allowed the tears, she might not be able to present a picture of strength for Tori. Tori would need her to be strong. The girl's death was awful, awful, awful. There was no way to change that. But she did not want this to damage Tori and her friends in some irreparable way. It was bad enough as it was.

When they'd pulled away from each other and settled around the island, Diana said, "Maybe Tori should stay home from school for a few days."

Kerri shook her head. "I'm not sure if that's the right move. Rumors are rampant at school already. All three girls are under scrutiny. And Renae Talley is going the distance to cover for her daughter."

"What do you mean?" Jen asked.

Steadying herself, Kerri went over her visit with Renae and then the confrontation in the street with Sykes and Peterson.

"That bitch," Jen growled. "How dare she make out like her daughter is more innocent than Tori."

Diana gave a dry laugh. "Hear, hear." Her expression turned somber. "Are you worried? I mean, really worried?"

"Of course I'm worried," Kerri admitted. "Not about what I know so far, obviously. But about what I don't know, and I don't know a lot. Which is why I'm *really* worried."

Jesus Christ, how could this be happening?

"Why are you worried?"

Kerri turned to find her daughter standing in the wide doorway between the living room and the kitchen. *Oh hell.*

"Hey, sweetie," Diana said, "would you like a Coke or something?"

Tori shook her head, the fear on her face breaking Kerri's heart. "No. I want to hear why my mom is worried."

Kerri stood and walked toward her daughter. "I'm so sorry to have to tell you this, but I just learned that Brendal didn't make it."

One, two blinks. "So, she's dead."

Kerri nodded. "I'm sorry, yes."

Tori started to tremble, and Kerri grabbed her just before her knees gave out. Her daughter clung to her and cried so hard her slim body shuddered. Kerri hugged her close and stroked her hair, all the while whispering soothing assurances. Diana and Jen wrapped their arms around the both of them, and they all cried together for a bit.

"Who died?" one of the twins demanded.

Diana pulled away. "Ryan, where's your brother?"

"Tell me," the older-by-two-minutes twin repeated. "What happened? The last time you were all crying like this, it was Amelia."

River came up next to his brother. "What's going on?"

Tori pulled free of her mother and turned to her cousins. "She died. Brendal died. And everyone thinks I had something to do with it."

"No," Kerri argued. "No one thinks you had anything to do with what happened."

Tori swiped at her eyes with the back of her hand. "Yes they do. Even Sarah's not talking to me right now. They think it was me. And now Brendal is dead."

Kerri tried to pull Tori into her arms once more, but she drew away. "No one—NO ONE," Kerri emphasized, "believes you had anything to do with Brendal falling."

"I wish I was the one who had died."

Tori rushed out of the house. Kerri started to go after her, but Diana held her back. They watched as Tori loaded into the Wagoneer.

"She's upset. Not thinking. She didn't mean what she said." Kerri looked from Diana to Jen and back.

"Kerri," Diana said, her expression dead serious, "don't even go there. You take those words as if you *know* she meant them. Do you hear me? Take no chances."

Her sister was right.

Tori was in a very dangerous place.

Kerri had no idea how to help her. But she would move heaven and earth trying.

—

Devlin Residence
Twenty-First Avenue South
Birmingham, 7:15 p.m.

"I don't want to talk." Tori tossed her backpack on the sofa and headed for the stairs.

"I'm sorry," Kerri said, "that wasn't a request. We are going to talk."

Tori halted, her hand on the newel post, but she didn't look back.

"Let's sit and talk now. Falco is bringing dinner."

Tori heaved an exaggerated breath, did an about-face, and strode to the sofa. She plopped down. "So talk." Even with her arms crossed so tightly over her chest, Tori's shoulders shook.

"What happened to Brendal is so, so awful. I understand you said what you did because you're hurt and afraid. I'm certain you didn't mean it. I also want to be certain you know I'm here for you. Whatever you need. We all are. We love you, Tori. Your family—Falco—we all love you so much. We want you to be safe and happy."

She looked at Kerri then, her eyes brimming with emotion, lips trembling. "Not my dad. If I was the one who died, he wouldn't care."

For the first time since Kerri had caught Nick cheating, she was glad she had called him. Filling him in on what was going on with their daughter was the right decision.

"I talked to your dad today," Kerri said. "He's worried too. He said if you needed him, he would be on a flight first thing in the morning."

A lone tear rolled down her daughter's cheek. Kerri's heart felt as if it were cracking apart.

"Are you just telling me that to try making me feel better?"

Even after a year of neglect, Tori still desperately needed her father to love her. Kerri would never forgive him for putting her through such profound uncertainty. But his rising to this challenge gave her a renewed, if marginal, ability to tolerate him.

"I'm telling you exactly what he said. In fact"—Kerri checked the time on her cell—"he'll be calling you any minute. He loves you too, Tori. We will get through this."

More tears flowed. "You promise?"

Kerri put her arm around her trembling shoulders. "I promise. In fact, I'm so certain this is all going to be behind us very soon that I told your dad it was fine if you went to New York for a couple of weeks when the school term ends."

Tori swiped at the flood of tears. "He actually wants me to come for two whole weeks?"

Kerri managed a smile. The bastard had allowed only weekend visits—and even those rarely—since the new baby was born. "He does, and I'm okay with that. I want you to be happy, Tori. Safe and happy, that's all I've ever wanted."

Tori searched Kerri's face, uncertainty clouding her expression once more. "What will you do?"

"Don't worry about me, kid. I'll find plenty to do." She had her work.

The doorbell chimed.

And she had Falco.

Tori shot to her feet. "Wait till I tell Falco. He won't believe it!"

Relief washed over Kerri as she stood. Chasing killers was easy compared to this parenthood gig. Watching her daughter's animated face as she shared her news with Falco almost brought tears to Kerri's eyes.

Falco hugged Tori, the take-out bags hanging from his hands. "This is great," he was saying. "You'll have to bring me a T-shirt."

Kerri's phone vibrated, and Nick's face appeared on the screen. "Tori." She held her phone screen out so Tori could see that her father was calling.

Tori gave Falco another hug and rushed to take the call. Chattering away to her father, she bounded up the stairs.

Kerri suddenly felt more tired than she had ever felt in her life.

"You did good."

She turned to her partner. When she'd called to tell him about Brendal's death, she'd also told him she planned to make the call, and he'd assured her it was the right decision.

He had been so, so spot-on.

"Thanks."

He placed the take-out bags on the coffee table and hugged her. "You're a great mom, Kerri. Don't ever doubt it."

Great was probably pushing it. But it was possible she wasn't half-bad.

They settled around the table, and Falco passed out the burgers and fries. "Wait"—Kerri pushed to her feet—"I'll get the beer."

"You," Falco ordered as he stood, "stay put. I'll get the beer."

She nodded and dropped back into her seat. Apparently, her exhaustion was obvious to her partner as well. She wasn't surprised. They were well attuned to each other's moods. Good partners always were.

Kerri picked up a fry and nibbled. By the time Falco reappeared with the cold, sweating bottles of beer, she'd gotten a second wind. "So tell me how the interviews went."

Falco unwrapped his burger. "There are seven names on the list—all small business owners in the area like Kurtz. I talked to five." He tore off a bite of burger.

Kerri nodded as she unwrapped her own. "You made good progress."

"Except"—he knocked back a swig of beer—"I got nothing for it. I pitched the story that Kurtz was working on a small business–owners' committee. None of these guys had talked business with Kurtz since before Christmas, when they discussed the holiday open house idea."

"What about the final two?"

"I'm waiting for callbacks from both."

No forward momentum on the case, but they were checking off more necessary boxes. That was something, she supposed.

Kerri focused on her burger, though she wasn't very hungry, mostly to give Falco time to finish his before she launched into her latest thoughts on the case. When they'd both polished off their beers, she said, "I've been thinking about Walsh's parents since the briefing, particularly after the meeting in the bathroom with his mother."

"Oh yeah. What're you thinking?"

"I'm thinking his father should be making more noise." Kerri braced her forearms on the table. "I love my kid more than anything. I have all these hopes and plans for her. Most parents do."

Falco nodded. "Course."

"So, what went wrong with Walsh and his father? Why bother with the prestigious education and clerkship, then come all the way to Alabama for a county DDA position? Sure, his aunt is here, but if his plan was to please her, why not attend Samford instead of Harvard? What happened between the clerkship and his taking the DDA position to change his mind about joining his father's law practice? Why would the hierarchy of power within the drug trade in Birmingham, Alabama, have any bearing on Asher Walsh's future? It makes no sense."

"First off, parents have killed their offspring for less," Falco pointed out.

Kerri made a face. "I'm not suggesting the father killed Walsh," she clarified. "I'm wondering how far the son would go to prove something to his father. You know"—she shrugged—"the in-your-face-dad scenario. Maybe Birmingham was the city he chose to do it because his aunt and fond childhood memories were here. He was no doubt aware how much his father despised the aunt and all things south—according to the aunt."

"Maybe in trying to prove whatever he intended to prove"—Falco picked up the theory from there—"the son got in too deep and got himself killed."

"Exactly." Kerri pushed back her chair and stood. "Maybe there's no big mystery here. Could be nothing more than a gone-too-far situation."

Falco nodded slowly. "You may be onto something, Devlin."

She grinned, feeling light for the first time since the call from the school. "I think I might be. I'll get the next round."

Kerri headed for the kitchen. There was nothing like feeling the weight of being a failed parent to make you see the possibility in others.

She shook off the idea. In any event, the parents had to be ruled out just like anyone else close to the vic.

Had nothing to do with her own failings.

At least that was what she told herself.

13

8:00 p.m.

Leo's Tobacconist
Oak Grove Road
Homewood

Sadie watched the small haughty crowd gathered around the bar. Mostly old white dudes. Their elegant clothes and fine leather shoes said plenty. Money. Lots of money. The privileged of Birmingham.

She sipped her bourbon on the rocks, ignoring the urge to down it and to order another. Keeping her shit together was important. It was the least she could do for Asher. In addition to finding that local power link to the cartel, he'd wanted to help her. This he had told her over and over. Eventually she would determine his actual motive. Not that she didn't believe he'd wanted to help her, but she'd learned the hardest way of all that even people who cared about you had a motive for every action. They might not be aware themselves of the underlying incentive, but it was there.

Human nature. Survival and all that bullshit.

Tara McGill had motive for what she had done too. With her, it was easy to figure out. She was the proverbial gold digger. Money was her goal. She didn't have enough. She wanted more. But McGill wasn't clever enough to be working directly for the cartel. If she was involved at all, someone would be feeding her orders, orchestrating her every move. McGill was the source Kurtz and Asher had suspected. Kurtz had discovered her little entrepreneurial endeavor. He'd been watching her for a couple of weeks when Asher approached him. Sadie's sources had pinpointed the shop as being a link in the distribution chain. McGill wasn't quite as discreet as she should have been. A mistake that would cost her big-time—whether from the good guys or the bad.

Kurtz had agreed with Asher's conclusion that if someone in his employment was working for the cartel, there could be other small business owners suffering the same treachery. Small businesses like his would be overlooked in the grand scheme of things when it came to law enforcement investigations. Too insignificant. *Unless* a significant number of insignificant establishments were pulled unknowingly into the game. Simple math. Little veins were far easier to hide than big bulging arteries.

Sadie's guess was that McGill had provided the information and access needed by whoever had offed Kurtz and Asher. Under the circumstances she likely considered herself innocent of the crime, but she was wrong. She was just as damned guilty as the shooter.

Another sip of bourbon slid down Sadie's throat as she watched McGill flit about, crooning over one customer and then another. Ensuring she touched each one on the arm or shoulder, sometimes the back. Dressed in a skintight black dress barely long enough to cover her ass, with a scooped neck that revealed lots of cleavage, along with black stockings and sexy black heels. The old bastards probably got hard-ons just watching her.

Sadie looked away. What she needed was the shot caller in whatever the hell went down. Her gaze shifted back to the group gathered in memory of the murdered owner. Could be one of these rich guys. Whoever it was, it would be someone in a position of power. As badly as she wanted the actual shooter, more than that she wanted the one who had given the order.

Taking down the ones who got their hands dirty scarcely slowed the flow. You had to find and cut off the head of the lead snake. Even then a dozen other snakes slithered seemingly out of nowhere to take its place.

It was all one endless, vicious cycle.

"Would you like another?"

Sadie looked up at McGill. She'd obviously decided to float over to the table in the deepest, darkest corner of the establishment. No surprise. Sadie had been nursing this one drink since she'd arrived. Establishments making money from the sale of alcohol didn't care for those who took up space and purchased only one drink.

Or maybe she had caught Sadie watching her one too many times.

"No thanks. I'm good." Sadie shifted her gaze forward in dismissal.

"I've seen you here a couple of times before. Did you know Leo?"

"No." Sadie took another sip of the now-watery bourbon. The two times she had patronized the establishment had been to be eyes and ears for Asher. Too bad she'd failed to recognize the full depth of the danger within these seemingly innocuous walls.

"That's a shame. He was a great guy. We're going to miss him terribly." McGill sighed. "I suppose the place will be sold." She made a vague gesture with her arm, sending the smell of perfume wafting over Sadie. "I'm running things until then. Someone has to."

Sadie lifted her gaze to the woman once more. "I'm sure you'll do a great job."

McGill smiled. "I saw you watching me. Is there something more than a drink you need?"

Now this was an interesting turn of events. Sadie manufactured a smile. "Always."

"I could meet you after the place closes. Say ten thirty?"

Softening the rejection with a smile, Sadie offered, "I'm afraid I'm already committed tonight. Another time?"

"You know where to find me." McGill began her float around the room once more. Laying on the compliments and doing her touchy-feely act.

The invitation was one Sadie definitely hadn't expected. She wore her usual—a black tee, jeans, and sneakers. It wasn't like she looked rich or powerful. Maybe McGill had been hoping for a night of slumming.

Sadie would be back tonight to see what McGill did after work. There were a number of perfect stakeout locations nearby. It was always possible the invitation had been a trap. Sadie doubted McGill had any idea about her involvement with Asher. Kurtz wouldn't have, either, unless Asher had told him. No reason for him to make that sort of move without informing her.

Whatever. She needed to get out of here for a while. To think. She wasn't going to learn anything until McGill closed up. Maybe she should go home with her. Find out her secrets. Dig up a little evidence to support the conclusions about McGill.

But then, Sadie had walked into a trap once too often. Whatever she decided, caution would be her watchword.

She had no desire to repeat past mistakes.

—

Eighteenth Street and Morris Avenue
Birmingham, 9:30 p.m.

Sadie sat down on the grimy concrete. She'd left her car parked at the Greyhound station, then walked around the corner to Eighteenth and found the exact spot under the overpass.

This was where she had been found in late November three and a half years ago, three years and seven months, to be exact. Unconscious. Broken. Loaded with drugs. The homeless guy who'd found her had thought she was dead. But she had been alive. Barely. Her right leg had been broken. The weeks-old injury had healed, but the bones hadn't properly aligned. The correction had required surgery. Left shoulder had been dislocated, the humeral head fractured. Weeks in a sling and months of physical therapy had salvaged most of the use of that arm. Her nose had been broken at some point, but it, too, had healed—not as straight as it had once been. An MRI showed evidence of recent and repeated head trauma. So many bruises and scars. Whoever had tortured her had been damned good at his work.

There were other things . . . things she didn't like to think about.

Do not go there.

The doctors had all agreed that the memory loss was a result of a combination of the head trauma and the extended overuse of hallucinogens, among other drugs.

Sometimes she had the most bizarre episodes. Possibly flashbacks but she couldn't be sure what was real and what was imagined. Dr. Holden had suggested that whoever had done this might have used video footage along with the drugs to imprint false memories.

Basically, she was seriously fucked up.

Ignoring the people just yards away, tucked into cardboard boxes for the night, she closed her eyes and let her mind go back.

"Hey! Hey, you okay?"

The man crouched over her that night had looked about as much like hell as she had. He'd worn dirty, torn clothes. His beard had been long, his face wrinkled and leathered. But his eyes had been keen, watchful.

It had hurt to move. Oddly, she'd grown accustomed to the pain. Probably from all those months of torture she couldn't really recall. She remembered opening her eyes to the old guy.

She hadn't been happy about it. The one thing she'd known for sure was that she hadn't wanted to wake up. Being dead would have been preferable. The realization wasn't actually a memory, just a knowing.

"What's your name?"

Sadie had lain there for about a minute, trying to figure out how to answer him.

"I'll get help."

He'd apparently realized she didn't know her name or couldn't speak, so he'd gone to the bus station to get someone to make the call, but there had been no need. A BPD cruiser had been at the bus station, so the old man had led the two uniforms to her.

An ambulance had arrived and whisked her away to the hospital. A few hours later her father had arrived and identified her. Most of the other stuff that had occurred those first few days was yet another blur in her life.

The concrete felt cold beneath her now. She remembered that cold . . . it had seeped so deep into her bones that night it had taken days before she felt warm again. She'd lost weight while she was missing. Nothing but skin and bones. They'd all said it was a miracle she was alive.

But it wasn't.

Very recently, maybe with Asher's help, she'd realized that she had survived by sheer force of will. Subconsciously she had determined to survive, possibly for nothing more than revenge. But years of recovery had been required to come to that understanding.

She laughed, the sound echoing in the night. The sad part was she couldn't remember precisely who the target of her revenge was. Yeah, yeah, the Osorio family for sure. The old man would have ordered whatever was done to her. But she wanted the others involved too. The ones who'd beaten her, cut her, and worse. So much worse.

She pushed away the thought.

Of course, she wanted to get Carlos, first and foremost. But there was something about the person or persons who'd inflicted the torture that made her want them even more. Faces she couldn't remember. Voices that were unfamiliar and unclear and came to her only in bits and pieces.

Nailing down the identities should be a piece of cake.

"Right," she muttered.

She pushed to her feet and started to pace the length of pavement under the overpass on the Eighteenth Street side. Back and forth. Back and forth. She'd eventually tracked down the guy who'd found her and gone for help. There was no way to gauge how many others had walked right past her. Lab tests on her clothes showed that at least one person had pissed on her. Whether that was before or after she'd planted herself facedown under the overpass, no one could say.

Witnesses in the bus station had stated that she'd gotten off one of the buses. The consensus as to which bus was mixed. Possibly the one from Houston, maybe the one from New Orleans. Drivers from every imaginable direction had been interviewed, and no one had remembered her.

Ultimately the answer to how she'd ended up at the Greyhound station and then under the overpass was yet another mystery.

She wandered into the station and watched the people coming and going for a while. Watched those waiting in the lobby, heads dropping forward or back as people fell asleep in their chairs. She noted the one hoodlum who watched those dozing off, his gaze going from them to their bags.

When he got up to snatch a bag, Sadie stuck her leg out in his path. "Don't even think about it, asshole."

The kid gave her a nasty glare and hustled away.

A few minutes later she felt as if she'd soaked up as much of the shitty atmosphere as she could tolerate. She decided to go back to Leo's and follow that lead.

Why not? She had nothing to lose.

If she got herself dead, her only regret would be not getting Asher's killer first.

Leo's Tobacconist
Oak Grove Road
Homewood, 10:35 p.m.

Sadie had backed into a slot in the rear of the parking lot at Leo's. She could watch the stockroom exit and McGill's car from her position. She'd made a quick detour on the way here for the gear she would need. It wasn't much. Something for copying McGill's house key. Decoding software in case she managed an opportunity to have a look at her computer.

At 10:39 the Vandiver guy exited, cell phone against his ear. He climbed into his vintage BMW and roared away.

Another five minutes elapsed before McGill came out. She strutted across the pavement in the direction of her car. Waiting until her target was at the halfway point between the rear exit and her Corolla, Sadie emerged and began walking toward her. Hearing the footsteps, McGill jumped and turned in Sadie's direction.

"Whoa. You scared the hell out of me." A hand on her bare chest, McGill said, "I thought you had other plans tonight."

Her voice shook ever so slightly. She wasn't completely sure of the situation or of Sadie. But she didn't run.

"I decided I liked your offer better." By the time Sadie reached her position, she had her hands on her hips and was looking all cocky. "Unless *you* made other plans."

"No other plans." McGill moved in closer to Sadie. The heels McGill wore put the two of them nose to nose. "Your place or mine?"

Sadie looked directly into her eyes. "Yours is probably closer."

McGill traced a finger over Sadie's lips, then a path down to her breasts. "You riding with me or following?"

"I'll follow. Makes the morning after less complicated."

McGill grinned. "I'm liking you more already."

Sadie headed back to her car and climbed in. She waited until McGill did the same and darted out of the parking lot. Sadie followed.

Her phone vibrated, and she checked the screen.

Falco.

She decided to answer since he might have an update from today's task force meeting. She touched the speaker icon. "Yeah."

"You got anything new on your end?"

Sadie considered holding back but decided if she wanted Falco to be on the up-and-up with her, she had to do the same to the extent possible. "I'm following Tara McGill to her town house."

The lady lived in a damned high-end community to be a barmaid. If Sadie'd had any doubts as to whether she was involved in illegal activities, discovering her digs had alleviated that doubt.

"Any particular reason?"

"It's possible she's the source Walsh and Kurtz suspected. Maybe. I can't be sure." Sadie wasn't ready to do a tell-all just yet.

"Sounds like you remembered something after all."

Sadie rolled her eyes at the thinly veiled innuendo. "Just doing a little feeling around, a little digging." No need to go into specifics. Falco was a smart guy. He knew what it took to get the job done.

"Be careful. If McGill is involved, she could be more dangerous than she looks."

"I got this." Sadie made the next left, staying close to McGill. "What's happening on your end?"

"Devlin and I are supposed to stay away from the Walsh aspect of the investigation and focus on Kurtz. Your old man wants us out of his way."

"That's his favorite MO." Sadie knew him like a damned book.

"I guess you heard the news that the Myers girl died."

"Yeah. That's too bad. How's Devlin's kid taking it?"

"She's having a rough time."

A couple of beats of silence elapsed, and Falco got to his point. "Look, if you can find anything on Myers or Talley or this new girl, Alice Cortez, I would appreciate it. I need to help Devlin with this. She's too close, and I'm not sure she can see beyond her daughter."

"You're sure her daughter isn't guilty?" Sadie hadn't met the kid, and she had no reason to believe she was a bad one, but she had to ask.

"I'm positive. Tori is a really good kid."

"Is that Falco the cop talking or the substitute father?"

"You're a jerk sometimes, you know that, Cross?"

"Came by it naturally." She pulled into the lot at the row of high-end town houses. "You've met my father."

"Bottom line, Tori is a good kid. Period. But whatever happened, she's tied into it somehow."

"I'll see what I can dig up. Gotta go." Sadie ended the call and put her phone away as she climbed out.

It was time to get into character.

She'd always been really, really good at being someone else.

14

11:00 p.m.

Cross Residence
Eagle Wood Court
Birmingham

His phone buzzed.

Mason Cross stared at the screen. He exhaled. Had little or no effect on the frustration that swelled inside him.

Ignoring the situation wouldn't help. It wasn't going away.

"Yes."

He listened. What else could he do? The molehill he had allowed to linger all these years had grown into a mountain. There was no easy way out at this point. Not for him.

"I'm outside. We need to talk."

The sound of her voice still had the power to unsettle him. It shouldn't. Nothing about her should do anything except fill him with fury . . . and yet *she* profoundly disturbed him on every level.

Rather than respond to what was clearly an order, he severed the connection and placed his phone back on the table next to him.

He picked up his glass and swallowed a slug of scotch.

He stood and walked over to the window. He didn't know why he bothered. It was too dark to enjoy his view. Moonlight flickered on the water. He'd loved this place the moment he'd laid eyes on it nearly forty years ago. He'd barely been able to afford to buy the land at the time. Even forty years ago waterfront property was outrageous. Sadie had been a toddler before he'd been able to have the house built.

Mary Ellen had loved it. The lake. The woods. The house. She'd been so happy. Those next ten years had been like heaven on earth. Then they'd found the cancer, and everything had gone to hell.

His beautiful wife had died for almost two years. Six hundred ninety-eight days. He'd watched her waste away. Had watched the light fade from her incredible gray eyes—the same eyes as Sadie's.

He knocked back the rest of his drink. Sadie was the utter reflection of her mother. He could hardly bear to look at her. He'd withdrawn from her after Mary Ellen was gone. It was a mistake. He recognized that now. At the time he hadn't been able to see beyond his own pain.

The trouble had begun then.

Another of his mistakes.

Nothing he could do to change that now.

But he intended to make amends before he took his last breath.

Better late than never.

He sighed, walked to the front door, and exited the house. He could make her wait, but he couldn't avoid her. The result of a long-ago mistake—one that would haunt him the rest of his days.

The black sedan idled at the curb in front of his house. *Was pulling into the driveway too much trouble?* The driver stood at attention next to it. Mason gritted his teeth and followed the stone path to the street. Without a word, the man opened the rear driver's-side door for Mason. He settled into the leather seat and the door closed solidly next to him. The driver remained outside the vehicle.

What else could she possibly want? The investigation was his now. He could do what needed to be done. His gaze met hers, and for a single moment he couldn't breathe. She was so beautiful . . . even after all these years.

The moment disintegrated, and reality snatched him back to the present. "What would your husband say if he knew we were meeting like this?"

She smiled, but it was not an expression of amusement. "I need to impress upon you once more how very delicate this situation is," she said as if he didn't fully understand the circumstances.

"I am aware."

"Asher's father is very, very upset, as you might imagine. He wants justice. Whoever did this must be found. *You* must find that person and the proper evidence to assuage his grief."

Mason wondered if she thought this late-night rendezvous would in any way change the steps he would take. He understood exactly what he had to do. Certain choices had stopped being his own long ago.

"I've already assured you that I will handle this investigation personally. Mr. Walsh may rest assured that a shooter will be found, as will the person suspected of having given the order. Both discoveries will be supported by the appropriate evidence."

"Forty-eight hours," she warned. "I want this business completed. None of us want this tragedy to play out in the media like a bad movie."

"Forty-eight hours," he echoed. "I'll do all within my power to meet your deadline."

She stared at him, the dim interior lighting more than sufficient for him to see how her perfect, refined features hardened. "I don't want your assurance, Mason. I want your guarantee."

He gave a single curt nod, and then he exited the car.

There was nothing else to say. He would take care of it.

Even that might not be enough. Asher Walsh had been a fool. He'd gotten in way over his head. He'd left a hell of a mess, and Mason was supposed to clean it up.

In forty-eight hours, no less.

Cleanup he could handle. It was keeping Sadie out of the investigation and alive that might prove difficult.

15

Session Two

Three Years Ago

"I am Dr. Oliver Holden. With me is my patient, Sadie Cross, age thirty-one. This is regression therapy, session number two."

Holden takes Sadie through the same relaxation steps as the first session. Her breathing becomes deeper, slower. The only other sound on the recording is the whisper of the air-conditioning.

"Sadie, we're going back to the compound in Mexico. The one you first visited on September 7, eighteen months ago."

"The Osorio compound." She sounds resigned. Sad or weary.

"Yes. Are you comfortable with going back again?"

"I have to go."

"If you want to remember, yes, going back is necessary."

"Let's do it, then."

"The date is October 31. You've been living at the Osorio compound for more than a month, but something happened this day that changed you. You've stated that your memories beyond this date are scattered, foggy."

"The Day of the Dead. Yes. There was a party. The household staff was busy preparing all day. Eddie was in meetings somewhere. Someone special was coming to the compound for the party."

"Who was this special person?"

"I don't know. Someone who mattered a great deal to Eddie and the old man. The task force wasn't aware of any other family, so I had no idea."

"To that point had your mission gone as expected?"

"Mostly. There were some kinks I had to work out, but I managed."

"But something happened at this party?"

A long gap of silence follows the question.

"Sadie?"

"That's the night something essential changed."

"What do you believe changed?"

Another lapse of silence.

"Sadie?"

"I don't know. That's why I'm here."

16

Wednesday, April 14

8:40 a.m.

The Coffee Bean
Seventh Avenue
Birmingham

"I understand this is asking a lot." Kerri kept her hands clasped tightly around her mug of coffee and waited for her partner's reaction. She'd asked him to meet her at the coffee shop across the street from Tori's school.

Falco's arms rested against the scarred Formica top, his untouched coffee abandoned next to the napkin holder. "I got no problem covering for you, Devlin." He shook his head. "You don't even have to ask. But I need to know you can do this on your own without crossing the line."

He had every right to be concerned. She'd crossed the line last year on their first case together. Who was she kidding? She hadn't simply crossed that line; she'd hurdled over it as if she were racing toward some unseen finish line. She had killed a man. Depending upon how closely you looked, what she'd done could be considered self-defense. If she had not chosen to go after the bastard on her own—unofficially—the situation would not have happened. Take your pick: self-defense or cold-blooded murder?

Falco and Sadie Cross knew what had happened that day. Both had helped to ensure Kerri's secret was safe.

Except . . . no secret was ever truly safe. She pushed the thought aside and promised, "I'll be careful. I won't make *that* mistake again."

Falco picked up his coffee and seemed to consider whether it would taste as old and overheated as it smelled. "Anything you do could damage the investigation and reflect badly on Tori."

"I'm aware. I just need to know that every rock has been turned over and every potential lead followed through to the end. I can't sit back and risk that something will be missed." Any mother in her position would do the same. "I'll stay in the background. Sykes and Peterson won't have a clue I'm checking up on them."

Falco dared to take a sip of the coffee, then made a face. "With the DEA lead in our case, we're not likely to get more than busywork. The stuff no one else wants to do, like checking all the p's and q's related to Kurtz. I can handle that." His gaze settled onto hers once more. "The LT will never know you're not taking every step I take. If you're sure that's what you want."

"It's what I want." Leaving Tori at school this morning had been one of the hardest things Kerri had ever done. But Tori had wanted to go. Like Kerri, Tori understood that her absence would only lend credibility to the rumors.

"All right." Falco set the coffee aside. "But we keep each other informed. It's the only way to properly cover our asses. If something happens to one of us, the other will be up to speed. We're less likely to get caught that way."

"Agreed."

"No keeping secrets," he reiterated.

"No secrets." Secrets led to mistakes. She wasn't going there again.

Falco nodded. "Okay. I'll get those final two on the Kurtz list interviewed. What's your first step?"

"I have a friend who works at Walker Academy."

Calling Sue Grimes a friend was a stretch. They'd gone to high school together, but they hadn't been close. Getting a list of the staff members had been easy enough from the website. Sue was the librarian. She might not have worked directly with Alice Cortez or either of the students who had attempted suicide, but she would have heard the talk among the teachers. She certainly would have known the students and perhaps their parents. Though it was preferable to go to a direct source, talking to Grimes was less likely to get her caught, since the detectives on the case would be questioning the teachers and staff who interacted directly with Cortez and the others—assuming they bothered to check out Cortez's background. At this point Kerri wasn't convinced about the thoroughness of her colleagues.

But that was the mother in her—not the detective—obsessing on the idea. Sykes and Peterson weren't bad detectives.

"I want to hear from you at noon," Falco urged. "Maybe we can rendezvous for lunch."

"Sounds good." Kerri felt a weight lift from her chest. Having her partner onboard was a genuine relief. Not that she'd expected him to say no, but the fact that he hadn't pushed the idea of her actions being a mistake gave her a better sense of balance.

When she would have scooted from the booth, he placed a hand on her arm. "Be careful, Devlin. I like having you as a partner."

She smiled. "Same here."

Kerri felt as if she were drowning in a case that wasn't hers and a situation that grew more dire for her daughter each day.

Walker Academy
Daniel Payne Drive
Birmingham, 10:00 a.m.

Unlike Brighton Academy, which was in a historic building, Walker was a fairly new build. The school had been around for decades but in a different location. Walker was, as was Brighton, a top-notch private school. Brighton, however, was attended by the children of the elite of Jefferson County. Walker had its share of the offspring belonging to doctors and lawyers, but the real power sent their kids to Brighton.

Kerri flattened the visitor's pass onto the lapel of her jacket as she walked the central corridor of the main building. The offices, cafeteria, nurse's station, and library were all housed in this building.

The library stood at the end of the corridor, its glass front filled with posters about books and upcoming reading events. Inside was as hushed as a tomb. The space was fairly massive with a ceiling that soared well over twelve feet. Rows and rows of shelves packed with books, and desks loaded with state-of-the-art computers filled both sides. Near the back was a staircase that went up to a mezzanine level, where more books lined the walls from floor to ceiling. On this first level to the right of the staircase were rows of tables surrounded by chairs, some occupied with students, heads stuck in their chosen reads.

The office was to the left of the staircase, glass walls allowing those inside to see the working students. Kerri spotted Sue behind the reception desk, phone handset to her ear. Kerri recognized her easily since she'd attended their fifteen-year reunion three years ago. Sue was married but had no children. She explained to anyone who listened that the children at her school were all she needed.

When Kerri entered the door, Sue looked up. Surprise and then a smile claimed her expression.

"Thank you so much," she said to the person on the other end of the line. "I will let you know. Bye-bye." She put the phone down and pressed her hands to her throat. "My goodness, Kerri Devlin, what in the world are you doing here?"

Kerri glanced across the room at the other woman, seated at a desk. "I hoped you might have a few minutes to have coffee with me. Or just to chat."

"Don't tell me they've hit you up for the reunion committee. It'll be the big twenty in no time!"

"True," Kerri agreed without answering her question.

"Absolutely." Sue glanced at her coworker. "Gwen, I'll be back in a few minutes."

"I'll be here," Gwen promised without looking up.

"Let's grab coffee in the lounge."

Kerri followed Sue back to the central corridor and to the teachers' lounge. Thankfully it was deserted.

"Cream or sugar?" Sue asked as she filled two paper cups.

"Black is fine. You look great, Sue." The last time Kerri had seen her, she had been incredibly thin and her hair super short. Now it was chin length and styled in one of those fashionable cuts that made her look years younger. Kerri had wondered if she'd been ill but hadn't wanted to ask.

"I'm really good." Sue passed Kerri a cup of coffee, and they moved to a table. "I didn't want to talk about it at the reunion, but the last time you saw me, I'd just finished my final round of chemo."

"Oh no. I'm sorry to hear that. I had no idea." Kerri held on to her coffee but didn't drink. She'd already had four cups today.

"Only my family and work friends knew. It made things easier that way." She stirred creamer into her coffee. "I'm certain people mean well, but all the questions can be difficult. I found it easier if I just did what I had to do and didn't dwell on the situation."

"I can understand," Kerri said. "Sometimes, it's far less stressful not to be reminded over and over about things. When Nick and I divorced, it was so much simpler not to talk about it. The questions." She shook her head. "It's amazing how many people will blatantly ask what happened. I didn't want to dwell on the reasons. I just wanted to move on with my life."

"Exactly," Sue agreed. "You can't believe how many people asked me if I was optimistic about my survival chances." She made a sound of disbelief. "I did understand they meant well, but really? Was it necessary for them to know if I didn't bring it up? Bless their hearts. It was just so awkward."

"The worst," Kerri said, "were the ones who couldn't stop saying how sorry they were, like I was pathetic and needed their sympathy."

"Yes! I swear, I hope I never catch myself doing that." Sue's expression turned sad. "I am sorry, though, about your divorce."

They laughed together; then Sue sipped her coffee.

"I'm not here about the reunion," Kerri admitted.

"I know. It's too early. I just said that so Gwen wouldn't think the police were investigating me."

"I didn't think of that," Kerri said. "I don't want to cause any trouble for you."

Sue waved a hand. "I adore the woman, but she does love to gossip."

"I wanted to ask you about what happened with those two students who attempted suicide last fall."

Sue's eyes rounded. "Are they reopening the case?" She leaned forward. "I always thought there was more to the story, but no one wanted the ugly details to end up on the news."

"I'm not aware of the case being reopened," Kerri clarified. "It's more about one of the students who was involved."

Sue glanced around the room and then toward the door. "The two who did the suicide pact seem to be fine now. No one talks about it. There was some chatter at first, but Mr. Billings didn't budge on the matter. If a student was caught discussing it, there were consequences. I've never seen an incident locked down and closed into a dark room so fast. Really, I think the kids understood." She shrugged. "The school has doubled the number of counselors on staff. Every effort is being made not to miss anything like that again. I believe Mr. Billings took it personally that it happened on his watch, you know? Like he'd failed the kids somehow."

"I can see how he might feel that way. I always feel as if I failed somehow if I can't close a case the way I believe it should go," Kerri said. "I'm glad to hear the students involved are doing better. But what about the other student, the one who transferred to a different school?"

"Alice Cortez." Sue nodded. "Now there's a story."

Kerri's instincts sharpened. "Do you think she was involved somehow? I'm sure you saw her in the library from time to time."

"Oh, I saw her all right. By the time the *incident* happened, she was the star pupil here at Walker. The two girls who tried to hurt themselves once held that place. Two of our brightest shining stars. It's a terrible thing to say." Sue sighed. "But it's like Alice arrived and decided she wanted to be those girls, and it happened."

"Do you believe she took steps to make that happen?" The two students who had attempted to take their lives were both in the same grade as Tori. If they were as bright as Sue had suggested, how had they been taken down so low?

"That's the truly bizarre part. Alice was nice to everyone. Everyone loved her." Sue leaned forward again. "The rumor was that she lured the girls into some secret club, but I can't be sure. The one student who mentioned this idea to me begged me never to tell. She was afraid, and I don't blame her."

Rather than demand the student's name as she so wanted, Kerri said, "It's a miracle she told anyone."

"You know, I'm like a bartender; I hear all sorts of things from the kids. But this was a little more bizarre than usual. This student," she said with a pointed look at Kerri, "said she and Alice, along with the two girls from the *incident*, would meet in the woods after school and do these strange rituals."

"The two students involved in the suicide attempts," Kerri ventured, restraining her need to reach across the table and shake more information out of the woman, "never mentioned any of this?"

"Not a word." Sue moistened her lips and shot another glance at the door. "When it was clear they weren't going to tell, I told the girl who came to me that we couldn't not share this with Mr. Billings. It had to be done."

"But you didn't tell him the girl's name." Kerri held her breath.

"No, I couldn't break her confidence. We put our heads together and found another way. I used the book Alice had checked out of the library to back up my concerns."

Kerri stilled. *Book?* "Will you tell me about the book?"

Sue inhaled a deep breath. "It was a book about Santeria. It's a religion, cult—whichever you prefer to call it—that originated in West Africa and eventually spread through Latin America. Like any other religion, some take it to extremes with rituals and animal sacrifices. Alice seemed to be obsessed with the darker side of Santeria."

Something cold crept through Kerri. "Obsessed in what way?"

"I can't show you because I gave the book to Billings when I spoke to him, but Alice had made notes and drawn images in the book. I don't think she intended to return it, but the girl who came to me took it from her locker after what happened as a sort of insurance policy to protect herself. When she finally came to me, she'd been holding on to it for a while."

"Can you describe some of the drawings or recall any of the notes?" Kerri's heart was thundering now. Why had Billings not come forward with this information? There was nothing in the news reports Kerri had reviewed online about a third student or any bizarre rituals.

"Most of it made no sense. There were statements about cleansing and ruling. Apparently, she considered herself some sort of princess. A lot of it was gibberish."

Tori's words, one in particular, echoed in Kerri's brain. *Princess.* "And the drawings?"

"Stick people hanging from ropes. Piles of stick people on fire. The images were quite disturbing considering what happened."

"Did Mr. Billings give this book to the police?" As the head of the school, he had an obligation. Jesus Christ, as a human being, he had an obligation. Kerri swallowed back the choke of outrage.

"I don't think he did. He told me not to discuss the book or Alice with anyone, that he would handle it. He insisted Alice probably watched too many horror movies. He said he would speak to her guardians about it as well. But I'm convinced he never went to the police. Think about it; one of the girls set her room on fire, and the other hanged herself. The only thing that saved either of them was that someone found them in time. The girl who hanged herself used the ceiling fan in her room and it broke, hit her on the head, and knocked her out cold. Her mother found her before she regained consciousness." Sue searched Kerri's face. "I don't think what they did and those drawings were a coincidence."

Kerri didn't either. "Sue, I need to speak to the other girl." If she attempted to talk to one of the two involved in the suicide attempts, Sykes and Peterson would be on her so fast her head would spin. But if they didn't know about this third girl . . .

Sue didn't respond for a bit. Finally, she asked, "Can you tell me why? The students involved survived. If the police aren't reopening the case, what's the point? I've kept this child's secret all this time." She shrugged. "In all honesty, partly, I suppose, because I understood my job likely depended on it."

"The Cortez girl, Alice," Kerri said, her gut in knots, "goes to school with my daughter. She's friends with my daughter."

"Oh my God." Sue's hand went to her mouth. "Did she have something to do with the girl who fell? The one who just died?"

Kerri had to be careful here. "It's possible. The trouble is I need to know for sure." She frowned then. "No one from the BPD has been here about what happened?"

Sue's hand fell back to the table. "Two detectives talked to Mr. Billings. At least I heard they did, but no one has mentioned anything about Alice being involved in what happened at Brighton. I had no idea she had transferred there." Sue shook her head, her face growing pale. "The girl that died . . . this could be my fault. I should have gone to the police myself."

"No, no, this wasn't your fault," Kerri argued, though she wasn't entirely convinced. "First, we don't know yet exactly what happened with the Myers girl. And warning Brighton when Alice transferred there was Billings's job, not yours. Just as going to the police was."

Sue chewed her lip a moment. "Let me talk to her and see if she's willing." She put her hand to her chest. "Don't worry; if she won't talk to you, I'll tell whoever I need to everything I suspected about Alice and the book. I can't pretend anymore that it doesn't matter."

"Let's not jump the gun here," Kerri countered. What Sue had was a serious accusation, but she didn't have any proof unless Billings was willing to hand over the book—assuming it was still in his possession. "Talk to the girl," Kerri suggested, "see if she's willing to come forward. If not, we'll go from there."

Sue nodded. "All right. I'll do that today and call you no later than tomorrow morning. I'll need your number." She blushed. "I'm sorry we haven't really kept in touch. Life." She shrugged. "It's a little busy most of the time."

"No kidding." Kerri reached into her pocket and withdrew a business card. She passed it to Sue. "There's just one thing." God, she hated to do this part. At her old schoolmate's expectant look, she went on. "I'm going to need you to keep my visit here to yourself for now. I'm not the detective assigned to the case. Technically, with my daughter in school with Cortez, I'm not supposed to get involved."

"I may not be a mother, biologically," Sue said, "but I know what a good one is. What kind of mother would you be if you didn't get involved?"

Good question.

17

Noon

Brighton Academy
Seventh Avenue
Birmingham

They were talking about her.

Tori stared at her lunch tray. She couldn't eat. She'd barely slept last night. This morning when her mother asked if she was okay, she'd lied and said she was. She wasn't. How could she be?

Brendal was dead.

Her mom had wanted her to stay with Aunt Diana today. She had assured Tori again that she and the other detectives would get this straightened out. Not to worry. But Tori couldn't stop worrying. She'd known that if she didn't show up at school, the ones talking about her would make something even worse of it. She couldn't give them any more ammunition.

She had to be strong.

An assembly had been called this morning to announce the news. Like there was anyone who didn't know.

Everyone knew.

And everyone thought Tori had something to do with it.

Without daring to raise her head, she stole another glance at Sarah and Alice. They were huddled together, whispering. Tori knew they were talking about her. Otherwise they would have sat at her table. She and Sarah had been besties since kindergarten. She always sat with Tori. Always.

Tori was certain Sarah and Alice had seen her when they headed this way from the lunch line, but they'd pretended not to. They'd sat at a table with the two meganerds who never sat with anyone much less talked to anyone. The nerds were at one end of the long table, while Sarah and Alice were at the other.

Two of the extra counselors the school had brought in were walking around the cafeteria, asking kids if they wanted or needed to talk.

Tori couldn't talk to them. She couldn't talk to anyone. Not her mom. Not anyone. Not about her secret. She couldn't do it.

But Alice had plenty to say—to Sarah.

And Alice knew. She'd sworn Sarah did too.

They glanced at Tori, not even attempting to hide the fact that they were doing just that—talking about her. *How could they be so mean?*

Tori stared at the food she couldn't eat if her life depended upon it. She wished Amelia were still alive. Tori could talk to her. She could tell Amelia anything. She missed her so much.

Her whole life had fallen apart in the past year. First her dad left her for a new family. He hardly ever even called anymore. When Tori called him, he was always too busy to talk more than a minute or two. He had a new child now, a three-month-old baby boy. He had no time for Tori. She instantly felt bad. Her dad had called her last night and talked for a whole hour. He missed her. Was worried about her and wanted her to visit as soon as school was out. He was trying. That was what her mom said. But it hadn't felt that way for a long time, especially last year.

Worse, Amelia had gotten murdered. Even after that her mom still worked all the time. Tori didn't really like spending a lot of time at Aunt Diana's. She loved her aunt, but she was always so sad.

On top of all that, this year Tori had started to get pimples instead of bigger boobs. No one took a second look at her. People were looking at her now because they were all suspicious of her about what happened to poor Brendal.

And now she was losing her best friend.

As if all that wasn't bad enough, she'd failed her algebra test this morning. She had never failed a test in her whole life. She was an A student! Always on the honor roll. But not this time.

She'd failed that test.

Tori pushed her tray away. She couldn't look at the food anymore. Couldn't stand the smell.

She had never felt so alone.

Why did she even bother being nice to people? Working so hard to make good grades?

She was a loser. An ugly, too skinny, pimple-faced loser.

She'd asked Alice what she thought of her outfit the other day, and Alice hadn't wanted to answer her. Finally, she'd admitted that the outfit didn't look right on Tori because she was too thin. She needed to fix her hair and wear makeup.

Tori was sorry she'd asked.

She was sorry about a lot of things. Most of all for being nice to Alice.

She wished Alice had never come to her school.

Tori scanned the crowded lunchroom. At every table there was someone staring at her. Alice and Sarah were still whispering about her. She didn't have to hear them. She could see the way they glanced at her, and they didn't care that she could see.

She wanted to go home.

Anywhere but here.

Would anyone besides her mom even miss her if she disappeared? Or died like Brendal?

Probably not.

Life sucked.

Tori closed her eyes and reminded herself of her father's phone call. Her mom loved her even if she wasn't home as much as Tori would like. Falco liked her a lot too. Aunt Diana and Uncle Robby, even the twins loved her.

She had to stop feeling sorry for herself and just be strong.

Her mom would find the truth. Tori knew she would.

She just hoped it wouldn't be too late.

18

12:45 p.m.

McGill Town House
Hampton Heights Drive
Birmingham

Sadie checked the street again before emerging from her car. She'd parked at the far end of the unit of town houses and on the opposite side of the street. There were no security cameras unless a resident had installed one, but Tara McGill had not. The neighborhood was quiet, just as it had been late last night and early this morning. Sadie watched for afternoon dog walkers as she strolled leisurely along the sidewalk. Walking too fast would draw attention. She made it a point not to look around. People also considered that behavior as suspicious.

McGill had still been asleep when Sadie left, but she'd mentioned having to go to work early today for preparing a supply order and another interview with Falco—one where they would have the place alone. The woman liked Falco. Sadie smirked as she unlocked the door to McGill's town house with the key she'd had made. Falco better watch himself; McGill was a maniac. Since she'd said she had to be at Leo's by one, Sadie had arrived at twelve thirty and watched until she left. Then she'd waited a few minutes more to ensure she wouldn't come back. By twelve forty-five she'd felt confident McGill was gone for the rest of the afternoon and evening.

Inside the living room a staircase to the second level stood on the far-right side. A kitchen, dining room, and powder room were along the back of the first floor. Two bedrooms, two baths, and a laundry closet were upstairs. McGill had a home office set up in the second bedroom. Starting there would get the more complicated steps out of the way.

Sadie took the stairs. She checked McGill's bedroom, noted the unmade bed and clothes strewn around the room. The lady was not exactly a neat freak. Not judging. Sadie was the same.

In the bedroom turned office, the computer and printer sat on the small, cheap desk. An old dresser sat where one would expect a file cabinet. Shelves had been added to the closet for storage. Christmas decorations and more shoes. A couple of high school yearbooks and photo albums. Sadie opened the storage container and sifted through the decorations. She checked the insides of the shoes lining the floor. Then flipped through the yearbooks and photo albums. No hidden papers, no secretive notes.

Saving the desk for last, she prowled through and under the drawers of the dresser. She slipped her Mini Mag from her back pocket and aimed the light at the narrow crack between the back of the dresser and the wall. Nothing taped to the back. Nothing hidden behind it. The drawers held office supplies. Paper for the printer. Printer cartridges. Pens, tablets. File folders. But no files. She removed the floor vent cover and checked in the duct. Nada.

Sadie moved on to the desk. She sat down in the chair and awakened the computer, noted the log-in box that appeared. Tucking a thumb drive into one of the slots, she allowed the program to do its job of determining the necessary password to get into the system. The middle desk drawer held more office junk. A couple of erasers, sticky notes. Two smaller side drawers were basically empty except for a tube of lotion in one and a pack of condoms in the other. Sadie opened the lotion and ensured nothing other than lotion was inside. She did the same with the small box of condoms. In the box she found McGill's secret stash of oxy. A dozen of the 40 mg pills.

Not surprising. The whole world seemed hooked on that shit.

The two lower file drawers actually held files. McGill had written the contents on each. "Property Papers." "Taxes." "Medical." "Credit Cards." The usual. Sadie picked through the contents of each manila folder.

A sound announced that the computer was now unlocked. She moved the mouse, lighting up the screen. One by one, she read through McGill's emails. There weren't that many. McGill had deleted anything older than a month, and then she'd emptied her trash. She'd also cleared her search history.

"Savvy lady," Sadie muttered.

Clearly, Tara McGill wasn't the airheaded blonde she pretended to be.

Other than the apps, only one folder existed on the desktop. The label read "Files." Sadie attempted to open the folder, but it was password protected.

Sadie ran the security breaker app again. Didn't work. She had McGill's username and password, which allowed her to view the stored usernames and passwords for websites and apps. But not for the "Files" folder. McGill appeared to have everything backed up on a cloud, which might work to Sadie's advantage. She could pass what she had along to her computer guy, and he would most likely find a way in. He'd never failed her before. She doubted this security system was anything he hadn't encountered in his long history of hacking.

A five-year stint in prison had only sharpened his skills. He'd met all sorts of other geeks. The powers that be should consider what those sorts of geniuses could do when they put their heads together.

Sadie removed the thumb drive and slipped it into her pocket. She went into the adjoining bath and found nothing but hand soap on the counter and toilet paper on the wall-mounted holder. Toilet tank held only water.

Sadie moved on to McGill's bedroom. The search in here would take considerably longer. The woman had a lot of clothes. Her walk-in closet looked as if she'd decided to start her own boutique. Sadie went through the most likely places first. In the ventilation duct. Under the mattress and the bed. In and under the drawers. On the backs of the pieces of furniture. She found another stash of oxy in a makeup compact and lots and lots of silky, racy lingerie.

Sadie progressed to the closet. The door was an in-swing louvered style, allowing for airflow into the large closet. Starting on the left, she checked one article of clothing after the other. Thankfully, there weren't a lot of pockets other than in her jeans and the few pairs of slacks.

A sound . . . a solid thud froze Sadie in place. The door. *Front door.* Then McGill's frustrated swearing preceded her up the stairs.

Sadie turned off the light and burrowed into the row of dresses near the corner, where the door would block her if McGill came into the closet. She twisted her sneakered feet to the side and hoped that would be enough.

McGill stopped at her home office first. Sadie closed her eyes and restrained a groan. Had the computer gone dark by now? Most people set them to go dark after ten or so minutes of inactivity. If that was the case, Sadie was safe. The screen would be black. She'd been in the bedroom a half hour at least. But if the setting was much longer . . .

Hurried steps rushed into the hall. Sadie held her breath. McGill entered the bedroom. Sadie heard her moving around the room, swearing under her breath every few seconds. She couldn't see what she was doing but assumed McGill was searching for something she'd forgotten.

Couldn't be anything important, because Sadie hadn't found anything important.

McGill walked into the closet, all the way to the far end—the end Sadie hadn't reached yet—and began to rifle through the garments hanging there. The sound of hangers swiping across the metal rod prodded Sadie's pulse into a rapid fire.

Only two or three feet from Sadie, McGill stopped.

"Here you are." She removed a garment from its place and hurried out of the closet.

Sadie dared to inhale a deep breath.

McGill abruptly rushed back through the door. "For fuck's sake," she griped as she walked through the closet again. The sound of fabric rustling and then a "Now."

It wasn't until Sadie heard the front door slam again that she relaxed and emerged from the rack of fabric. A quick glance around told her McGill had taken a pair of shoes in addition to whatever garment she'd grabbed. The empty spot was where a pair of red high heels had been resting, waiting their turn to show off the owner's sleek ankles and toned legs.

When she'd finished in the closet, Sadie moved to a window that looked out over the street and verified that McGill's Corolla was gone before going downstairs. She quickly went through the rooms on the first level. Discovered McGill's workout gear in a large closet intended for coats.

The downstairs search was carried out the same as the one on the second level and yielded nothing other than the name of the gym McGill used. There could be a locker there. Something else to add to her list of places to check out.

When Sadie was sure the coast was clear, she exited the town house, locked the door, and walked casually to her car. As she drove away, she called Wesley Bryant, better known as Snipes. She'd given him that nickname after the first few times they'd worked together. Every damned time she had required his services and made the call, the man had been in the middle of watching a Wesley Snipes movie.

Snipes was glad to hear from her—no matter that she called only when she needed his help—ASAP, of course. He had plenty of other customers, but he was always happy to put Sadie at the front of the line.

Loyalty was a characteristic she greatly appreciated and found all too rarely.

Taylor Residence
Eighteenth Avenue South
Birmingham, 3:00 p.m.

Sadie gave a nod to the new guy, Tim Barton, as she walked past his car. She'd had to bring in another set of eyes to keep up the surveillance on Naomi's house. It was the least she could do. She should have done more before Asher had ended up shot in the back of the head.

Regret pierced her. Sadie rarely allowed herself to feel any sort of emotion, but this she couldn't keep at bay. She cleared her head and focused on the here and now. Naomi Taylor was never less than happy to see Sadie. The feeling was mutual. Sadie didn't like a lot of people, but she liked Naomi.

The bag she'd brought clutched in one hand, Sadie knocked on the door with the other and waited for the woman to answer. After a second knock, the locks rattled and the door opened.

Naomi smiled. "I'm so glad to see you, Sadie. Come in."

Sadie had never liked her first name—mainly because her father had picked it out—but she didn't mind Naomi using it. Most anyone else would get their ass kicked for calling her anything other than Cross.

After the expected discussion about tea, Sadie followed Naomi into the kitchen and watched while she prepared the kettle.

The older woman announced, "Asher's parents are in town."

Sadie imagined they had come to ensure their son's case was being investigated properly—the old man was a lawyer, after all—and to make arrangements for his body. Asher and his father had had the sort of relationship Sadie had with hers. He hadn't talked about the reasons, and she hadn't asked. She'd learned long ago that when you asked personal questions, you generally ended up having to answer the same.

Sadie cleared her throat. "Are they taking him back to Boston?"

"I imagine so." Naomi sighed. "I'm certain he would prefer to be buried here, but his father will have none of that."

"Has your sister called you?" Despite their differences, one would think Asher's mother would want to be with family now. Particularly considering how much Asher had loved his aunt.

But not Lana Walsh. All the more reason Sadie did not like the woman.

"She won't call me. I won't even be invited to the funeral." She sighed. "But that's fine by me. I'd rather remember Asher as he was."

"Has anyone come by to speak with you besides the two detectives, Devlin and Falco?"

Naomi shook her head. "Not a soul. Should I be expecting someone?"

"Not that I know of. I was just wondering." It seemed Falco and Devlin had stuck by their word and kept Naomi, as well as Sadie, from the task force. Maybe one day her confidence in humankind would be restored.

She mentally smirked. *Not likely.*

"Did the detectives take anything from his room?"

Naomi shook her head. "They took photos but didn't take anything else. I was glad. I think they recognized that I really wanted to keep everything possible. I'm sure his parents will be taking all his things from his condo."

"There's one thing they won't be taking."

Naomi's eyes widened in expectation as Sadie reached into the bag she held. "I dropped by his condo and got this for you. I knew he would want you to have it." She passed the framed photograph of Naomi and Asher to the lady.

"Oh, thank you so much." She clutched the photograph in both hands and smiled sadly. "This is my favorite picture of us together." She lifted her gaze to Sadie. "I'm certain they would have tossed it out."

Sadie smiled too. Something else she rarely did. Naomi made her want to smile. Asher had, too, for that matter. He was the first person she had allowed so close in a very long time.

"Is there anything new on the case?" Naomi held the photograph to her chest as if she were hugging her nephew.

"Nothing yet. A task force has been set up to work on the investigation. Hopefully things will move along quickly. The parents coming will put a living face on the loss and prod the efforts—particularly if they go public. Asher's father is a powerful man. The people in charge will not want him suggesting they aren't doing anything other than a stellar job."

Naomi gave a little nod. "At least the bastard is good for something."

"Did you ever like him?" Sadie couldn't help being curious. Besides, maybe there was something in that broken relationship between father and son that pertained to her investigation into Asher's death. There was definitely something off with the mother.

"I tried to in the early years," Naomi admitted. "But it was clear he didn't care for me right off the bat. I think he was intimidated by my credentials."

"Really?" A frown furrowed across her brow. "But he's a Harvard-educated attorney. Rich. Powerful. Well respected."

Naomi held her gaze for a moment. "I think because he recognized I saw through him."

"Saw through him how?"

"I did a little research on Leland Walsh. His academic record is quite impressive, but I spoke with a good number of others who attended Harvard at the same time as he, and they couldn't believe he'd done so well. They insisted he wasn't nearly so brilliant as he would have the world believe. He's built his empire on the backs of others, my friend. He is an evil man. Asher despised him."

"Do you have any proof that he's involved with anything shady or illegal, or are we talking about evil in the sense that he's ruthless and will do whatever necessary to win?" She'd never met a really good attorney who wouldn't.

"Probably the latter. I know how ruthless he is. He turned my sister against me. Tried to take Asher from me. His firm has quite the reputation for winning. Their record appears to be unblemished, and we both know you don't win like that without crossing certain lines. It's the corroborating it that most often proves impossible."

Sadie recognized part of Naomi's hatred for the man was nothing more than the fact that he had stolen her family. But Sadie also knew Naomi had a keen, highly intelligent mind. She was no fool. There was likely some merit to her claim.

"Do you feel his sheer ruthlessness is what ruined his relationship with Asher?"

Naomi nodded slowly. "I do. Asher was a kind, loving soul. He was one of the rare few who truly believed in justice for all. The older he got, the deeper his hatred grew for the mentality of people like his father."

"Would you like me to have his ass kicked while he's here?"

Naomi laughed so hard she lost her breath. "I suppose not, since I would surely be blamed. But the thought is marvelous."

Now for the part she dreaded. "Naomi, I've looked into your sister and her husband a bit. Like you, I couldn't find anything off about Leland, but I did discover something odd in Lana's activities over the past year or so."

Naomi's eyes lit with hope. "Please tell me that she's been cheating on the bastard. That would make my day."

"Afraid not." Sadie wondered if this lady would be hurt by what she was about to learn and if it mattered in the grand scheme of things. She couldn't risk that it might. "Did you know Lana has been coming to Birmingham once a month for a day, sometimes two, for the past fifteen months? Maybe longer, but that was as far back as I could find data."

Surprise claimed the older woman's face. "I could see her coming to visit Asher since he moved to Birmingham, but as far as I know, she didn't. Are you certain you have the right Lana Walsh?"

"I am. Can you think of any reason Lana would come here without telling you or Asher?" Though he hadn't been here so long, one would think Lana would visit her only child if she came all the way to Birmingham. Obviously, she had not, or at least Asher hadn't admitted as much to Sadie or Naomi.

Naomi appeared baffled by this news. She shook her head. "Lana has always hated everything about the South, particularly Alabama. I can't imagine any reason she would visit so frequently. Did you say every month?"

"Yes. Could she have some other family or friends here? Maybe there are distant relatives your mother never told you about."

Naomi shook her head. "There are no other relatives on either side. As for friends, all my sister's friends are in Boston. She only came here a couple of times. Asher most always traveled alone when he came for his visits. Lana would put him on a plane in Boston and pick him up when he returned. She hates Alabama. Always has."

Moving on, Sadie asked, "Is it possible your father left her some sort of property or share in some kind of investment?"

"Absolutely not. I executed my father's will. Lana was not mentioned."

"But could he have passed something along to her before his death? Something you didn't know about?"

She exhaled a heavy breath. "Just because I adore you," she said to Sadie, "I will double-check. I have an old friend who retired from public records. I'll see if she can dig anything up." Naomi's gaze connected with Sadie's. "However, there were no secrets between me and my father. I am utterly confident that you're barking up the wrong tree on this one, my dear."

Sadie hoped Naomi was right.

19

4:00 p.m.

Jefferson County Morgue
Sixth Avenue South
Birmingham

Kerri parked. Shut off the engine and collapsed against the seat. She had spent the past five hours tracking down information on the Cortez family and surveilling their house. She'd watched as the black Cadillac Escalade arrived home with Alice in tow. The woman and the girl had climbed out of the vehicle and walked into the house. Alice had a haughty walk about her. Kerri hadn't noticed that before. Maybe she only noticed it now because of what Sue had told her.

Tori had sent a text saying Diana had picked up her and the boys. They were going for ice cream. Kerri had called Tori back immediately. A text wasn't good enough anymore. Not after Amelia. She had needed to hear her daughter's voice.

Tori had sounded tired and . . . depressed. The idea that Kerri couldn't protect her daughter from this kind of pain broke her heart all over again. But she couldn't. All she could do was support her, love her, and try to find the truth. Before ending the call, she'd spoken to Diana and urged her to keep a close watch on Tori. Her emotions were so fragile and unstable right now. She needed to feel their unwavering support.

At three thirty Falco had called with news that the ME wanted to meet with the two of them at his office. Moore wouldn't call for a face-to-face unless something was up. As much as she wanted to stay on the Myers case, this was a meeting she couldn't miss. It wouldn't take long.

Falco's Charger pulled into the lot, and she climbed out. Met him at the halfway point between their vehicles.

She summoned a smile. "You have any idea what this is about?"

He shook his head as they walked toward the entrance. "No idea."

Moore's assistant waited for them in the lobby. Kerri exchanged a glance with Falco. This couldn't be good.

The assistant ushered them toward an autopsy room and left them at the door. Falco took a moment to survey Kerri. "You okay?"

She nodded. "I'll catch you up after this."

He opened the door, and they entered the room. Moore stood next to the table where Leo Kurtz's body lay covered with a sheet from the waist down. The usual closed incisions made after an autopsy were visible.

Once they'd gathered around the table with Moore, he began, "Leonard Kurtz died of a single gunshot to the back of the head. The weapon used was a .22 caliber. All his lab work came back clean. No drugs were found. His blood alcohol content was well below the level considered to cause impairment."

He couldn't have told them this on the phone? Kerri liked the man, but dragging her over here for this was a little frustrating. She could have picked up her daughter from school and spoken with her face-to-face if not for having to come to this *urgent* meeting.

"Kurtz isn't why I asked you here," Moore said quietly, as if he feared someone overhearing even though the door was closed.

Kerri's frustration fizzled as Falco asked the question that suddenly cleared through the worry in her brain: "You have something to share on Walsh?"

Moore nodded. Kerri and her partner shared a look.

"Dr. Moore," Kerri cautioned, no matter that the cop in her was dying to hear what he had to say, "as much as we appreciate anything you're willing to share, we don't want to put you in the line of fire. You're aware of the protocol established for the task force investigating this double homicide."

Moore chuckled. "Your concern is duly noted, but I'll take my chances. This is *your* case. I've never cared for the way certain federal agencies play."

Kerri nodded her understanding.

"Asher Walsh died by the same manner and cause as Mr. Kurtz. Except," Moore qualified, "his lab work came back with a positive hit. He had used cocaine before he died."

Kerri and Falco shared another look. Asking the ME if he was certain wasn't necessary. He was, or he wouldn't have released the information.

"Thank you, Dr. Moore," Falco said. "This could be very helpful."

Kerri thanked him as well before following Falco from the room. They didn't speak until they were out of the building and halfway to their vehicles, but tension throbbed as thick as coagulated blood between them. Words weren't necessary to understand something was way, way off.

Falco stopped and turned to her. "Are you buying this?" He shrugged. "I mean, there's plenty of people out there who preach one thing while doing the other. Just because Walsh stayed on his soapbox about drugs doesn't mean he didn't dabble."

"No question," Kerri agreed, though every instinct she possessed was screaming at her that this was wrong, wrong, wrong. "But his aunt seems awfully certain he was squeaky clean." Kerri was the one shrugging now. "Then again, sometimes family is the last to know." On a purely personal level the idea scared the hell out of her.

Falco's gaze narrowed, and his lips thinned. "But not Cross." He moved his head side to side. "Cross is adamant about Walsh's anti-drug standing. The aunt might have missed the mark when reading her nephew, but Cross wouldn't have. No way. He wouldn't be able to fool her."

"I have to agree with you there. I can't see Sadie missing that about him." Kerri drew in a deep breath, mostly to slow the pounding in her chest. She watched the anger dance across her partner's face.

"They want us to believe Walsh was buying from Kurtz," he said, the fury simmering in his voice.

Kerri could see the beauty in the plan. It flipped everything. "It was a simple drug deal gone wrong. Territory dispute or something like that."

Falco braced his hands on his hips. "I saw this kind of cover-up all the time when I was undercover. This is the way you shift attention to make the potential witness or, in this case, the victim, look dirty. Walsh loses credibility, and the investigation turns in a whole different direction."

"How do you suppose his father is going to react to this?"

"I was wondering the same thing." Falco's nostrils flared with a big breath. "Someone is working hard to change the direction of this investigation. Someone who was there the night Walsh and Kurtz died."

"The shooter," Kerri suggested, "or the one who gave the order."

"Cross thinks McGill may have been the source Kurtz and Walsh were going to confront."

Kerri considered the idea, then said, "What do you think?"

"I think she's onto something. McGill had opportunity. She could be the link between the shop and the cartel's local, low-level distributor. Cross thinks her motive is money. She's doing some more digging." He held Kerri's gaze for a moment. "Whatever she finds, this is going to get ugly, Devlin."

"This case isn't the only one getting ugly."

Falco cocked his head. "What'd you find out from your friend?"

"Sue says there was a girl—she wouldn't ID the kid—who came to her about Alice Cortez's bizarre behavior." Kerri shrugged. "Rituals related to Santeria. Allegedly, Alice and the two girls who attempted suicide were practicing these bizarre rituals. Sue insisted on speaking to the girl before giving me her name. She's supposed to call me as soon as she has talked to her."

"There are extremists who do some weird shit in the name of Santeria," Falco said. "Did you learn anything about the family who took in the Cortez girl?"

"That's another strange aspect of all this. I can't find anything on these people before August of last year. It's like they appeared out of thin air to be available for Alice. Their Alabama driver's licenses were issued in August of last year. They rented the house here in the same month. Bought the big Escalade they drive in August. The man, José Cortez, started his job at a warehouse over by the port in August. The woman has a nursing degree from UAB, yet I couldn't find any record of her attending the University of Alabama here or anywhere else."

"Sounds like someone set up new identities for these folks and planted them here."

Kerri nodded. "Like a bought-and-paid-for, ready-made family."

"Damn." Falco shook his head. "What about Alice? Did you find anything on her?"

"Not one thing except that she supposedly lived in Mexico with her parents, who died in a car crash, and now she's here. It's all very vague. The dead father was supposedly the brother of the man, José Cortez, who took Alice in. It's all too clean but at the same time very ambiguous."

"Less information provides less to dissect," Falco offered.

"Exactly." Kerri frowned. "It's hard to follow leads when there are none."

"Maybe," Falco said slowly as if he were still laying out the theory in his head, "these people are in witness protection?"

"I considered that possibility," Kerri granted, "but I figured if it was the feds, they would have moved the family out of Alabama as soon as that first trouble happened at Walker Academy."

"Yeah, yeah. They would have. Definitely." Falco considered their limited information. "Unless no one informed the family's contact. Alice's name didn't come up—publicly, anyway—in the Walker Academy incident. So far, no one's fingered her in the Myers girl's death. It's possible there's a lapse in communication. Whatever is going on, it's way wrong."

"It is, and I can't confirm enough facts to make any movement in the right direction," Kerri admitted. "I feel like I'm spinning my wheels."

"How's Tori holding up?"

"She's sad, depressed, scared." Kerri should be at home with her right now. *Damn this job!*

"Look." Falco reached for her arm, gave it a squeeze. "You can't do this alone or even with just my help. This thing just gets bigger and creepier. You need to take what you've learned to the LT."

Kerri shook her head. "He'll be pissed I've been nosing around."

"He'll get over it. If something else happens with this Alice girl, no one can say you didn't do all within your power to head it off."

He was right. "Okay. I'll go see the LT; then I'm going home to my daughter. Did you learn anything else from McGill that might substantiate Cross's suspicions?"

He scrubbed at his unshaven chin. That was something else about her partner that had driven her crazy at first. He didn't shave every day like the other male detectives in MID. He seemed to prefer that scruffy look. Not that it was a bad look on him, just not the norm for his current position.

"I think she's trying to play me."

"Play you or play *with* you?" Kerri teased.

"Ha ha, Devlin. She has all these elaborate excuses and alibis. You were just talking about vague; hers are too full of detail. She's covering her skinny ass. I just don't know if her motive is murder."

"Sounds like she has something to hide. She was the last person to see Kurtz alive—besides his shooter, I mean." Kerri squared her shoulders, ignored the exhaustion pulling at her. "Anything else I need to know?"

"Not yet. Go." He jerked his head toward her Wagoneer. "Talk to the LT."

"I'm going. I'll catch up with you later."

He gave her a two-fingered salute. "Yes, ma'am."

Kerri laughed as she climbed into the driver's seat. Her partner was right. It was better to give her thoughts to the LT than risk more trouble by keeping potentially significant information to herself.

Birmingham Police Department
First Avenue North, 5:00 p.m.

"You just caught me, Devlin," Brooks said as he shouldered into his jacket.

Kerri closed the door behind her, giving them privacy from anyone else who might stroll by the LT's office. "I have some information I need to pass along." She braced herself and said the rest. "It's about the Brendal Myers case."

Pushing back the sides of the jacket he'd only just slipped into, Brooks sat his hands on his hips. "Devlin, I warned you to stay clear."

"I know, but a friend who was concerned about my daughter called me," she improvised. Lied. Whatever. At this point all that mattered was ensuring this aspect of the case was investigated thoroughly. "She and

I went to school together. She's the librarian over at Walker Academy. Has been for years."

"All right, I'll bite. What did this friend have to say that you feel I need to hear?"

"Alice Cortez attended Walker Academy last semester. There was trouble, and she transferred to Brighton at the beginning of the new semester. January."

The LT stopped prepping to leave the office. "What kind of trouble?"

She had his attention now. "Two girls attempted suicide. Thankfully they weren't successful." Before he could ask how that tied into the Brighton Academy situation, she told him the rest of what Sue had shared with her.

"If I'm understanding you correctly," he said, sounding dubious, "you think this Alice Cortez might be playing some sort of cultlike games to prompt other students into doing her bidding."

When he said it that way, it sounded like something from a *Scooby-Doo* episode. "I'm saying there was trouble last fall when Alice attended Walker Academy, and now there's trouble at Brighton. She was friends with the girls involved in the incident at Walker, and she's friends with the girls involved at Brighton. Coincidence? Maybe. But it's something Sykes and Peterson need to check out."

Brooks mulled over her story for a bit, his brow lined in concentration. The LT was barreling toward sixty, but he looked like a forty-year-old. The man was a health nut and addicted to working out. More importantly, he was a good listener, a fair leader, and a damned good cop.

"What you're telling me is an interesting twist and one that bears further investigation," he agreed. "I'll have Sykes and Peterson give it a go. I appreciate the heads-up, Devlin, as I am sure they will."

Kerri managed her first decent breath since walking into his office. "Thank you, sir. No one wants this case solved more than me."

"I'm very much aware of your personal interest in this case, Devlin." He grabbed his briefcase. "But I will remind you again; stay out of the investigation. Sykes and Peterson have got this. I don't want to hear about you digging around again. Are we understood?"

"Yes, sir."

"Go home, Devlin. That's exactly where I'm going."

"Good night, sir."

Devlin Residence
Twenty-First Avenue South
Birmingham, 6:30 p.m.

Kerri had left the office, driven straight to her sister's house to pick up her daughter and then home. She needed some alone time with Tori. She wasn't sure exactly how she would go about this diplomatically, but she wasn't going to sleep until she'd had this talk with Tori.

She started with, "You want me to order Chinese?"

Tori tossed her backpack onto the sofa. She never bothered taking it to her room if her homework was done. "Sure."

Kerri made the call and then sat down on the sofa next to her daughter. "Can we talk until the food arrives?"

Tori shrugged. "Guess so."

"I spoke to someone at the school Alice attended last fall."

Tori's eyes rounded. "About what?"

"I wanted to find out if there was any trouble there when Alice attended. I have a friend who works at Walker Academy, and I asked her."

"Did she tell you something?" Uncertainty, hope welled in her voice and eyes.

Kerri nodded. "She told me about a group of girls Alice hung out with. There was some trouble, but no one died, thankfully. One of the girls talked about this religious stuff Alice was into. I think they were doing some sort of rituals. Not at school, of course."

Tori looked away.

Kerri's gut clenched. "You mentioned that you didn't like visiting Alice's house. Can you tell me more about that? It could be really important."

Tori moistened her lips. "Are you going to tell the other detectives what I say?"

"Only Falco—if that's okay with you."

Tori nodded. "You can tell Falco anything. He's my friend."

He was. He was Kerri's too. Her heart lightened at the thought.

"Did Alice do some sort of ritual when you and Sarah were there?"

Tori took a breath. "She would like wear this creepy mask and do all this chanting. It was really weird."

"Did she tell you things you should be thinking or doing?"

Tori frowned. "What do you mean?"

"When she did the chanting, was she suggesting things about either of you or suggestions for any actions you should take? Like being mean to other kids or hurting yourself in some way?"

Tori shrugged again. "I don't know. It was all totally creepy, and it made me feel creepy. I don't remember all of it. It's kind of . . . I don't know . . . blurry. Like a dream."

A new worry nudged Kerri. "Did you eat or drink anything before this chanting ritual began?"

Tori bit her lips, seemed to search for the right answer.

"Just tell me what you remember," Kerri urged.

"We had dinner." She thought some more. "Then cookies and milk later."

"Did Alice's aunt make you cookies and milk?"

Tori shrugged. "Alice brought them into her room on a tray. Three cups of milk and a small plate of cookies."

Another knot tied in Kerri's stomach. "Was it after you ate the cookies and milk that she started the ritual?"

Tori nodded. "A little while later, yeah."

Anger unfurled inside Kerri. "I need you to listen carefully to me, Tori."

She blinked, searched Kerri's eyes.

"I want you to do your best to avoid Alice, okay?"

Uncertainty stole over her daughter's face. "But she'll be mad at me."

"Possibly," Kerri said, "but I think it's really important that you stay as far away from Alice as possible. If she says anything to you, just tell her you're not feeling well, and you don't want her to catch whatever you have."

It was an old reliable excuse.

"She won't believe me." Tori picked at her cuticles.

"You could stay with Diana and just skip the rest of the week. I'm sure—"

"No way!" Tori shot to her feet. "Then everyone will think the rumors are true. That I hurt Brendal and I'm staying home because I'm guilty."

"Tori." Kerri clasped her hands in her lap to prevent reaching for her. She knew her daughter well enough to know that look. She did not want her mother touching her or treating her like a baby at the moment. "You are not guilty of anything. I know you and I trust you. I need you to trust me."

"What if I did?" She wilted back down onto the couch. "What if I accidentally pushed her?"

Terror chilled Kerri's veins. "Do you think you pushed her?"

Tori shook her head. "No. But other people do."

"Sometimes other people can be hurtful when they're unsure of something. They get scared and try to find someone to blame."

Tori rubbed her hands over her face, then clasped them together in her lap. "I'm just so . . . I feel like I can't remember, and I'm scared."

Kerri pulled her close, hugged her, and struggled not to let the tears slip past her lashes. "Sometimes I get scared too, sweetie. We'll figure this out. I promise."

Tori pulled back and looked her mom in the eyes. "I hope so."

"That day," Kerri ventured, "did Alice bring any cookies or a snack of some sort from home?"

Tori frowned, concentrating. "I can't remember. Maybe. She used to do that a lot. Alice said her aunt was trying extra hard to be like a real mom."

"You think about it," Kerri said. "If you remember something, let me know, okay? It could be important."

Tori nodded. "I will."

The doorbell rang. Kerri smiled. "Come on. That's the food. Later we can have ice cream."

"With M&M'S?"

"Definitely."

Kerri wished ice cream and M&M'S would make everything better. She wasn't sure anything could, but she refused to give up trying.

20

9:00 p.m.

Chez Fonfon
Eleventh Avenue South
Birmingham

Mason sat at the bar, perfectly positioned to watch the entrance.

Leland Walsh had asked for a private meeting. Mason had no problem with giving the man a few minutes of his time. After all, Walsh had just lost his son. The issue would likely be what the man expected from the meeting.

If he'd asked for this meeting for the same reason *she* had, there wasn't much to tell. At this time, he had nothing new regarding the investigation. At least nothing the man would want to hear.

Walsh entered and glanced around. Mason didn't bother raising a hand to call his attention to the bar. The hostess would bring him over. Mason had tipped her well for the trouble.

Walsh glanced at Mason, then headed his way. Mason had done his homework on Leland Walsh. His firm took no prisoners when it came to courtroom battles. He was accustomed to winning and to having those around him do as he asked without question. Though Mason had never met him before, he knew his sort. The sort who thought he ruled his slice of the world. Anyone who blocked his path was to be removed by whatever means necessary.

"Agent Cross." Walsh approached Mason's position and extended his hand.

"Mr. Walsh." Mason shook his hand, then gestured to the stool next to him. "Please join me. I'll order you a drink."

Walsh slid onto the stool. "Bourbon. Neat."

Mason nodded to the bartender and placed the order. When the bourbon had arrived, he kicked off the conversation by reaffirming what he'd already said after the task force briefing. "I am genuinely sorry for your loss."

Walsh nodded. "So am I. So am I." He downed his drink. "But there's one thing I recognized in Asher." He turned to Mason. "Whatever he decided to do in life, he was not going to be stopped. Unfortunately, this attitude may have been the death of him."

Mason hummed a note of understanding. "I have a daughter exactly like that. There's no changing her mind once it's made up." He gestured to the empty glass. "Would you care for another?"

Walsh placed his hand over his glass. "I'm not going to waste your time, Agent Cross. I want this investigation into my son's murder over as quickly as possible."

Mason stared into his own glass, considered throwing back the contents but decided to hold off for a bit. Where had he heard this before? Just further indication of how jumpy everyone had grown. "I can assure you I'm doing all within my power for a speedy closure."

"I saw the medical examiner's report. I do not want that information to become public knowledge. My wife is already devastated. I don't want her hurt further by learning about the cocaine."

Strange. Mason had expected the man to insist his son would never be involved with drugs. Perhaps he had overestimated the man's grief. Or perhaps his need to protect the family's reputation simply outweighed the grief. "It's possible the report could come into evidence if there's a trial. I have no control over what the district attorney does with evidence. However, I don't expect a trial."

"Both the mayor and the chief of police have assured me," Walsh pointed out, "that you will take care of the situation. I appreciate your personal assurance as well."

Why was Mason not surprised? Of course the powers that be had provided assurances. "I'll do what I can," Mason allowed.

"Thanks for the drink."

Walsh slid off the stool and walked out.

Mason prided himself on keeping his finger on the pulse of the goings-on in his home turf. He was beginning to suspect he had missed something here.

Something bigger than he'd expected.

21

Session Three

Three Years Ago

After the usual steps to prepare for the regression therapy, Dr. Holden begins.

"Sadie, this is session three. In our last session we went back to October 31. There was a party with a special guest attending. Can we discuss this night further?"

Silence.

"Unless we move forward, we'll never get to the memories you've lost."

"Something was wrong that night."

Her voice sounds too soft and too small. Sadie is hard and cold and far fiercer . . . like her father. But this is her voice. No mistake.

"Explain how you mean. Wrong in what way?"

"I felt strange. Like I was on a bad trip. Someone must have put something in my drink. At one point I had to leave my glass on the nearest table and brace myself so I didn't fall. The room whirled around and grew dim."

"Did you collapse?"

Silence.

"You need to state your answer aloud, Sadie. Shaking or nodding your head isn't a sufficient response."

"No. Not at first. I went to the bathroom. I washed my face in the sink and studied my reflection. Crazy images kept transposing themselves over my face. It must have been all the masks some of the others were wearing at the party. The whole night messed with my head. Maybe the tequila was getting to me. But I think it was more."

"What happened next, Sadie? Did you return to the party?"

"I opened the door to step out of the bathroom, and it was dark. Like someone turned off the lights in that part of the house. The corridor was long, but I knew which way to go to get back to the big gathering room where the party was happening, yet I couldn't move. I leaned against the wall. Felt as if I was falling."

"Were you alone at that time?"

"At first . . . but then someone appeared. I saw the mask, the flowing white dress or robe as if whoever wore the costume was glowing. It was totally otherworldly. I told myself I was hallucinating. But the child—and it must have been a child because the person was so small—took my hand."

Silence.

"Isabella?" Sadie says. Pause. "I called her name, thinking maybe it really was her, but when I saw Isabella last, she wasn't wearing a mask or dress-like robe. She was in her pj's in her bed. I went in to say good night. Unless a guest brought a child, there weren't any other children, so . . . I don't know. I couldn't be sure. I was probably hallucinating."

When the silence goes on for thirty seconds, Dr. Holden asks, "What happened after the child or small person took your hand?"

"I was guided to another room. It was dark, but I could tell that I hadn't been in this room before. There were lots of stairs. I believe we were going downward. I think it was a cellar or basement of some sort. But then we were outside. I smelled the night air, felt the slight breeze against my face. When I looked up, I saw the moon. It felt close enough to have reached out and touched it."

"Where did you go then?"

"A house or shed. Some place on the compound a good distance from the house. There was an old woman inside. She was doing some kind of ritual. Chanting and waving her arms. There were bizarre drawings on the wall. Blood. Bones. When the old woman turned around, she was wearing a mask too. I started to back away, but the little girl or whoever was wearing the mask looked up at me and said I shouldn't be afraid."

"Do you remember leaving this house or shed?"

"No. I remember the old woman turning toward me; her mask was like the child's. White with horns sticking out on both sides. There were holes for the eyes but nothing else. She continued chanting and walking around and around me and the child. The room started to spin, and I thought I might puke. Then she stopped right in front of me. She placed her hands on my waist. She whispered words I couldn't understand, and that was the last thing I remembered. I passed out, I guess."

"When did you wake up again?"

"The next morning. I was in our bed—in Eddie's room. He was already up. I showered and dressed. There were bruises on my upper arms and my torso. Obviously, there was a lot more that happened; I just can't remember. When I found Eddie at breakfast, he said he was glad I was feeling better. Apparently, I told him I needed to go lie down at some point during the party. But I don't remember telling him anything. I just remember the child and the old woman in the masks."

"Did you ask Isabella about what happened?"

"I was careful not to say too much, but I did talk to her about the party. She wanted to know all about it. She didn't seem to have any idea about the night's events. She kept saying she wished she could have been there."

"So, she was not the child in the mask."

"I guess not. Maybe the whole thing was a hallucination."

"So you never met this special guest who was supposed to be at the party."

"No."

"If these events were only hallucinations, what about the bruises?"

"I don't know. Maybe those happened during sex that night. Later, Eddie mentioned that I went a little primal on him."

"Were there other episodes of this sort after that night?"

"No. Not until . . . I became invisible."

22

Thursday, April 15

7:45 a.m.

Brighton Academy
Seventh Avenue
Birmingham

"Mom, I don't want you to walk me in."

Judging by Tori's mortified expression, one would think Kerri had suggested Tori strip off her clothes and run naked through the school.

"No hugging either."

"Fine." Kerri held up her hands. "I don't want to embarrass you." The teenage years, especially in the beginning, swung from one extreme to the other. The girl who wanted ice cream and cuddling last night wanted nothing to do with her mother this morning. One of her friends might see the potentially humiliating event.

But her daughter had come downstairs this morning, head held high, determined to go to school.

"See you later," Tori mumbled.

"Love you," Kerri said before her daughter could escape the Wagoneer.

"Love you," Tori muttered before closing the door and rushing to join the other kids pouring into the front entrance of the school.

Kerri watched until Tori was inside. Her gut clenched. Tori seemed better this morning. More optimistic, particularly about her upcoming visit to New York. Kerri exhaled a breath chock full of anxiety. Was she doing enough to protect Tori? To solve this terrible case?

She stared at her cell phone lying on the seat next to her. Still no callback from Sue. She'd hoped to hear something by now, anyway. The idea that the anonymous girl didn't want to talk was becoming more and more likely. Kerri felt sick. She needed the whole story on this Alice Cortez. The one that Sykes and Peterson would never know about otherwise.

"Damn it." Kerri shifted into drive and prepared to merge into traffic. Since turning twelve, Tori had insisted her mom let her out at the sidewalk in front of the school. No public displays of affection and certainly no pulling into the car line to let her out nearer the building. But with all that had happened, Kerri had hoped to drop her off closer to the entrance. Mostly to avoid the huge display of pink flowers and teddy bears piled around the fountain in front of the school in memory of Brendal. Not that Kerri resented the display. Of course she didn't. It was just so hard for Tori right now, and she wanted to do all in her power to protect her.

Kerri took a deep breath and prepared to ease into traffic. Before she could, a black Charger nudged up to the curb behind her. She looked from her rearview mirror to her side mirror, confusion lining her brow. The driver's door of the Charger opened, and Falco emerged.

What was he doing here? They weren't supposed to meet up until later.

Kerri kept her foot on the brake, expecting him to come to her window and give her whatever news wouldn't wait. Possibly there had been a break in their case. When he'd called last night, he'd learned nothing from the final two names provided by Caldwell. He had managed to get a few minutes with Lucky Vandiver's father, who claimed to be as lost as the rest of Kurtz's friends about why he would have been murdered. He had no easily verifiable alibi for his whereabouts on Sunday night. He'd dozed off in front of the television and didn't wake up until Lucky arrived home at nearly eleven. Then they'd both gone to bed. Had the father been covering for the son or vice versa? Falco had noticed the security cameras outside the stately home. Assuming they could scrape up sufficient evidence, a warrant for the security video would tell them if the son or the father had left the house that night during the time frame in question.

But that was a huge if.

The evidence techs had found more than a dozen different sets of prints in the stockroom of Leo's Tobacconist, but so far all had been matched to employees and Leo himself, as well as a few that belonged to Asher Walsh. Basically, other than the cocaine that showed up in Walsh's lab work, they had nothing new unless that had changed since their conversation last night.

Rather than come to Kerri's window, Falco slipped between their vehicles and came to her passenger-side door. Confused all the more, she shifted into park and hit the "Unlock" button. Falco opened the door and slid into the seat Tori had vacated.

"I thought we were meeting at the office." Kerri didn't like the closed expression on her partner's face. This typically meant there was something he had to tell her—something she wouldn't want to know.

"Did you hear from your librarian friend last night?"

Kerri frowned. "No. I would've told you if I had. In fact, I called and left her a voice mail this morning, but she hasn't called me back."

A new kind of worry crept into Kerri's thoughts. Before she could voice her worst fears, Falco spoke.

"She won't be calling you back, Devlin." He glanced forward before meeting her gaze once more. "There was what appeared to be an attempted carjacking on her way to work this morning. She stopped at a red light and . . . well, you know how it works."

Kerri sank deeper into her seat. "She's dead." It was the only explanation for the expression her partner wore.

Falco held her gaze, gave a slight nod.

"Because she talked to me about what happened at Walker Academy." Kerri started to shake deep inside.

"It gets worse," he warned.

Kerri swallowed back the bile rising in her throat. "Worse how?"

"A female student from Walker Academy, the same age as Tori, is missing. Her mother went into her room this morning to get her up for school, and she was gone."

The realization of what this news meant settled in Kerri's gut like a bucket of hardened concrete. "The only person I told about Sue and the anonymous girl was the LT. He must have talked to someone else. Maybe the chief. For sure Sykes and Peterson."

"Probably," Falco agreed.

"Somebody one of those people spoke to had Sue taken out." Kerri recognized she sounded like a conspiracy theorist, but she'd learned a difficult lesson last year. One Sadie Cross had warned she had been too naive to see at the time.

And she had been. Kerri had always felt she recognized the good guys from the bad ones. She had accepted that certain people, like her superiors and fellow detectives, were good guys, because that was the expected thinking. She'd been taught to trust the uniform, the titles of those in charge of making and enforcing laws. But she had been wrong.

People, no matter the position they held, had secrets. Sometimes those secrets were terrible things they had done or were doing.

But the idea that the Cortez girl and her family were in a position to make some event like this happen felt ludicrous.

She says she's a princess.

Tori's and Sue's words reverberated inside Kerri.

"What's the missing student's name?" Kerri needed a starting place. She could talk to the parents. The girl's friends. She suddenly needed to go. To do something. Anything but sit here and suffer this dread swelling into her chest.

"Violet Redmond. Only child. Lives in Mountain Brook."

Kerri cleared her mind and focused on the logical steps that needed to be taken. "Any change in our case?"

"Nothing new that I've heard this morning. I planned to pay Naomi Taylor another visit to explore the idea of Walsh being a drug user. We both know it's a dead end, but we can't ignore it."

Kerri reminded herself to breathe. "It's a setup to discredit him, no question," she agreed.

"They—whoever they are—want this tied up."

Kerri forced her brain to focus. Too many possibilities were bombarding her at once. "I'm certain Walsh's family will be up in arms. The father must be livid."

From what she'd found on her internet searches, the man was a perfectionist. He wouldn't have anyone believing such a thing about his only son. It made no sense. The mother's words echoed in her brain. *Find who did this. Don't be distracted or fooled by theatrics.*

"No question," Falco said.

"I want to visit Naomi with you." Kerri turned to her partner. "I can talk to the Redmond family later this afternoon." Whoever was investigating the girl's disappearance would be all over the family this morning. Kerri had stepped on too many toes already.

Falco nodded. "I'll meet you there."

When he would have climbed out, Kerri put a hand on his arm. He turned back to her. "Thanks, Falco. I appreciate you having my back in this."

"It's what partners do."

Taylor Residence
Eighteenth Avenue South
Birmingham, 9:00 a.m.

"It all happened very fast," the older woman said.

"Ms. Taylor," Kerri asked, "are you certain you're not hurt?"

"I'm fine, really. This nice young man stayed with me until I calmed down." Naomi smiled in the direction of the thirtysomething who sat on her sofa.

Tim Barton claimed he had been walking by and had seen the intruder slipping around to the back of the Taylor home. He had rushed to the front door and started knocking to warn the lady of the house about the potential trouble. After hearing a scream, he had burst through the door, splintering the wood around the dead bolt, forcing the intruder to retreat out the back door—the same way he'd broken into the house.

Kerri and Falco had arrived only minutes after the perpetrator disappeared. Their first clue that something was amiss was the damaged front door standing open. They had hurried inside to find Taylor being attended to by an alleged neighbor and Good Samaritan.

"You didn't get a good look at the intruder?" Falco asked the lady.

She shook her head. "He was wearing one of those dark ski masks." She tutted. "How very insipid."

Falco looked to Barton. "Was he wearing a ski mask when you saw him?"

"No. He must have slipped it on when he went around the back of the house. Like I said, he was probably six feet, medium build, brown hair. He had his back to me, so I didn't see his face."

"You didn't see the make of the vehicle when he fled?" Kerri asked. These questions had been asked already, but it was important to see if his story stayed the same.

"I didn't. I ran through the house after him, and by the time I was back around at the front, he was gone. To be honest, I'm not even sure which way he went from there. The guy had to be a serious runner to move that fast."

Like the intruder, Barton had brown hair, was about six feet and with a medium build. His face was nondescript. The sort a witness likely wouldn't remember. No visible scars, tats, or other identifiable markings.

"Remind me where it is you live?" Falco prodded.

"At the end of this street. I'm renting a garage apartment from a friend." He stood. "I should go, or I'll be late for work."

"We may have other questions," Kerri said. "You have a cell phone number?" The rectangular bulge in his back pocket provided the answer but not the number.

"Yeah, sure." He recited the number.

Kerri entered it into her cell. "You said you work at the Trader Joe's over on Summit?" That would be maybe twenty minutes away. She had shopped there a few times.

"Yeah." He looked away. "Feel free to call me if you think of anything else." He nodded to Taylor. "Gotta go."

He was lying or maybe just leaving out some relevant fact. His eyes were far too evasive, his expression too closed. Kerri called after him, "Thank you, Mr. Barton."

When he'd gone, she sat down on the sofa. "Ms. Taylor, we haven't reported your connection to your nephew." Considering the Walsh aspect of the case had been taken from them, she certainly hadn't felt compelled to do so. "Have you spoken to anyone about him? Or did he ever have friends or colleagues visit him here?"

"No one." She paused, frowned. "Except Sadie. Sadie Cross. She came over several times." Taylor smiled. "I think they were a bit more than friends." The frown deepened. "She said she would have someone watching after me. Do you suppose Mr. Barton is a friend of hers?"

Kerri's uneasiness lessened a fraction. Right there was likely the fact Mr. Barton had omitted. "That would explain him happening along just when you needed him."

Falco pulled out his cell. "Why don't I call someone to have a look at your doors? I'm not sure those locks are going to be reliable with the way the wood is cracked."

"I have a retired friend who lives in the neighborhood. I'll call him. He's always happy to help."

"All right then, I'll call Cross and confirm her association with your Good Samaritan," Falco said.

While he stepped outside, Kerri asked, "Ma'am, is there anything else we can do for you while we're here? Would you like to file an official report?"

Taylor shook her head. "No. No. That's not necessary. You and Detective Falco being here is quite sufficient." Her face fell. "Really, if you can find the person who killed my Asher, that's all I need."

"We're optimistic that we'll have more on that soon." Kerri gave her a smile and hoped she wouldn't have to explain how his murder was no longer theirs to investigate. Or the fact that Kerri desperately needed to be elsewhere because she was terrified for her daughter. "Ma'am, I realize this question may not be a pleasant one, but I have to ask. Is there any possibility Asher may have used illegal drugs, even occasionally? You've insisted that wasn't possible, but can you really be completely certain?"

Taylor's expression turned to horror. "Oh my word! I keep telling you that Asher was the most antidrug young man you would ever meet."

Before she could demand to know why she'd asked again, Kerri went on. "Was there something that happened in his past that made him feel particularly antidrug? Beyond the general reasons, I mean."

"Not to my knowledge. I don't recall him talking about drugs the few times I saw him during his high school and college days. I suppose there could have been something. But since he moved here, he spoke adamantly about it. In fact, his keen focus on the issue concerned me a bit."

"How so?"

"A person in his position as a DDA needs a certain amount of objectivity and the ability to spread his attention. The sort of single-minded focus could create issues in his career and certainly in his personal life."

"Thank you for clearing that up, ma'am." Kerri could see how an obsession of any kind could affect his work; possibly lessen his ability to be objective.

"None of this makes sense." Ms. Taylor shook her head. "Obviously, I understand that in his career, he made enemies. You can't be in the legal field without making a few. For God's sake, I'm still stunned about Lana's secretive visits. I had no idea, and I don't think Asher did either. I can't imagine what she was doing."

Kerri didn't have the faintest idea what Taylor meant. "Asher's mother visited him recently?"

"No, that's what I mean. She *didn't* visit him. She insisted that if he wanted to see her, he would come to Boston. I simply can't imagine why she made a trip to Birmingham every month without visiting her son. I've racked my brain, and I can't come up with a reasonable explanation." Exasperation claimed her expression, and she tapped her forehead. "Oh dear. It wasn't you who told me about Lana's visits. It was Sadie. Is she working with you and Detective Falco? She mentioned that you're friends of hers."

"We are friends, yes," Kerri confirmed. "You're saying your sister was making regular visits to Birmingham but not to see her son?"

"Apparently. I might even have chalked it up to her secretly checking on Asher, except according to Sadie's research she's been making those quick visits for longer than Asher lived here. It's very odd."

"You can't think of any reason she would do this?"

"None at all. She has no friends here. She owns no property in the state of Alabama, much less in Birmingham. Has no investments I can find." Taylor shrugged. "I suppose it's possible she's checking up on me, though I can't fathom why."

"Does she have reason to believe you're in poor health?" Taylor certainly seemed in great shape to Kerri.

"I would hope not," Taylor insisted. "Not that my health would matter. My sister has no interest in my health—good, bad, or otherwise."

This wasn't exactly a pleasant topic, but they might as well explore it. "What about *your* estate?"

Taylor frowned. "With Asher gone, there's no one else to inherit my estate."

"Except your sister," Kerri said.

Now the older woman laughed out loud. "My sister's husband is a very wealthy man. The property I own is hardly desirable. Particularly those old warehouses near the port." She waved a hand dismissively. "I'm certain nothing I own would be of any relevance to either of them—not that I'd want them to have it. There are numerous charities who would benefit from what I have to give."

"Understandable. Still, we should look at every possibility," Kerri explained. "Are the warehouses you mentioned empty?"

"Oh no. They've never been empty. Like my father, I lease them to small businesses who need storage. The warehouses closer to the port are far more expensive. But I have to tell you, the lease value is probably less than my sister spends on handbags each year. I'm certain this is a dead end, Detective."

Kerri didn't doubt Ms. Taylor's conclusion on the matter, but there had to be a reason Lana Walsh started visiting Birmingham. The possibility that she was checking up on Taylor's assets couldn't be dismissed out of hand.

Could a person ever be rich enough?

Kerri asked, "Do you own any other property besides the warehouses and this home?"

"I do not. I have some savings, but nothing that would impress my sister."

"We'll check out the warehouses," Kerri decided. "See if any of the business owners have spoken to your sister. Would you mind giving me a list of the businesses who hold the leases?"

It was another of those long shots that cops looked into that often turned out to be nothing, but it was sometimes the one they dismissed that would have made the difference. A good cop didn't ignore the possibilities no matter how seemingly remote. If Lana Walsh had no other connection to Birmingham, the property owned by her sister was as good a place as any to start.

"Of course." Taylor rose and walked to the side table where the landline sat. She opened the one drawer and gathered a pad and pen.

Now that she'd thought about it, Kerri had heard something about coming expansions at Birmingport. It was remotely possible that Taylor was too easily dismissing the future value. "You own the warehouses and other land in the port area?"

"More than a hundred acres. The warehouses aren't directly on the water, but they're close by." She handed the list to Kerri. "My father inherited the property from his father, who assumed ownership from his own father, but it will leave the family with me. With Asher gone, I have no reason to bother with it any longer."

"Ms. Taylor, may we have your permission to look around the property?" They would need permission from the tenants to look inside the warehouses, but Taylor could give them permission for the property outside any locked areas.

"Why not? I'm certain it's a waste of your time, but I'll make a few calls and ensure that no one gives you any trouble."

"Thank you—that would help tremendously. Would you also let me know if you hear from Asher's parents?"

She made a harrumphing sound. "Don't hold your breath."

Kerri gave her a nod. "I'll keep that in mind."

Falco appeared at the door. "Cross confirmed that she'd hired Barton to keep an eye on you and your home. So no worries there."

"Thank you for letting me know," Taylor said, looking relieved.

Before leaving, Kerri and Falco waited until Taylor had called her neighbor about the door repairs. The man was coming right over. On the sidewalk outside the Taylor home they spotted him headed that way with his toolbox in hand.

When they loaded into her Wagoneer, Kerri told Falco about the warehouses. She glanced at the view beyond the Taylor home as she pulled away from the curb. In a city expanding the way Birmingham was, you never knew what piece of property would suddenly be worth a fortune.

Birmingport Road
Birmingham, 11:30 a.m.

Kerri had been right to consider the Taylor assets. Falco had spent the time required to reach Birmingport Road searching the net and calling his sources in the property office for information about the warehouses as well as the home Taylor owned. A developer was already attempting to buy up the property in the area where she lived to tear it all down, making way for a new high-end development. The homes like Taylor's with the city view would be the most highly sought after.

The warehouses were located south of the Birmingham port on the lower loop of the Locust Fork. The property extended across the river and deep into the woods on the other side. The warehouses stood maybe a half mile from the actual waterfront, with a strip of dense forest standing between the buildings and the shoreline. In Kerri's limited knowledge it didn't appear that extraordinary effort would be required to carve a path between the warehouses and the river. Perhaps Taylor had underestimated the value of the property. But then Kerri was no engineer.

There were three warehouses. One was a local third-party seller for Amazon whose company had grown too big for the owner's garage, but he hadn't been able to afford a building in town, so he'd leased the smaller of the warehouses. He lived closer to the warehouses than downtown anyway. The second company was another local one that had developed a so-called natural brand of cosmetics, Iris. Kerri had heard of the brand, but it was available online only, so she'd never seen the actual products. A separate maintenance shed was also leased by the cosmetics company.

The third was a tire resale company. People who didn't like the nearly new or new tires on their vehicles sold to this company, who then sold the tires to people who were looking for that brand or size for a cheaper price. It was quite the enterprise, based on what Falco had found in his search.

Only one of the three actually used the port. The cosmetics company shipped their products to others who actually did the selling and shipping to individuals. Like a sort of Avon or Mary Kay. The manufacturer shipped to the sellers, who distributed to the individual customers.

None appeared to have any sort of connection to Leo Kurtz and his shop. And certainly not to Asher Walsh other than via his aunt.

The warehouses were older, circa the 1920s. But all had been updated with electrical and climate control. This was according to the only one of the businesses who had agreed to allow them inside. The third-party Amazon seller, one SouthernWorks, LLC. The owner insisted he had nothing to hide and even permitted them to watch the packing of boxes.

"How was Tori this morning?" Falco asked as they walked through the building, careful to stay out of the way of the employees readying products to ship.

"Hanging in there. That day on the stairs is still fuzzy for her." Kerri hesitated a moment. "Tori said Alice gave them cookies and milk whenever she and Sarah stayed the night. Her memories of events on those occasions are foggy and fractured. It makes me wonder if the same thing happened with Tori and Sarah at school that day. Tori mentioned that Alice was always bringing cookies and other snacks her aunt had prepared to share with her friends. I'm worried she and Sarah were drugged. Maybe even the Myers girl."

"We could take Tori to the lab. Have some tests run," Falco suggested. "It might not be too late to find something, especially in her hair. If she'd prefer, I could take a hair sample to the lab under an alias."

Kerri nodded. "Good idea. I'm not completely okay with putting the possibility out there that she's ingested some sort of drug. Sykes and Peterson could twist it into something it's not." And her partner was right; many drugs showed up in hair samples long after the last use.

"We should talk to Tori."

"Okay." Kerri was fairly certain her daughter had already considered the possibility but didn't want to say the words out loud. A new kind of worry knotted in her gut.

Focus, Kerri. Right now, she needed her mind in this investigation.

Back outside they walked around the other warehouses. They couldn't go inside, but they had the authorization to walk the property. The tire reseller, Wheels, Inc., had two vehicles, one SUV and a truck, parked in the small accompanying lot. Falco took a photo of each license plate.

Iris, the cosmetics company, had only one vehicle. A quick snap of the license plate and they headed back to the Wagoneer. Kerri hoped they hadn't wasted their time, but not checking it out could have been a mistake.

Considering the rising potential of the warehouses at Birmingport and the escalating value of Taylor's home, Lana Walsh could certainly be interested in her sister's estate. Did her interest have anything to do with Asher Walsh's murder? Not likely since Lana's unexplained visits started well before her son's death.

Didn't sit right with Kerri. She wasn't ready to consider the mother a suspect.

As they drove away from the warehouses, along the only entrance and exit to the property, Kerri shared her conclusions with Falco.

"I'm with you. I can't see it. Hold on." He fished his cell from his pocket and took a call.

In the distance, a dark vehicle appeared. As they drew closer, it was obvious the vehicle was headed toward the warehouses, but it was too far away to determine whether it was a truck or an SUV. The profile was too high for a sedan or hybrid.

As the expanse of highway between her Wagoneer and the other vehicle diminished, Kerri's pulse began to race.

Black.

SUV.

The emblem on the grill came into focus.

Escalade.

The driver—male, Hispanic—and Kerri stared at each other as their vehicles passed.

José Cortez.

Kerri hit the brakes and skidded to a stop, ending up sideways across the road.

"Whoa, Devlin." Falco put his phone away and looked around. "What did I miss?"

Kerri pointed the Wagoneer in the necessary direction and headed after the other vehicle. "Black Escalade. José Cortez is the driver."

They followed the Escalade to the Iris warehouse. Cortez was exiting the SUV when they parked next to him, cutting him off from the warehouse entrance.

Falco was out before the vehicle stopped rocking. "José Cortez, I'm Detective Falco, and this is my partner, Detective Devlin. We have a few questions for you."

Kerri had skirted the hood by then. She stood on one side of Cortez, and Falco stood on the other. He looked ready to bolt.

"This will only take a moment of your time, Mr. Cortez," Kerri reassured him with the best smile she could muster.

"What's going on here?"

A female had exited the warehouse and was headed their way. She looked to be in her forties. Brunette hair. Medium build. Dressed in jeans and a sweater, along with fashionable slides.

Kerri introduced herself and Falco to the woman, who didn't bother returning the pleasantry. "We have questions for Mr. Cortez."

The woman braced her hands on her hips. "Mr. Cortez is my employee, and he's already late. I suggest the two of you schedule a time with him for after work. Right now, he needs to get inside before he ends up in the unemployment line."

They made no move to stop the man when he followed his boss's order. Until they could prove Cortez was somehow involved in criminal activity, they didn't want to cost him his job.

"May I have your name, ma'am?" Kerri asked. "I'll need an explanation to give my boss for why we didn't interview Mr. Cortez." This was a lie, but the other woman had no way of knowing this.

"Elizabeth Grant. COO of Iris. Google me. That'll give you the rest of what you need." She turned her back and walked into the warehouse.

"Friendly," Falco muttered.

Kerri scoffed. "About as friendly as a rattlesnake."

"Considering the Cortez connection," Falco said as they climbed back into the Wagoneer, "I say we do some digging into this Iris Cosmetics."

"Start with the boss," Kerri suggested. "Shit rolls downhill, but it typically starts at the top."

Was it coincidence that José Cortez worked in one of the Taylor warehouses?

Had to be.

Kerri tried to shake the idea, but it wasn't budging. Not with the other facts she knew about Cortez.

One—he and his wife had appeared out of nowhere in August of last year.

Two—the high-end vehicle was purchased at the same time.

Three—Alice and the death of her parents seemed to be the catalyst for both.

Could the murders of Walsh and Kurtz be somehow tied to the Cortez family?

Was that even feasible, or was Kerri sifting through all the scattered facts and theories to reach the conclusion that suited her most? Needing to find answers so desperately, she was putting two and two together and coming up with ten?

Stop & Shop
Birmingham, 1:50 p.m.

Kerri wasn't sure she could eat, but Falco had insisted. She stared at the less-than-appetizing offerings beyond the greasy glass of the display case. Overcooked chicken. Potato wedges. The smell of stale cooking oil had her stomach churning.

Falco joined her. "This might be safer." He passed her a can of beanie weenies.

"You're right." She noted the drinks in his hand. "Crackers?"

He lifted his head in acknowledgment before disappearing down one of the three aisles to hunt down crackers. Kerri moved to the cash register and placed the can on the counter. Falco appeared and unloaded his selections. The soft drinks, another can of beanie weenies, crackers, and a couple of packs of Twinkies.

"The lunch of champions," Kerri muttered.

"Damn straight," her partner confirmed.

"Is that it?" The man behind the Plexiglas shifted his attention from Kerri to Falco and back, his darkly tinted glasses concealing his eyes.

"That's it." Falco retrieved his wallet to pay.

When Kerri would have insisted on paying her part, a breaking news bulletin flashed on the ancient flat-panel TV hanging above and behind the guy. Mayor Emma Warren and Leland Walsh stood at a podium.

"Hey, turn that up," Kerri said, jerking her head toward the screen.

The guy had Falco's money in his hand and seemed more interested in settling their bill than catering to Kerri's wishes.

"Turn it up," Falco echoed more sharply.

The guy huffed a sigh and grabbed the remote.

"With every passing hour," the mayor was saying, "the likelihood of finding those responsible for the murder of Asher Walsh grows dimmer, more fleeting. The Walsh family is now offering a one-million-dollar reward to anyone who provides information leading to the arrest and subsequent prosecution of those involved."

"Holy shit," Falco murmured.

"My sentiments exactly," Kerri agreed.

Reporters shouted questions at the mayor as the hotline numbers scrolled across the bottom of the screen. Leland Walsh stared somberly at the camera. Behind him, scarcely in the frame, his wife stood next to Agent Mason Cross. The expression she wore might have been pain, but Kerri sensed it was something else. Fury, maybe.

Why was the mother of the victim unhappy, possibly even angry about offering a reward?

"I guess the Walshes don't trust the task force to get the job done," Falco said as he accepted his change from the guy in the dark glasses.

Kerri hummed an uh-huh as she stared at the screen. There was just something wrong with that picture.

Maybe money was more important to Lana Walsh than Kerri had estimated.

23

2:00 p.m.

Brighton Academy
Seventh Avenue
Birmingham

Tori sat on the gym floor and watched the other girls in her class playing basketball. Everyone but Sarah. She hadn't come to school today. Tori had told the coach she had awful cramps so she could sit out.

The only cramps she had were in her chest. Everyone was still talking about her. Brendal's funeral was on Sunday, and the whole school now thought Tori was responsible for what had happened.

Sarah had barely spoken to her the past couple of days. Alice always had plenty to say, but Tori really didn't want to hear any of it. She wanted to go home and stay there forever.

Or maybe just disappear. None of these people would miss her.

Tori closed her eyes and banished the idea. Her mom and dad would miss her. Her whole family would. She was just feeling sorry for herself. She hadn't done anything wrong.

The coach's whistle shrieked, and Tori's attention shifted to the girls on the court. Alice had fallen. Two of her teammates helped her up. She walked as if she'd twisted her ankle. The game resumed as soon as Alice had hobbled over to sit on the floor next to Tori.

Great.

Alice rubbed her ankle and winced.

"You okay?" Tori found herself asking in spite of her intention not to say a word. Her mom had warned her to stay away from Alice.

Funny thing, since Brendal's fall Alice had suddenly turned into like the most popular girl in school. Tori didn't want to hate anyone, but right now she hated Alice. Maybe she even hated Sarah.

"It's nothing," Alice said. She hugged her knees to her chest. "I don't like this class. It's so boring and pointless."

This was one thing they could agree on.

When Tori said nothing, Alice turned to her. "Are you okay?"

Tori shrugged. "Cramps."

"I thought maybe you were upset about Sarah." She stared forward then as if she hadn't dropped a bomb.

"She's probably just not feeling well," Tori said. Sarah almost never missed school. She had to be really sick to be absent. Twice this morning Tori had started a text to her and then deleted the words. Sarah hadn't sent her a text. Hadn't called. Hadn't talked to her at school.

Why should Tori be the one to reach out?

"She had to be interviewed by the police again," Alice said. "She told me yesterday. She was really worried."

Tori made a face. "She didn't tell me."

"I'm not surprised."

Tori stared at Alice's profile. "What does that mean?"

"She told me she was going to tell the police the truth."

Dread swelled in Tori's stomach. "What truth?"

"That you were the one who pushed Brendal."

"What?" Tori hadn't meant to shout the word. Several girls in the game glanced their way, as did the coach.

"I told you," Alice said in a sharp whisper. "Sarah believes it was you."

Tori wasn't listening to this again. "Just stop." She scrambled to her feet. "You're making that up. Sarah is my best friend, not yours."

Alice stared up at her as if Tori had slapped her. Tears burned Tori's eyes, but she refused to let anyone else see them. She stormed to the dressing room. As quickly as she could, she stripped off her gym clothes and tugged on her jeans and sweater, then her shoes. She was going home. She would just call Aunt Diana and ask her to pick her up. Tori couldn't take this anymore.

"Tori."

She shut her gym clothes into her locker and turned around slowly. "Yes, ma'am?"

Coach Lawrence stood just inside the door, her hands on her hips. "Are you okay?"

"I'm sorry," Tori said, unable to hold back the new wave of tears. "I think I just need to go home."

"I understand this is a difficult time for you," Lawrence said. "Why don't you go on to Mrs. Leary's office and talk to her? I'd feel better if you did that first."

"Yes, ma'am." Tori grabbed her backpack and headed to the counselor's office.

Even the few students she passed in the hall stared at her as if she were some sort of freak. She just wanted to run away. To hide. To disappear.

Mrs. Leary waited at her door for Tori. When they were settled in her office, she started the conversation with, "If you'd like me to call your mom, I will."

Tori swiped her eyes. "I guess I can try to get through the rest of the day." She had to be strong. Her mom and Falco would figure this out. Wouldn't they? Worry twisted inside her. What if they couldn't?

"I intended to call you to my office this afternoon."

Tori stilled. "Why?"

"I've heard about the outbursts you've been having."

Tori stared at her as if her head had split open and an alien being had emerged. "What outbursts?"

"The anger episodes," Leary explained. "Like the one in the gym only a few minutes ago."

"That hasn't happened before," Tori said, suddenly terrified of what the counselor might say next.

"We all show our emotions in different ways," Leary assured her. "As long as our reactions don't get out of control, it's not a problem."

"Wait." Tori held up her hands. "I don't have anger episodes. Where in the world did you hear something like this?"

"Tori, let's not worry about that; let's focus on what we need to do to deal with your feelings."

The world felt as if it were spinning out of control. "I'd like to call my mom."

A knock on the door stopped whatever Leary intended to say next. When she would have stood, the door opened.

"I apologize for the interruption," Mr. Foster said. "I need a word with you, Mrs. Leary."

"Excuse me, Tori." Leary moved around her desk and stepped into the corridor with Mr. Foster.

Tori closed her eyes and exhaled.

"Oh my God!"

The words sifted through the door, had Tori turning toward it. The sound of a sob or gasp had her rising from her seat and moving closer to the door. It was sobbing! Mrs. Leary was crying! Pulse racing, Tori held her breath and leaned an ear to the door.

"We won't announce anything until we have further details regarding her condition."

"Sarah's parents must be beside themselves."

Sarah? Had something happened to Sarah? Tori curled her fingers into fists to prevent yanking the door open and demanding to know what was going on.

"For now," Mr. Foster said, "let's be thankful the suicide attempt was unsuccessful. My God, what next?"

Sarah had tried to kill herself.

Hurt twisted inside Tori.

This couldn't be happening.

24

3:00 p.m.

Taylor Residence
Eighteenth Avenue South
Birmingham

"I am so grateful for your friend who came to my rescue," Taylor said. "All these years since Father died, I never minded being alone. Never felt alone. I had my work. But then, after the ministroke and being forced to retire, I was lonely."

Sadie produced a rare smile for the lady, who had become unexpectedly important to her. "If you hadn't told me about the stroke, I would never have known. Asher never mentioned it."

"Because he didn't know. I didn't want him to worry. It wasn't such a bad one. Just a wake-up call the doctors identified as a TIA."

"The intruder didn't get beyond the living room; is that correct?" Sadie asked, steering the conversation back to the immediate issue. Naomi had told Barton this was the case, but now that the lady had calmed and regathered her wits, she might recall differently.

"He came in through the back door. When I walked into the kitchen to see what all the noise was, he pushed me down and plowed his way into the living room. By then your man was beating down the door. The intruder whipped around and exited the same way he'd entered."

Sadie nodded. "He didn't attempt to restrain you or disable your phone?"

"He did cut the phone line outside. Otherwise, he seemed to be in a hurry to get upstairs. I can only imagine that he was after the notes in Asher's room. There isn't anything else of negotiable value."

Something about the scenario didn't quite fit. The intruder couldn't have known how long it would take to find whatever he was looking for. He couldn't have known that Naomi hated cell phones and only had the landline. He damned sure couldn't know about the hidden notes upstairs.

Unless someone had briefed him on what to expect.

"Naomi, has anyone been in your home since Asher's death or shortly before, besides Asher, myself, and the two detectives, Falco and Devlin, who visited you?"

A frown furrowed the older woman's brow as she considered the question. "The day before I learned Asher had been murdered, the Alabama Power inspector came in to check my breaker box. There was some concern about the electrical meter, but all was well. I think it was the morning before . . ." She shook her head. "No, no. I'm wrong. That would have been a Sunday. It was on Monday. Early. Around eight thirty or so, just before I got the awful news about Asher."

"Did this man show you any sort of identification?"

"Of course. I would never have allowed him inside otherwise. What are you getting at, Sadie?"

"I'd like you to write down everything you remember about how this man looked and what he was wearing. While you do that, I'm going to have a look around."

"Very well." Naomi picked up the notepad and pen lying on the table next to her chair and set to the task.

Sadie started with Walsh's room. One by one, she went through each upstairs space, checking all the typical places for bugs. Lampshades, smoke detectors, movable decor objects. Beneath tabletops. On light fixtures.

Nothing.

Downstairs she did the same.

Beneath the table next to Naomi's chair was the first bug. When she retrieved it, Sadie put a finger to her lips to ensure Naomi said nothing.

"Did you finish up with your description?"

"Finishing now," Naomi said with a nod. She focused on writing the description of the visitor as Sadie continued around the downstairs area. She found bug number two in the kitchen. At the kitchen sink, she ran a glass of water and dropped each device into the water. When she returned to the living room, Naomi looked astonished.

"You think the man who came by Monday morning claiming to be from the power company planted those devices?"

"I do. I don't mind keeping twenty-four-hour surveillance on your home, but I'm not sure that's enough to keep you safe. I'd feel a lot better if you'd allow me to set you up someplace to stay until this is over."

"Really, I'm fine," Naomi argued.

"I need all my resources. It would be better for my investigation if I could focus all those resources on finding out what happened to Asher."

"Well, I certainly can't argue with that."

Sadie would bet money that was the first and only time this lawyer had ever said those words.

"I know just the place," Sadie assured her.

A quick call to Doug Angelo, a friend she'd met through Pauley, and Naomi's minivacation to an exclusive spa resort for seniors just south of Birmingham was in the works.

"Did your detective friends mention if they discovered anything at the warehouses?"

Sadie slid her cell into her back pocket. "What warehouses do you mean?" She hadn't spoken to Falco or Devlin today.

"The ones I lease down by the port. Like you, they were attempting to come up with a reasonable scenario for why my sister flies into Birmingham each month. God knows it isn't to see me." She removed the page from the notepad upon which she'd written the description and handed it to Sadie. "I passed along what you discovered about her monthly visits. Like you, they seemed to think it was worth a follow-up."

"I'll give Falco a call and see what—if anything—they found."

A knock on the door drew Sadie's attention there. "I'll get it. It's probably Barton."

She checked the peephole, and it was him. After opening the door, Sadie stepped onto the porch. "Did you get a hit on the guy's license plate?"

Luckily Barton had captured the plate number in a pic on his cell. He had a friend at the DMV who helped him out at times like this.

"Darius Washburn. Forty, lives on—"

"I know who he is." Fury detonated in Sadie. "He's one of the people my father hires when he needs something outside the law taken care of." Sadie gritted her teeth to hold back the litany of things she would love to say about the bastard.

"You want me to pay him a visit?"

Sadie shook her head. "I'll do it. You stay with Naomi until Angelo gets here to pick her up. She's taking a little vacation. As soon as she's off, I want you to search this house top to bottom. Whatever Darius was here for, I want it."

"Will do."

Sadie reassured Naomi once more that she would be in good hands, and then she headed for Eighteenth Street.

DEA Field Office
Eighteenth Street
Birmingham, 4:15 p.m.

Beyond the intimidating fence and the fortresslike security, the old man's office was on the third floor of the austere building.

Security always looked at Sadie suspiciously and called the special agent in charge's assistant before allowing her up. This ensured her father—if he was in the office—would be ready and waiting for her.

She hated that part.

Surprise visits were always the best.

Catching him off guard was a difficult thing to do.

Rather than board the elevator, Sadie took the stairs. He would be braced for all hell to break loose. She hadn't come to his office in a really long while. The last time, she'd been so angry about the way he'd stuck his nose in her personal business she'd swiped all the shit off his desk and then walked out.

She wasn't sure what she could do now—without a weapon—to top the look on his face when his papers and other crap had flown across the room. His assistant had hovered outside the door, prepared to call security on his command.

Security had not been called.

Mason Cross wouldn't have wanted the embarrassing episode to leak beyond his office area.

Instead, he'd asked Sadie to leave and return when she had calmed down.

Sadie hadn't gone back. That was maybe fifteen months ago. Once in a while he showed up at her door. She didn't answer. Why would she? She wanted nothing from him. Not his advice, his pretense at affection, or any damned thing else.

"Good afternoon, Sadie," Francine Wright said as Sadie entered her domain—the small lobby outside her father's office. "He's waiting for you."

"Thanks." She had nothing against the woman. Wright couldn't help that she worked for an asshole.

Sadie opened the door and walked into the boss's office.

"Sadie, to what do I owe this pleasure?" Smiling broadly, he skirted his desk, arms open as if he intended to hug her.

She drew back when he tried. "Your boy Darius broke into the house of a friend of mine. Why?"

Mason Cross frowned as if he hadn't a clue what she meant. "I haven't utilized Washburn's services in quite some time. Is your friend all right?"

Like he gave a shit. "Naomi Taylor. Asher Walsh's aunt. I would be stunned if you didn't know about it. Aren't your people heading the task force working that case?"

"We are, yes," he allowed as he settled against the edge of his desk. "Why would this aunt have anything to do with the case?"

"I don't know. Maybe you should ask Darius."

Her father shook his head. "As I said—"

"I know what you said," Sadie cut him off. "I'm telling you it was him, and I know you sent him, whether you choose to tell the truth or not."

He exhaled a big breath. "How are you? You've been avoiding my calls and visits for what? Nearly a year now?"

"I'm fine." She stared directly into his dark eyes. He would never know how happy it made her that she had her mother's eyes. Her nose, mouth, and just about every damned thing else. She looked nothing like this bastard.

"That's your stock answer," he reminded her. "I'm interested in how you really are."

Like he cared. "Do not mess with Naomi Taylor again."

When she turned to go, he said, "You should stay clear of this investigation, Sadie. This is not going to end well."

"It already ended badly," she tossed back. "Asher Walsh is dead."

Rather than wait for him to make some other lame comment, she walked out. Gave Wright a nod and headed for the elevator. A few minutes with Mason Cross and she was ready to flee.

She slid behind the wheel of her Saab and fished for a cigarette. She tucked it into the corner of her mouth and lit up. He knew better than to suggest she walk away from a case or any damned thing else. She always finished whatever she started.

Except that once with the Osorio op.

But that hadn't been because she'd walked away. She'd been taken away, drugged, tortured. Otherwise she would have finished that too.

She started the engine and drove to the gate, waited for the bar to rise, then pulled out of the parking lot.

Her cell vibrated against the console, and she grabbed it. *Barton.* "Make me happy."

"I found what our intruder was probably looking for. A thumb drive. I plugged it into my laptop, and whatever is on this thing, it's going to take someone above my pay grade to break into it."

"Take it to Snipes. Tell him I need whatever's on it ASAP."

"On my way."

Sadie tossed her phone aside. Why the hell would Walsh keep something so important from her? Had he been protecting her? His aunt? Or someone else?

Whatever the answer, she needed it . . . *now.*

25

7:15 p.m.

Devlin Residence
Twenty-First Avenue South
Birmingham

Lieutenant Brooks had been out of his office all afternoon, and he hadn't taken calls on his cell. Kerri had wanted to talk with him about the carjacking and Sue's murder. She'd gone to the Redmond residence in hopes of speaking with Violet's parents, but the media had been all over the place, along with an official BPD cruiser.

Her frustration had hit overload. She'd had to close all of it out of her head, at least for a few hours.

She decided to focus on dinner and some quality time with Tori. She prepared an old reliable: spaghetti. She and Tori both loved it. When Tori was a toddler, Kerri had made it almost every day.

But her little girl wasn't a toddler anymore, and she was hurting.

Sarah Talley had tried to commit suicide. The girl had taken an overdose of her mother's sleeping pills. Fortunately, her mother had discovered what she'd done in time to avoid the worst. Sarah would remain in the hospital for observation and a psych evaluation for the next seventy-two hours.

For Tori, this was a stunning blow. Fear, hurt, and anger were no doubt tearing her apart.

Additionally troubling was that Tori didn't want to talk about it.

A truly frustrating and infuriating part for Kerri was that Sykes hadn't called to let her know. She'd had to find out from Diana when she picked up Tori. At this point, Kerri was so angry with Sykes and Peterson she wasn't sure she would ever be able to work with either one again. On top of that she was absolutely terrified by the idea that she had shared the story she'd learned from Sue Grimes with the LT, and now Sue was dead, and very possibly the student to whom she had been referring was missing. It was far too big a coincidence to be just any Walker student gone missing. It had to be the anonymous girl.

Kerri had always considered the folks in MID—in all the BPD, really—as family. The past week, today in particular, had greatly damaged that relationship.

As insane as it all was, she couldn't bring herself to believe the LT would have passed along this information to anyone who would have hurt Sue. Not intentionally.

Yet somehow there had been a leak. Sue had been perfectly fine all these months since the incident. Then when she'd shared the story with Kerri, she'd ended up dead less than twenty-four hours later.

This could not be coincidence.

Oh, and she couldn't forget the big reward the Walsh family was offering. Following up on the leads called in would do nothing but slow down the task force. Agent Cross would probably delegate that detail to her and Falco.

"Mom."

Kerri shook off the disturbing thoughts, moved the pan of pasta from the stove, and poured it into a colander in the sink to drain. "Hmm?"

"Do you think it's possible to do something awful and then forget you did it?"

Shutting off the burner beneath the sauce, Kerri turned to her daughter. "It's not impossible. There are cases of trauma-induced amnesia. Why do you ask?" She knew why, but her daughter didn't need to know she'd already considered the scenario.

Whatever answer Kerri had expected, the deluge of tears and sobs was not it. She hurried around the island to hold her daughter. "Please tell me; what's happened?"

It was a foolish question considering the Myers girl's death and now with Sarah's suicide attempt.

Tori stared up at her mother, her face red and damp. "I can't remember doing anything wrong, but Sarah thinks I pushed Brendal."

"She told you this? When?" Kerri had never known Sarah Talley to be purposefully hurtful. But situations like this often brought out the worst in all involved. Like her mother, Renae, looking the other way whenever she saw Kerri.

"Alice told me what she said." Tori dragged in a shuddering breath. "Sarah told Alice she was telling the police I did it." Tori searched Kerri's face. "Mom, I swear if I did this, I have no memory of it. I was standing there. We were all arguing, and then Brendal was falling." She shook her head. "I can't believe I would do such an awful thing."

All the trouble seemed to lead back to Alice. "First of all, you don't know for sure that Sarah said this. Alice may not have been telling the truth."

Tori shook her head as if tired of fighting the battle. "Yesterday they didn't sit with me. They kept whispering to each other and looking at me. I think she might be telling the truth. Even Alice kept saying that I should just tell the truth, as if I should know what really happened. I swear I don't." Her tears began again in earnest.

Kerri held her for a long while. When the sobs quieted, she drew back and made her daughter a promise. "We will figure this out."

"Today Mrs. Leary asked me about my anger issues." Tori shook her head. "I don't have anger issues. I *had* anger issues when Dad first left, but I got over all that. According to Mrs. Leary some of my friends have been talking about my anger. I've hardly spoken to anyone at school all week. Only Sarah and Alice. I don't understand what's happening. It's like my whole life is falling apart." She squeezed her eyes shut. "I failed an algebra test. I've never failed a test."

Kerri hugged her daughter again. "There will be more algebra tests. Everyone has an off day now and then." Fear pulsed in her veins. She wanted desperately to say something profound and inspiring . . . but what could she say that hadn't already been said? The only thing she knew to do was to hold her daughter.

Tori drew back and hugged her arms around herself. "I don't understand what's happening to me. It's like everything is wrong or going wrong."

The more Tori talked, the more concerned Kerri grew. "First, I want you to try and stop worrying. I know I've said this already, but when things like this happen, everyone wants to find someone to blame. It's the same in homicide investigations. No one wants a crime to go unpunished. Your friends at school are trying to make sense of what's happened. They want someone to blame. It's human nature." No matter that they had talked about this before, emotions were preventing her daughter from reasoning.

Tori blinked, searched Kerri's eyes. "I'm glad I've got you, Mom. I don't know what I'd do without you."

Kerri pulled her into another desperate hug. "You'll always have me."

She decided this was as good a time as any. Kerri ushered Tori to a stool and sat down next to her. "Falco and I have a theory."

Tori searched her mother's eyes and waited as if lacking the wherewithal to ask what that theory might be.

"It's possible you and Sarah may have ingested drugs, and that could explain why your memory of what happened to Brendal is so fuzzy."

"Drugs?" Tori made a face. "You mean from like the stuff Alice brings from home."

Kerri nodded. "Yes."

Tori shuddered visibly. "After you asked me about whatever I ate or drank at her house, I started to think about it. And I think maybe it's possible. I've never been unable to remember like this before."

"I know," Kerri agreed. "Falco and I would like to take a hair sample to a lab for analysis."

Tori's eyes went wide. "To the crime lab?"

Kerri shook her head. "Falco has a friend at a private lab. Would that be okay with you?"

"Yes." Tori nodded. "I want to know what happened to me." She blinked back new tears. "I need to know."

Kerri hugged her tightly for a long while; then they grabbed a plastic sandwich bag and took care of the hair sample Falco would need.

Some persuading was required, but Kerri eventually convinced Tori to eat. Devouring the spaghetti conjured dozens of memories, and they even shared a laugh or two. But Kerri was still worried. The shadows in her daughter's eyes scared her. By the time they got around to ice cream, Kerri had decided Tori wasn't going to school tomorrow. She needed a break. She needed to be under the watchful eye of a loving family member to protect her and to help her heal.

"I know we've talked about this before, and you weren't good with it," Kerri ventured as she tucked dishes into the dishwasher.

Tori was busy wiping down the counter. She met her mom's gaze. "What?"

"I think you should take a break tomorrow. Hang out with Diana. Go to the dance studio. Have pizza. Shop. Anything but go to school."

Tori nodded. "Okay."

Kerri kissed her on the forehead. "We'll get through this."

Tori threw her arms around Kerri and held tight for a moment. When she let go, she actually smiled. It was a small one, but it was there just the same. "I'm going to shower. Get my homework done and then zone out with some new series on Prime."

Kerri tapped her nose. "Sounds like a good idea."

When she was gone, Kerri reached for her phone. She needed backup here. It felt as if an elephant was sitting on her chest.

Falco answered on the first ring. "Funny thing, you calling."

"Funny how?" Kerri pushed "Start" on the dishwasher.

"I just parked in your driveway. Cross is right behind me. We got stuff to talk about."

More than he knew. "Great. I have spaghetti." She always made too much.

"Heading for your door now."

Kerri ended the call and went to the door and unlocked it. Falco had a six-pack of beer. Beer would be really good right now. Cross trailed after him. She looked as weary as Kerri felt.

When they'd gathered in the kitchen and Kerri had prepared plates for her visitors, Falco got to the point. "Cross found a hidden thumb drive at the Taylor house. She thinks maybe that's what the guy who broke in was after."

Kerri twisted the cap off a beer, her gaze settling on the other woman. "Anything interesting on it?"

"Don't know yet. I've got my guy working to get into the files. Evidently Walsh—assuming it was his—didn't want just anyone looking at it."

"And he didn't mention this whatever it is to you?" Falco asked.

Cross shook her head. Downed a slug of beer. "Nope. But if it's important enough for the DEA to want it, it must be good."

"The DEA?" Kerri asked.

"A guy who does jobs for my old man was the one who broke into her house. I confronted the almighty Mason Cross right in his office, but he pretended he had no idea what I was talking about. He lied. I could always tell when he was lying."

Kerri understood. She did not like Agent Cross. She doubted many people did. There was no need to offer the BPD's assistance with the hacking. Kerri knew firsthand that Cross's computer guru was the best.

"Did you notice he stood next to Mrs. Walsh during the press conference announcing the reward?" Kerri still couldn't get right with the way the mother had looked.

"Yeah, I heard about it. The real question," Cross offered, "is why was he even there? In front of the camera? He usually likes to stay away from the media."

"Another mystery," Falco noted.

"Speaking of mysteries, what did you two find at the warehouses?" Cross asked. "Walsh never mentioned any warehouses to me."

"We didn't find anything, really," Falco said. "But there is this odd connection to the case at Tori's school."

He looked to Kerri, and she took it from there, explaining the black Escalade and José and Alice Cortez. She finished off her beer and reached for another.

Before Cross could comment, Falco asked Kerri, "What happened today?"

She had wondered how long it would take her partner to see through her pretense that she was okay. She didn't hold back; she gave him everything Tori had told her. Inside, she was shaking by the time she'd recounted the whole story. This was wrong. Completely wrong. Tori was innocent, but someone—maybe Alice Cortez—was trying to make her look and feel guilty.

"Why would this Alice go to all these lengths?" Cross wanted to know. "What's in it for her?"

Kerri told her about the girls at Walker Academy and what had happened there. The story Sue Grimes had shared and then about Sue's death and the student, Violet Redmond, who had gone missing.

"That's one hell of a coincidence," Cross said slowly, as if her mind were somewhere else. "What else do you know about the Cortez girl?"

Kerri explained how staying the night with Alice had freaked Tori out because of the bizarre religious elements and the inability to recall things that had happened at Alice's house and just before the Myers girl's fall. "There is something off with this girl, and I need to find it before anything else happens."

Falco asked, "You still want me to take that hair sample to the guy I know?"

"Definitely." Kerri opened the drawer next to the sink and retrieved the plastic bag. She passed it to Falco. "How long do you think your friend will need for the analysis?"

"Twenty-four to forty-eight hours."

Kerri nodded. "As much as I hope my daughter hasn't been drugged, it would sure explain a hell of a lot."

"I could do some digging," Cross offered. "Falco mentioned you could use some help. Do you have a photo of this Alice Cortez?"

"Several." Kerri reached for her cell, passed it to Cross.

Examining each one closely, Cross went through the photos. Finally, she tapped one. "Send me that one."

Kerri sent her the photo in a text. "Her uncle working at one of Ms. Taylor's warehouses could be nothing more than a coincidence. I get that. But it feels like more when I consider all the things about this girl I've learned the past couple of days."

"Think about it," Falco suggested. "What kind of warehouse employee drives an Escalade and sends his niece to the most expensive private school in the state?"

"There could have been a sizable estate from her parents," Kerri offered, playing devil's advocate to her own theory.

"Like I said, I'll dig around. See what I can come up with." Cross stood. She seemed unusually agitated. Suddenly ready to go. "If I get anything from the thumb drive, I'll let you know."

Kerri walked her to the door. Before opening it, she said, "I really appreciate any help on this thing with my daughter. The whole situation makes me feel helpless."

Cross nodded. "I'm familiar with that territory. I'll get back to you soon."

As Kerri closed the door behind her, she decided not to take Cross's sudden need to leave personally. The woman wasn't one to do the "friend" thing. Kerri returned to the kitchen, where Falco was cleaning up. She joined him, drying the big pot she'd used for preparing the pasta and the smaller one she'd used for sauce.

"I know this is hard." He dried his hands on the towel and tossed it aside.

Kerri exhaled a big breath. "Now I know how Diana felt last year when she couldn't help Amelia."

"This is not going to be like that," Falco assured her.

"You can't be certain," Kerri argued. "Look at what Sarah Talley did just today."

"Tori is stronger than Sarah," Falco argued.

"I hope so." In addition to feeling helpless, Kerri felt guilty too. "I should be helping you with the Kurtz investigation. The case is too much for one person."

"I've got this. You keep your focus on Tori and this Cortez girl. There's something more than adolescent bickering in all this. To tell you the truth, it sounds a whole hell of a lot like plain old murder."

Her partner was right, and that was the scariest part.

26

10:00 p.m.

Mulligan's Pub
Sixth Avenue, Twenty-Seventh Street
Birmingham

Mason watched the man enter the pub and survey the place. Darius Washburn spotted Mason and snaked his way through the jam-packed tables and around booths. The place was crowded for a Thursday night.

No surprise. Pauley, the son of a bitch, had always known an Irish pub would do well on this corner.

Washburn pulled out the chair across from Mason and sat. Even in the dim lighting Mason noted the sprinkle of gray at the man's temples. The first time he'd hired Darius for a job, he'd been twenty-five and fresh out of prison. The man was good, very good. Possibly the best at getting in and out of places and, more importantly, finding things. But there were drawbacks with Darius.

Now that he'd cultivated such a respected reputation for himself, he honored the highest bidder.

Darius ordered his preferred ale and turned his attention to Mason. "You have a job for me?"

The only time they ever met in person was when Mason gave him instructions on a new assignment. Mason didn't leave trails to be followed. No texts, no calls, no emails. Nothing. Face-to-face. That was the way he conducted this sort of business. It was best for all concerned.

Meeting here, with his daughter just upstairs, was a sort of irony only he understood for now. Perhaps Darius would come to see it later.

"Not at this time," Mason said. "I'm going to ask you a few questions, and you're going to answer."

Darius smirked but said nothing because the waitress had appeared with his beer.

When she had flitted away, the younger man said, "You know I don't answer questions about my other assignments, so don't ask. I wouldn't want our relationship to become awkward like that."

Mason felt himself smile. Oh yes, the cocky little shit had decided the price of his stock had risen significantly.

"Darius." Mason shook his head. "Your memory must be failing you. However valuable your services are to others, however much they choose to pay you for those services, I"—Mason patted his chest for emphasis—"*own* you. Forgetting that fact could be very awkward for you."

Fury tightened the younger man's face. "What do you want, Cross?"

Much better. It was infinitely useful to have information on anyone you might one day need. Mason had learned this lesson particularly well from someone far more ruthless than him. Take the fact that Darius Washburn had murdered his own father after his release from prison. Not that anyone could prove it or that Mason blamed him. The old bastard had set up his son to take the fall for his own bad deed. Never underestimate how far your offspring might go for revenge if you screwed them over badly enough.

Those words were inscribed across Mason's brain. His own offspring would likely one day have her revenge. Maybe sooner than he had anticipated.

"Who hired you to hit Naomi Taylor's home?" Mason asked. "Or more specifically, who hired you to stage such a blunder. We both know that job would have been a piece of cake. Apparently, someone wanted to send a message, and I want to know who that someone was. Particularly since the message appears to have been intended to prompt trouble for me."

And it had worked. Sadie had immediately put the blame on him.

"What's it to you?"

"Shall I rephrase the question?"

Darius leaned forward. "Are you trying to get me killed? You've never asked me to do this before. Why now?"

"Was it *her*?" Mason demanded.

Darius blew out a breath. "It was Lana Walsh."

He shouldn't be surprised, and yet somehow he was. Mason moved on to the next question. "What else did she hire you to do?"

"Nothing," Darius snapped. He chugged down his beer, wiped his mouth with the back of his hand. "She wanted something her son had hidden in the house."

"How did she know he'd hidden something?"

Darius shrugged. "Who knows? I wasn't hired to know the why; I was only hired to do the job."

"Yet you ensured the job was not done and that even the police discovered what had been done."

Darius ignored the accusation. "I did what I was paid to do."

Obviously, Lana Walsh had been outbid. How curious.

"I'd like you to stay away from anything or anyone related to Asher Walsh," Mason warned. "This one is mine."

Darius dared to smile. "Sure." He pushed back his chair and stood. "Don't call me again unless you have a paying offer." Before going, he leaned down and said, "I wasn't going to mention just how loyal I've been to you, but since we're here, like this, why not? Old friend,

I turned down a premium offer to take out your daughter. Since she's still breathing, I'd say that makes us even now."

Mason didn't bother rushing after him to ask who had hired him to hurt Sadie.

He already knew the answer with the kind of certainty only a father could understand.

27

Session Four

Three Years Ago

Dr. Holden waits for her to speak. The sound of fabric rustling suggests he crossed or uncrossed his legs. Or perhaps Sadie shifted her position.

Her silence goes on and on. Finally, he asks, "Do you still want to participate, Sadie? I've told you on several occasions that these sessions are optional—totally voluntary."

"I need the truth."

Her voice sounds hollow, as if she would rather be anywhere but here. Except she clearly understands she has no choice but to try.

"Very well, let's get started. It's January now. Eduardo's family seem to have embraced you," Holden prods.

"Things changed at Christmas. I missed my period in November, maybe even in October. I don't remember. Didn't matter at the time. It happened fairly often. I didn't really think anything of it until December passed and there was still no period. I asked one of the household staff members—Valerie—to pick up a couple of pregnancy tests in town. She promised not to tell, and I trusted her. I don't trust easily."

"Meaning you felt entirely comfortable sharing this potential bombshell with her."

"Yes."

"Did she bring what you needed?"

"She did, and both tests showed positive. I was pregnant. Not a good thing, considering my position."

She says these things with such detachment. Perhaps because of the subtle form of hypnosis. There were times when she grew emotional. But not now. Not about the pregnancy.

"I would think this new development would have bonded you even closer to Eduardo."

"It did. He asked me to marry him. He was thrilled. The old man didn't appear to hate the idea, but who could say. He rarely got excited."

"And the girl? The daughter, Isabella?"

"Eddie didn't want her to know in the beginning."

"I see." Holden hesitates a moment. "What happened to the wedding plans? I'm assuming you did not marry him."

"Around that same time there was growing unrest in another cartel. There was talk of a war. The tension was mounting. I could feel it thickening with each passing day."

A long silence follows this explanation. Does she fear what comes next? Who wouldn't?

"Did something happen in January, Sadie?"

"There was a meeting. I can't remember the exact day. But, at some point in January, I overheard a telephone conversation between Eddie and his father and a female. The woman was on the phone; she wasn't there at the compound. The call was on speaker, and the three were arguing. The woman seemed to be winning. It was very strange. Whatever she suggested, the old man agreed. Eddie not so much."

"Did you know this woman?"

"No. I didn't know her . . . *don't* know her."

"She was never addressed by her name?"

"No. Carlos referred to her only once or twice by *manita*."

"Little sister."

"Yes."

"Were you or those in your task force aware Carlos had a sister or someone to whom he referred as sister?"

"No. The existence of a female relative was never proven. To my knowledge, it was decided she was some sort of business partner. An outsider with some other source of power besides blood."

"Eduardo didn't refer to her as aunt or by any term of endearment?"

"No. He was very angry during what I heard of the conversation. I can't remember specifics, but I got the impression he didn't like her."

"Was there anything about the conversation that proved particularly important to your assignment?"

"Yes. The decision was made to initiate a strike against the other cartel. I passed this information along to my contact that same day."

"Why would a strike against a rival cartel be of significance in your operation?"

"It was the DEA's plan to boost the rival cartel's means so they would be able to defeat the Osorio family. A surprise attack wouldn't bode well for that end."

Holden says nothing else for a while. Eventually, he asks, "Is this common practice for an agency to use a criminal element to help accomplish their goal?"

"Happens all the time."

"How did this development affect your situation?"

"Passing along this information blew my cover. I was taken into custody by the old man's security regime."

"Did Eduardo intervene on your behalf?"

"No. When the commander of the security team told him what I had done, he turned his back and walked out of the room."

"He said nothing to you or to the commander?"

"'Make the call.' That's all he said."

“Meaning the decision or an actual call?”

“I don’t know. My memories of that time are less than reliable.”

“You were extremely lucky.”

“I guess that depends on how you define lucky.”

“You lived.”

“Did I?”

28

Friday, April 16

8:30 a.m.

Birmingham Police Department
First Avenue North

The LT wasn't buying the scenario that Sue Grimes was dead because the BPD had a leak.

Kerri wanted to scream. Right now, this minute, she should be working the Kurtz case with her partner. Falco was handling this high-profile damned case alone. Because Kerri was terrified for her daughter.

Actually, at this point, Kerri was beyond desperate. "You are the only person besides Falco I told about Sue's story."

The accusation hung in the thick-with-tension air. Brooks stared at her in a sort of stunned silence.

"Are you accusing me of something, Detective?"

Kerri refused to back down. "No, sir. I'm accusing someone you may have spoken to regarding the situation. Sue Grimes is dead. I can't believe her murder, less than twenty-four hours after telling me that story, is a coincidence."

The LT had offered her a seat the moment she'd entered his office, but Kerri hadn't been able to sit. She stood there now, hands on her hips, waiting for his reaction like a prisoner about to be executed. She felt exactly as alone as a prisoner on death row. Her entire career, this was the one place she had never felt alone or out of place.

Until now.

"You see, that's the problem, Devlin," he said, leaning forward to brace his forearms on his desk. "What you told me was a 'story.' Hearsay from the librarian at the school where a tragedy occurred. If your friend had proof of what she said, why not go to the police? Why allow this dangerous girl to go to another school, unfazed, and hurt someone else? What kind of person was this friend?"

Fury erupted inside Kerri, but she held it back. Now he was just trying to make her angry. "She was afraid for the other girl. The girl begged her not to tell."

"The girl that might be missing now?" he tossed back.

"She disappeared shortly after I shared the information." Kerri held his gaze. "With you."

Her boss took a breath. "This is what I can tell you, Detective. I shared this information with exactly three people. Sykes and Peterson because they are working the Myers case. I also briefed the chief in a private meeting. Are you prepared to accuse one of those three people of leaking this information?" He held up his hands. "Better yet, which of the three do you believe would have wanted to harm Sue Grimes and this missing child, Violet Redmond?"

No matter that she knew in her gut she was right, his words made Kerri's face burn with something besides anger. "I am not accusing anyone, sir. What I am suggesting is that someone along this loop may have unknowingly shared the information with someone else who allowed a leak—either accidentally or on purpose."

Brooks hit the intercom on his desk phone. His assistant responded immediately with a "Yes, sir."

"Get Sykes and Peterson in my office ASAP."

Another "Yes, sir" echoed in the room.

The LT gestured to a chair in front of his desk. "Sit, Devlin. We may have to wait a bit."

Kerri lowered into the nearest chair. He was the one angry now. She refused to regret this confrontation. It had to be done. Today. Now. Should have been done yesterday. "I tried to talk to you yesterday."

"I'm aware," he said. "For your information, I had a funeral to attend. Does that excuse my not getting back to you before this morning?"

Now she felt like a total shit—at least on that point. Before she could apologize, he went on, "Should I call the chief and request his presence as well?" His glare warned that he wasn't entirely joking.

Neither was she. She met his glare without flinching. "I'll leave that to your discretion, sir."

He looked away.

A knock on the door had Brooks announcing, "Come in."

Sykes and Peterson swaggered into the room. "You wanted to see us," Sykes said.

The two glanced at Kerri and audibly exhaled.

Perfect. Now they were all pissed at her.

"Take a seat, Detectives."

The two did as they were told, making no attempt to conceal their dark glances at Kerri.

"Let's talk about the Myers case," Brooks said. "Have you looked into the Walker Academy connection as we discussed yesterday morning?"

Surprise lanced through Kerri. He hadn't told Sykes and Peterson until yesterday morning? Sue was murdered yesterday morning. These two wouldn't have had time to pass along the info to anyone who may have had something to do with her death.

Well, hell.

"No, sir. After what happened with Sarah Talley, we were a little busy."

"So you haven't discussed Sue Grimes or Walker Academy with any of your sources? With anyone, for that matter?"

Sykes shook his head. "We haven't talked to anyone about it."

"We did hear she'd been murdered," Peterson chimed in. "Which pretty much put trying to talk to her on the back burner."

What an ass. Kerri turned to the man. "Really? You're going to joke about a woman's murder?"

"At least I ain't hiding my kid from a homicide investigation."

"What the hell are you talking about?" Kerri demanded.

"We went to the school to talk to Tori, and she wasn't there," Peterson said.

"You went to talk to her without calling me first?"

"We were going to call," Sykes interjected. "We hadn't gotten that far."

"Just as far as the school and asking for her," Kerri shot back.

"You don't get it," Peterson growled. "The Talley girl didn't just try and off herself; she left a note."

Sykes glared at him. Peterson shrugged.

"What does that mean, Peterson?" Kerri demanded.

"Sarah Talley left a note confessing to pushing Brendal Myers down those stairs. She said Tori was the one who came up with the idea to get rid of Brendal. Alice Cortez tried to talk them out of it, but . . ." Sykes turned his hands up. "You know how it turned out."

"I have no idea why," Kerri argued, her voice quavering, "but Sarah lied. Tori would never do that." The sting of betrayal was sharp. Why in the world would Sarah have made up such an awful lie? Following that hollow burn of betrayal was a stab of outright fear that she refused to acknowledge. Tori would not hurt anyone or urge a friend to do so. Not possible.

It was like Tori said . . . everything was wrong . . . upside down.

"You can't be sure, Devlin," Peterson argued. "Kids do stupid shit sometimes."

"You see," she shouted at him, tears way too damned close to the surface, "that very attitude is why this investigation is so screwed up. You two are only looking for the easiest and fastest way out of this."

"I know you're upset," Sykes allowed, "but that's going too far, Devlin."

"Is it?" she roared.

"Stop. Now," Brooks commanded. "This discussion is over."

"Sir," Kerri began.

"Enough," Brooks ordered.

When the room was silent, he turned to Sykes and Peterson. "You two will follow through with the information provided to Devlin by Grimes, and you will follow up on the Redmond girl's disappearance. Talk to her parents. Talk to the head of Walker Academy. Check in with the detective assigned to both cases. If these events are in any way linked to the Myers case, I want to know. Are we understood?"

*Yes, sir*s sang out.

"Go," Brooks ordered. "I don't want to see your faces again until you have something concrete for me. This investigation is dragging on way too long. Find some damned answers."

The two walked out without another glance at Kerri.

After the door closed, Brooks settled his attention on her once more. "Detective, as of this moment, you are on paid leave."

"What?" Kerri surged to her feet. "But, sir, I—"

"No buts, Devlin. This is all too close for you."

She shook her head. Before she could argue, he said, "You think I don't know something happened last year?"

Shock kept her quiet.

"Oh yeah, Detective, I'm aware. I know you far too well not to have seen it. That case changed you, and it's because of whatever part you and Falco left out of your final reports. I may never know what that part was, but I will not watch history repeat itself. Now go home and take care of your daughter."

Kerri wanted to argue. She wanted to show how offended she was that he would even suggest such a thing. But she couldn't.

Because he was right.

She had crossed a line during that investigation.

The memory would haunt her for the rest of her life.

29

9:05 a.m.

Sadie's Loft
Sixth Avenue, Twenty-Seventh Street
Birmingham

Sadie sat cross-legged on the floor, leaning against the door to her loft.

She'd slept here last night. On the floor. Her body pressed into the wood like a wedge to make sure no one got inside.

Hours and hours she had studied all those damned pieces of paper—fragments of her past she had posted on her wall. Trying to remember more. To somehow shift those pieces together in a way that made sense.

Hadn't happened. Eventually she'd collapsed into a nightmare-filled sleep—without the aid of alcohol. The two beers she'd had at Devlin's didn't really count. This crash had been caused by utter exhaustion.

What she needed now was caffeine, preferably an IV infusion, but since that wasn't possible, she'd have to make do with the brewed stuff. As soon as she could convince herself to get up and walk across the room.

She stared longingly at the coffeepot on the counter about twenty feet away.

In a little bit.

She'd dreamed about Eddie.

Sadie closed her eyes. He'd kissed her stomach and smiled up at her. *Te quiero.* He had loved her. Air shuddered into her lungs on a harsh inhale. She'd felt something for him. Naming the feeling love wouldn't be precise. But she had felt something for him. Something she'd never felt for anyone else.

She coughed, wished for a cigarette.

Blocking the concept of deeper emotions, she reminded herself that she'd played the part. She'd pretended to adore the family, even the old man. No one had suspected her of being anyone other than the food truck girl who'd stolen Eddie's heart.

Even Isabella had grown attached to her. The feel of her small hand in Sadie's filtered through her brain. Her laughter and the way she had twirled around the room like a ballerina. She had giggled and begged Sadie to join her. Sadie had danced around the child, clapped and smiled. She could see herself smiling, but it didn't feel like her . . . it felt like someone else. Someone from another life.

Those months had been another life . . . a lie.

Screams of agony. Pain like she'd never endured before roared through her body. She'd felt the baby moving . . . and then it was dead.

Cries . . . a baby's cries echoed inside her.

Sadie flinched. Only her imagination. The baby had died. She'd seen the tiny body. Felt the cold flesh . . . the little chest that failed to rise and fall.

Maybe it was for the best. She was too broken to take care of a child. Hell, she couldn't even take care of herself. And if the baby had lived, it probably would have ended up growing up in the cartel.

Her dead baby was buried on the compound somewhere. She would never know where. Maybe next to Eddie.

He was dead too. Though, like the rest of her memories, the parts about him during that time were fragmented and unclear.

Over the months and years there had been speculation that he was still there, in hiding at the compound.

Anything was possible, but deep in her gut she was certain he was dead. She should know. She was the one who had killed him.

At least he'd sure as hell looked dead.

Sadie squeezed her eyes shut and blocked the scattered voices and images from those missing months. No one could help piece the puzzle together. She was like Humpty Dumpty. All the king's horses and all the king's men couldn't put her together again.

Asher had tried.

Asher.

He was the first person she had allowed so close since her infamous disappearing act. He'd made promises about finding the truth and stopping Carlos Osorio where it counted—through his backers. One night after they'd had sex he'd laughed and promised to bring her the old bastard's head.

She'd tried to pretend he might even be able to do it. To win.

But she had known he wouldn't.

She'd warned him that it was too dangerous. Then he would insist she had survived; why couldn't he?

Maybe because deep inside she was made out of the same shit as the Osorios. Maybe that was why she'd fit in so well and ultimately survived.

Asher had been too good.

It didn't actually matter who'd pulled the trigger that had put the bullet in his head; Sadie knew who had ordered his execution.

Carlos Osorio.

She might not be able to get to him, but there could be another way.

Was it possible this girl, this Alice Cortez, was Isabella? She had many of her facial features and her coloring. Sadie thought of the photos Devlin had shown her. It had taken every ounce of willpower she possessed to maintain her composure after seeing those pics. She'd had to get out of there before she went over the edge.

But she couldn't be sure. Her mind played tricks on her far too often for her to be sure of anything from that part of her past.

What Sadie needed was to see this girl up close. To hear her speak . . . to see her move.

Then she would know for sure.

30

Noon

Cortez Residence
Eleventh Avenue South

From the passenger-side window of Jen's car, Kerri stared at the Cortez home. She shouldn't do this. It was bad enough to take the risk herself, but to ask someone else . . .

But she was desperate.

"I know that look," Jen announced. She twisted in the seat to look directly at Kerri.

Kerri blinked. This was wrong. Just wrong. "Jen, I shouldn't have come to you with this. I'm sorry."

Jen reached across the console and took Kerri's hand in hers. "Your daughter calls me Aunt Jen." Her lips trembled. "The same way Amelia did." A lone tear escaped and rolled down her cheek. "You and Diana—you're all family to me. I would do anything to help you."

Kerri rode out the hurt that hurtled through her, took a breath. "This is wrong. What I'm asking you to do. To impersonate a state official. If I could do it myself, I would. But these people know who I am, so I can't. And if I weren't scared to death for Tori, I would never ask you anyway."

Jen squared her shoulders and lifted her chin defiantly. "I want to do it, Kerri. Had I known what to do to help, I would have done it without you asking. Please, let me help." She shook her head. "Not for you or for me, but for Tori. I can't lose anyone else I love."

Kerri nodded. "Okay." She took a deep breath. "We've done the sound check. You have everything you need." Now or never. "Let's do it."

Jen smiled. "On it, sister."

Jen climbed out of her car, crossed the street, and stepped up to the sidewalk leading to the Cortez home. She looked sharp even in such a modest skirt and jacket. When she had called Jen, Kerri had suggested she wear a reserved, professional suit and keep the makeup light. To bring a notepad or portfolio and be ready to behave like a social worker.

Jen had nailed it.

Kerri smiled. She and Diana had always called Jen their other sister. She was a dear friend who would do anything for the people she loved.

Kerri desperately needed this to work. To know what was going on with Alice Cortez and her family.

"Here we go," Jen whispered, the breathy sound soft in Kerri's earpiece.

She heard the faint chime of the doorbell after Jen pushed the button. Three, four, five seconds elapsed before the door opened. From the car, it looked as if only a crack appeared.

"Mrs. Cortez?" Jen asked.

"Yes."

"My name is Wanda James. I'm from the Child Services Division, and I just need to ask you a few questions. May I come in?"

"You have . . . ID?"

The lady's accent was thick. José Cortez was the one who had done most of the talking the first time Kerri dropped her daughter off to spend time with Alice. He'd spoken perfect English with only the slightest Mexican accent.

Kerri held her breath as Jen flashed the fake credentials. It wasn't that Kerri had a stash of fake credentials, but she had a couple. Falco had taught her that sometimes it was necessary to skirt the perimeter between right and wrong to get where you needed to go. There had never been a more necessary time than now.

The door opened wider, and Jen was in.

Kerri wasn't sure whether to be relieved or further on edge.

"What a lovely cross," Jen said as she moved into the house. "You have a lot of beautiful crosses. How nice."

In the background the lady thanked her. Her voice was small. She was nervous.

"Now. As I said, my name is Wanda, and I have a few questions for you. May I call you Cora?"

"Yes, of . . . of course."

"How is Alice doing? I know this whole thing at the school has been just awful for all of you. The school counselors are working hard to help all the children, especially those closest to what happened."

Kerri was impressed. Jen should be an actress. So far she hadn't missed a single point Kerri had laid out.

"She isn't sleeping." The other woman hesitated. "I wake up and she is walking the floor. Talking to herself. It's so sad."

"Oh my," Jen said, "have you spoken to her counselor about this?"

Pause.

"Why haven't you?" Jen asked.

Kerri presumed the woman, Cora Cortez, had shaken her head in a no.

"My husband doesn't want to get involved. We keep to ourselves. It's easier that way."

Interesting.

"Your husband works with Iris Cosmetics?"

Another long pause.

"I'm not sure. He does not discuss his work with me. I wouldn't know."

"Alice's father was his brother?" Jen asked without hesitation.

"No. He is—was a friend. Longtime friend. They grew up together like brothers."

The abrupt silence told Kerri the woman realized she'd said too much.

"That's good," Jen said. "Friends are so important. It's good when we're there to help one another."

The woman made a soft sound of agreement. "Adopted," she added quickly. "He was José's adopted brother."

"Oh," Jen said, "I see."

Good comeback, Mrs. Cortez, Kerri granted.

"No other problems with Alice?" Jen asked.

Pause.

"Great."

Another unspoken answer apparently.

"How long have you lived in this country, Cora?"

Kerri held her breath.

"I . . . don't understand the question. Why do you ask?"

"When did you move from Mexico?" Jen rephrased. "Never mind. It's not really important. I was just curious. You have an excellent command of the language. And your home is so cozy. It looks as if you've been here ages."

"Thank you. Last year. August."

Kerri's heart started to beat faster.

"To take care of Alice," Jen suggested.

"Yes."

Another of those pauses elapsed.

"I . . . I lived here before," Cortez blurted. "I went to university here. I'm a nurse. I don't work any longer . . . because of Alice."

Another last-second save. The woman had her part nailed. Except Kerri wasn't buying it.

"You and your husband have sacrificed a great deal for Alice. That's very kind of you."

Good job, Jen!

"Well, all right then. I think I have everything I require except for having a look at Alice's room. I'm sure it's fine, but I have to follow the rules."

The silence was longer this time.

"I'll only take a moment, I promise," Jen reassured her.

The swoosh of fabric told Kerri someone had moved.

"This way," Cortez offered.

Kerri surveyed the block in both directions. Just a few minutes longer. If her heart beat any faster, it was going to jump out of her chest.

Footsteps echoed in Kerri's ear. The squeak of hinges warned when a door opened.

"Alice loves crosses, too, doesn't she?" Jen said, sounding bright and maybe a little too cheery.

"Yes, very much."

"What are the masks?"

Ice formed in Kerri's gut.

"Just . . . you know . . . decoration. She loves playing dress-up."

"Are these Alice's drawings?"

"She has big imagination also."

"She does," Jen agreed. "Well, I'll just take a couple of photos with my cell phone, and I'll be on my way."

"Sure . . . sure."

Kerri didn't breathe again until Jen was at the door, thanking the lady for her cooperation. She had started toward her car when an approaching vehicle snagged Kerri's attention.

Instinctively Kerri eased down in the passenger seat.

When the vehicle stopped on the Cortez side of the street, Kerri's heart surged into her throat.

Sykes and Peterson.

Assholes. Her lips flattened into a thin line as she watched, scarcely able to see over the upholstered part of the door where it met the glass of the window. Maybe she had gone too far in coming here like this, but by God they had pushed her to this point.

Jen flashed the two men one of her trademark sexy grins as their paths crossed on the sidewalk of the Cortez home. Peterson, of course, looked back at her ass as they walked on. *Perv.*

The detectives stopped at the Cortez front door and rang the bell. Kerri eased lower in the seat as Jen climbed behind the wheel.

"Friends of yours?" Jen asked without looking down as she fastened her seat belt.

"Get us out of here," Kerri urged.

Jen started the engine, checked both ways, and then eased away from the curb. When she'd reached the intersection at the other end of the block, Kerri sat up.

"Those were the detectives assigned to the investigation."

"In that case," Jen suggested as she handed Kerri her cell, "we were cutting it close."

"Too damned close for comfort." She took the phone and opened the photo app.

"There's some weird shit in that house, Kerri. I'm here to tell you. There are crosses everywhere; nothing against crosses or religion, but this is way over the top. I'm surprised your detective friends haven't mentioned it."

"The masks," Kerri muttered. This was what Tori had been talking about.

"You talk about creepy." Jen snorted. "If that little girl isn't a future serial killer, then I'm Mother Teresa. And we both know that ain't so."

Kerri had a very bad feeling Jen was right about the girl.

31

1:00 p.m.

Swanner Residence
Twenty-Third Avenue South
Birmingham

The phone rang, and Tori wondered if it was her mom checking up on her again.

Her aunt Diana answered the extension in the kitchen. Judging by the way she laughed, it was probably Aunt Jen. Jen had a way about her that could make even the saddest person laugh.

Except her. Tori doubted anything would ever make her laugh again.

She pushed up from the sofa, left her lunch on the coffee table. She couldn't eat. Had zero interest in watching any more television. She'd spent the morning helping Aunt Diana at the dance studio. The class had been the three- and four-year-olds. The thought almost made her smile. The little kids were so sweet. She hoped they didn't grow up to be mean teenagers like so many other kids.

Like Alice. And poor Brendal.

Tori wished Alice had never come to Brighton. She'd ruined all their lives. Brendal was dead. Even though she wasn't very nice, she didn't deserve to die.

Trudging up the stairs, Tori decided she might as well play a game in the boys' room. Anything to get her mind off life.

Before reaching the boys' room, she paused at the door to Amelia's room. She swallowed the emotion that instantly swelled into her throat. She missed Amelia so much. Her fingers lit on the doorknob before her mind made the decision. She opened the door and walked inside. Diana came in here every morning. She'd told Tori how she would sit down on Amelia's bed and talk to her. It made her feel closer to her daughter.

Tears burned Tori's eyes as she stepped into the room. It was exactly the way it had been when Amelia died. All the dance posters and fun throw pillows. Her cousin had a flair about her. Her closet was full of trendy clothes. Amelia had been the kind of person who could take thrift store finds and turn them into the hottest fashion.

Tori dropped onto her bed and stared at the framed photo of Amelia and her brothers on the bedside table. "I miss you."

If Amelia were here, she would tell Tori to suck it up and stop feeling sorry for herself. Amelia had been strong and brave. Far stronger and braver than Tori.

Dragging her cell from her hip pocket, she held her breath and took the plunge. She was not going to be afraid to look at her own social media pages. Whatever ugly things people were saying, it was all lies.

First in her news feed was a post by Alice.

The truth is out. Sarah did it. She killed poor Brendal. But it was Tori who told her to do it. #Brighton #deadgirl #meangirls #murder #killerteens #wtf

The bottom fell from Tori's stomach as if she'd just gone around the Ferris wheel after having way too much cotton candy.

Why would Alice say something like that?

Post after post from classmates echoed the same news. The killer teens hashtag was trending.

Tori clapped a hand over her mouth. How was this possible? None of it was true. Tori had never told Sarah to hurt Brendal. Sarah would never have pushed anyone, not even someone as mean as Brendal.

Sick, Tori tossed her phone on the bed. What about Alice? She was the one who had told Tori that Sarah thought she'd pushed Brendal. The day before that, Alice had been huddled and whispering with Sarah. Tori had known Sarah forever. She wouldn't come up with such a deceitful plan.

It had to be Alice. All that religious or voodoo crap she did was just further proof that she was evil.

Way more evil than Brendal ever was.

Tori glanced at her phone. But everyone thought she and Sarah were the evil ones.

How would she ever make them see otherwise? Her mom swore she was going to help, but Tori wasn't sure she could fix this no matter how much she wanted to.

Maybe Sarah had been the smart one when she'd tried to free herself from all this insanity.

Why should Tori hang around? She no longer had any friends. She had gotten completely ugly the past few months. Too skinny. No boobs. Pimple face. She'd failed a big test. Now she couldn't even go to school.

Her life was over anyway.

The tears rushed from her eyes. The sobs rose and tore out of her.

"Tori? Sweetie, you okay?" Diana appeared at the door.

Tori shook her head. "No. I'm not okay. And I don't know what to do."

Diana hurried to the bed and sat down beside her. She pulled Tori into her arms. "You tell me whatever you're thinking, precious girl. Don't hold anything back."

The words spewed out of Tori on violent sobs. She wasn't sure they would ever stop.

Not until she was empty.

32

1:50 p.m.

Brighton Academy
Seventh Avenue
Birmingham

For such an elite private school, the security was surprisingly lax. The guard had waved Sadie through the maintenance entrance as if they were old friends. It helped that she wore coveralls with the Southern Comfort Heating and Air logo. Drove one of their trucks too. Sadie had all sorts of friends who owed her favors.

She supposed the truck and getup or maybe her big smile kept the guard from checking with the office to see if anyone had called for HVAC maintenance. Complacency. Never a good thing.

She'd gone from floor to floor, room to room, checking thermostats until she'd found Alice Cortez in an art room. Sadie took her time removing the thermostat from the wall and pretending to examine the device.

As closely as possible she watched Alice interact with the other students. Observed her mannerisms and listened to her speech in hopes of noting something familiar. Her voice sounded vaguely recognizable, but it had been more than four years since she'd been in the same room with the child of Eduardo Osorio.

Her dark eyes . . . the shape of her nose and chin were Eddie. No question. But he wasn't the only Hispanic man with big brown eyes and full lips to pass along to his offspring. If this Alice was Isabella, she was still as beautiful as she had been as a much smaller child.

Just then Alice whirled around and said something to the girl behind her. That move, the little ballerina-like twirl was so familiar.

Dark eyes bumped hers, and Sadie looked away. She definitely did not want to get caught staring at one of these kids.

She should get the hell out of here. She'd seen enough.

As quickly as possible, with her fingers suddenly fumbling, she mounted the thermostat back on the wall and hit "Reset."

"What's your name?"

Sadie froze.

The other kids were still chattering and laughing, but not Alice. Alice stood right next to her. Sadie had no idea where the teacher had gone. What kind of teacher left a stranger in the room with her class?

Knowing she couldn't pretend she hadn't heard the girl, Sadie kept her focus on the device and said, "Mel. What's yours?"

"Alice."

The girl stared at her as if expecting some response.

"I like your eyes."

The words radiated through Sadie, through time . . . she had heard those words from this girl before.

"They're so gray, they're almost blue. Like a stormy sea. I love the sea. Do you?"

"Sure." Sadie grabbed her tool bag and backed away. "Have a nice day, kid."

She was almost to the door when a hand tugged at her sleeve. Sadie froze again, her hand wrapped around the doorknob. She'd almost gotten away.

"Do I know you?" Alice asked.

"Doubtful." Sadie opened the door and walked out.

If the girl followed her into the corridor, she was going to run.

Thankfully she did not.

Sadie walked as quickly as possible toward the stairs. She didn't want to break into a run, but she was damned tempted. Sweat had broken out on her skin. Dread clawed at her throat. Her heart thumped a frantic drumbeat.

She hadn't gone into all-out panic mode in more than a year. She was damned well headed there now.

The girl had recognized her on some level.

Sadie gritted her teeth and slid into the borrowed truck. She spotted the security guard headed across the parking lot as she rammed into drive and burst out of the parking slot. Rather than keep going, she braked, took a breath, and powered the window down. *Stay calm. Do this right.*

"System checked out fine. There was one thermostat offline, but it's all good now."

The guard narrowed his gaze, then nodded. "Thanks for the update."

She powered her window up and rolled away. He wouldn't be so thankful when he reported to the office and no one could recall a work order for the HVAC system.

Still struggling to get the panic under control, Sadie drove the ten minutes required to reach the building where her friend and his team were installing a new system. She shed the coveralls, tossed them into the seat, and left the truck. She waved a thanks to him and climbed into her Saab and drove away.

She needed to know for sure who this girl was.

More than that she needed a drink.

But she wasn't going there. Sober was necessary right now. She'd had that one lapse the other night, and she wasn't about to allow it to happen again.

Calm down. Slow, deep breaths. Keep it rational. Think clearly, logically.

Could Alice Cortez be Isabella Osorio? The age was right. The features.

Had the old man sent her here for protection of some sort? There was growing unrest in the region over which he reigned. The old man's time on this earth was limited. Others were champing at the bit to take over as the leader of the largest cartel in Mexico, with a reach that extended all the way to Canada. For that to happen, any remaining heirs would have to be eliminated.

Images of the child in the mask—the one that had haunted her for the past four-plus years—expanded in Sadie's head.

Take my hand and you'll be invisible.

Sadie blinked. Turned up the radio to block the voice.

Can't be her. Osorio wouldn't send her here . . . not this close to Sadie. Not after what she'd done. The idea that he might not know Sadie was in Birmingham was ludicrous. He would know. He hadn't successfully grown the largest drug cartel in Mexico because he was stupid or shortsighted.

All this time she had never stopped looking over her shoulder, but none of his people ever showed up on her tail or at her door. She'd expected him to. At times had even hoped he would. Then it would be over.

But no one had come to finish her off.

He wouldn't send his granddaughter here. No way. There had to be another explanation.

A flash of memory slammed into her brain. A voice. *His* voice whispered in Sadie's ear . . . warning that she would never be free of him.

She would always belong to him because of what she took from him.

"No." She shook her head, slapped the heel of her hand against the steering wheel. Carlos Osorio had never come after her. He didn't care about her. He'd made sure she wouldn't remember anything important. This was just another fragment of memory that likely was nothing more than a hallucination.

She had invaded his compound. Stolen his son's heart and then taken his life. Yeah, she had taken something from him all right, but she'd lost plenty as well.

Was that why he had allowed her to live? He wanted her to suffer with those particular demons for the rest of her days?

Bastard.

Watch for the sign.

The air stalled in Sadie's lungs as the voice rang out in her head, louder than the heavy metal band on the radio blaring in her ears.

There will be a sign when the time comes.

Was the girl . . . a sign?

Could the old bastard finally be coming for Sadie? After all this time?

She spotted the stopped truck a split second before she would have barreled into it. She cut right. Hard. Her Saab bounced off the shoulder of the road and into the ditch.

Her head banged into the driver's window before the vehicle came to a jarring stop against a culvert. The airbag blew up in her face.

When she could move, Sadie smacked the deflated bag from her body. She coughed. Her chest would be sore as hell tomorrow. Rubbing at the side of her bruised head, she stared out the shattered windshield at her damaged front end.

"Idiot."

She should have stopped somewhere after returning the truck and walked off the damn panic attack. She'd done it hundreds of times before. What had she been thinking?

"Damn it!"

She dug out her cell and called a wrecker. With one en route, she climbed from behind the wheel and propped against the wounded vehicle.

An Uber home would be the quickest way to get out of here. She could get another car to use until hers was fixed.

Right now, she really needed that damned drink.

Not true. What she needed was to know more about Alice Cortez and her family. She considered calling Falco, but Devlin would be the best source. And Devlin was far more desperate at the moment than Falco.

Sadie tapped the name in her contact list. Devlin answered on the second ring.

"Can you give me a ride?"

Sadie's Loft
Sixth Avenue, Twenty-Seventh Street
Birmingham, 2:40 p.m.

Sadie pointed to a grainy photo she had printed from the internet. "This is the image a sketch artist did right after I came back. That's what I could recall of the girl, Isabella."

Devlin stared at the wall of notes Sadie had made. Pieces of memories. Fragments of time. "She could be Alice," Devlin said. "No question."

"The voice is right." Sadie shrugged. "More mature, but right."

Devlin shook her head. "I can't believe you got into Brighton Academy so easily. Geez. What am I paying for?"

"Good question," Sadie concurred. "I was able to watch her for a few minutes—the girl, I mean. She did this little twirl around like a ballerina. I saw Isabella do it a hundred times."

"Most girls want to be a ballerina at one time or another in their lives," Devlin countered.

"Yeah, yeah." Sadie didn't have kids. She knew nothing of what little girls did or wanted.

"Walk me through what you actually remember," Devlin said.

Sadie grabbed her mug of coffee from the table and stalked toward the sofa. "I was assigned to the task force in July. By September I was in tight with the son, Eduardo—Eddie to his friends. By October I was living at the compound. By Christmas we were engaged."

The other part Sadie had long ago decided she wouldn't talk about. To anyone. Her father knew because the doctors had told him there were indications Sadie had given birth a few months prior. She'd never told anyone else.

"Were you able to pass along usable intelligence while you were undercover?"

Sadie downed a hefty swallow of coffee. "I did. Not as much as I would have liked but more than anyone else had ever managed before. I was the first undercover to get inside the compound. It took getting really close to the family. Digging in deep."

"I imagine it was difficult to play the part so completely."

"I don't know." Sadie stared at her half-empty cup. "Part of me became my cover. It's the only way to make it real. You pull on that skin and become the person you're pretending to be. After a while, it feels . . . right, and you do what you have to do."

"What happened before you vanished?"

"I overheard a conversation. Passed along the intel, and that was the end of my cover."

"Someone saw you or set you up?"

"The last bit of intelligence I passed along was too close. No one knew except Eddie, his father, and the woman on the phone. They knew it had to be me. There was no one else in the house that day."

"What about the woman? Did you recognize her?"

"I only heard her voice on the conference call. For a moment. A dozen words, maybe. She never came to the compound." A snippet of memory about someone important visiting at the party on October 31 flashed in her brain. Was that why she'd ended up drugged that night, so she wouldn't see the visitor? Sadie shook off the memory. "She's the big mystery that remains even after digging in so deep and all that hard work."

"And sacrifice."

Sadie nodded.

"Where did they keep you?"

"A containment facility away from the compound, I think. But I can't be certain."

"You were tortured and drugged all that time. Why keep you so long and then let you go?"

A baby crying echoed in her brain. *It's dead. It's dead.*

Sadie blinked at the painful reverberation. "They wanted to make sure I forgot anything I ever knew, I guess. They did this whole brainwashing thing."

Devlin considered this a moment. "Why didn't they just kill you?" She picked up her mug but didn't bring it to her lips. "Sounds like they were waiting for something. Maybe some sort of deal with the DEA or BPD."

"There was no deal." Sadie shook her head. "No one knew if I was even still alive."

"Maybe you just weren't told about it. Your father could have—"

"He had nothing to do with it," she snapped, cutting Devlin off.

The other woman held up her hands in surrender. "Okay. Got it."

Those emotions she didn't like to feel roiled inside Sadie. She should have known Devlin wouldn't stop digging. Damn it. "They kept me alive because I was pregnant with an Osorio heir. A boy. Okay?"

Devlin looked as stunned as Sadie felt at having told her. She'd never told anyone that part. Not even Dr. Holden—at least as far as she knew. If she had, he'd never mentioned as much. He would have told her, wouldn't he? Wasn't he supposed to share everything that came out during her regression sessions?

Sadie forced away thoughts of Holden. Didn't matter. The kid had died at birth. What would have been the point of telling anyone? The omitted detail might have kept her story from being considered suspicious and being dissected repeatedly by the BPD and the DEA when she first reappeared. But she couldn't be sure of anything . . . couldn't bear talking about it then or now.

Why the hell had she just told Devlin?

Weak. Rattled. Losing her fucking mind. *Take your pick.*

"You were pregnant. Oh my God. What happened to the baby?"

"It died just before or during birth. I can't be sure. I only know it . . . *he* was dead. I saw him. Touched him." The foggy memory of cold flesh swam in her head. "I guess I fell over the edge completely then, because I went batshit crazy."

Devlin waited for her to go on. Sadie had gone this far; she might as well tell her the rest. Maybe she was at that batshit crazy place again . . . just a little less violent.

"I don't remember more than a voice here or there after that. My next real memory is of waking up under that overpass on Eighteenth."

Devlin absorbed this statement for a bit, then said, "I'm stunned you were able to escape. Why didn't the old man ever send anyone after you?"

"How the hell should I know?" She tossed back the last of the coffee. How many times had she asked herself that same question? She. Did. Not. Know. "I gotta go."

"Wait." Devlin stared at her as if trying to see inside Sadie's head. "Why would Carlos Osorio send his granddaughter to Birmingham under a fake identity? Particularly considering this is where you live."

"That's the million-dollar question, Devlin. Who the hell knows?" Speaking of a million dollars, she thought of the reward the Walshes had offered and wondered what Naomi thought about it. Was that the family's estimated value of their son's life?

Sadie felt sick. Devlin asked questions, raised possibilities she didn't want to think about.

"There has to be a reason," Devlin countered, pulling Sadie back to the conversation. "Something so important that Osorio would be willing to take the risk."

Since Devlin appeared determined not to let it go, Sadie took a breath and forced herself to mull over the concept before tossing out a possible scenario. "Isabella was kept a secret. She never left the compound. It's possible if there has been some sort of trouble in the area, they've sent her away to protect her. Birmingham has become a major stronghold for Osorio. He may feel she's safer here despite my presence. I guess it depends on how bad the trouble is and what his assets here are. Besides, I'm not supposed to remember anything, right? Frankly, what little I do makes basically no sense."

"Whatever the reason," Devlin said, "I believe Alice is Isabella, and she's here. She's killed at least one girl and tried to kill two others." Devlin pulled out her cell. "A friend of mine posed as a social worker and spent some time with the woman taking care of Alice—the alleged aunt. My friend said the house is full of crosses. But the strangest part is Alice's room." Devlin handed her phone to Sadie, the photo app open.

Sadie's gaze landed on the masks hanging on the wall. Ghostly white. Two dark eyeholes. Horns protruding from the sides. Fear crowded into Sadie's chest. This was the kind of mask the child in her dreams . . . or memories had worn. Fingers trembling, she swiped, stared at the next photo. This one showed crude drawings. A bloodred moon in the middle of a paint-blackened page. Yellow flames, flickering across another page. The red coals beneath the flames bleeding.

Doing all within her power to keep her hand from shaking, Sadie passed the phone back to Devlin. She struggled to find her voice. Her heart pounded harder and harder. "You better keep your kid away from this girl, Devlin."

She's had some problems . . . we've had to be very careful with her.

The words whispered through Sadie's mind. Eddie's voice, his words. Had he said this to her about Isabella? Or had he been speaking of someone else?

Devlin's cell vibrated in her hand. She answered. Listened for a few seconds, then said, "I'll be right there." She put her phone away. "I have to go. My daughter needs me."

"Thanks for giving me a ride," Sadie managed to say without her voice breaking.

Devlin paused at the door. "Like I said last night, anything you can do to help is greatly appreciated."

Sadie nodded. "Yeah."

Devlin left.

All this talk about Alice being Isabella was nothing more than speculation, a potential scenario. A theory. Sadie couldn't be sure. Maybe her mind was playing tricks on her again. That happened sometimes. Okay, more than sometimes.

But the photos on Devlin's phone were real. The drawings belonged to Alice Cortez. Dark. Sinister. Those drawings were way too similar to ones Sadie had seen before . . . in that shack or shed at the Osorio compound. The shaking started deep inside Sadie and spread outward, through her limbs.

The place the masked child had led her into the night of that party.

33

4:15 p.m.

Devlin Residence
Twenty-First Avenue South
Birmingham

"Please, Tori," Kerri pleaded, "tell me if there's anything else we need to talk about? I can't help if I don't know."

Tori sat on the sofa, her elbows resting on her knees, her face in her hands. Kerri had never seen her so desolate. To say she looked as if she'd lost her best friend was the understatement of the century. She *had* lost her best friend as surely as if she had died, but this went well beyond that kind of loss and pain.

This was the agony of betrayal. The level of betrayal only a best friend could wield.

Tori leaned back against the sofa. "They all believe her. And why wouldn't they? We've been friends forever." Her eyes closed in misery. "I just can't imagine why she said such a thing."

"Did Sarah ever talk to you about wanting to hurt Brendal? Or to Alice that you know of?"

Tori moved her head side to side. "She said she hated her. We all said that at one time or another. You know when you get angry, you say things you don't really mean. At least not completely."

Kerri nodded. Her back to the arm of the sofa, she pulled one knee under her so she could sit facing Tori. "I know exactly what you mean. There was someone in my freshman class who made me feel that exact same way." Kerri sighed as the memories instantly tumbled into her mind. "My sort-of-hate girl was Lola Gray."

"Lola?" Tori's lips twitched as if she might smile. "Are you talking about Piper Knox's mom?"

"She was a Gray back then," Kerri admitted. "She was the mean girl that year. She'd come into her more grown-up assets earlier than most of us, and she had perfect skin and perfect teeth—no braces required. She lived to make the rest of us girls feel inferior—which was completely unnecessary, because we already did."

"But she didn't die." Tori's face fell. "And your best friend didn't finger you for pushing her down the stairs."

"No. But I did play a dirty trick on her once." Kerri had never admitted this to anyone. Ever. Not even Diana or Jen.

Tori's eyes widened in disbelief. "What did you do?"

"We were seated on the bleachers awaiting the start of the pep rally. Lola was on the row above me, her feet sort of between me and the girl next to me. Lola was always so full of herself and bragging to anyone around her that she never noticed me fiddling with her sneaker laces."

"You did not?" Tori said in disbelief, her eyes even wider now.

"I did. I tied those suckers together. When the pep rally was over and it was our turn to leave, she took a tumble. She busted her lip and hit her nose, so there was lots of blood. Scared the heck out of me. Luckily there were no serious injuries. She was, at least temporarily, mortified with the swelling and bruising."

"Did you feel like you'd made her pay just a little?" Tori asked, her eyes closely searching her mother's.

"For about three seconds and then I felt like a total jerk. I kept thinking of all the terrible things that could have happened. She could have been gravely injured. I was lucky it wasn't far worse."

"Wow. I can't believe you did something like that."

"We all have our moments, Tori, where we say or do something we regret later. Maybe it feels or sounds right at that moment because we're upset or hurt. But we realize in the end that it was a mistake."

Tori seemed to realize what her mother was getting at then. "I didn't do it, Mom. I didn't push Brendal or tell Sarah to do it. I don't know why she said I did. It's not true." She shook her head. "I didn't do it."

"I never believed you did," Kerri assured her. "I just wanted you to understand that we all make mistakes. If the idea was discussed prior to what happened—"

"It wasn't," she cried. "I swear. We never talked about hurting Brendal. Never. We did talk about how we hoped everyone saw her for what she was one day, but we never—at least I know I didn't—took any sort of step to make that happen."

"Let's talk about Sarah," Kerri offered. "Have you noticed any issues with her recently. Depression? Anxiety? Anything going on with her parents?"

"No way. She was hurt by the things Brendal was saying and doing, but she knew it would pass eventually. Brendal never stayed focused on one person too long. Sarah and I knew she would move on eventually."

"What about Alice? How was she in all this?"

Tori took a big breath. "She's the one who kept saying Brendal needed to understand she couldn't treat people so badly. She didn't like her at all. Honestly, I think she was jealous of her."

"She never suggested any recourse one or all of you should take?"

"No. She just kept bringing Brendal up. Rubbing it in, sort of. I didn't consider that was what she was doing at first, but looking back, I can see how she wanted to keep the drama going."

Kerri thought of all that Jen had seen in the Cortez home. "Did Alice talk much about the masks and the drawings she likes so much? The ones at her house, I mean."

"They're part of her beliefs." Tori shrugged. "Like her religion. She thinks they give her magical powers because she's a princess."

"Did she ever try and prove this theory to you?"

Tori bit her lip as if she wasn't sure she should tell this part.

"Don't hold back," Kerri urged. "It's the only way I can help."

"The last time Sarah and I spent the night at the same time, Alice talked about how if we were her real friends that we could become like her—a part of her. She said we'd be the most popular girls in school if we stuck with her. She told us this over and over. Kept reminding us of how amazing we'd be."

"Was she attempting some sort of brainwashing?" This was sounding more and more like exactly that sort of pressure tactic.

Tori shook her head. "I don't know. Maybe."

Kerri reached out and squeezed her hand. "Whatever she was attempting to do, I don't believe you or Sarah did anything bad. We are going to get to the bottom of what did happen."

Tori nodded.

Kerri's chest tightened as she thought of what she needed to ask her daughter next. But she couldn't pretend it hadn't happened. As soon as Kerri had arrived at her sister's house, Diana had pulled her aside and told her what the boys had found on the computer in their room.

"Tori, have you been feeling like maybe you want to die too? I mean, as in take your own life?"

Tori's gaze shot to her mother's and just as quickly shifted away. "Why would you ask such a lame question? I already told you I didn't mean what I said after I found out Brendal had died. I was just upset."

"Diana noticed someone had been searching suicide on the upstairs computer. If it wasn't you, it was one of the boys. She needs to know if one of them is having trouble."

Kerri held her breath.

"It was me."

Kerri's heart sank. "I hope you would never feel as if that were the only answer. You have people who love you and who would do anything for you. Suicide is not an option."

"I know. I was just feeling sorry for myself and I . . ." She fell silent for a moment. "No, that's not right. Yes, I was feeling bad, but it was Alice who told me I should probably take myself out of the narrative. It made me wonder how people—people like Sarah—could feel bad enough to actually do it."

Outrage roared through Kerri. "Has she ever suggested such a thing to you or Sarah before?" Kerri thought of the two girls at Walker Academy, and more of that white-hot fury flamed inside her.

"A few times lately." Tori shrugged. "I think she mostly does it to see how we'll react. You know, the whole shock-value thing."

"I'm certain you understand by now that Alice is not and never has been your or Sarah's friend."

"For sure." Tori stared at her cuticles for a moment. "There's something else I need to tell you. Something Alice found out and has been bugging me about."

Kerri held her breath and waited for her daughter to go on.

"I think I might be gay. I mean, I'm not sure, but . . . I think so." Tori squeezed her eyes shut and seemed to hold her breath as well.

Surprised at not having recognized her daughter was wrestling with her sexuality, Kerri reached out and pulled her into a hug. "Sweetie, you don't have to be afraid to talk about that or anything else with me. You're my daughter. I love you no matter what. Do you understand that? I love whatever makes you *you*."

Tori held on to her mother for a long while; when she finally drew back, she said, "Can we not talk about this for a little bit? I'm not ready to tell other people right now. I have to get used to these feelings before I feel comfortable sharing them. Maybe we can order pizza or something."

"Absolutely." Kerri leaned over and kissed her daughter on the head. "Relax. I'll place an order now."

After ensuring Tori had found something on television, Kerri went into the kitchen. She placed the order for pizza and put through a call to Sykes. She struggled to calm herself before he answered. She wasn't entirely successful.

"Tell me you have something concrete in this investigation," she demanded. Her daughter was suffering. Being a teenager was damned hard enough without all this insanity.

The rough exhale that sounded in her ear was not the answer she wanted to hear.

"The LT told you to back off, Devlin," Sykes warned. "We cannot discuss this case with you."

"I don't want to hear the dirty details, Sykes. I want to know if you're making any headway. A yes or no will be sufficient."

His silence was answer enough. *No.*

"Let me tell you what I know." Kerri told him about the masks and the bizarre drawings. "Did you miss all that when you visited the Cortez home?"

"We didn't miss shit," he snarled, defensive now.

"What about the two suicide attempts at Walker Academy and the missing girl? Alice was involved with those girls. You can't see how what happened there might be relevant to this case? I know you're a better detective than this, Sykes."

One, two, three beats of silence.

"Yes, Devlin. We've been looking into what happened at Walker. Remember, the LT ordered us to. At least we were until we were told to back off."

And here Kerri had thought nothing could shock her at this point. "What does that mean, Sykes? Did the LT tell you to back off?"

"No. What it means is little Miss Alice Cortez is in Mayor Warren's mentoring program. She's off limits. We got the order straight from the chief. We don't get to question her or her family again. If we discover something that ties the girl to what happened, we take it straight to the chief. Otherwise, we keep our mouths shut about her. The kid's untouchable."

Kerri took a moment to ride out the shock and outrage and to digest this news. "I see."

"Yeah. We're doing all we can—including looking more closely at the Walker situation. We just have to walk that line I told you about. And FYI, we finally got to talk to the two girls at Walker Academy. They both said Alice tried to talk them out of what they did. I guess your dead friend failed to tell you that part."

Rather than tell Sykes what she thought of his smart-ass remark, she said, "Thanks for giving me a heads-up." She ended the call and fought the urge to call the LT and rant.

Ranting wouldn't help. She was on thin ice with the LT already.

What she needed was evidence. The evidence Sue Grimes might have been able to give her if she hadn't ended up dead and if that poor girl hadn't gone missing.

Why the hell would the mayor put her program—no matter how prestigious—above a murder investigation? Why would she protect Alice Cortez? Was it because the girl was a minority like her? Did she believe that Tori and Sarah were being treated differently than Alice because they were white?

Maybe, but Kerri's instincts were humming far too loud to ignore the other possibility. They needed to take a much closer look at the mayor, even if only to rule her out. She could only imagine the LT's and the chief's reactions to this conclusion.

The doorbell rang, dragging Kerri away from the troubling thoughts.

"I'll get it," Kerri told her daughter as she moved back into the living room. She didn't want Tori answering the door, in case it was a rogue reporter.

Thankfully it was only the pizza delivery. A few minutes later the pizza and drinks were spread on the coffee table, and Tori was picking at a slice. Kerri forced herself to eat in hopes of encouraging her daughter to do the same. But the idea that Mayor Warren had taken such a drastic step wouldn't let go. *What the hell?*

Kerri's cell vibrated against the table. Falco's face showed on the screen. She answered. He needed to know about this as well. "Hey."

"How's our girl?"

Kerri pushed to her feet and walked into the kitchen. "She's okay. We're muddling through. Anything new on your end?"

"Cross was able to get some bank statements belonging to McGill."

Before Kerri could respond, he said, "Don't ask how. Just know that she got them, and there are very large monthly deposits to a sweet little overseas account McGill set up two years ago—about the same time she started working for Kurtz. The deposits are far healthier than her monthly salary. Looks like Kurtz was right, and McGill was the source inside his business."

Definitely an interesting turn of events. "Is there a chance what she was doing might have been something less complicated, like skimming profits at the tobacco shop?"

"With the income he took in weekly, it's not impossible," Falco said.

"If that's the case, maybe Kurtz discovered her sticky fingers and confronted her?" Which could mean his murder wasn't related to drugs or the cartel, ultimately blowing all to hell their theory that he and Walsh were working together.

Falco said, "We're talking a sizable chunk of change. She would've done some serious time if he'd pressed charges. Previous employers could potentially have started coming forward if McGill has done this before. But," he allowed, "this could also be about the distribution of drugs. Cross believes McGill was the source Kurtz and Walsh intended to confront. This could be the first piece of tangible evidence."

True. "But there's a big difference between taking money or even low-level drug distribution," Kerri reminded him, "and killing someone—especially two someones."

"No question," Falco agreed. "But what do we really know about McGill? She may have a history of violence we haven't uncovered yet. Maybe they confronted her, and she killed them. In fact, Walsh being there actually worked in her favor by drawing suspicion farther from her. She doesn't know the guy and had no connection to him."

Kerri wasn't ready to buy into the scenario. "Maybe someone else figured out what she was up to and used it to blackmail her into providing the opportunity to take them both out."

"Only one way to find out," Falco said. "I'll drop by the shop and interview her again."

Worry gnawed at Kerri. "I don't like you doing this alone. We don't know what McGill is capable of." Right now was not a good time for her to leave Tori.

"I'll take Cross with me. She seems to know a lot more about McGill than we do."

"Be careful and keep me up to speed," Kerri ordered. "I don't want to hear from someone else about you getting into trouble."

"I'll call you, don't worry. Just take care of Tori. She needs you more than I do."

"Look, I learned something from Sykes that doesn't make sense."

"I'm listening."

"He and Peterson were instructed to back off where Alice Cortez and her family are concerned. The girl is in the mayor's mentoring program, and Warren wants the family left alone. The order came straight from the chief."

"That means just one thing to me," Falco said. "We need to turn over some rocks from the mayor's past. See what crawls out."

"I was thinking the same. I'll do what research I can from home tonight. You be careful."

He laughed softly. "I'm beginning to think you're attached to me, Devlin."

"I just don't want to have to break in a new partner."

Kerri ended the call rather than risk saying something else that would incriminate her. The truth was she didn't want to lose him. Tori wasn't the only one who needed him.

With a deep breath, Kerri pasted on a smile and went back to the living room.

The mayor's connection was curious. She grabbed her phone from the side table.

Now to learn just how curious.

34

7:30 p.m.

Elyton Hotel
First Avenue North
Birmingham

Mason finished off the scotch and placed his glass on the bar. He hadn't been in this bar since it had been renovated. He'd heard the one on the rooftop had quite the view.

But he wasn't here for the view or the elegant atmosphere. He was here for *her*.

Fury burned through him, but he didn't move. Waiting for the right moment was crucial. She'd arrived for dinner a few minutes ago. A trip to the powder room was inevitable if for nothing more than to freshen her lipstick.

His ability to outwait the enemy had been well honed over the decades. He would wait all night if necessary.

A third scotch had landed on the counter in front of him by the time his target excused herself from the table and headed in the direction of the ladies' room.

Mason slipped from the far end of the bar and skirted the perimeter of the room until he reached the side corridor where she had disappeared.

His hand was on the door in front of her before she could push through it. She gasped, turned to him. Even in the low lighting her startled expression was visible. He almost smiled at the idea that he could still surprise her.

"Mason, what're you doing here?" She glanced toward the other end of the corridor.

"Not to worry. This will only take a moment. Your husband will hardly have time to miss you."

Fury tightened her lips. "What is it you want? I believe I've already made myself clear on where we stand."

Oh, she had made herself clear, crystal. Now it was his turn to be equally clear.

"I have one question, and I need the truth."

"Very well." She faced him, hers scarcely more than half a dozen inches from his. "What is so important that you had to stalk me to the ladies' room?"

Her voice—soft and alluring—sent fire searing through him. He was a fool. "Someone attempted to hire a hit on my daughter. I only need to confirm who that person was before I take steps to rectify the situation."

Her far-too-perceptive gaze narrowed. "Why would you assume I know anything about your daughter and her enemies?"

Please. "Don't toy with me. I want an answer."

"I'm afraid you've wasted your time coming here." She reached for the door once more.

"It was *him*."

She paused, visibly startled once more. "If you know it was him, why come to me?" She lifted her chin, stared defiantly into his eyes. "Don't play games with me, Mason. If you're trying to tell me something, just say it."

He leaned his face closer still to hers. "You shouldn't have allowed this. You're slipping. Fair warning—if anything happens to my daughter, there will be severe ramifications."

Something like amusement lit in her eyes. “Good night, Mason. I’m certain you’ll find the answer you’re looking for.”

This time he didn’t try to stop her when she pushed into the ladies’ room.

Instead, he walked away.

He had his answer.

35

8:00 p.m.

Leo's Tobacconist
Oak Grove Road
Homewood

Sadie slid onto the nearest stool and ordered a sparkling water.

Falco's eyebrows rose ever so slightly.

"What?" she demanded. "You think a zebra can't change its stripes?" The glass of water landed on the counter in front of her, and she picked it up and sipped the fizzing liquid.

"Glad to see you're taking your health seriously for a change." He ordered a beer. "What's up with the yellow Bug? You get a new car or something?"

"I borrowed it from a friend. Mine's in the shop. Didn't Devlin tell you?"

"Tell me what?"

Clearly Devlin was off her game as well. "I had a little fender bender. Now can we please stop talking about me? Do you see our target?"

The place was packed. The owner's death hadn't slowed patronage at all. Sadie leaned from one side to the other, surveying the tables as well as the length of the bar.

"Doesn't look like she showed up," Falco said.

"Oh well." Sadie sipped her water. "I guess we wasted our time on this one, pal."

Sadie knew where McGill lived. She'd wait her out if necessary.

Falco propped his forearms on the bar and leaned closer to her. "What's going on with you, Cross? I thought you wanted to help find Walsh's killer?"

She blocked out the background noise of conversation and clinking glasses. "You wouldn't have this lead if not for me. I submit to you that's evidence enough of my interest in solving the case."

Maybe it was just all those photos from the girl's bedroom—the Alice that looked so much like Isabella—and going to the school that had Sadie off balance. Fact was she was having a little trouble keeping her shit together. Other voices were whispering to her as well.

Voices she didn't want to hear. She'd searched for the truth all this time, and now she couldn't bear to hear it. She couldn't shake the damned voices. There was a time when she'd had meds that sent the panic and the voices away, but then she'd realized she might never remember the rest of her past unless she allowed all those haunting voices and images to come as they would. In retrospect, maybe that hadn't been such a good idea.

Here and now those damned voices were driving her crazy. She couldn't stay focused. Could barely sit still.

"There's Vandiver," Falco said, drawing her attention back to the crowded room.

George Caldwell, the man in charge tonight, had already told Falco that McGill hadn't shown up so far. Hadn't even bothered to call, leaving him shorthanded. Explained why the guy was huffing and puffing and all red faced trying to keep up with customers' orders. Two other waitresses floated around the room. They could be clones of McGill.

Vandiver walked around with a tray, taking discarded glasses and empty peanut and pretzel bowls. He wore his typical jeans and sneakers, but the shirt was classier than usual, and his hair was slicked back into a ponytail. He smiled at customers as if he was glad to be here.

Had to be whatever drug he was on. According to McGill, Vandiver—Lucky, as she called him—hated his job.

Sadie scanned the place again. Still no McGill. Frustration nudged her. Or maybe it was worry. Nah. She never worried. Except she couldn't help wondering if her visit to McGill's town house was the reason she was now missing. If the woman was actually in any way related to the drug business, someone might have been watching her and her place. Particularly with Kurtz and Walsh dead. The cops weren't the only ones needing this case wrapped up.

Any time a high-profile situation potentially involved the local drug supply, even the bad guys wanted closure.

Bastards.

If something had happened to her . . .

Sadie shook off the thought. Sipped her water. Wished she'd ordered something stronger.

"Lucky, my man," Falco said as the younger guy passed.

Vandiver paused. "I don't have time to talk. We're crazy busy."

Sadie stuck out her leg when he would have tried to move on. "Too bad you're shorthanded."

"Yeah, it sucks. Tara's a bitch."

"I hear she had some trouble with the boss," Falco said.

"Not that I heard about." Vandiver shrugged. "Like I told you before, Leo was too good to her in my opinion."

"Did you ever see her take anything from the cash register?" Sadie asked. "You closed with her plenty of times. Maybe she gave you a little something to look the other way."

He snorted, sent Sadie a glassy-eyed stare. "The only thing she ever gave me was a hard time." He looked from Sadie to Falco. "I wouldn't put it past her to steal from the boss, but even that would have been better than what she was really doing."

"And what exactly was she really doing, Lucky?" Falco asked, keeping his voice below the level of the conversations around the room.

Vandiver laughed hysterically. Definitely high on something. "You still haven't figured it out, have you?" He shook his head. "Leo's been dead five days, and you're no closer to the truth than you were when you first showed up."

"Why don't you enlighten us?" Sadie suggested. "If you're so in the know. Or maybe you'd prefer my friend here took you downtown for a more intimate conversation."

"Okay. Okay." Vandiver visibly struggled to compose himself. "Tara is using this place to distribute drugs. The packages come in, and she passes them along to her foot soldiers, who do the selling. She never gets her hands dirty, and no one ever suspects a classy joint like this would be serving as a distribution center."

Sadie couldn't say she was surprised. Walsh had suspected this was the strategy being utilized. She shrugged. "Tara said she got her drugs from you."

Vandiver gave another of those snorty laughs. "Of course she did." He placed his tray on the counter and looked Sadie square in the eye. "I've been around enough folks in the business to recognize her scam. Yours too."

"You didn't think it was important to tell us this before?" Falco demanded. "Maybe we could do our jobs if people like you didn't hold back crucial information."

Vandiver scoffed. "Whatever. I had to protect myself. If I don't stay clean, my old man will make my life more miserable than it already is. Tara told me if I told anyone she would go to my dad." He grinned. "Guess it doesn't matter now. Apparently, she's out of here." He made a poof sound. "She'll have to find herself some other way to do her moonlighting."

"Whatever," Falco parroted, then thrust one of his business cards in the guy's face. "If you see or hear from Tara, call me."

"It would make my day," Vandiver assured him.

Falco headed for the exit. Sadie followed. "We going to her town house now?"

"We are."

"Good thing I have a key."

Falco glanced at her and grunted. Didn't ask questions. He knew better.

McGill Town House
Hampton Heights Drive
Birmingham, 8:40 p.m.

McGill wasn't answering. Falco called her cell phone, and the distinct sound of it ringing echoed through the door.

He put his phone away. "Use the key. If need be, we can say the door was unlocked."

"And ajar," Sadie added, giving him a fake smile. "I remember how it works." She unlocked the door.

"Don't touch anything," he ordered as they entered the premises.

Sadie was the one grunting this time. She knew the deal.

Nothing looked disturbed as they moved into the living room.

"Ms. McGill, you home?" Falco shouted. "This is Detective Falco. Your friends at the shop are concerned for your welfare."

Yeah, right, Sadie thought.

Falco jerked his head right and nodded to the left. They split and began the slow, careful move around the first floor. Didn't take long.

Falco led the climb up to the second floor. A moment later they were at McGill's bedroom door. Bed was unmade, clothes discarded on the bed.

Sadie moved into the en suite ahead of Falco.

"Damn." Tara McGill was in the whirlpool tub. Sadie didn't need a medical examiner or a closer inspection to tell her the woman was dead.

Her body, including her head, was submerged beneath the water.

A small handgun and an empty bottle of vodka lay on the floor alongside an empty medication vial. Sadie crouched down and looked at the label on the vial. Tranquilizers. Falco eased down next to her and checked out the small handgun.

"No surprise," he muttered. "It's a .22."

Sadie glanced around, spotted a handwritten note on the closed toilet lid. Based on the notes she had seen on the kitchen bulletin board and at McGill's desk, the handwriting was the vic's.

Falco leaned Sadie's way, reading the note along with her.

I fucked up. Got in too deep. I loved Leo but he found out about the money. I had to do it to stay out of jail. His friend was there. I had no choice . . .

Sorry.

"All tidied up in a neat bundle," Falco commented.

"Looks like"—Sadie stood—"you can close your case now. How nice is that?"

Falco chuckled, a dry growl. "Yeah." He pushed to his feet. "When were you here?"

Sadie glanced at the woman in the tub. "Around one in the afternoon on Wednesday."

"Caldwell said she was at work last night until closing, which means this," Falco surmised, "happened in the past twenty or so hours."

Sadie shifted her gaze from the bathtub and the body in the water. "I'd say in the past four or five hours. No way she's been in that water overnight or even all day. You know the shit that happens when a body has been in water that long."

Falco nodded. "Let's have a look around. Tell me anything that looks different than when you were here on Wednesday afternoon."

They moved through the second floor one room at a time. In the bedroom turned office, it was clear what the killer had taken.

"The computer is missing." Sadie walked over to the desk. "It was here. I pulled the info I gave you from it."

Falco scrubbed a hand over his chin. "Good thing you were one step ahead of whoever ordered the hit."

"Yeah." Sounds and images from the hours she had spent between the sheets with McGill whispered through Sadie's head. "I'm thinking now if anyone had spotted me coming or going on Wednesday, she would have been dead before today."

"There would likely be signs of an interrogation as well," he reminded her.

No signs of interrogation. Didn't make Sadie feel a hell of a lot better.

"Don't forget," Falco added, "McGill made her own choices. You didn't do this to her; she did it to herself."

Maybe.

"I guess you have to call this in." Sadie started backing toward the door. "I should go. See you later, Falco."

Sadie was out of here. She had shit to do. Otherwise the damned voices were going to take over.

—

Cortez Residence
Eleventh Avenue South
Birmingham, 10:30 p.m.

She should have brought something stronger than coffee.

Sadie screwed the lid back on the thermos and tossed it into the passenger seat of Heck's shitty yellow car.

She stared at the Cortez home. There were no outside lights. Just the moonlight sifting through the trees, spotlighting the house in an eerie glow. The windows were like boxes outlined in gold. The curtains blocking most of the interior lights caused a gold-colored edge to encircle each one.

The girl was in there. *Isabella.* Maybe it was Sadie's inability to maintain a coherent thought between the blasts of voices from the past intruding in her head, but she was pretty much convinced at this point that it was *her*.

They'd had trouble with the girl. She'd remembered Eddie telling her how the behavior problems had started at age five. Before her death, the girl's mother had refused to allow any sort of real discipline. Eddie had blamed himself and his father mostly. She was the only grandchild and spoiled completely. Everyone, the staff, the guards—they all spoiled her, were enchanted by her.

She was the perfect angel. As entertaining as any child movie star.

Except when she didn't get her way or failed to receive all the attention. Then she became cruel and violent.

Eddie refused to try the medication route. His thinking was that the child would outgrow the tantrums.

All those pieces of memory had sifted through Sadie's brain the last couple of hours as she sat here watching the house. The words, his voice, had slid over her as if he'd touched her. She shivered even now. Shaking off the sensation, she focused on the house. Her mind conjured up the images from inside . . . the masks, the crosses, the drawings Devlin had shown her. All far too familiar.

Now, if this Alice was in fact Eddie's daughter, she was up to far worse than tantrums.

But the big question still hung like a flashing caution sign in Sadie's brain. Why send her to Birmingham?

Why not keep her hidden away as they had before?

Made no sense. Sadie closed her eyes and dropped her head back against the seat. She was so tired. For years now she had struggled to remember all the missing fragments. But they had refused to come beyond a snippet here and there.

Suddenly they were like a meteor shower.

Maybe the old man couldn't deal with the kid any longer. There had been a nanny. Maybe the kid had killed the nanny or tried to hurt the old man. He was too old to deal with that kind of shit.

Sadie wanted to smile at the thought of the kid hurting the old man, but she had a bad feeling she could actually be right.

Her mind drifted back to that night . . . the night when the girl—wearing that bizarre mask like the one in the photos Devlin had shown her—had led Sadie to the shack at the far back corner of the compound. It had been dark. Or maybe Sadie had been dreaming. She couldn't tell anymore. The sound of laughter and music had still wafted from the main house. Inside people had been dancing and drinking, and probably a few had been hidden in quiet corners doing other stuff.

Isabella's little girl voice had been saying that she was taking Sadie to her secret place to meet her secret friend. She'd twirled around in the night, whispering things Sadie couldn't quite make out.

That was right, she realized. It was definitely Isabella who'd led her down those stairs and then through the darkness.

Sadie had been so drunk that night. Like so many nights since her return. Her mind had refused to stop revisiting those dark places she couldn't quite remember. Some errant brain cell kept stirring the pieces of her fragmented memories in an attempt to put them together like a puzzle that had scattered over the floor.

Only she couldn't find all the pieces. They wouldn't all come together.

She was like the nursery rhyme, she thought again. Old Humpty Dumpty in too many pieces to manage.

Oh, but that had abruptly changed. Whether it was seeing all those photos or the girl herself, something was happening in Sadie's brain, and she couldn't shut it off.

She'd followed the girl in the mask that night nearly five years ago. To the shack where the little old woman lived. The one who served as the compound's healer. She was a tiny, bent woman, not much bigger than a child herself. Her gray hair was long and worn in a braid. Her clothes old and clearly homemade.

Sadie's breath caught at the new rush of sensations, not exactly memories. Images, voices, a knowing.

"*Toma*," the old woman said, ushering a cup toward Sadie.

"Drink it," the girl in the mask said.

The child was blurry, but Sadie had understood that it was the alcohol level in her blood, not the child, really.

She wanted to ask what was in the cup, but she couldn't. Her tongue wouldn't work. Instead, she accepted the cup and drank the contents.

The world spun, and then the blackness took her. Two words followed her into the darkness. *Be gone.*

Sadie jerked upright in her seat.

She blinked. Shook herself. She was in the car. The ugly yellow one. Parked outside the Cortez home.

She blew out a breath. Water. She needed water.

What time was it?

She checked her cell. Almost midnight. She'd dozed off and slept for more than an hour.

"Damn." She tossed her cell back onto the passenger seat.

She licked her lips as she stared into the darkness around the house. All the windows were dark now.

In the corner of her eye she spotted movement. A wisp of white fluttered around the back corner on this end of the house. Sadie sat up straighter. Peered harder through the darkness.

"What the hell?" she murmured.

She waited and watched. Then she saw it again. Something small but ghostly white in the distance of the backyard.

Opening the car door, she eased out, then pressed it shut. Keeping her head low, she moved around the rear of the car and across the street.

She disappeared into the tree line between the two houses. Soundlessly she crept along the property line until she was in the backyard of the Cortez home.

Holding as still as stone, Sadie waited and watched.

Maybe a minute later the ghostly apparition swept from around the opposite corner of the house and twirled around the backyard. The dress or covering was dark, maybe black like the night. The slip of white was the mask.

A mask exactly like the one the little girl had worn that night all those years ago in Mexico at a cartel compound.

Maybe she was dreaming. Or hallucinating. She'd done it before.

Sadie squeezed her eyes shut and held them closed to the count of five. She told herself she was dreaming.

But when she opened her eyes, the white mask was still dancing around the yard. Its two dark holes where eyes would be seemingly empty. Two garish horns curled up, one on each side.

Sadie dared to take a step forward, toward the dancing apparition.

Something hard collided with the back of her head.

Pain shattered in her skull.

Her face was suddenly in the cool grass.

"You shouldn't have come."

Not the child's voice.

36

Session Five

Three Years Ago

The digital recording drones with silence for a good thirty seconds.

"Are we finished with this session before we start?" Holden asks.

"What do you want me to say?"

"It would be helpful if you said you were prepared to begin."

"Get it over with," Sadie grumbles.

The doctor releases a heavy sigh before beginning the steps that would relax Sadie and allow her to go back to the time when she was a prisoner of the Osorio cartel.

"It's late October, more than a year since you first arrived at the compound. More than eight months since anyone on your team has heard from you."

"I clutched at my belly."

Sadie's voice is low and small.

"Why did you clutch at your belly?" Holden asks.

"The baby was gone. He was born already. But he was dead."

"The child was stillborn?"

"Yes. That's what they told me. And I saw him . . . touched him. He was dead."

"Where are you, Sadie?"

"I don't know. There were no windows. I had no grasp of time. Night or day. The passing of seasons. The temperature was always the same. The lights were always on."

"Were you alone?"

"Yes."

"Were your medical needs attended to?"

"I'm not sure. I believe so."

"And you're certain you were alone."

"At first, but then he came into the room."

"He?"

There is a delay in her answer.

"Eddie."

"I thought he was dead."

"He would be in a few more minutes."

"You intended to kill him?"

"Yes. I hid an ink pen in my waistband."

"Tell me what happened."

"I waited until he was close enough. He hugged me. No matter that I was a traitor; he still felt something for me. I took advantage of the moment and jammed the pen into his jugular. The blood spewed and flowed like a river. I remember his eyes and the way he looked at me as he died in my arms."

"Were you taken away when his body was found?"

"No . . . wait." A long pause. "That's wrong."

"What do you mean *wrong*?" Holden prods.

"Eddie was dead before . . . a long time before. I killed him when they first discovered who I really was. The old man wanted me dead. Eddie pleaded with his father to keep me alive until the child was born."

"Are you saying you didn't kill him?"

Silence.

"No," she says. "I did. Except it was when he came into the room to tell me my life would be spared long enough for the child to be born."

"But you said the child was stillborn."

"I don't remember telling you about the baby."

"You did, Sadie. Just a moment ago. You told me the baby was dead."

"I don't remember telling you, but it's true. He died." Her voice is high now, strained. "I remember the voices."

"Whose voices?"

She doesn't answer for several seconds.

"Someone I trusted. *His.* And . . . and hers."

"Whose voices?" Holden repeats.

"I don't want to talk anymore."

37

11:55 p.m.

Finley Boulevard
Birmingham

Mason had listened to Sadie's regression therapy sessions at least a dozen times. The past few days he'd put himself through the torture once more. His daughter had come so very close to learning his secret during the therapy. The final session was the reason he had halted the appointments and taken possession of the recordings. Holden hadn't argued. After all, Mason had paid him a great deal of money. Initially, Mason had intended to destroy the recordings, but he could not bring himself to do it. Each time he listened, he was reminded of how very much Sadie had paid for his mistakes.

He would see that she never paid for anything he did ever again.

This would end now.

Before leaving home a half hour ago he had carefully packed the recordings of the sessions in the box with the rest of the things he wanted Sadie to have when the time was right. Much would be explained when she had an opportunity to go through the items he had saved. Her name and phone number were on the box to ensure it was passed on to her in the event he was unable to tell her about it.

It was time to finalize one last step.

He watched as the rented luxury sedan pulled into the parking lot of the abandoned warehouse on Finley Boulevard. Mason emerged from his Lexus and strode toward the dark sedan without hesitation. The engine continued running, the parking lights on. As he approached the front passenger-side door, the auto lock disengaged. He opened the door and settled into the leather seat. The dim interior lighting closed in around him and the man he'd asked to meet him. Mason placed his hands loosely in his lap.

"I was surprised you called," Leland Walsh announced. "I thought our business was finished after our last meeting."

"I thought so, too, until I spoke with *her*." Mason knew her better than she knew herself. When she did not refute his allegation, he had known he was right. She would never have permitted Mason the leeway to move on a conclusion that was unfounded. She was far too exacting for such an allowance.

Walsh had the audacity to laugh. "Really, Agent Cross. I can hardly see the problem. She has every reason to feel exactly as I do, wouldn't you say?" He turned to face Mason. "An eye for an eye, after all. Except we aren't talking about eyes, are we?"

Mason gave a nod, primarily at having his conclusion confirmed straight from the horse's mouth. "No, we are not." As he spoke, he slid a hand beneath his jacket and wrapped his fingers around the butt of his weapon. "You made a mistake, Walsh."

"She made no move to stop me," he tossed back. "We both know who's in charge here."

"Always recognize your limitations." Mason withdrew his weapon, pressed the silenced barrel to the man's forehead. The dim interior lighting cast an eerie glow on his suddenly pale face. Fear bloomed in his eyes. "Never cross a man who is more merciless than you."

He fired the weapon, relaxed at the sharp ping that sent the bullet through the other man's skull. Then he got out of the car.

Now to end this.

38

Today

Saturday, April 17

7:20 a.m.

Birmingham

I don't want to die.

Turning fourteen hadn't made her as brave as she'd thought. She had to run . . . she should never have taken that call. She should have stayed home and not sneaked out of the house.

She needed a way to contact her mom and . . .

The car door opened.

It was too late.

Alice slid into the back seat of the car. She glanced at Tori.

Tori tried to act normal as the driver pulled away from the curb in front of Alice's house. *Stay calm.* She didn't want Alice to see how terrified she was. She had to play along at least for a while longer. The only thing she could think to do was pray. Didn't matter whether God had ever answered her prayers before or if she didn't really know how. Praying was her one option at the moment.

It wasn't like she could call for help. After picking up Tori a block away from her house, Alice had thrown Tori's cell phone out the window. She should have started screaming then. She should have shouted for the driver to stop. At first, she'd been too shocked at what Alice had done to react. Then she'd realized she couldn't do either of those things . . . not if Sarah needed her.

Alice had explained that Sarah had slipped out of the hospital and run away because her parents wanted to send her to a psychiatric hospital. Alice had insisted Sarah intended to try suicide again, but she'd persuaded her to wait until they could talk face-to-face.

Tori couldn't ignore the possibility that Alice was telling the truth this time.

A glance at the black bag on the floorboard reminded Tori of another reason she had to try to be calm for a while longer. That big knife was right there in that bag. She'd sneaked a look inside while Alice had gone into her house for something she'd forgotten. If Tori dared to scream or to tell the driver . . . Alice would probably kill her before he could even stop the car—if he even stopped. The driver may have been hired by her family. Maybe he was a killer too. Either way, that knife was intended for hurting someone. Tori was not going to let Alice get away with hurting anyone else.

"Our destination has changed," Alice said to the driver. "Birmingport Road. I'll tell you where to turn."

"What the hell is out there?" the driver demanded, speaking for the first time since Tori got into the car. "I'll have to call in the change. Your card—"

"Keep the charge on the card." Alice dug into the pocket of her jeans and pulled out a wad of cash, large bills, twenties and fifties. "You think this might take care of the extra trouble?"

The driver shot another glare at Alice in the rearview mirror. "I have to call it in."

Alice laughed. "There's five hundred dollars here. Maybe you can make an exception this time."

He shifted his attention to the street and kept driving. His silence confirmed his agreement. Tori's heart sank.

Alice rolled her eyes before leaning down, picking up the bag, and tucking the money inside.

Tori's heart thumped harder and harder as a new wave of fear crashed against her. Why hadn't she gotten out back there while Alice was in her house? She could have run. Even if the driver had chased her. She should have tried. What was wrong with her? She had allowed Alice to convince her Sarah needed them. After all the lies she had told, how could Tori believe her this time?

Now she was probably going to die. For all she knew Sarah was already dead.

No. No one else was going to die.

Anger shot through Tori. "Where is Sarah?" The thin, not-so-steady voice was hers. The words had burst out of her. Tori blinked, stared at Alice. "When you called, you told me she'd run away from the hospital and was in trouble. We're supposed to be going to help her. Where is she?"

Alice exhaled a dramatic sigh as if she had no patience for Tori's questions. "I told her to wait at the warehouse. It was the only place I could think for her to hide. Her parents would never look there."

"At the port?" Tori demanded, her bravado rallying. "How did she get there? She couldn't have walked that far." Hitchhiking would be too dangerous. Sarah would never do that.

Alice nodded to the driver. "How do you think she got there? She called an Uber. Don't be stupid, Tori. She's our friend. We're going to help her. That's what friends do."

Tori held back the other words she wanted to shout. How could she not have realized the guy behind the wheel was just an Uber driver? She really could have run, and he probably wouldn't have cared. She was an idiot. She had to think. Alice could be lying. Why would Sarah run away and ask Alice for help? Why hadn't she called Tori? They had known each other the longest—way longer. Why hadn't the police had a guard on her hospital room? Sarah had confessed to pushing Brendal. Wouldn't the police be watching her or something? Tori squeezed her eyes shut. The whole thing—the whole story was some kind of crazy lie that Alice had probably convinced Sarah to believe. No way had Sarah pushed anyone.

Tori understood now what kind of liar Alice was. But she couldn't risk letting Sarah down if she needed her. Ignoring Alice's call hadn't been an option any more than not seeing this through was.

But she should have told her mom instead of leaving a note and sneaking out. If this was another lie . . .

"I don't believe you."

Tori froze. She'd said the words. Out loud. To Alice.

Alice held the bag closer to her chest; one hand slid inside. "Just shut up, Tori."

Tori dared to meet her gaze. Alice's eyes were wild and fierce. She was not kidding.

"We're doing this together," Alice said calmly. "Just like we planned." She even smiled.

Probably for the driver's sake, since he watched in the rearview mirror.

And they hadn't *planned* anything. Alice had told Tori what they had to do, and Tori had done it.

Tori said another hasty prayer. Since he apparently didn't work for her family, she hoped the driver wasn't one of those people who didn't like getting involved.

Help me, please.

Tori stared at that rearview mirror and silently repeated the words over and over. Maybe her eyes would somehow telegraph her plea to the man.

39

7:30 a.m.

Devlin Residence
Twenty-First Avenue South
Birmingham

Kerri cradled her coffee mug in both hands. She and Tori had talked and cried until late in the night. They'd eaten pizza and popcorn and ice cream. It hadn't been until after midnight that Kerri had left Tori asleep in her bed and made her way to her own.

She'd slept like the dead. Kerri hadn't opened her eyes until seven this morning. She never slept past five. Never. Tori was generally up by six, seven at the latest. Kerri glanced toward the living room. Still no sign of the popcorn queen. Her daughter had won the popcorn-eating contest. Kerri made a face. Personally, she might never eat popcorn again.

Kerri finished off her coffee and set her mug aside. The urge to call Sykes writhed inside her. He was supposed to call her if there was any word on the missing Walker Academy student, Violet Redmond. He had promised to look more closely at the situation.

Falco had called late last night with an update. Tara McGill was dead. They'd found her body in her bathtub. An autopsy would be coming, but for now it looked as if she'd swallowed a fistful of pills, then proceeded to drown her sorrows in a bottle of vodka and her tub. She'd left a note confessing to the murders of her boss and Walsh. The proper caliber of weapon was even right there next to the tub. How convenient was that?

Except her computer was missing.

Cross had confirmed the computer had been there on Wednesday afternoon, which was likely how she'd obtained the info on McGill's financials. Kerri wasn't judging. Cross wasn't a cop anymore. She wasn't bound by the same rules. All she had to do was not get caught.

The suicide note, along with the news that McGill was possibly stealing money from the tobacco shop and, according to Lucky Vandiver, using the shop as a way to distribute drugs, might seem like a break in the ongoing case. It was in reality a distraction. McGill's death, in fact, elevated the case from a double homicide to a triple.

Not exactly an ideal break. She and Falco were meeting this morning to strategize how to prove their scenario to the LT. The wrap-up with McGill was obviously what the task force wanted, since a "speedy closure" had been underscored on numerous occasions. Especially by the mayor. In every single press briefing she'd tossed out that promise.

McGill's confession also ensured there was no further need to talk to José Cortez. The mayor's desire to protect the family simply because Alice was in her mentoring program didn't sit right with Kerri. Sure, having the father involved in a murder case would reflect badly on the mayor's choices, but wasn't she supposed to be the big antidrug advocate? Was stopping crime less important than her program?

Kerri's research last night had uncovered a couple of potential kernels that merited further digging. She had been under the impression the mayor had been born and raised in the Birmingham area. Not so. She'd moved to Birmingham from Galveston, Texas, when she was fifteen. Like Alice Cortez, she'd been raised by a family that wasn't her own. Her parents, too, had died, and she had no other family. Possibly neither of those similarities was anything more than coincidence, but they could explain why the mayor felt especially protective of Alice.

Still, the part of Warren's early history that nudged at Kerri was the other similarity to Alice's. The Odell family, who had taken in the future mayor, had suddenly come into a great deal of money about that same time. Or at least their lifestyle had changed dramatically. They'd moved from a modest home in Gardendale to a mansion in Mountain Brook. More research would be required to determine the details of the transition, but the cost of the new home didn't fit with Mr. Odell's employment at Alabama Power.

Interviewing the Odells wasn't possible since the couple had died in a car crash shortly after Emma entered college, and there were no other children. Emma—the mayor—had no other family and no children of her own. There was only her husband.

Basically, the mayor's history could be whatever she chose since there was no one to say otherwise.

Kerri shook off the thought. Maybe she was reading too much into the connection. Either way, she needed to talk to Falco about this. They should do more digging into not only the mayor but the Walshes. Considering the secret trips to Birmingham the mother had been making, it was possible she had hired someone to take out her son. The scenario didn't fit with how she'd urged Kerri to find his killer. Then again, she'd looked almost furious about the reward being offered. There were just too many conflicting vibes coming from the woman. The mayor, too, for that matter. Until Kerri found something more concrete—if she found something more concrete—there was nowhere to go with either of those theories.

She should make breakfast and then drop Tori at Diana's for a few hours. Not the whole day, just enough time for her and Falco to do some research and determine where they went from here on this case. If Tori wasn't game for that scenario, Falco could come to the house and work with Kerri. They'd done it plenty of times before.

There wasn't a whole lot they could do related to the Kurtz-Walsh case until after the ballistics report came back on the handgun Falco had found at McGill's town house.

She exhaled a big breath, opened the fridge, and checked for the necessary breakfast ingredients. French toast was sounding good to her this morning. It was one of Tori's favorites.

Speaking of Tori, Kerri glanced at the clock. It was twenty before eight. Tori was always up by now even on Saturday after a late night. Kerri headed for the stairs. She stopped at her daughter's door and knocked before opening it. "Good morning, sleepyhead."

Standing in the doorway, Kerri stared for a moment before her brain assimilated what her eyes saw.

Tori's bed was empty.

She had passed the bathroom on the way to Tori's door. The bathroom door had been open, the room empty. She wasn't in the bathroom.

When Kerri would have taken a step back to go to her own bedroom and check there, something on her daughter's bedside table caught her eye.

A note.

Fear slowly overtaking her, Kerri crossed the room and picked up the handwritten note.

> Mom,
> Please don't be mad. I know I can't trust Alice, but Sarah has run away and she needs my help. I need Sarah to help me figure this out.
>
> Love you,
> Tori

Fear burst inside Kerri's chest, spreading icy cold through her body. She snatched the cell from her hip pocket and called Tori's cell. Ring after ring went unanswered. When the call went to voice mail, as calmly as possible, Kerri said, "Call me. Love you."

Hands shaking, she called Sarah's mother next. Each unanswered ring had Kerri's heart beating harder.

"Hello." Renae Talley sounded exhausted, defeated.

"Renae." Kerri caught herself. This woman's daughter had tried to kill herself. She had to tread softly. "How is Sarah?"

For a long moment there was nothing but silence.

Was it true then? Sarah had run away, and Tori was out there somewhere trying to help her? Anguish knotted inside Kerri.

Renae cleared her throat. "She's better. Until this morning she hadn't spoken a word to us or anyone."

Shock joined the fear tugging at Kerri. "You're still at the hospital?"

"Yes."

Kerri moistened her lips and dared to hope. "Has Tori spoken to you or Sarah?"

"No." Renae took a deep breath. "I'm not supposed to talk about any of this since the detectives talked to Sarah only a few minutes ago, but there is something I need you to know—from mother to mother."

Kerri's heart stumbled.

"Sarah swears she doesn't remember pushing Brendal. She also said Tori never suggested she do so. We didn't press her about why she'd said so in the note. When she's stronger, we'll get to the bottom of this. I'm sorry . . . I don't understand what's happened or why."

The tears streaming down Kerri's face were filled with relief. She should be elated, but what she was beneath the brief flash of relief was terrified.

"Thank you for telling me," she managed. "I'll check in on Sarah later."

Kerri ended the connection and called Falco. He answered on the first ring. Kerri blurted the words burgeoning in her throat, "Tori is missing."

Every bit of restraint Kerri possessed was required to hold back a howl of misery. "She left a note saying Sarah had run away and she'd gone to help her. But I just spoke to Sarah's mother, and she's still in the hospital. They haven't heard from Tori."

"Call it in," Falco said. "I'm on my way to you."

40

7:50 a.m.

Sadie's Loft
Sixth Avenue, Twenty-Seventh Street
Birmingham

Her head ached.

Sadie touched the back of her skull. Groaned at the new sore spot. She told her eyes to open, but the dreams weren't quite ready to let her go.

She was back there . . . in Mexico. In the place where they'd kept her locked away. Eddie was there, holding her, telling her everything would be all right. The baby was crying in the background.

No. That wasn't right. Eddie couldn't have been with her then. He was dead.

She had killed him.

He had asked her why. Why she'd betrayed him. Sadie had told him the truth. She was a cop. Working undercover. Her real name was Sadie Cross, and she was carrying his child. She loved him, but she had a job to do, and his father was evil. What he was doing was evil.

Eddie had moved his head slowly from side to side and told her the truth. "I cannot save you."

The weapon had been lying on his desk. It hadn't been a pen as she'd thought; it was a gun. The two of them were in his office alone. She had a chance—slim, but still a chance.

Sadie grabbed the gun and fired without hesitating, without thinking.

He stumbled backward. Fell to the floor. Blood spreading across his chest.

She ran.

But the guards caught her before she could escape.

The girl was there . . . the one wearing the mask. She seemed bigger, older. Sadie must be mixing up the Isabella from nearly five years ago with the Alice now.

"Shh-shhh. You must be quiet."

It was dark. Where had the day gone? Where was Eddie's body? Sadie was confused.

"Take my hand."

Sadie stared at the hand. Not the hand of a child. The wrinkled, gnarled hand of someone old.

"Take my hand," the voice demanded, "and you will be invisible."

Sadie didn't understand, but she took the old woman's hand. She fell into the darkness. Deeper and deeper. There was nothing but darkness. Then the voices came. *His* voice. Demanding that she be kept alive. And *hers* . . . the woman she'd heard in the conference call. The one who seemed to be making the decisions. Then Sadie had awakened under the overpass on Eighteenth.

How had she gotten there?

Sadie didn't know the female voice she'd heard.

But she knew *his* voice.

It was not Carlos or Eddie.

It was her father. She'd heard him demanding that she be allowed to live.

Sadie's eyes flew open. She blinked. Stared out the windshield of her borrowed car—the piss-yellow one.

The taste in her mouth was of vomit and something else. A drug she had tasted before.

Pain split her skull.

She touched the back of her head. Where the hell was she?

Sadie looked around. A frown pulled at her face. Made her head hurt worse. She was home. The borrowed car parked in the alley next to her place. How the hell had she gotten here?

She stared at the steering wheel, the keys . . . her hands.

Oh yeah, she'd obviously been drugged and driven here. But by who?

Her last memory was of being at the Cortez house. She had seen the girl in the mask.

Was it the girl? Alice/Isabella?

Couldn't have been the old woman. Hell, she was probably dead by now. She'd been ancient nearly five years ago when she was serving as the healer at the Osorio compound. Eddie had said she'd been with the family since before he was born.

Eddie was dead.

Sadie had killed him.

She blinked, held perfectly still. The rest of the dream rushed in on her.

She'd heard her father's voice.

That wasn't possible. She must have confused the timing. She had awakened in the hospital, and he had been there. But he hadn't been with her before that. Not under the overpass and certainly not in Mexico.

Had he?

Cross Residence
Eagle Wood Court
Birmingham, 8:30 a.m.

Sadie beat her fist against the door. She winced at the pain the sound made in her skull.

The door opened, and her father stood there, dressed as he always was when he was off duty—in khakis and a button-down shirt. She didn't have to look to know he would be wearing his favorite leather loafers.

This was the dad side of him. Not the hard-ass agent.

Good. This was the Mason Cross she wanted.

"Sadie, what a pleasant surprise. Come in. I've been thinking about you." He said these things as if they hadn't been estranged for nearly a year.

"No." She started to shake her head but thought better of it. She probably had a concussion, maybe two, considering how hard she'd hit her head when she'd wrecked her car. "I have a question for you."

He frowned now. Likely taking in her wrinkled clothes, unbrushed hair. No doubt he smelled the sweat and vomit emanating from her every pore.

"Are you all right? You don't look well."

That was his fatherly way of saying she looked like hell.

"You were in Mexico after I killed Eduardo Osorio."

He stared at her, his face, his eyes abruptly shuttered. "You should come inside."

"No. We'll talk right here." She tried to moisten her lips, but her mouth was too dry and bitter—probably whatever drug they had used on her. "You were there. I remember hearing your voice. You pleaded for my life." This part should make her feel good about him. She should be grateful. Except she wasn't.

He had been there. At the compound. There was no other explanation.

He exhaled a big breath. "I knew you would remember eventually. There was no guarantee the drug therapy would be permanent."

She stared at him, startled that he'd actually told the truth. What the . . . ?

"I listened to the recordings of your sessions with Holden. He gave them to me. Unwillingly, of course."

Fury belted her. "You blackmailed my shrink into giving you my private files."

Her father nodded. "Don't blame him. He had no choice. He genuinely felt bad for you, but his need to protect himself overrode his sympathy. Besides, I paid him well."

Sadie held up a hand. "So you were there—in Mexico. You're admitting this?"

He nodded. "I was there. You'd gone missing, and no one in the official operation seemed able to figure out what happened. I went directly to the compound."

"Wait. Wait." Sadie held up her hands stop-sign fashion. "They let you in and then allowed you to leave." She laughed. This was crazy. He was lying or leaving something out. Maybe he was the one who'd had a breakdown. Maybe insanity ran in the family.

Or maybe this was another of her bizarre dreams. She could be hallucinating. Last night and this morning could be just one long hallucination. Maybe she wasn't even here, standing at her father's door, talking to him.

Holy shit, she was so screwed.

"Everyone has secrets, Sadie. There was one person in the Osorio family with whom I could negotiate. That person made a deal with me. I agreed, but first I insisted on proof of life. I wanted to see you for myself. Once I knew you were alive, I agreed to the terms of the negotiation."

A sound burst out of her. A kind of laugh but not. "You came there, saw me, and left. You left me there to be tortured and brainwashed for months."

He nodded. "I did. Those were the terms. You would be released alive at a place and time they chose. I was just grateful I would get you back alive."

Okay, so maybe this wasn't a hallucination. "You made this deal with a woman, not with the old man. I remember a woman's voice."

He stared at Sadie now, his face rearranged into that blank she knew so well.

"Who set the terms of the agreement?" she demanded.

"I'm afraid I can't share that information with you."

"Did you share it with your superiors? With the BPD?" She was yelling now. She didn't care. "Was this an under-the-table deal? Is that what you're saying? Did your superiors even know about it?" Of course they didn't know! All this time everyone had looked at her as if she'd done something wrong. Had something to hide. Because no one could figure out what happened. Why she was even alive.

"You son of a bitch," she snarled.

"You should come inside and have coffee with me."

Jesus Christ. Her old man, the hard-ass DEA agent, had crossed the line. Oh, he'd left the "father" line behind decades ago . . . but this . . . this was that holier-than-thou, self-righteous asshole-of-the-century *line.* The one he revered above all else. Mason Cross, the decorated hero, had just confessed to crossing—or at least blurring—the line of honor, of duty.

Sadie backed away. "No way. You made a deal for my life, and I want to know who else was involved. It was *my* life." She pounded her chest. "I have a right to hear the details."

"I kept you from being executed," he stated, his patience thinning. "You should be grateful, not questioning my methods. Especially in light of the sacrifice I made."

Sacrifice? She held up her hands again. "Fine. Fine. Then tell me this, *Daddy*. What did you give them? A negotiation is about give-and-take. What did *you* give? What was your *sacrifice*?"

"I can't answer that question either."

Outrage blasted her. "Can't or won't?"

"It's the same thing, Sadie. You're alive because I did what I did. Please, let that be enough."

Her cell vibrated in her pocket before she could say anything else. She dragged it out with the intention of stopping the damned distraction, but Falco's face flashed on the screen. She crammed the device against her ear. "What?"

"We need your help. Tori is missing. We think she's with Alice. We just pulled up at the Cortez house."

Worry sloshed over her fury, dousing it as surely as water pouring onto a fire. "I'm on my way."

Sadie shoved the phone back into her pocket and glared at her father. "I will have the answers to my questions." She turned and headed for the shitty yellow car parked at the curb.

"Sadie!"

Despite her best efforts to ignore him, she couldn't. She turned back and waited for him to impart whatever the hell fatherly wisdom or asshole warning he had on his mind.

"If you continue down this path, I fear I won't be able to protect you. I've done all I can."

A new rush of outrage detonated inside her. "This time, I'd rather take care of myself."

Then she was gone. Devlin and Falco needed her.

She stared one last time at her father before squealing tires as she peeled away from the curb.

She would have the truth. If it was the last thing she did.

41

8:45 a.m.

Birmingport Road
Birmingham

Tori peeked out the crack left by the partially open door. She couldn't see Alice. Couldn't hear her either. But she couldn't have gone far. There was nothing out here but woods and these old warehouses.

And the maintenance shed, according to the sign on the door, where Alice had left Tori.

She glanced around the room. At least there were lights. There were big electrical boxes and all sorts of tools and a commercial-size riding mower.

Tori glanced out once more. She should make a run for it. She should have refused to get out of the car when they'd first arrived.

But she'd been afraid. What if she'd done that and Sarah really was in trouble?

Alice had told Tori to wait here and she would bring Sarah to her. Tori waited.

What she needed to do now was find a weapon to protect herself.

A thump had Tori spinning around.

The hum of whatever mechanical things were running was the only sound.

"Alice?" she dared to whisper.

What if Alice had just brought her here to play a trick on her?

Or to kill her. She'd probably try to make it look like Tori had killed herself. Then they could all blame Brendal's death on her.

"Alice!" Anger burned inside Tori. She wasn't getting away with this.

Fear abruptly coiled around Tori's chest. What if it was Sarah and she was injured? Or someone else?

"Sarah?"

More thumping and what sounded like rustling.

Tori listened, focused on pinpointing where exactly the sounds were coming from.

The rustling and thumping increased. The door of a tall locker-like cabinet moved. Tori held her breath and eased toward the locker. Her heart thudded harder and harder, rising in her throat as if it might pop like an overinflated balloon.

She touched the door. It moved.

Tori jumped back.

The next sound she heard was a moan-like scream. As if someone were trying to scream with their mouth full . . .

"Sarah?" Tori grabbed for the door again. She tried to open it, but it wouldn't budge. The sounds on the other side grew more frantic.

She tugged harder at the latch. Then she realized she needed to push down the latch and slide it sideways.

The locking mechanism released.

The door sprang open.

A bundle fell out onto the floor.

Long blonde hair. Pink tee. Jeans.

The smell of urine and feces.

Tori blinked and stared at the sobbing girl.

Not Sarah.

Blonde girl, around Tori's age. She'd wet and soiled herself. There was a cloth stuffed into her mouth. Her hands were tied behind her back. She lay on her side, whimpering and rocking.

Emotions spinning inside her, Tori stared at her. Why didn't she stand up?

Then Tori spotted the reason. Her hands were tied to her ankles. Knees bent. She was tied up like one of those calves in rodeos.

"I'll get you loose." Tori knelt beside her. The girl was sobbing now. The ropes were made of nylon and tied really tight. "I need scissors or a knife."

Tori shot to her feet and searched the shed. She didn't find scissors, but she did find a large metal tool that looked kind of like scissors. She thought she had seen a neighbor trimming bushes with something like this.

Might work.

Tori rushed back to the girl. "Hold still."

It took some maneuvering to get the rope between the cutting blades without hurting the girl. Finally when the tool was in place, she squeezed the handles together. Nothing happened. She squeezed harder, gritted her teeth.

What if this didn't work?

Alice could be back any moment.

The rope snapped. Tori set the tool aside and pulled as much of the rope away as possible. She needed to cut one more section. The one around her ankles.

With her hands free, the girl reached for her face and pulled at the cloth in her mouth. Tori snapped the rope holding her ankles together.

The girl scrambled away.

Tori placed the tool back on the floor. She glanced at the door. Hoped Alice didn't walk in for a few more minutes.

"Who tied you up here?"

The girl's eyes were wild as if she'd turned feral.

"What's your name?" Tori asked.

She stared at Tori. It was at that moment Tori recognized her.

Violet Redmond. The missing student from Walker Academy. Her face was all over the news and the internet.

"Oh my God. Are you okay, Violet?"

"Help me," the girl whispered, her voice rusty.

Realization of the situation flashed in her brain. Tori rushed to Violet, grabbed her hand. "We have to get out of here."

They moved to the door. Violet stumbled a couple of times. Probably from being cramped up in that cabinet for two days. Tori eased the door open enough to check outside. She didn't see Alice or anyone else.

"Come on." Holding Violet's hand tightly in hers, Tori led the way from the shed toward the road. The driver had turned off Birmingport Road and driven down a fairly long drive that ended at these warehouses. If they could make it to the main road, they might be able to flag down a car.

"What're you doing?"

Tori froze. Violet started to sob.

Alice.

Tori turned around, ushered Violet behind her. "We're leaving," she announced.

Alice smiled. She waved the big knife in her hand. "No you're not. You two are my only loose ends. I have to take care of you. If you run, I'll just have my grandfather send his soldiers to kill you."

Was the threat more of Alice's tales about being a princess? Tori reached behind her, grabbed Violet by the arm, and pulled her closer. She whispered over her shoulder. "Run to the road. I'll stall her, and then I'll run in the other direction. Don't stop running until you find help."

Violet whimpered.

"Run," Tori growled.

Violet tore away.

Alice started after her.

Tori rushed toward Alice. Threw her full body weight against her shoulder.

They slammed down onto the asphalt.

42

9:00 a.m.

Cortez Residence
Eleventh Avenue South
Birmingham

Kerri had called the LT. He'd issued an endangered child alert and sent Sykes and Peterson to the Cortez residence.

Kerri couldn't help remembering how he'd put her off about issuing an alert when Amelia was missing. But Tori was younger than Amelia had been at the time. Still, Kerri was fairly certain the LT remembered making that decision.

Pushing the thoughts away, Kerri centered her attention back on the woman who refused to answer her or the other detectives' questions. She'd finally begun to talk when Falco had threatened to arrest her.

"My husband went looking for Alice as soon as he realized she was missing. He hasn't returned or called, so I am sure he is still looking and contacting her friends' parents."

"Funny," Kerri said, her voice tight, "he hasn't checked with me."

The woman picked up her cell phone from the coffee table and called her husband again.

Falco held up his hands in a let's-take-it-down-a-notch manner. "She's talking," he said in an aside to Kerri. "Let's be grateful for that."

Kerri bit her lips together. It was difficult to be grateful at the moment. She had called Tori's cell phone repeatedly, but it just kept going to voice mail. She should have put that tracking app on her daughter's phone, but she'd never worried that she would need it. Tori never got into trouble . . . she was a good kid. Trustworthy.

Jesus Christ, she needed her little girl to be okay.

Sykes sidled up next to Kerri. "Peterson is giving Foster a call to have him put the school's weekend guards on alert. It's possible they may have gone there. We've also got people watching the hospital where the Talley girl is."

Kerri nodded. "Thanks." She should have thought of those moves herself.

Goddamn it.

She'd called Diana and Jen and had them checking with everyone they knew. The twins were surfing social media. Robby was driving around the neighborhood.

And Kerri was standing here doing nothing with no idea where to go next.

The door opened, and Peterson swaggered back inside. On his heels was Sadie Cross.

She walked straight to Kerri and looked her dead in the eyes. "If you can clear the room, I'd like to talk to Mrs. Cortez alone."

Kerri looked from Sykes, who was watching the two of them, to Falco. "We need to step outside a moment."

Falco gave her a nod and executed an about-face and strode straight to the door. Sykes and Peterson shared a look and did the same. When the door had closed behind the men, Kerri nodded to Sadie and walked out.

"Whatever happens in there," Peterson warned, "is on you, Devlin."

Falco backhanded him on the shoulder. "Shut the fuck up, Peterson."

Sykes swallowed hard, the movement visible along his throat. "He's right. Shut up, Peterson."

A minute ticked by. Then another. Kerri felt ready to explode. The sound of sobbing seeped past the front door, and Kerri wasn't sure she could take it.

The door suddenly opened, and Sadie exited the house. Cora Cortez lingered in the open doorway. Other than being shaken, she looked unharmed.

Relief trickled inside Kerri. "What did she tell you?"

"She thinks they went to the warehouse where her husband works. He called her right before you came and said he was going there next."

"Let's go," Kerri urged.

"What'd you do, Cross?" Sykes demanded as the whole group headed for the street. "Threaten her life. Jesus."

Cross glared at him. "I just told her that I knew who she and her husband really are and that I would use that information if she didn't cooperate."

Sykes watched Sadie round the yellow VW. "Who the hell are they?" he demanded.

Sadie didn't answer. She climbed into her vehicle and drove away.

Kerri and Falco loaded into his Charger and did the same.

Kerri's cell vibrated. Dispatch appeared on the screen. "Devlin."

"Detective Devlin, I'm patching a Junior Ridley through to you. He's an Uber driver who says he has information about the alert on Tori."

Kerri's heart thumped as she thanked the dispatcher and waited for the call to be connected.

"Hello?"

"Mr. Ridley, this is Detective Kerri Devlin."

Ridley explained that he had picked up two girls. One girl kept referring to the other one as Tori. He described the two girls and how that by the time he reached the drop-off point, he felt as if something wasn't quite right.

"Where was the drop-off point?"

He gave the address and the time of the drop. Kerri thanked him and ended the call.

"What the woman told Cross was right," she told Falco. He glanced at her. "An Uber driver dropped Alice and Tori off at the warehouses an hour ago."

Falco floored the accelerator.

Kerri didn't have to say the rest.

A lot could happen in an hour.

43

9:50 a.m.

Taylor Warehouses
Birmingport Road
Birmingham

As they reached the end of the long drive, Kerri spotted a dark sedan and the black SUV in the parking lot already.

The Escalade Kerri recognized. It belonged to Cortez.

"Who the hell is that?" she muttered, more to herself than anyone else.

"Looks like the mayor's car."

Kerri scowled. Falco was right. The license plate read: WARREN1. "Why would the mayor be here?" She thought again of the mayor's *personal* involvement in this case and the similarities between her early years and those of Alice Cortez. Was she attempting to save this girl Alice or save face?

The idea that there was more nudged at Kerri.

The Charger had scarcely stopped moving, and she was climbing out. She all but ran toward the maintenance building, where a door stood open. Falco caught up with her by the time she reached the entrance.

Kerri drew up short as Mayor Emma Warren emerged, Cortez right behind her.

"Where is Tori?" Kerri demanded.

Warren stalled for a single moment. "Tori? Excuse me, Detective . . . ? Why are you here?"

"That's a good question," Falco said, "for you, Mayor."

She blinked once, twice. "I'm here with Mr. Cortez."

Cortez stared but kept his mouth shut.

"He believes Alice has run away from home, and since she is the student I'm personally mentoring, I felt compelled to assist him. She's been very upset since the Myers tragedy."

Falco glanced around the parking area. "Where's your driver? Your security?"

Warren's perfectly polished facade cracked just a little, showed a flash of frustration. "Again, why are you two here?"

Sykes's car rolled into the lot. Cross followed in the yellow Beetle.

"My daughter, Tori, is missing," Kerri said. "She was last seen with Alice Cortez. An Uber driver brought them here."

Cortez said something in Spanish to Warren. She ignored him, but recognition registered in her eyes. She understood.

"Let's get out of this doorway," Warren suggested, stepping forward and forcing Kerri and Falco to back away.

Determined to get inside, Kerri walked around the obstacle the two made and entered the maintenance shed.

Warren called out something about a warrant, but Kerri ignored her. She didn't bother explaining that they had exigent circumstances. Warren was an attorney; she knew this.

Nylon ropes and a wrinkled cloth lay on the floor. Judging by the short strips of nylon rope, someone had been bound with it. Fury knotted in Kerri's gut. She stormed back out just in time to see Sykes and Peterson marching toward the first of the three warehouses.

Cortez hustled after them, shouting about the need for a warrant. At the door, Sykes paused long enough to say, "Exigent circumstances, my friend. A child is missing, and this was her last known location."

Grateful tears welled in Kerri's eyes. She had to find her daughter. She started toward the second of the three warehouses. Warren ordered Falco to call the chief of police.

Cortez rushed back to the mayor, speaking in Spanish to her once more. This time Warren responded in kind. Her tone was far from the mesmerizing, sophisticated one she generally used. Instead it verged on feral and was filled with warning, the cadence clipped. As her volume and the intensity of her voice rose, the words obviously grew increasingly threatening.

Sadie Cross moved up beside Falco, her head canted as if she were deciphering the exchange between Cortez and Warren. Considering her past undercover work, she probably was. She no doubt had an excellent command of the language they were using.

Kerri told herself to move, to hurry into the waiting warehouse . . . Tori was here somewhere, but something—call it intuition—held her frozen in place. She couldn't stop staring at the woman she'd watched charm the city with her benevolence and brilliance . . . the one she had admired so much.

Warren abruptly stopped speaking. She stared at Sadie.

"I know your voice," Sadie said, her tone accusing.

Her expression icy cold, Warren demanded, "And who are you?"

Cortez ran for his SUV.

"You were part of Carlos Osorio's organization. You were the one . . ."—Sadie took a step toward the mayor—"the one who gave the orders."

Falco, his phone clutched to his ear, fell silent.

"Are you insane?" Warren demanded; she glanced around. "Who is this woman?"

"You're the one," Sadie said, her voice dark with rage. "The one Walsh was looking for. The power—here—who supports the cartel." She nodded. "Just now"—she pointed a finger at the other woman—"when you snapped orders at your minion . . . not the cultured, smooth voice you use to hide behind. This voice . . . *this* is the real you."

A scream echoed in the morning air, reverberating from the woods and between the buildings until the sound pierced Kerri's very soul. "Tori!" Her heart flailed helplessly in her chest.

Kerri bolted toward the woods, in the direction of the sound.

By the time she reached the tree line, Falco was racing ahead of her. Kerri shouted her daughter's name. A responding cry of "Mom" rang out.

Kerri ran faster, her pulse pounding in time with her frantic pace.

The roar of the river in the distance seemed to muffle all else. Blood roaring in her ears, Kerri paused to listen for anything else from her daughter.

Where was she?

Please, please, please let her be okay.

"This way!"

Kerri jerked toward the sound of Falco's voice. He lunged deeper into the woods, straight for the river.

The underbrush slapped at her legs, but Kerri didn't slow. She darted between and around trees. "Tori!"

"Mom!"

Kerri's brain instantly analyzed her daughter's voice. *Terror. Extreme agitation.*

Was she okay? Kerri spotted her then. Ten . . . fifteen yards ahead. Her daughter stood among the waist-deep underbrush, her face pale, her body shaking like a leaf fluttering in an icy wind.

Falco reached Tori first.

He dropped to his knees, and the fear already strangling Kerri tightened like a vise. Was Tori injured? Kerri couldn't see any blood. She lunged faster through the brush.

She pushed past Falco and threw her arms around her daughter. "Are you okay?"

Tori sobbed so hard Kerri could barely understand the confirmation that she was okay. She ran her hands over her daughter's arms and legs, her slim waist, and shuddering chest. "You're sure you're not injured."

The relief rushing through Kerri almost undid her.

"I'm okay." Tori stared down at where Falco still crouched. "She was going to kill me."

Kerri spotted dark hair tangled in the bushes. The air fled her lungs. She leaned to one side to see beyond Falco.

Alice Cortez.

Was she hurt? A knife lay next to her, but there was no blood.

"She was chasing me with the knife and she fell," Tori cried. "She hit her head on that log. She won't wake up."

Kerri pulled her daughter close. "You're okay now." What the hell happened out here?

Tori drew back, stared up at her mother. "Violet was here too. The girl from Walker Academy. She was tied up in that shed. Alice was going to kill her too."

"She's breathing," Falco muttered, then pulled out his cell and called for paramedics.

Alice moved a little, moaned. She was alive.

Pulse racing, Kerri searched Tori's tearstained face. "Where is Violet?"

"I told her to run for the highway and look for help." Tori's thin body shook harder. "It was the only thing I knew to do."

Kerri hadn't seen anyone on the highway. She pulled her daughter in close again, trying to soothe her quaking body. "Don't worry. We'll find her."

She closed her eyes to hold back her own tears. Her girl was okay. She was really okay. *Thank God. Thank God. Thank God.*

Falco's arms came around them. "It'll be okay now," he murmured.

Falco carried Alice out of the woods. Following, Kerri held tight to Tori.

They reached the lot and the warehouses, and more official vehicles had arrived. Kerri spotted Brooks, her LT, and several uniforms. Cortez was being cuffed and loaded into a cruiser. A young blonde girl was talking to a female uni.

"Violet!" Tori tore out of her mother's arms and ran toward the other girl.

Kerri managed to keep herself upright and moving forward. All three girls were alive. The sense of relief was very nearly overpowering.

The next person Kerri spotted was the chief of police. She remembered then that the mayor had ordered Falco to call him. Cross's accusation rang in Kerri's ears. If Cross was right . . .

Kerri searched the crowd for Cross, found her at the fringes of the ongoing activity. She looked shaken and alone—totally un-Cross-like. With a glance toward Tori to see that she was still okay, Kerri adjusted her course to intersect with where the other woman lingered.

"What's going on?" Kerri asked when she stood next to Sadie.

"The chief is here to escort the mayor to his office," Cross said, her voice oddly flat.

"Does this mean they believe you?" Not that Kerri didn't, but Cross was an ex-cop with a troubled history, and Warren was the mayor with a stellar record. Even Kerri had started to consider that the mayor might be somehow involved with all this. But all she had were suspicions, no hard evidence.

Sadie shrugged and shifted her attention to Kerri. "I don't know. Maybe. The chief didn't say."

"Wow. This is . . ." Kerri shook her head. She was too physically and mentally exhausted to say or do more. "I'll catch up with you later. I have to be with my daughter."

Two ambulances arrived. One took Alice Cortez, along with a female officer. The other took Violet Redmond and another officer.

The LT had already notified the Redmond family that their daughter had been found.

The chief left with the mayor.

At the moment, for Kerri, all that mattered was that her daughter was safe.

44

4:30 p.m.

Birmingham Police Department
First Avenue North

Sadie slid behind the wheel of Heck's shitty yellow car. She'd been forced to spend the past five-plus hours at the BPD, giving her statement and being interrogated.

Some uptight asshole from the DEA had spent more than an hour questioning her about her father. She learned her father had turned himself in this morning. No one would tell her what the charges consisted of, but she understood it was about his involvement with the Osorio cartel. She had no idea what level of involvement or when this involvement had occurred.

Sadie dug for her pack of smokes and lit one. If she was really lucky, she'd get the truth about what had happened to her during all those months. Maybe Warren would want a deal for whatever part she had played in supporting the cartel. If her role was as vital as Asher had suspected of the source of power in Birmingham, the woman would know many things. Maybe the fallen Mason Cross would finally tell Sadie everything he knew. Apparently, he'd shown up at the chief of police's door early this morning, shortly after Sadie's visit to him, and had started talking.

Sadie suspected her father or Warren, maybe both, knew a hell of a lot more than he or she had admitted so far.

Before this was over, Sadie intended to know the rest of the story.

It would be her luck the whole damned thing would be labeled *need to know* and no one would believe she had the need.

The best news was that Carlos Osorio was being interrogated in Mexico right now. The DEA in a joint op with Mexican authorities had raided his compound a few hours ago.

The Osorio family was done.

This was the extent of what Sadie had been told. She suspected her father had somehow been instrumental in the raid down south. Or maybe she just wanted to believe he had done one last good thing.

The saddest part, she decided, was not knowing who had killed Asher. He and Leo Kurtz deserved justice too.

Sadie made up her mind then and there that she wouldn't let the case go until she had uncovered the last of the dirty secrets. Put the final pieces together. Devlin and Falco wouldn't let it go either. She could count on those two.

She turned into the alley at her place, noting the overflowing crowd already lining up for happy hour at the pub. She planned on having her own happy hour just as soon as she'd taken a nice, long shower. Limit two beers, though. No more hard stuff. She glanced at the cigarette pack. Maybe she'd even give those up.

If she was going to get happy with staying alive, she might as well make the most of it. "One step at a time," she mumbled.

As she braked to a stop next to her fire escape, she spotted a woman sitting on the rusty metal steps. She looked vaguely familiar.

Sadie parked and climbed out. She grabbed another smoke and lit it as she walked toward the waiting stranger. She'd quit smoking tomorrow. Step one had to be the hard liquor.

"Sadie."

The woman's identity registered then. *Lana Walsh.* To say Asher's mother showing up like this after everything that had happened today was odd would be the understatement of the decade.

There were still a lot of unknowns about this woman. Sadie wouldn't trust her until she knew all the answers.

Maybe she never would.

Lana Walsh stood. "Coming here was a bit of an impulsive decision. Perhaps not a good one."

Wary, Sadie paused a few feet away. "What can I do for you?"

Asher's mother was attractive, far prettier than her more practical sister. The trouble was she didn't seem to be as nice as Naomi. Naomi had plenty to say about her, none of it good. Asher had never spoken badly of her, but he hadn't really mentioned her a lot. And she hadn't visited him. That was the part that bugged the shit out of Sadie. What kind of mother did that? And if she hadn't been coming to Birmingham to see her son, what the hell had she been doing here, and how the hell had she concealed her activities so carefully that even Sadie couldn't find her out?

"Asher liked you. More than a little, I think." Lana smiled at Sadie. Didn't seem to notice that Sadie looked like hell, wearing the same clothes she'd had on yesterday and without a shower. Or that she didn't trust her one little bit. *Or* like her, for that matter.

"He was a good guy." Sadie took a deep breath, ignored the desire for a drink of something stronger than beer. She wasn't going there ever again. Instead, she sucked on her smoke.

"He trusted you."

Sadie was relatively certain that was correct. He might not have shared everything with her, but Asher had his reasons.

"I want the person responsible for his death to be brought to justice, and I'm terrified that isn't going to happen."

Sadie didn't bother telling her that if his death involved the Osorio cartel, then the person responsible—Carlos Osorio himself—might already be going down. Then again, maybe she was wrong. Maybe this woman was the one who'd given the order. Or soon-to-be ex-mayor Warren? Maybe it was McGill, though Sadie highly doubted that one.

"Asher believed what I had suspected for years," Lana went on when Sadie said nothing. "His father and Naomi are involved. An affair, I think. But Asher wouldn't tell me if he'd confirmed as much since moving to Birmingham. I didn't want the idea to consume his life as it has mine, but I'm convinced he knew far more than he was telling me."

Whoa. Okay. The lady had Sadie's attention now. "He never mentioned anything about this to me. He didn't talk about his father often, and, for the record, he was really close to his aunt."

"He didn't want to believe she would betray me," Lana admitted, "but I'm certain of it. Either way, I fear Asher was determined to find the truth if for no other reason than to reassure me in the event he discovered I was wrong. I confronted Lee about my suspicions yesterday, and he walked out. I haven't seen him since. I've driven by Naomi's, but his car isn't there. He isn't answering his cell. God only knows where he is. Maybe he went back to Boston, but no one at his office or the house has seen him."

Her voice sounded so weary, so sad.

Maybe she was telling the truth. Maybe her husband was involved with someone else. But it couldn't be Naomi.

"There were things Asher didn't tell me. I guess this was one of them." Sadie had been aware he'd kept certain things from her. She just hadn't expected it to be so personal. This lady wasn't sharing everything either. Sadie recognized the tactic. She didn't meet Sadie's eyes for more than a moment. She kept her points vague rather than going into detail. But then, who did share everything? It was a self-defense mechanism. Survival instinct.

"I think," Lana ventured, "Asher believed his father was involved in something more than simply an affair with my estranged sister."

She dared to meet Sadie's gaze. "I could be wrong, and God, I hope I am, but this was the impression Asher gave me. He would never say as much, but I knew my son, Sadie. I believe he had found more. Far more. If this is true, I don't want the bastard to get away with whatever it is. I'm certain Asher is dead because he felt that way too." Her lips trembled as she fell silent.

Her words took Sadie aback. "Are you suggesting your husband was—is involved in something illegal, and this involvement is somehow relevant to Asher's murder?" Sadie was relatively certain she hadn't misunderstood.

"Whatever my husband is doing, I know in my heart he is the reason Asher is dead."

Sadie thought about the way the woman had looked when her husband had stood next to the mayor, offering that big reward. Did she have an actual reason for hating her husband so much? Would Asher's father really kill his own son? Or was the mother trying to play Sadie?

Sadie had a few questions. Now was as good a time as any to ask them, particularly if the woman wanted something from her. "Why have you been coming to Birmingham for a day or two once a month for more than a year?"

Lana was the one who looked taken aback now.

"If you expect me to be up front with you, you need to be up front with me," Sadie warned.

Lana nodded. "Fair enough. In January of last year I discovered my husband had been coming to Birmingham in his private jet each month for ages." She smiled at the subtle lift in Sadie's eyebrows. "Yes, he has one of those. He thinks I don't know, but I do. I couldn't imagine why he would come to Alabama. He never had anything good to say about it when the subject came up, especially after Asher accepted the position here."

"You suspected he was coming to see Naomi." The idea was totally ridiculous. Naomi hated the guy.

"I believe so. I tried to catch them, but I wasn't successful, so I hired a private investigator. You must have known him, Pauley Winters. He died about this time last year. His office was here." She gestured to the loft above them. "He was a truly nice man."

Sadie couldn't respond immediately. Pauley had worked for this lady? For Asher's mother? Why were there no notes in his files? Why hadn't Sadie known?

"The last time I heard from Mr. Winters," Lana went on, "he left a message on my cell phone, saying we needed to talk. This was the same day he died. I believe my husband had something to do with his death."

Sadie snapped out of the shock. She shook her head. "Pauley died of a heart attack."

"You did know him."

"Yeah . . . he was . . . yes."

"Then you know he was the best."

Sadie did know. She also knew that he'd died of a heart attack . . . and that he hadn't told her about or left any files related to a Lana Walsh case.

Focus, Sadie. She cleared her throat. "You have to understand, Mrs. Walsh, whatever your husband has been doing, I consider Naomi a friend. I can't see her doing this."

Okay, so maybe that wasn't entirely true. Naomi might engage in an affair with her sister's husband just to get even. But Sadie wasn't ready to go there.

Lana pursed her lips and gave a single nod. "I understand." She seemed to consider for a moment what she would say next. "I would ask that you do something—not for me, but for Asher."

Still reeling with the bombshell that Pauley may have been working with this woman, Sadie managed an "All right."

"Look into my theory. Objectively, if you can. If I'm wrong, then I'm wrong. But I want justice for my son. If it means anything to you, Pauley—Mr. Winters—believed me. I also believe my son had documented whatever Lee was involved in beyond an affair with Naomi. I know Asher kept a file. I just have no idea where. But I am absolutely certain whatever it is, my son was killed because of it. I went to the trouble of hiring someone to search Naomi's home in case it was there, but he failed to find anything."

So she was the one who had hired Darius. "How did you find the man you hired to do the search?"

"Pauley introduced me to him once." She shook her head. "I don't know why I kept his number all this time. He certainly proved useless."

Few people knew about Darius. Her father and Pauley were two who did. This knowledge lent some credibility to her story. Possibly. "All right, you have my word; I will look into your theory. Objectively and thoroughly."

"Thank you." Lana opened her purse and fished around. When she closed it again, she held out a card. "Call me when you find the truth. If you're half as good as my son believed you were, you will find it."

Sadie accepted the card with the woman's name and number on it, then watched her walk away. When Lana Walsh's car had disappeared in the distance, Sadie pulled out her cell and called Snipes. "Hey, you got anything on that thumb drive yet?"

"I'm working on it. This one is a little more complicated. Someone didn't want anyone to get their hands on whatever is on this one."

"Call me the minute you break in."

"Will do."

Sadie ended the call. When she'd worked up the nerve, she climbed the stairs and locked herself away in her loft. Even though she'd been through the place a dozen times and had rifled through Pauley's files even more often, she intended to go through them again.

If Pauley believed the woman . . . how could Sadie not?

She surveyed the loft. If she had to tear this place apart, she would find whatever notes Pauley had made.

There had to be something here.

45

5:30 p.m.

Birmingham Police Department
First Avenue North

Kerri glanced at Falco once more as they waited for the LT to begin. He had called them to his office as soon as the dust settled.

In truth, Kerri couldn't be sure at this point if both she and Falco were about to be suspended. She'd already been on leave. She had been too busy to consider exactly what lines they might have crossed and exactly how much trouble they were in.

"Well," Brooks announced, "it looks as if—"

"This is on me," Kerri blurted. "Falco was only doing what I asked him to do. I'm the senior detective. It's my responsibility."

Falco stared at her. She didn't have to turn her head to know. She felt his gaze burning into her.

The LT frowned. "As much as I would love to hear whatever it is you're referring to, Detective, it's late. I'm sure we'd all rather just wrap this day up and go home."

Kerri's stiff posture deflated. She hunkered down into her chair and kept her mouth shut. She might as well prepare for the worst.

Thankfully, whatever happened, Tori was safe and had been completely cleared of anything related to Brendal Myers's death.

At this point, the Myers case was basically closed. Alice Cortez hadn't admitted anything yet, but Sarah Talley had confirmed all that Tori had been saying from the onset. The statement from Violet Redmond helped to prove Alice was involved with the trouble at Walker as well. Contact hadn't been made with the school head from Walker just yet. Sykes and Peterson were on top of locating Billings. In the meanwhile, José Cortez's testimony had backed up Violet's. As it turned out, Cortez and his wife had paid a hefty price for their involvement with Alice. He insisted they had lived in fear of her for the past nine months. There was no question at this point about who had done what.

The court would assign Alice an attorney and guardian ad litem.

As for the Cortez family and Alice, whatever had brought them together fell within the DEA's purview. The information had not been shared with the BPD at this time. Alice was, apparently, the granddaughter of Carlos Osorio—who had been taken into custody today. As for the mayor, her connection had not been clarified—at least not as far as Kerri knew. She imagined some sort of deal was being made before details—if any—were released.

For Kerri and Tori, the nightmare was over.

"I called you into my office," the LT went on, yanking Kerri back to the here-and-now, "to commend you for your excellent work on the Myers case. Sykes and Peterson have given most of the credit in solving the case to the two of you. I am certain the parents of children from both schools, Brighton and Walker, will be grateful as well. Not only did you help to resolve the Brighton Academy situation; you shed new light on what really happened at Walker. The department, the city, owes you a debt of gratitude. I'm certain there will be more coming on this for the two of you as well as for Sykes and Peterson."

Kerri shared a look with Falco. "Thank you, sir," they said simultaneously.

Brooks nodded. "As for the Walsh-Kurtz investigation, the two of you will continue working with the task force. However, in light of certain new insights, you will be lead. I trust that you'll solve this case in the same thorough and speedy manner."

"Yes, sir," Kerri assured him.

"Absolutely," Falco echoed.

"Good." Brooks stood, fastened his jacket, and gave a nod. "Excellent work, Detectives. I'll see you on Monday."

Kerri pushed to her feet. Falco did the same. They both thanked the LT and filed out of his office.

In a sort of shock, they descended the stairs and headed into the parking lot. The LT was right. It was late. Kerri couldn't wait to celebrate with Tori and the family. The nightmare was over.

At the door to Falco's Charger, Kerri hesitated. "I want to do something with the family tonight to celebrate. You up for dinner with my crew?"

He smiled at her over the top of the car. "Always."

Kerri really liked seeing that smile. "I think I need another vacation after this."

They got into the car. Falco started the engine. "Damn. You read my mind. I was just thinking I needed one."

Kerri hummed a sound of acknowledgment. "Yeah. A vacation sounds really good."

Really, really good.

46

Sunday, April 18

8:15 a.m.

Sadie's Loft
Sixth Avenue, Twenty-Seventh Street
Birmingham

The pounding on her door forced Sadie off the sofa. She'd heard the notification that someone had approached the fire escape and then the second notification that whoever the hell it was had started up the rusty metal steps. But she hadn't wanted to move. Not even her eyelids.

She'd been up until five this morning searching, digging through papers.

She stood. Swayed for a bit until she found her bearings.

"Cross, it's Snipes. Open the fucking door."

The concept that Snipes had what she needed prodded her into action. She staggered to the door and unlocked all the dead bolts. Pulled the door inward.

"Holy shit." Snipes made a face. "You look like hell."

Sadie blew out a breath. "Feel like it. No sleep."

Snipes made a knowing face. "You need coffee and a shower."

Sadie held up a finger. "Coffee I can do. The shower will have to be later, when I'm feeling reasonably human."

She turned and launched herself toward the counter, where the coffeepot waited to revive her. The sound of the door closing confirmed that Snipes had let himself in.

"What'd you find?" She asked this while going through the steps to load the machine that would ultimately resuscitate her.

Snipes laid a stack of spreadsheets and the thumb drive on the counter. "Lots of numbers and dates. I don't know what any of it means, but there it is." He tapped the stack. "Enjoy."

The scent of brewing coffee awakened a few more of her senses. He was halfway across the room before she managed, "Hey. Thanks, man."

He waved without looking back.

Sadie shuffled to the door, closed it behind him, and engaged the four dead bolts. As much as she despised the idea, she headed for the bathroom. A hot shower would help clear her head. By the time she was finished, the coffee would be ready.

She peeled off her clothes on the way, leaving them wherever they fell. While the shower spewed out cold water, she took a piss. Once the steam started to fill the tiny room, she climbed into the thirty-two-inch-by-thirty-two-inch shower stall and leaned against the plastic wall while the water pummeled her body.

Why was it that everyone she cared about ended up dead?

The whole thing had started with her mother. Cancer had taken her and left Sadie with her coldhearted father. Who was currently being held for whatever the hell he'd done. She could only imagine. Apparently, he'd had some affiliation with the Osorio cartel and had made a bargain for her release. No doubt whatever he'd given in return for her release was official information that made him a traitor to the DEA. That would be the sacrifice he'd mentioned, she suspected. If she was a really good daughter, she would pretend her gallant father had crossed the line only to save his only daughter. But that was bullshit, and she knew it.

Whatever line he'd crossed, he'd done so for himself. Not just for her.

She had spent most of her life trying unsuccessfully to impress him for reasons a dozen shrinks would never be able to help her understand.

Then there was Eddie. He'd really loved her. She had known it, which made her screwed-up life even more complicated, considering she had killed him.

Don't kill her . . . think of the child.

She never allowed the baby she had lost to enter her head beyond a fleeting thought. She could never go there. Ever.

Then there was Pauley. The idea that someone could possibly be responsible for his death made her want to scream murderously.

No matter how unrealistic she deemed the possibility, she would be looking into it. The autopsy lab work had confirmed the medication Pauley had been prescribed for his heart had not been present, which meant he hadn't been taking it. This was the reason he'd had the fatal heart attack. She wasn't an idiot. There were ways to make that happen without Pauley being the one responsible. Fury tightened her lips. She'd never once considered it. Pauley was like her. He'd more often than not allowed work to blind him to everything else . . . even taking care of himself.

But now she had reason to believe his death might not have been that simple.

Knowing the coffee would be waiting for her by now, she ran the soap over her body and even managed to shampoo her hair. When she shut off the water, she realized she'd forgotten a towel.

"Shit."

She walked out of the bathroom, dripping water as she went. She needed that coffee. *Now.*

The first eight ounces she sucked down burned her tongue and scalded her throat. She didn't care. Another cup followed. Three were required before she no longer cared if the world ended.

When she'd dried her skin and hair, and pulled on clothes, she picked up the spreadsheets and had a look. Lots of columns, representing dollars. Lots of dates, representing what appeared to be deliveries. Everything seemed to involve two individuals or entities.

"Who the hell are Iris and Harvard?"

She picked up her cell and the card lying next to it and called Lana Walsh. The woman finally answered after the third ring. "Hello."

Judging by the devastation in that one word, she had been crying. "This is Sadie Cross. Did your husband show up?"

There was a sniff, and then the other woman cleared her throat. "No. I was just on my way out the door to file a missing person report." She exhaled a shaky breath. "At this point it's the only thing I know to do."

"You should," Sadie agreed. The urge to ask her about this Iris and Harvard burned on her tongue, but the jury was still out on the lady. Better to work it out with someone she trusted. "I'll . . . ah . . . call when I have something to share."

Besides, she had an idea already about both Iris and Harvard.

Devlin Residence
Twenty-First Avenue South
Birmingham, 9:50 a.m.

Sadie wasn't surprised to see Falco's Charger at Devlin's house. The two were partners and friends, maybe closer than either of them realized. Devlin had gone through hell the past few days. Not to mention some screwed-up shit the past year. If anyone deserved a strong shoulder to lean on, it was her.

Falco was a good guy.

For the most part.

Sadie knocked on the door and waited. She hadn't called before coming. It was a bad habit of hers. She liked catching people off guard even when it wasn't necessary. Responses were more honest when a person wasn't expecting whatever showed up.

As she knocked again, she considered that some scumbag attorney had called and left her a voice mail saying her father wanted to see her and permission had been granted for her to visit him today. Sadie rolled her eyes. Like she wanted to bother.

Well, maybe she did. There were questions she needed to ask. For her own peace of mind. If he could fill in more of those missing fragments, she would be relieved if not exactly grateful.

The door finally opened, and Falco gave her a nod. "Hey, Cross. Come on in."

Sadie followed Falco to the kitchen, where Devlin sat at the island drinking coffee.

Devlin gave one of those same nods Falco had given. "Morning."

"Coffee?" This from Falco.

"I'm good." Sadie scooted onto a vacant stool. She placed the envelope holding the folded spreadsheets on the counter. She looked from Falco to Devlin. "The Myers case is closed, I hear."

Most people would probably have asked Devlin how her kid was, but Sadie figured the detective would get around to that in the course of giving her answer to the question asked.

"Sykes and Peterson have some follow-up and reports to finalize, but, yeah, it's pretty much done." Devlin set her mug on the counter. "Billings, the head of the school, came forward this morning and confirmed what Sue Grimes shared with him last year. So, it's over for us, yes."

"Alice Cortez," Falco chimed in, "a.k.a. Isabella Osorio—is the one who caused Brendal Myers to fall down the stairs. She leaned toward the girl, making threats with some crazy chants, and Brendal tried to step back and ultimately fell."

Tension sifted through Sadie. So the kid's identity had been confirmed. "I remember Eddie—Eduardo—saying once that his daughter had behavior problems. Too bad I didn't remember sooner."

Devlin said, "Cora Cortez stated that Isabella had issues. The problems started when she was a child. She killed small animals. Chickens, cats, dogs. She couldn't have pets."

The memory of waking up with a bloody, headless chicken in her bed zoomed into vivid focus in Sadie's head. She flinched and banished the image. That was one piece of her memory she could have done without recalling.

"The problems became so bad they had to send her away," Devlin went on. "Even members of the family's household staff were afraid of her. They called her a witch. Cora Cortez said she had crosses all over her house because she was terrified of Alice. A truly twisted little girl."

Sadie wondered if Eddie could have helped his daughter—if Sadie hadn't killed him. She blinked. *Not going there.*

"Yes," Devlin said, "to answer the question you didn't ask, Tori is fine. It'll take some time to put this behind her, but she'll get there."

Sadie nodded. "Good to hear."

Falco gestured to the envelope. "What's this?"

"My case isn't closed." Sadie opened the envelope. "I still don't know who killed Walsh or his friend, Kurtz."

"Technically, Cross," Falco countered, "the case is ours, and we're still trying to figure that out as well."

Sadie's eyebrows reared up in surprise. "The task force?"

"We're still working with the DEA," Kerri explained, "but this time, we're lead in the homicide portion of the case."

Sadie let her surprise show. "Good to know. Before I forget, I had a visitor last night." As she pressed the folds out of the pages, she brought Devlin and Falco up to speed on Lana Walsh's theory about her husband.

"She gave you the spreadsheets?" Devlin asked.

"No. My computer guy finally hacked his way into the thumb drive I found at Naomi's house where Asher—Walsh had hidden it."

Devlin leaned toward the pages in question. "Did you find anything that will help us with solving the murders?"

"I don't know." Sadie pointed to the columns. "There are lots of numbers, like deposits or transfers and delivery dates." She tapped the headings of the main two columns. "There appears to be only two names associated with whatever all this means. Harvard and Iris."

Falco leaned forward and scanned the top page. "There's the cosmetics company called Iris."

"Ironically the company rents one of Taylor's warehouses," Kerri pointed out. "I doubt that's a coincidence."

"Yeah, that was my first thought," Sadie said. "Both Asher and his father attended Harvard, but I'm certain this is the father."

"The father gets my vote," Falco said.

"Me too," Kerri agreed. "Not that there's really any question."

Sadie allowed a hint of a smile at Devlin's smart-ass remark. "Exactly. So, I called Lana Walsh this morning. Leland Walsh is still missing."

"Is she making an official report?" Falco asked.

"Yeah, she was headed to the BPD when I called. With all that happened yesterday, it's possible Leland Walsh has cut and run—if his wife's theory is on target." She gestured to the pages on the counter. "And if our conclusions on all this are right."

Kerri looked up from her study of the columns. "So, Harvard and Iris are silent partners, and they're using the cosmetics company as a cover for whatever illegal activity they're involved in."

"Like drugs," Falco said. "Cortez worked at the warehouse Iris Cosmetics used. We know he's connected to the cartel. A trusted connection since he was given custody of the granddaughter."

"Has Warren," Sadie interjected, "given up the cosmetics company or anything about the Walsh case? You'd think any large distributor in the area would be a serious bargaining chip for her. Whatever her relationship with the cartel, it had to be influential, powerful. Is she saying anything at all?"

"Not that we've heard," Devlin said. "But with the DEA involved, we could be the last to know."

"You could ask your father," Falco suggested.

Sadie shrugged. "He probably won't tell me, but I can ask. Apparently, he has requested to see me."

"Hold on a sec." Devlin made a face as if she'd just thought of something unexpected. She picked up her cell and started tapping on the screen.

Sadie wished she had eaten something and downed some aspirin. Her head was throbbing with lack of sleep and caffeine overload.

"That's it." Devlin turned her phone around for Sadie and Falco to see the screen.

"You planning some landscaping?" Sadie asked, unimpressed with the blue blooming clumps in the photo Devlin pointed at her.

"Irises," Falco said knowingly.

Devlin nodded. "Taylor's favorite flower. They're blooming all around her house. Maybe the lady is in this for more than just the affair."

Sadie shook her head, making it throb even harder. "Wait. Naomi loved Asher. She wouldn't be involved in this. She's . . ."

A cold, hard reality slugged Sadie, pushing the air out of her lungs. It didn't matter that Naomi claimed to love Asher. Sadie's father claimed to love her. It definitely didn't matter that Naomi presented herself as a good person . . . Sadie's father did the same.

Sadie gasped for a breath. "Holy shit." Her gaze collided with Devlin's. "You could be right."

"We need a warrant for that warehouse," Devlin said as she scooted off her stool. "The search yesterday was for my missing daughter. No one opened packages or boxes prepared for shipping."

"I know just the judge to ask," Falco agreed.

"I've got Naomi," Sadie said, outrage pounding inside her.

"We want her alive," Devlin warned.

"So do I," Sadie assured her. If Devlin's scenario was correct—Sadie wanted Naomi to face her judgment day publicly. What better way to punish an attorney than in a court of law?

Devlin hesitated. "You go," she said to Falco. "I can't leave Tori."

He nodded. "You're right. No problem. I can handle it."

"No."

They all turned toward the newcomer to their party. Tori stood in the doorway.

"I've already called Aunt Diana to come pick me up," the girl said, looking directly at her mother. "Go do your job, Mom. I like it when you get the bad guys."

Sadie grinned. She liked this kid, and she never liked kids.

47

Noon

Taylor Residence
Eighteenth Avenue South
Birmingham

After stopping by her place to pick up her weapon—leaving this morning without it just went to show how out of it she really was—Sadie made a quick phone call to Angelo and confirmed Naomi Taylor's location. Apparently, the woman had left the resort the same day she'd been dropped off.

Obviously Naomi had only been playing along with Sadie. Placating her to avoid suspicion. Naomi hadn't been afraid at all, because she was one of the bad guys.

Outrage boiled inside Sadie.

Ignoring the multitude of blooming irises seemingly mocking her, Sadie knocked on the door. It opened immediately, as if Naomi had been standing on the other side waiting for Sadie's arrival.

Naomi smiled. "Come in," she said, opening the door wider.

Sadie's lips tightened to prevent lashing out at her. She stepped inside. Had to play this right. She wanted the bitch to confess everything. The door closed behind her.

Keep your cool.

Naomi floated past her and toward the living room without a word. Sadie's nose wrinkled at the smell that wafted behind her.

"Are you . . ." Sadie wandered into the living room. "Are you smoking weed?"

Naomi picked up the generously sized joint and took a long drag. She held the smoke deep in her lungs; then, as she exhaled, she said, "I am. So, I'm outed, am I?"

For a moment Sadie wondered if Naomi already realized just how far she'd been outed.

"You are." Sadie took a seat across the coffee table from her. The weapon nestled against the small of her back scrubbed at her bare skin. "You aren't supposed to be here."

"I couldn't stay at that lovely resort," Naomi announced with a big breathy sigh. "Though I do appreciate your thinking of my safety. I was never afraid."

"Yeah. I get that." Sadie removed the thumb drive from her front pocket and tossed it on the table. "I thought you might want this."

Naomi stared at the incredibly small device and laughed. "Well, I'll be damned. I searched this house from top to bottom and never found that thing. I caught Asher with it once, and I knew he had something incriminating hidden on it, but I just couldn't find it."

"I have only one question for you, *Iris*."

Naomi laughed again. Probably the weed.

"Did you kill Asher?"

Shock claimed her face. "Of course not! How could you say such a thing? I loved him."

Images of Asher's smile, his eyes, flashed across Sadie's vision, sparking a powerful need for revenge. "Why don't you tell me who did?"

Naomi carefully tapped out the fire at the end of her joint and settled the remainder on the edge of the ashtray. "I thought Lee had done it."

"His father?" Surprise trickled through Sadie, though it shouldn't have. The bastard apparently had a lot to lose.

"I'm sure you've established the identity of Harvard." Naomi said this with a sort of nonchalance that warned she was as high as a kite.

Sadie nodded. "I never could get right with the whole parent-killing-the-kid thing." Not entirely true but she had to keep the conversation going. Either that or she would put one between the woman's overly dilated pupils here and now.

Devlin would be pissed. She wanted to solve the whole case, not just Asher's murder.

"Please, men like Leland Walsh have no true moral compass behind the facade they present to the rest of the world. He would kill his own mother if necessary."

"The two of you are partners in the distribution game with the Osorio cartel. Asher found out and planned to take you down." No need to beat around the bush.

"Actually, it was Lana who figured out there was something between myself and her husband. But she was never able to catch us. She was never that bright, you know. Frankly, luring her husband into business as well as my bed was quite easy. She thought she'd married into this fine, upstanding family when, in fact, dear old Harvard is as underhanded as they come. As soon as he figured out what I was doing, he wanted a slice of the pie. Helped cultivate new distribution channels all the way to Canada. Everyone was pleased."

"Why would you set out to steal your sister's husband?" Sadie didn't actually care; she was merely curious for the purposes of putting all the pieces together.

"Our mother, God rest her no-good soul, left me here with my father. I put up with his mental abuse my entire life until the COPD killed him. By then I'd considered all sorts of ways to kill him myself, but thankfully I didn't have to. I realized, of course, what mother chose to do was not really Lana's fault. But Lana's decision to take her son—to whom I had grown quite attached—away from me was her fault. She shouldn't have been so cruel. I decided it was only fair that I make her pay for that shameless decision. Oh, and I made her pay in all sorts of ways."

Sadie gritted her teeth and let the woman carry on with her confession. Too bad she hadn't turned on her phone's recorder. Just went to show it was never good to be emotionally involved in a case.

Just her fucking luck to make the same mistake twice in one shitty lifetime.

"Why did you let Asher go too far?" Sadie said, her voice catching in spite of her best efforts. "Why didn't you do something?"

"That was her fault," Naomi said miserably. "Asher found out his mother believed his father was having an affair, and he started digging around. Sadly he found far more than the affair. He even had me fooled at first." She sighed. "I had no idea the only reason he took the appointment here was to get close to me again. To find the truth."

"You understand," Sadie said, barely holding on to her emotions, "his murder is as much your fault as the shooter's."

Naomi nodded, her expression distant. "I do, and for that I cannot forgive myself." She made a dry sound that was likely intended to be a laugh. "Or her." Her lips tightened. "My idiot sister even called me in the middle of the night last night demanding to know if her husband was here." She snorted. "Like I would have told her if he had been. Twisting the knife a little harder was all I had left."

Sadie's spine stiffened as her instincts kicked in more fully. "Have you spoken to or seen him?"

"Not since the day before yesterday," Naomi said. "As I said, I presumed Lee had killed Asher, and I needed him to tell me I was wrong. Not that it mattered who pulled the trigger. Asher's death was like my own. Worse, actually. My one goal from that point was to survive long enough to see that his killer was found."

All those years she had spent as a cop nudged at Sadie to call for backup, but she didn't dare slow the momentum of the conversation.

Despite her concern for what Naomi might have in mind, Sadie had to ask, "Did he tell you what happened?"

"He said he knew who had killed Asher, and he was going to have his revenge the old-fashioned way. The way they did things in the Bible." She laughed, another of those dry, brittle sounds. "I wasn't sure I believed him, but he refused to meet with me. Just as well, I suppose. I would probably have killed him with my bare hands, and that would have been a mistake. You see, when Lana called last night, quite hysterical, she said all sorts of unpleasant things. Including the fact that on Sunday night she and Lee had a terrible fight. She actually slapped him. Obviously, Lee couldn't have killed Asher if he was in Boston arguing with his stupid wife."

"Maybe your friend Emma Warren killed him," Sadie suggested. Naomi had said she had a friend in the mayor's office. Who knew it was the mayor herself and that they were more than friends?

But Sadie got it now. They were business partners. The puzzle pieces were all falling into place.

Naomi made a face. "Emma gives the orders. She never executes them. She has always been the real power." Naomi smiled. "She's just like me. Born into a man's world. But she, too, took the power. She found herself pregnant at fifteen, and her father, who was already disappointed she wasn't a boy, shipped her to Galveston and then to Birmingham to be rid of her. But she showed him. She achieved her law degree at Samford just as I did. We became very good friends. We had so much in common—powerful, abusive fathers. I helped her find her place in Birmingham. Introduced her to her future billionaire husband. I helped mold her into an unstoppable force, and her father had no choice but to see she was his ticket to great things in this country. A doorway. A very important one."

For the first time in her life, Sadie found herself at a loss for words. "What're you saying?"

The older woman smiled. "Emma's father is very much alive. His name is Carlos Osorio. The child she had at fifteen was Eduardo. I think you knew him."

Shock quaked through Sadie. "That's not possible."

She laughed. "Trust me, dear Sadie. Carlos sent her away, and she clawed her way to the top; she became the one with the power. Carlos took orders from her. Raised her son like a wet nurse." Naomi laughed long and hard; this time the sound was full of amusement. "He became the wife and mother. How ironic is that?"

Fury burned through Sadie. Now she had her answer. "So if what you said is true, even if Warren didn't kill Asher, she must have given the order."

"No, no," Naomi contended. "Emma wouldn't do that to me. She understood what he meant to me, that he was my life. Someone else did this without her consent. It's the only possible explanation."

Sadie was the one who laughed this time, a dry, weary sound. "You keep telling yourself that if it makes you feel better." She pushed to her feet. "If Warren is really who you say she is, I guarantee you she gave the order."

"You can't possibly know that," Naomi argued, staggering to her feet.

Sadie drew her weapon. "You might want to get back to that joint. Finish while you can, because I'm calling this in." Sadie fished out her cell with her left hand. "I regret that I can't do the honors myself, but I'm not a cop anymore."

Naomi collapsed back into her chair and reached for the lighter. "The sooner this is over, the better."

Sadie made the call to 911.

Then she sat down to wait and keep an eye on the woman. Naomi Taylor wasn't going anywhere before the police arrived.

She should have known better than to worry. Just before the sirens sounded in the distance, Naomi had a seizure and stopped breathing.

Sadie started CPR.

Probably something the crazy old woman had added to the weed.

The cops arrived and took over the situation, but there was no reviving the woman.

She was gone.

Sadie walked away. Whatever happened next didn't matter to her. She had what she wanted.

She knew who had killed Asher.

She should have known from the beginning.

48

4:00 p.m.

Federal Holding Facility
Birmingham

Sadie waited in the interview room.

Like all interview rooms, even those operated by the feds, the walls and floor were a bland grayish-whitish beige. The table was utilitarian with enough wear and tear to be called vintage. A clock hung on the wall. Something to remind whoever was on the wrong side of the table how much time had passed. To make them sweat. To ensure the tension continued to build. Just watching the second hand tick, tick, tick around the face of that basic, no-frills clock was frustrating. The sound it made was similar to a leak in a faucet. That drip, drip, drip that echoed in the night, the sound carrying through the darkness.

The air was stale, the temp too warm. Later it would be too cold, then too warm again. But it was the chairs that were the worst. Hard, slick. Uncomfortable for five minutes, downright painful after half an hour.

She'd been waiting five or so minutes. The attorney had set up everything. All she had to do was show up with her ID.

The door opened, and a guard escorted the fallen Mason Cross into the room. His hands were cuffed at his waist. A longer section of chain connected the cuffs on his wrists to the ones on his ankles. The latter making him shuffle forward a few inches at a time rather than taking his usual confident strides.

The guard pulled out the chair opposite Sadie, and her father dropped into the seat; then the guard left, closing the door behind him.

"Thank you for coming."

Sadie had barely kept her emotions in check since talking to Naomi. She didn't want to lose it now. Not until she had what she came for.

"What is it you want to talk about?" she demanded. "Did you make some big deal for your freedom? I'm sure you know all kinds of good shit to bargain with."

"No. I'm not taking any deals, though several have been offered. I'm providing all that I know with no strings attached."

His declaration surprised her, but she refused to give him any credit for doing the right thing. For all she knew, he could be lying. He'd done it plenty of times before.

"There are things I need to tell you before you hear them other ways," he offered.

"I have two questions for you," Sadie said flatly. "The only things I want to hear are answers to those questions."

"Let me have my say, and then I'll answer any question you ask."

If playing his little game would get this over with more quickly so she could get out of this room, why not?

"I used to be a good man. A good agent. Maybe even a decent father and husband."

No comment.

"After your mother died, I was lonely. In time I met a woman. She was an attorney for one of my informants. She made me smile when I had nothing to smile about; my wife had died. I was working all the time. I had no time for my only child. Ultimately, Emma and I started an affair."

Sadie made a dry sound. "You had an affair with Carlos Osorio's daughter. Wow. I guess I inherited my ability to get involved with the wrong people from you. Looks like we both got screwed by the cartel."

He nodded.

Jesus Christ. Naomi had been right. Warren was the old man's daughter.

"As time went on," Mason continued, "Emma and I grew closer, and I began to share things with her." He shrugged. "Pillow talk. I had no idea she was using me to plant bugs in my office. I didn't know until much later. All along I thought she was some vibrant, selfless attorney, and she was merely amassing markers. Building her reputation and power, and I helped her. Eventually I learned the truth, and we broke it off. But the damage was done. She had me. I watched the news, read about her in the paper as she gained power and influence. So many times I wanted to out her, but I couldn't. Not without ruining everything. My career—all those years of hard work. I couldn't go to prison and leave you. Your mother was gone. You had no one else." He made a dry snort of a chuckle. "You see, that's how it begins. You make a mistake—a misstep. The next one is easier. You begin to see how much you can benefit professionally and personally from yet another step across the line. Until you're in too deep. You've gone too far."

Sadie wanted to rant at him for using her as an excuse, but she couldn't find the words or the wherewithal to hurl them at him. This was a side of him she had never seen. Helpless, disgraced. Defeated.

"The one good thing I managed was to keep you away from *her*. I never talked to her about you. When I learned you were taking part in that operation five years ago, I tried to stop you."

Renewed fury fired inside her. "Were you afraid I'd learn your connection and out the great Mason Cross?"

"No. I was afraid they would learn who you are and kill you just to hurt me. Didn't matter. You were bound and determined. The next thing I knew you were in, and there was no turning back. Then you went missing, and I was certain the worst had happened." He made that sound again, the half laugh that was no laugh at all. "But she didn't have you executed. Instead, she was all for making a deal. It seemed we both had something she wanted—you and I, I mean. From that day, I belonged to the cartel."

"What the hell are you talking about?"

"Whatever else I've done," he said rather than answering her question, "I will never regret doing what I had to do to save your life."

She'd heard enough. "My turn," she snapped. "Two questions. You gave your word." For what that was worth.

He drew in a deep breath. "Fire away."

"Did you kill Asher Walsh?"

Sadie held her breath.

"Your involvement with Walsh placed you in the line of fire. My options were limited, so, to answer your question, yes. I was ordered to neutralize Walsh and Leonard Kurtz, or someone else would do the job, and you would be part of the package."

Sadie had thought when she learned the truth, there would be some sense of relief, but there was none. She felt empty. Ill. Lost . . . and then mad as hell.

At her lack of a response, he continued, "Walsh and Kurtz were preparing to contact other business owners and digging around in cartel business. They veered too close. Leland Walsh tried to stop his son, but, like you, he wouldn't listen."

Sadie felt her lips tremble, felt the emotion burning her eyes. She would not cry in front of this son of a bitch. "My father, the cartel's private assassin." She shook her head. Launched to her feet. "I need to get out of here before I puke."

"Everything I did was to protect you. Leland Walsh wanted you dead. He figured out I was the one who killed his son, and he wanted revenge. A life for a life."

"I guess you killed him too."

"It was the only way to protect you. All of it, every move, was to protect you."

"Except." Sadie pointed a finger at him, emotion pulsing so loudly inside her she felt ready to come apart at the seams. "*Except* when you started fucking around with the cartel princess because your wife was dead. What were you doing to protect me then?"

He lowered his gaze, unable to look at her.

Maybe that last part wasn't fair. He hadn't known she was an Osorio. Didn't matter. He deserved no sympathy. No leeway from her. Head spinning, stomach churning, Sadie turned for the door. She couldn't look at him a second longer. Couldn't share the same air.

But she couldn't go yet. Not until she knew the answer to her other question. She shifted her attention back to him, took a breath. "Did you do something to cause Pauley to have that heart attack?"

For the first time she noticed how very tired her father looked. Not that she cared. Damn him. She had known—she had—that he was cold and heartless. Ruthless, really. But she would never have imagined him capable of taking so many lives without hesitation.

"Leland Walsh told Emma that his wife had hired Winters. Emma ordered me to watch him. When he got too close with his investigation, I had no choice but to stop him. The heart condition made the job simple. I replaced his medicine with placebos."

Hatred whipped through Sadie, mixing with the fury, forming a bitterness that stole her breath. "I guess you did that for me too."

He shook his head. "No. I did that for me. Pauley was taking my daughter away from me."

Sadie turned away, grabbed the doorknob.

"You have my word, Sadie; I've made right my biggest mistake."

She didn't want to hear any more.

"I only asked for one thing, and it wasn't for me. I suppose perhaps that constitutes a deal, but it was something I needed to do."

"What the hell are you talking about?" she demanded.

"Just know that I've taken care of the mistake I regret the most. The bargain I negotiated before—I allowed them to keep something I shouldn't have. But I've made it right now. You'll see. I love you, Sadie."

She yanked the door open and walked out.

Maybe a good daughter would have said she loved him back. But she wasn't a good daughter, and he damned sure wasn't a good father.

49

5:40 p.m.

Birmingham Police Department
First Avenue North

Sadie walked across the bullpen. One of the detectives she'd met in the stairwell had told her which cubicle belonged to Devlin and Falco. She spotted Falco as she moved in that direction.

She wasn't sure what she was doing here. Her first thought after the meeting with her father was to go home and get shit faced—but that was the old her. She was free now. Maybe she didn't have every single piece of her past intact. Some parts she might never know, she supposed. But today had explained a lot. The past that had haunted her so darkly was out in the light now.

For example, why she was able to escape the cartel. Why she was even alive. Why her father had stopped looking at her the way he had before her mom died. His mounting guilt had put distance between them. His inability to control his daughter had kept him worried.

She couldn't forgive him for all the terrible things he'd done. He'd killed at least two of the most important people in her life.

Whatever had been left of their relationship was gone now.

No big loss. He'd been preparing her for this complete break for most of her adult life. She understood that now. Maybe he'd known all along he couldn't do the father thing without his wife to keep him on the straight and narrow.

"Hey," Falco said when he saw her coming. "How'd your meeting go?"

Devlin was pulling on her jacket. "You okay?"

Sadie still wasn't sure how down she was with this friendship thing. Barton and Snipes and Heck—they didn't ask her personal stuff like this. Very possibly they were afraid to do so.

She shrugged. "It went. There was a lot of spilling of guts. Mostly his."

Devlin said, "The LT told us he confessed to the hits on both Asher and Leland Walsh as well as Kurtz."

Sadie nodded. "Pauley Winters too."

Falco made a face. "No shit?"

"No shit. Who knows if there were others. He's giving a tell-all to the good guys and passing on any bargains."

"I'm surprised his attorney hasn't talked him out of that route," Devlin said.

"Maybe he's lost it. I don't know. Whatever happens next, he and I are done."

"Understandable." Falco shrugged into his leather jacket. "There are some things that can't be fixed."

Enough about her and her bullshit. "How'd the raid on the warehouse go?"

"The DEA is seriously jealous," Devlin said, a grin tugging at her lips. "This was a big one. Evidently, several huge shipments had just come in. The COO, Elizabeth Grant, is doing some spilling as well."

"Word is after the deal Warren cut," Falco said, "Carlos Osorio was taken into custody. The compound has been overrun by locals. A couple of other cartels are running scared. Apparently, our esteemed mayor has the goods on a lot of folks south of the border."

"Lana Walsh is taking her son's ashes back to Boston," Devlin tossed in. "Rumor is she requested her husband's body be donated to science. And two major cases are closed."

"And we are going to Devlin's," Falco said, "to celebrate with Tori. I'm making dinner."

"You should join us," Devlin offered.

Before Sadie could respond, Falco added, "We make a good team. The three of us." He shrugged. "Just saying."

"I guess we do," Sadie admitted. She looked to Devlin. "I appreciate the invitation, but I have some loose ends to take care of at my place. We'll grab lunch or something next week."

Devlin gave her a nod. "For sure."

Falco gave her a fist bump, and Sadie headed out. As weird as this was, it felt good. Maybe she should do some celebrating of her own sans the alcohol, even the beer.

Sadie's Loft
Sixth Avenue, Twenty-Seventh Street
Birmingham, 6:40 p.m.

Sadie was fairly sure that beyond the morning she woke up under the overpass on Eighteenth, she had never felt so exhausted in her life. She could sleep forever.

As she neared the turn into her alley, she spotted a big black SUV parked at the curb. Her instincts went on alert, no matter that this could be a patron of the pub. Still, in her line of work and with her history, it was better to be cautious. She parked in her usual spot and got out of the piss-yellow Beetle. She hoped to hell she had her Saab back soon. Before closing the door, she reached under the seat and grabbed her Beretta and tucked it into her jeans at the small of her back. She locked up the borrowed car and walked around it.

When she would have started up the fire escape, the driver's-side door of the SUV opened, and a man climbed out. Big guy. Broad shouldered, dark jacket and trousers. Sunglasses even at night. Typical muscle guy.

Well hell. Maybe old man Osorio had managed one last order before his capture. She reached for the weapon at her back. The big guy held up a hand.

"There is someone who wishes to speak with you."

Couldn't be her dad or the mayor. Naomi was dead. Maybe Lana Walsh had decided to stop by on her way to the airport.

The big guy opened the door behind the driver's door and reached inside.

Sadie kept her right hand on the butt of her weapon just in case.

The first thing she saw was a colorful skirt that reached the ankles of the woman stepping down. Her shoes were gray-leather, well-worn flats.

When she moved beyond the vehicle door, her gaze locked immediately on Sadie.

Old.

Petite—no, tiny.

Long gray hair lay in a thick braid. Wrinkled face as if she were a couple hundred years old.

"Do you remember me, *la muchacha*?"

Sadie blinked. Her hands fell to her sides. "Yes." Her pulse started to race. "You're the healer who took care of me." Oh shit. Was she hallucinating again? This couldn't be real . . . could it?

The old woman nodded. "I kept you safe and invisible until it was time for you to go."

Take my hand and you'll be invisible.

It hadn't been Isabella behind the mask that last time. Sadie had lost the baby, and all she wanted to do was die . . . this woman had saved her life. Even during the months of torture and mind games, this woman, this healer, kept her breathing. She suddenly knew this with the same certainty she knew her own name.

"Thank you." Sadie wasn't sure what else to say. Her entire being hummed with some kind of anticipation. Not fear. Something far more intense. Something she couldn't name.

"When they learned what you had done, you were to die. Eduardo had begged for your life and for the life of the child you carried. He came to tell you he could not save you, and you killed him." Her thin chest rose with a shuddering breath. "A deal was made. A trade. You were returned to your father, barely alive, but alive."

The voices and images Sadie could never quite grab on to, never fully see or understand, filtered through her mind now. Her father had talked about a trade. "I can't remember. What kind of trade?"

She nodded to the driver, and he reached inside the back seat as the old woman turned back to Sadie. "Now there is a new deal."

Sadie watched, her heart pounding, threatening to rupture.

The driver drew back from the vehicle, a small child in his arms. He stood the child next to the old woman. *Boy.* The child was a boy. The boy looked up at Sadie. Gray eyes—gray eyes exactly like hers—stared back at her. This wasn't possible.

Her heart lurched. "But . . . but my baby didn't make it."

"Another baby was brought to you . . . one from the village who did not live past birth."

Unable to keep her eyes off the child she had believed for years didn't exist, Sadie shook her head. "Why?"

"You took her son, and she took yours." The old woman pulled something from a pocket in her skirt and thrust it at Sadie. It was a small photo of her and Eddie. "I did what I could. I have shown him this picture every day of his life. I have kept him safe from his sister and other threats until this day came. I knew it would come."

Sadie looked from the child to the woman, long-dormant emotions crowding inside her. "I don't know what to say."

The healer smiled and turned to the boy. *"Esta es tu madre."*

Sadie's breath caught. She closed her eyes a moment, certain this had to be a hallucination.

"This is your son," she said to Sadie.

Sadie forced her eyes open. They were still there, the three of them, including the beautiful boy. It wasn't another hallucination.

"His name is Edward. He belongs with you now."

Sadie couldn't speak, much less move. She could only stare at this child with his beautiful dark hair, his big gray eyes.

The driver went to the back of the SUV and removed two suitcases and placed them on the sidewalk next to the boy.

"You will find his papers there," the old woman said. She looked down at the boy. "Go to your *madre*, Edward."

The boy took the few steps that separated him from Sadie. He looked up at her and smiled.

Sadie dropped to her knees, every part of her bursting with some foreign emotion that overwhelmed all else. "Nice to meet you, Edward."

He nodded and offered his hand.

Sadie took his hand in hers and gave it a shake. "I'm really glad you're here."

"Take good care of him."

Sadie looked beyond the boy to the old woman. "I'll do my best."

The healer gave a final nod, and the driver assisted her back into the vehicle. He slid behind the wheel and drove away.

Sadie stared down at this child. *Her* child. Her son.

I allowed them to keep something I shouldn't have. But I've made it right now.

Her father had traded whatever deal the feds might have offered him for her son—the son no one else knew existed . . . the one she thought had died.

More of those overpowering sensations fired through her. Her chest felt so full she could scarcely breathe. Whatever she was feeling, she understood that when the shock wore off, it would evolve into sheer terror.

What did she know about kids? She had no idea what to feed him or . . . anything. She couldn't possibly be a good mother.

Sadie dragged in a deep breath and reached for his hand. "Let's take your things and go inside. Then we'll go meet some friends of mine."

Devlin was a good mom. She would know what to do.

50

8:15 p.m.

Devlin Residence
Twenty-First Avenue South
Birmingham

Kerri watched Falco and Tori going at it with whatever video game they were playing. Put a game controller in his hand, and Falco turned into a big kid.

He'd made the most amazing rice and orange chicken for dinner. They'd devoured the meal as if they were starving. And maybe they were, a little. More for the unfettered companionship than the food. The past week had been hell, but it was over now.

Kerri was taking a couple of weeks off. She and Tori were going on another vacation. This time Falco was going with them. Warmth and a kind of happiness that made her feel giddy spread through Kerri at the thought. She didn't know where this relationship between her and Falco was going, but she was ready to take the risk and explore it.

She had called Diana and Jen and given them the good news that the nightmare was finally over. She'd also shared her little secret about

Falco going on vacation with her and Tori. Kerri had never heard such uninhibited squealing.

Eventually, she and Falco would figure this all out, and life would get back to normal.

Whatever normal was for a couple of detectives who spent most of their time investigating homicides.

The doorbell rang, and Kerri wandered to the door. She peeked around the blind, and Cross gave her an odd little wave.

"Looks like Cross decided to join us," Kerri called out to the others as she unlocked the door.

"Better late than never!" Falco tossed back.

Kerri pulled the door open, and Cross had the strangest look on her face. Kerri blinked, realizing she hadn't come alone.

A child—a little boy, maybe three or four—stood next to her. "Hey," Kerri said to the child before her questioning gaze shot back to the other woman's.

"This is my son, Edward." Unadulterated terror shone in her eyes. "I'll explain later." Cross took a big breath and pasted on a wide smile. "I'm determined to do this right—I have to—but I have no idea where to start. I was hoping you could help."

Her son? But her baby . . . wow. Kerri reminded herself to breathe. This was incredible. She smiled, grateful for one more good thing to have come of these tragedies. "Come on in. I think we can figure this out."

She ushered Sadie and her son inside and made the introductions. Falco did a good job of recovering quickly from his own shock. Tori immediately got down on her knees and started talking to the little boy, who spoke perfect English.

They solved complicated, high-profile homicides every day. She and Falco could certainly handle whipping Cross into a good mommy in no time.

"Come on," Kerri said to Cross, "we have a lot to talk about."

Maybe that vacation would have to wait a bit.

Sadie Cross was pretty much family now.

And family came first.

Always.

ACKNOWLEDGMENTS

There are many amazing authors out there who write incredible series. I have too many favorites to name. When I first started writing with the hope of publication, I created a cast of characters I wanted to expand into a series. Thankfully, that dream saw fruition, and I went on to write many multibook series. I always fall in love with my characters—it's my weakness—and I like keeping them around for a while. They become a part of my life.

But it's really you, the reader, who allows me that privilege. Thank you so very much for buying and reading my books. You have given me the opportunity to live the dream of a lifetime. I was nine when I wrote my first story, and from that moment I knew—no matter what else happened in my life—I would continue writing stories, if only for my own entertainment. I am so very grateful that I can write my stories for you. I hope you enjoy this one as well as all the ones to come. I plan to write many, many more.

Oh, and please do leave a review at Amazon. It means so very much.

Cheers!

ABOUT THE AUTHOR

Photo © 2019 Jenni M Photography LLC

Debra Webb is the *USA Today* bestselling author of more than 150 novels. She is the recipient of the prestigious Romantic Times Career Achievement Award for Romantic Suspense as well as numerous Reviewers' Choice Awards. In 2012 Webb was honored as the first recipient of the esteemed L. A. Banks Warrior Woman Award for courage, strength, and grace in the face of adversity. Webb was also awarded the distinguished Centennial Award for having published her hundredth novel. She has more than four million books in print in many languages and countries.

Webb's love of storytelling goes back to her childhood, when her mother bought her an old typewriter at a tag sale. Born in Alabama, Webb grew up on a farm. She spent every available hour exploring the world around her and creating her stories. Visit her at www.debrawebb.com.